T0285368

THE KING-KILLING QUEEN

Also by Shawn Speakman

The Annwn Cycle

The Dark Thorn
*The Everwinter Wraith**
*The Splintered King**

Battle's Perilous Edge

Song of the Fell Hammer

The Chronicles of Antiquity Grey

The Tempered Steel of Antiquity Grey
The Undone Life of Jak Dreadth

Edited by Shawn Speakman

Unbound
Unbound II
*Unbound III**

Unfettered
Unfettered II
Unfettered III

*Forthcoming

THE KING-KILLING QUEEN

SHAWN SPEAKMAN

GRIM OAK PRESS
SEATTLE, WA

The King-Killing Queen is a work of fiction. Names, characters, places, and incidents either are the product of the author's imagination or are used fictitiously. Any resemblance to actual persons, living or dead, events, or locales is entirely coincidental.

Cover artwork by Magali Villeneuve
Interior artwork by Donato Giancola
Map on pages vi–vii by Jared Blando
Interior design and composition by REview Creative

eBook ISBN 978-1-956000-36-8
Trade Hardcover Edition ISBN 978-1-956000-35-1
Signed & Numbered Edition ISBN 978-1-956000-37-5
Signed & Lettered Edition ISBN 978-1-956000-38-2
Rare Edition ISBN 978-1-956000-39-9

Grim Oak Press First Edition, November 2023
2 4 6 8 9 7 5 3 1

Grim Oak Press
Battle Ground, WA 98604
www.grimoakpress.com

For my wife, Kristin, and our two sons, Soren and Kael,

Who infuse my life with the most powerful of magic—their love

The Old World
Leagues
Misty Isles
Dubhlinn
Lundenburgh
Mont-Saint-Michel
Cliffside
Rouen
Paris
Marly-le-Roi
Macet
Royaume de France
Bordeaux
Dundleloren
Sea of Atlas
Bay of Vizcaya
Iberia
Castillo de Butron
N
S
E
W

Stavangr
NORGE
NORTH SEA
BURGHAM
River Rake City
The Rhine River
COLONIA
ALLEMAGNE
FOREST
Rouen
Paris
Clair-de-Lune Abbey
PRAHA
TWILIGHT LANDS
VOSGES MOUNTAINS
MIROIR LAKE
ALPZ MOUNTAINS
MILLAN
ITALIE

THE KING-KILLING QUEEN

PART I

THE KING-KILLING QUEEN

1

igh King Alafair Goode lay dying, and Death advanced to finish the work.

It was not upon a battlefield, where a glorious end fighting enemies led to an afterlife of honey-soaked crème cakes, rivers of rubywine, and the warmth of a woman's flesh. It was not at the hands of a jealous lover, which always resulted in the King hale and women disappearing. And it wasn't the result of one of Serath the Shadow's many assassination attempts. Or the Fall Hunt, when the great tusked boar Barak skewered the High King's chest. Or being exposed to the feverpox that struck down the northern city of Herrick. No, Death did not have a hold on High King Alafair Goode as it did others. After all, a witch had magicked the orphan boy during his quest to destroy Mordreadth the Great Darkness, and that enchantment held true for all his days as foretold. Until the death arrived that none may escape—that of singular old age.

Sylvianna Raventress strolled Mont-Saint-Michel's seaside market and breathed in salty morning air, wishing the High King could also enjoy such a day and hoping that death would remain at bay a while longer. Though he'd been bedridden for weeks in the King's Tower at the island's pinnacle, his final days upon him, Alafair had remained hale enough to regale Sylvie and Master Historian Kell, his stepbrother and Sylvie's mentor, with stories of his life. She longed to hear more before his end. She had grown up with many of the tales; everyone in the kingdom had. Writing down a few more would add further weight to such a storied life.

She glanced up at the lording spire as if she could see High King Alafair there. To hear directly from the man who slew the Great Darkness and spent the rest of his life unifying a kingdom was a privilege. Almost every day for months, she had scribbled his words upon paper with quill and ink, documenting his history. She enjoyed the act, even as Master Kell questioned the more embellished events of his stepbrother's accounts. Some of her favorite moments, like the High King's wit and laugh, had nothing to do with his past. He had even taken interest in Sylvie herself—her young life after being adopted by Kell, her studies and how they progressed, where she ventured when not with the Master Historian, and her philosophies on life and her hopes for the future.

She almost felt like she could call him a friend, if such a relationship could exist between King and commoner.

Once High King Alafair Goode entered Annwn's hereafter, and only legend remained, Sylvie would cherish the time she'd been given with him. It saddened her to know that day rapidly approached. But this morning Master Kell had advised her that life would go on and, to that end, they needed more supplies to complete Alafair's memoir.

So, she walked the early morning on errands, an empty canvas sack slung over her shoulder for her second stop and her first destination, her favorite of the two, right around the corner.

When she entered the bustling bakery, even the open windows could not dispel the amazingly sweet smells permeating the space. A couple of people observed her entrance but paid her little mind. Few knew her as the Master Historian's apprentice; most would not care if they did know. She liked it that way. It gave her freedom to observe the common people as well as those who governed, a key asset to becoming a great and impartial chronicler.

"Good morn, Sylvie!" a tall, heavyset man shouted over the tumult of breakfast orders being yelled at him. The Sweet Start Bakery's owner, wearing an apron smeared with flour, jam, and bacon grease, was a blur of movement as he catered to his customers.

"The same to you, Dandrews," she said, her mouth already watering. She shuffled her way to the side away from the chaos. "It's a beautiful one, for sure."

"Too busy for me to notice. The usual?" Sylvie nodded as Dandrews kept working, fetching various pastries he had made early that morning for awaiting patrons.

Sylvie waited while the baker and his apprentices helped others. She'd known Dandrews since she was a girl, Master Kell teaching her not only the skills necessary to be the High King's historian but also introducing his young charge to the ways of the people outside the castle. Looking back, she saw the wisdom of his choice. While Alafair Goode and his dozens of family members enjoyed every comfort that wealth and status could provide—creating a sea of spoiled brats who deserved none of it, as her teacher put it—Master Kell's decision had taught Sylvie how others worked, dreamed, hoped, and even died. Partly through visiting people like Dandrews, who played an integral role in Mont-Saint-Michel's lifeblood.

During a lull, Dandrews came over to Sylvie, his voice hushed for privacy. He wiped a damp brow with his forearm even as he handed her a cloth containing three sweet cakes. "I need a break. How fares the High King, Sylvie? Heard he fails faster every day."

"Thank you." She took the pastries to enjoy upon leaving and gave him two silver pennies, which joined the jingling coins already within his apron pocket. "The High King is strong. He is made of stern stuff. Master Kell is not sure how much life remains in him, so we are enjoying our time by his bedside as much as we can."

"When it happens, it will be the end of a hero. End of an era," Dandrews said, rubbing his gray-stubbled chin and sighing. "To have seen the things he has seen. My grandfather fought for him against the armies of the Great Darkness. Once I was old enough, my grandfather related the terror of battle and the nightmarish things he witnessed on the field. He called Mordreadth a terrible fallen angel; I've heard others call him a demon. No matter. Without the High King, these very stones we stand upon would have been struck down and tossed into the sea. Given the nature of the witch magic placed upon his house, I thought he'd live forever."

"Was Mordreadth an angel, a demon, a Fae? Or just a man empowered?" Sylvie mused, and shrugged. "Who knows the truth. Even Master Kell doesn't know from where the Great Darkness sprang, and he's the most educated person I know. Only that Mordreadth's coming was prophesied by the light-weavers of Clair-de-Lune, as was that a son of Pendragon would rise to meet it."

"Ahh, the light-weavers of Clair-de-Lune. All women, right?" Dandrews grinned with a wicked glint in his green eyes. "Now that's a place I would like to visit one day before I'm dead. If I hand this bakery over to my eldest son, think the light-weavers would take me in?"

Sylvie laughed. "Few are given admittance to Clair-de-Lune. Fewer still are men. So I doubt it."

"In my youth, I could be rather persuasive," he said with a wink.

"Of that, I'm sure." She laughed again.

He sobered and gripped her shoulder in friendship. "Regardless, I had better return to work before my apprentices start throwing my own pastries at me. Give my best to Kell. I've lost two brothers. I know how painful it can be."

"I will."

Giving her a nod of farewell, the large man went back to work.

Sylvie had always appreciated Dandrews, and his baked goods were Mont-Saint-Michel's best. As she took a sweet cake and let its sugary tartness break her fast, she returned to the crowded marketplace to finish her second errand. Vendors who knew her gave greeting, and she spoke to a few of them. For twenty winters, she had been apprenticed to one of the most powerful men in Royaume de France, but sometimes she was glad to get away from castle intrigues and her

Master's work to just be alone, see the city, and absorb what interested the citizens living in less rarified circles.

After following several streets that took her away from the marketplace's busiest shops, Sylvie finally arrived at the Ink Spot for stationery items. She pulled the door open, its bell ringing her arrival and awakening a merlin within his hanging cage.

The gray-blue bird gave his customary shrill and chattering song at her entrance. Why Jacqueline and Edouard needed the bell above the door when the mother and son had the bird, Sylvie would never quite understand.

"Oh, you shush, Boron," she said.

The falcon cocked its head at her, brown eyes wary.

"Is Boron giving you grief again, Mistress Sylvie?" a middle-aged woman said as she exited the curtained doorway leading to the back room with a grin on her round face.

"Good morn, Jacqueline," Sylvie said, nodding to the older woman and perusing the tables along the shop's one window. Tall urns held a menagerie of long feathers, and bottles of various inks joined them. "Looks as though you have new quills in stock. Goose?"

"Swan, actually," the other corrected. She straightened a few items on the front counter, a habit Sylvie had seen her perform a hundred times. "The best. Perfect for a scribe such as yourself."

The Ink Spot was peaceful in comparison to Sweet Start Bakery. Then again, most needed breakfast, while few needed writing supplies. As a result, the Ink Spot's selling area was barely larger than Sylvie's washroom, though she knew the back room to be of considerable size, as that's where they stored and prepared inks and paper. Up front, Jacqueline and Edouard used every bit of wall, table, and floor space. There were dozens of different ink bottles and quills for even the most demanding writer to choose from. Paper examples were available in four bound books at the counter. After many winters of visits, Sylvie could spot the newest items easily.

She took her time looking over the wares, though, instead of conversing with the shop owner. Jacqueline meant well, but she prattled on about her son ad nauseam—his worth, his prospects, his good looks, and especially how Edouard and Sylvie would make a perfect romantic match due to their complementary professions. Jacqueline's husband had been murdered three winters earlier when a thief became too cavalier with his knife, leaving her with an only son and his future to worry over.

Before Sylvie could select the items needed for Master Kell and the continuation of the High King's memoir, Jacqueline threw open the back curtain. "Edouard, get out here! Mistress Sylvie is visiting," she said before returning to the counter.

Sylvie cursed her luck but managed to turn with a smile as Edouard joined them.

"Well, say good morn to Sylvie," Jacqueline coaxed.

"Good morn, Mistress Sylvie," Edouard repeated, looking anywhere but at her. He was her age and handsome, with a roguish look and a striking combination of black hair and hazel eyes. No doubt other women their age found him attractive.

But he had the personality of a turnip, which disinterested Sylvie entirely.

"And to you," Sylvie replied politely. "How goes the work? I see four new ink varieties here to choose from. That crimson is of particular note. It's lovely. I might just have to buy it."

Edouard nodded, still unable to meet her gaze. "It took me a few days, but I meant to capture the color of the roses growing along the front of the Citadel."

"You did it then," Sylvie said, trying to set the shy young man at ease.

"Are you still with that squire, Mistress Sylvie?" his mother asked, uncaring if such a question made her son squirm, which it did.

"I am. Darian is his name. He is near to knighthood."

"It is a hard life, being married to a Knight of the Ecclesia. Or so I have been told." Jacqueline clucked, as if she hadn't said the same thing a hundred times before. "Edouard here would be a safer bet, if I can be so bold. Fewer wounds for you to bind, fewer bones to set. You know, that sort of thing. And the babies you'd have. My goodness, they'd be beautiful."

Sylvie kept a straight face while Edouard turned the very crimson of his ink and fled to his back room. "I will consider all your words, Jacqueline. Really, I will," Sylvie said, thankful for Master Kell's teachings on diplomacy and amused at the woman's audacity and its result.

That seemed to satisfy the stationery owner, as she beamed at Sylvie. "What are your needs today? Those swan quills caught your eye, I know."

Sylvie was about to ask for the items she wanted when a loud commotion from outside drew her attention.

"Well," Jacqueline said, coming around the counter with a frown and joining Sylvie at the window. "What is all the fuss about?"

Men, women, and children in the streets looked confused as they watched others running among them, the latter's shouts indiscernible from inside the Ink Spot. Sylvie saw a range of emotions on the faces outside—fear, sorrow, worry, and puzzlement. Boron began singing his song repeatedly, adding to the tumult. No one seemed to be in danger, from what she could tell.

But when Jacqueline opened the door and stepped beyond her shop, Sylvie heard the words she had hoped not to for a while yet. Before Jacqueline could say anything, Sylvie was already in the street and rushing back toward the castle, two sentences repeated around her as more people took them up and made them their own.

"The High King is dead! Long live the High King!"

2

ith the news spreading like wildfire, Sylvie found the main castle a flurry of chaos. As she hurried to return to the suite she shared with Master Kell, multiple people yelled at her to stop, to share what she knew. She ignored them. The Naming of the Heir had not occurred. Master Kell would need her now—and not only for the historical records.

Once upon a time, when High King Alafair Goode knew not his royal lineage, he had been adopted into Kell's family, the boys raised together like brothers. Sylvie had chronicled that story directly from the High King, with the Master Historian sharing memories of their boyhood and the trouble they'd been fond of finding. For decades, inseparable the two men had been. Now, having accomplished so much together, one had left for Annwn's hereafter while the other remained.

Sylvie had no family besides Master Kell. She would never know what it was like to lose a brother or sister.

But she knew she had to be there for him during one of his darkest moments.

When she finally gained the collection of rooms she shared with Kell in the Masters Tower, Sylvie burst through the front door and into the living room, already heading to her own room to change into more appropriate attire. The extensive Goode family would undoubtedly be gathering to pay their respects to their patriarch, and she had decorum to consider.

Then Sylvie came to a sudden stop, the fire in her legs from the stairs going cold.

Master Kell sat before the smoldering fireplace in his favorite chair, legs crossed and an unreadable expression on his wrinkled face.

"The High King has gone to Annwn," Sylvie said tentatively.

Master Kell held up his hand, eyes boring into her. He was dressed appropriately for such a moment, and what remained of his white hair was neatly combed back, but he had none of the urgency. There was no hint of fallen tears, no aspect of sorrow in his demeanor. It made her suddenly uncertain.

"Listening to street rumors once again, Sylvie," Kell asked with no question in his voice. "What have I told you about that?"

She sighed, realizing what had happened and feeling ten years old again.

"Verify. Verify. Verify," she said.

"That is correct. Verify. Because most people are daft pigeons, walking in circles, unable to forage let alone fly." He stood, adjusting his ceremonial robe. He smiled at her then to soften the lesson, and she saw a hint of his sadness in it. "Do you think my brother would be so foolish as to not fulfill the Naming? The High King yet lives, though the healers have said my brother is nearing his end. He has called us all. Including Pontiff Scorus of the Citadel, Lord Alent of the Ecclesia, and I'm assuming a great many Goode scions. The time has come. Dress accordingly."

Feeling sheepish, Sylvie moved toward her room.

"And Sylvie?"

She stopped and half turned. "Yes, Master Kell?"

"This is the first moment of many that I have trained you for," he said, serious in a way that denoted a lesson. "History will be recorded today. The Naming. It is our duty to see that every aspect of the day is observed and preserved for the future. You must be as sharp as you've ever been. For today will be remembered long after you and I are both gone."

Sylvie nodded, understanding the import. "I will not let you down."

"I know you won't. Now prepare," Kell said. As he turned away to gather the items they would need, it was all Sylvie could do not to hug the old man. She steeled herself instead. Moments of emotion would not aid them now.

"Will you be all right?" she asked.

Kell, head down as he prepared the gold-filigreed steel elixir box, didn't turn. "I love my brother. It is time, though," he said, not answering the question, shoulders slumped under unseen weight. He seemed elderly in a way Sylvie hadn't seen before. "Let us go to the King's Tower. Many of those joining us are vultures, only wishing to know who the heir to the throne will be. It's all about power. They don't care about Alafair Goode, the man. And we do, right?"

Sylvie nodded and went to dress. It didn't take her long. Soon they left the suite, taking stairs downward through the Masters Tower until two Ecclesia knights met them at the spire's base to escort them through the castle to the King's Tower. A few people asked questions of them or offered condolences, but Master Kell kept quiet, his eyes forward and stride sure. Sylvie did the same, carrying the elixir box. Once they gained the King's Tower, they climbed toward the High King's suite of rooms at the top, where Sylvie had spent most of her time as of late.

But when she followed her mentor into the grandiose sleeping quarters of the High King and saw the bedridden form of Alafair Goode clinging to life, Sylvie shivered. This was a man she had grown to admire despite his faults; this was a man who had shaped history.

"Child, be mindful," Kell growled as they walked through the parting sea of onlookers who already filled the bedroom, all there to witness the Naming and the passing of their monarch. "You stepped on my robe. I nearly tumbled."

"Apologies, Master Kell."

"Remember what I told you, Sylvianna. We are here to aid a man to Annwn. It does not matter that he is the High King. Or my brother."

It matters a great deal, she wanted to say.

She remained as silent as a mouse, though. She was no child; she would not embarrass her Master in front of the kingdom's royalty and religious and political leaders.

But she knew her history. This was a day for decorum—a day that would see the passing of a High King whose exploits had long been legend.

Sylvie would likely have questioned that legend were it not for Master Kell's account of the High King's fight to destroy Mordreadth. Then there were the relics, which authenticated the stories too. The sword Lumière, forged from fallen-light. The ring Vérité, a truth circle discovered in the crook of a willow tree near the Fae rivers of the Twilight Lands. And Pridwen, a shield hammered into being from a scale of the dragon Shurtuth. Sylvie had seen them all—even touched Vérité—and they were as real as the terrible poisons and restorative elixirs she carried in her Master's box.

All of that mattered little. The man would die, and one of the people in this room would be Named heir to the kingdom the High King had carved out of blood and death.

Master Kell ascended the steps to the circular dais that held the King's bed, and Sylvie steeled herself for what was to come. The future of the kingdom depended on this moment. Wielding his gold staff of office, Pontiff Scorus stood behind the High King's head, his crimson vestments failing to conceal his massive paunch. He was there not only to oversee the spiritual needs of High King Alafair's end, but to hear the King's choice of successor. Also standing about the bed were five men and a woman, royal scions like others in the room but considered the High King's favorites. Each was as invulnerable to death as Alafair, a strange aftereffect of the witch's curse. They awaited their father's Naming. Over the two decades Sylvie had been Apprentice Historian, they had barely registered her existence; she, on the other hand, knew them well, having quietly observed and recorded their interactions with one another. Most were deplorable, interested only in selfish ambition.

Sylvie joined Master Kell at the side of the High King's bed. There was no doubt he was dying. Pain lingered in every deep line of his face. Blue eyes that once sparkled with life seemed muted, as if leached of color. Even his white beard, which had always appeared as alive as he was, lay limp like wilted moss. Time had caught up with the legend. Lumière, the High King's fabled sword, lay alongside him.

"My High King, my brother," Master Kell said, sitting down on the edge of the bed, his white robe a stark contrast to the High King's royal blue bedspread. He took the other's hand.

High King Alafair squeezed Kell's fingers in return, but Sylvie noted his grasp lacked strength. "Brother. The day has come, hasn't it?"

Master Kell nodded. "The Mother willing, it will not be today."

"You've never been good at lying."

"You've never been good at anything besides being who you were born to be."

High King Alafair croaked a laugh. "We did great things together."

"You stole the whole world from the Great Darkness and created one kingdom from many," Master Kell said, eyes welling with tears. "Peace. Prosperity. And a world in which your children have no want. You did this. You."

The High King closed his eyes and took a deep, shuddering breath. Sylvie heard the rattle in his throat. The love the stepbrothers shared almost brought tears to her eyes. The day would be difficult for most in attendance, but it would be hardest on her mentor.

"Do you think she will come? At this end of all things?" High King Alafair asked.

Master Kell smiled but it was tinged with sadness. "If she yet lives . . . perhaps. She said one day she would return to the House of Goode. Up until now, she has not. You were in such pain then, only a boy really. Those were her only words, if I remember correctly."

Sylvie knew of whom they spoke. The witch. She had saved young Alafair Goode during his quest to find Lumière, when a dark agent of Mordreadth wounded him. Some called her Morgause or Gwyar or Anna, names often attributed to a powerful woman known to have been born centuries ago. However, separating folklore from history had never been easy, and Master Kell's account of that day had stunned Sylvie when she first heard it—a boy given life without injury for the rest of his mortal days. No one could have known then that the magic would pass down to High King Alafair's children, grandchildren, and even those great-grandchildren who now stood waiting in the bedroom.

Sylvie wondered what life would be like if nothing could kill you.

High King Alafair took another deep breath. Pain made him twist to the side. Then he fixed his watery eyes on Sylvie's.

Blue eyes to blue eyes. She couldn't look away.

"Child, are you prepared for this day?"

The way he said it seemed to suggest something other than the obvious. Sylvie nodded. She didn't want to upset her liege. And she certainly didn't want the High King's family or her mentor to think she held any disrespect toward him.

"We have gotten to know one another well, haven't we? When you look at me, do you see a perfect High King?" High King Alafair asked. The sincerity of the question caught Sylvie off guard. "Or a flawed man?"

She didn't respond immediately. Master Kell had taught her to treat every question as important, and every answer as a possible trap. "I see a man who is High King, and that man has done right by his kingdom," she said.

The High King snorted. "Are you sure about that?"

"No, High King Alafair," she answered. Sylvie felt all eyes upon her.

The High King chuckled until it became a cough that shook the bed. Once he had recovered, he stared at her. "Honesty. Such a rare trait here among my children and children's children." He paused, his gaze never deviating. "Your eyes, so blue. Like mine. That pleases me a great deal."

Sylvie had no idea why it would. Many people had blue eyes this far north. Rather than reply, she thought it best to simply nod. High King Alafair only had so long left to live, and it shouldn't be spent focused on her.

"My King," Lord Pike Goode said, stepping forward to place a caring hand upon his father's arm. An act of tenderness that would only upset the High King, Sylvie thought. Pike was Alafair's eldest son, a grandfather in his own right, but the two had always had a contentious relationship. "Are you well enough to fulfill your duty this day, Father?"

"No, I am not well enough, you dolt," High King Alafair growled. "I'm dying. Let me do this day my way before the vultures pick my bones."

Lord Pike's face darkened and he stepped back. Lady Erlina looked away, the King's daughter repressing her amusement at her half-brother's ineffectual attempt at drawing their father's attention. Lords Idlor, Collin, and Yankton remained quiet. Each hoped to be Named heir to the High King. Only the youngish Lord Kent seemed to take no interest, intent upon studying his fingernails, as if he had better things to do with his day.

Sylvie kept hidden her satisfaction at Lord Pike's discomfort. She hoped to be Master Historian one day, shaping the kingdom's future as the High King's personal counselor, and that meant treading carefully amid the family.

"Now, since Pike opened his yap, let him be the first," High King Alafair said.

"The first what, Father?" Lord Pike asked.

"To receive the first question," he replied. Sylvie saw a glimmer of impish life in his eyes. Alafair was enjoying this, she realized, and had a plan beyond merely selecting his heir. "Of the Seven Virtues, which would best aid the High King to keep the peace between the Fae and the Winter Trolls?"

Lord Pike cleared his throat, stalling as he searched for an answer. "I believe Morality," he said tremulously. "Yes, Morality. Morality leads to the justice that is clearly needed to keep the two factions from killing one another. Fairness is needed. Balance. Morality gives that."

"And Erlina," High King Alafair continued, as if he hadn't even heard his first son. No woman had ever been crowned before. It made her inclusion all the more interesting. "A High King—or in this case, a High Queen—is faced with an invasion from the Isles of Raston. They've been hit hard with winter, are starving, and are in search of the hunt. Which Virtue best serves?"

Having seen how her older brother was caught off guard, Lady Erlina answered with conviction. "Fortitude," she said. "Courage to do the right thing. Fortitude to confront the attack, courage to repel it."

High King Alafair nodded. "And what of you, Idlor. New fall-en-light is gifted us from the stars, and you as High King have the chance to forge a new weapon from the metal. Which Virtue helps you make that decision?"

"Prudence, Father," Lord Idlor said, eyes hard-set. He clearly did not like the questions. Sylvie knew him to be vain, and in his vanity he already owned the crown. "Prudence is the wisdom of our age. The needs of the kingdom would determine how best the fallen-light should be used, and that requires wisdom."

The High King then turned his gaze upon Lords Collin, Yankton, and Kent. They were younger than the others and rumored to hold great favor with their father. The only one who ever spoke to Sylvie was Lord Kent, though she thought he did so only to retain Master Kell's high opinion. She doubted any of them were being truly considered for High King of the united Royaume de France, but she couldn't discount it either.

"Collin. Yankton. Kent. Which of you would make the best High King?" Alafair asked, surprising everyone with the directness of the question.

Lord Collin, known for his quick wit, began, "Becoming High King would be an honor I'd take wi—"

"I would," Lord Yankton said, standing tall.

Lord Collin frowned. "No, it'd be *my* honor."

"It'd be an honor for you, all right." Lord Yankton laughed. "An honor for all of those concubines you keep locked in your bedroom."

Collin and Yankton erupted into a finger-pointing argument. Master Kell shook his head. Lord Kent hadn't answered.

"Father, I protest this," Lord Pike said over the commotion, drawing his father's glare. "If this were to be a test, we should have been made aware—"

"Life is a test. Ruling is a test every moment," the King said as everyone quieted. "And these are my choices?"

"Temperance," Lord Kent said out of nowhere. All eyes turned to him. No one dared cross him, given rumors detailing how people in his life had a tendency to go missing. Even his older siblings kept clear of his machinations. "Extremism is a path a ruler cannot afford to embrace," he said, looking back and forth between Sylvie and his father as if no one else in the room mattered. "Recklessness has destroyed kingdoms. The choice of your successor, Father, must be determined by moderation and tradition. Any choice outside those boundaries could be disastrous for the kingdom and your family."

Sylvie realized then that the King's questions were planned and directed specifically at each family member based on their weaknesses. Lord Pike was known for his unwillingness to compromise. Lady Erlina knew nothing of war. And no amount of wisdom could overcome Lord Idlor's selfish heart. The sons and daughter of High King Alafair had been given serious questions, but, Sylvie now realized, it had all been a ploy.

"It is clear these children of mine have a lot to learn. Though as my Master Historian is fond of saying, 'Wisdom is found if it is willingly sought,'" the High King said, his voice growing raspier. He gazed at Sylvie again. "Can you answer these questions, child?"

Sylvie had spent all her years with Master Kell in study. Whether it be history, philosophy, anatomy, or the chem of elixirs and poisons, her training had been rigorous, especially with word games. The High King had phrased this question with purpose too. His scrutiny of her only intensified. It put her in a terrible situation. She did not want to become an enemy of the next person to wear the crown and sit upon the throne.

"Not answers, Your Highness. Answer," Sylvie said, trying diplomacy in hopes of threading the proverbial needle and upsetting neither her liege nor his children.

"Go on."

Sylvie stared at the royal blue bedding as she spoke rather than at any of those who had just spoken. She didn't want the King's scions to think she was rising above her station, or that she was making them look like fools. "A ruler requires all of the Virtues," she said. "Therefore, each of your questions has the same answer. All the Virtues."

Sylvie thought High King Alafair would respond to her answer. Instead, he lifted a weak finger toward his stepbrother.

"Will you aid me in my final burden, Kell?"

"You know I will, my brother. Then I will give you the Last Shade." Master Kell motioned toward Pontiff Scorus. Then the Master Historian stood once more and raised his voice. "High King Alafair Goode shall plant the future in this present with the help of Pontiff Scorus, for all of us in this room and for everyone who lives in this Royaume de France we have sworn to protect."

At that, Pontiff Scorus summoned his assistant from the crowd below.

A boy of no more than ten winters, flanked by two Knights of the Ecclesia, hurried up the stairs holding a large tome, bound in black leather and clasped and hinged with the same fallen-light metal that forged Lumière. There, within the pages of the Covenant Codex of Saint Emmer, High King Alafair Goode would write the name of his successor, continuing the peace between Fae and Man with a stroke of pen and ink, the Naming such potent magic that even the Fae would know the chosen heir.

The boy knelt before Pontiff Scorus, and the leader of the Bishops of the Citadel took the tome in his plump-fingered hands. The boy returned to his place among the dozens of observers below while the knights remained. Pontiff Scorus turned toward the High King, and Alafair tried to push himself up into a sitting position. Sylvie was about to help him, but Kell shoved a pillow behind the High King's back. Alafair took a deep breath and placed his hand on Lumière, the magnificent sword lying lengthwise along his right leg.

"High King Alafair Goode, He Who Wields the Light of Lumière, the Final Bane of Mordreadth," Pontiff Scorus said, his voice echoing about the chamber. The man loved attention. "We are here to witness the Naming. By which Man once again renews his oath of peace with the Fae, and the Fae again consent to the terms of the original Compact of so long ago." He gently put the book on the High King's lap, and then returned to his position just behind him.

"The Covenant Codex is our most sacred of texts," High King Alafair began, picking up the book of peace with hands that had killed thousands of his enemies. The irony was not lost on Sylvie. "Once, war raged between Man and Fae. It was the bitter evil of the time. It divided not only Man and Fae but Man and Man. Saint Emmer managed to discover peace with the Fae. The words within this Covenant Codex are the bridge to that peace. With my Naming and signing of this book, that peace is renewed once more.

"My children," High King Alafair continued. "Each of you represents a different aspect of me. My strengths. My weaknesses. The hopes and dreams of a dying father. Each of you has a role to play when I am gone, which I hope will preserve what we've worked so hard to build. The kingdom needs you. Remember this if you falter from the path I have decided." He drew in a steadying breath as if he were going to war one last time. "It is time for the Naming."

Pontiff Scorus stepped to the High King's side, offering a quill while holding an inkwell. Alafair opened the book and turned the pages to the one he wanted. It was all Sylvie could do not to lean forward to see the name that would be written. This moment would decide who she would serve, one day, as Master Historian.

She and the others watched High King Alafair draw another deep breath, steady his hand, and press his quill to the paper.

And magic filled the room.

"By my own hand, with quill and ink to mark the Covenant Codex of Saint Emmer, I Name my heir." Alafair scribbled into the book, his breath labored. A hush hung over the room. The King's children around the bed tried to see what he wrote, but the High King clutched the book so close, Sylvie doubted anyone other than Pontiff Scorus could view it. When the High King lifted his quill free from the page, he sank back into his pillows, the book falling to his lap with the pen in its inner hinge. Magic lingered in the air about them, renewing the Compact between Fae and Man, and raising the hairs on Sylvie's arms.

"It is done," High King Alafair Goode whispered.

Then he closed his eyes, his breath shallow, his skin pasty white. Kell took the gold-filigreed box from Sylvie, opened it, and began mixing two vials. Pontiff Scorus withdrew the Covenant Codex of Saint Emmer from the High King's lap. He stared at the open page. Then he closed the tome and clutched it to his chest.

"Read the name," Lord Pike snarled.

Pontiff Scorus took a steadying breath. "High King Alafair Goode, Slayer of Mordreadth the Great Darkness, Wielder of Lumière, and Strength of the Kingdom, has chosen his successor," the robed man said. "The newest name inscribed in the Covenant Codex of Saint Emmer is legible and clear. On this day and all of those henceforth, the light from the heavens above illuminates those below in our blessed Royaume de France."

"Out with it, Scorus!" Lady Erlina hissed.

"High King Alafair Goode has selected Sylvianna Goode," Pontiff Scorus muttered. "The first of her name and the first High Queen of the kingdom. As ordained by the Compact between Saint Emmer and Wise Belloch, the heir has been Named before the careful regard of the Citadel, the Ecclesia, and the Masters."

Sylvie couldn't believe her ears. She went rigid, then, baffled, she glanced around her, hoping her ears had deceived her. The dozens of scions of the House of Goode whispered among one another, most looking at her, their murmured voices growing to curses and shouting. All the while, Alafair breathed upon his bed, eyes closed, as if worries could no longer touch him.

Sylvie looked to Master Kell, but even he was not looking at her.

He continued to mix the concoction that would aid his brother to Annwn with neither pain nor awareness.

As though he had known all along.

"That cannot be!" Lord Pike shouted, bringing Sylvie back to the moment.

"This is outrageous, Father!" Lord Idlor roared, and he stepped down from the dais to storm from the room.

"She isn't of your blood!" Lady Erlina spat.

High King Alafair did not open his eyes. "Kell, the dagger," he said.

Master Kell drew his weapon from the folds of his white robe. "Come sit, Sylvianna," he said, patting the bed. "For all to see and witness."

Master Kell moved aside, and Sylvie sat. Dagger in hand, High King Alafair opened his eyes and looked at her. Conviction burned there despite the frailty of his appearance. He watched her closely. She turned to ask Kell what was going on—and suddenly felt like she had been punched in the lungs by a red-hot fist.

She looked down and saw the hilt of the dagger jutting from her chest.

"Pull it out, Sylvie," Kell said.

Sylvie gulped. With a shaking hand, she gripped the knife's handle and pulled the blood-slick blade from her body. As she withdrew it, power swept through her. It was magic, she realized. She couldn't pinpoint its source, but it felt potent, ancient, a warmth like none she had ever experienced. Barely any blood stained her robe. The magic knit bone, muscle, and skin back together until the wound closed, her body tingling all the while. Then the unknown power left her as though nothing had happened. She met the eyes of the High King, who watched her with a mixture of exhausted life and hope.

"Am I . . . your daughter?" Sylvie asked, still trying to grasp it all.

"Remember Mikkel," Lord Pike growled to his siblings, before the High King could answer. His face was red with anger. "Father chose a boy to become his heir apparent and gave him full command of all the Knights of the Ecclesia. Mikkel had to be stripped of his titles and imprisoned when he rebelled. He wasn't ready. This girl isn't ready. It's the same thing!"

"None of you are as prepared as Sylvianna," High King Alafair rasped. "I have gotten to know her well, as she has been by my side more often than any of you. She is educated, well-informed, humble—unlike most of you—and worthy of my Naming." He drew in a rattling breath, almost unable to find enough strength to speak again. "She is ready."

"And for you, my brother, I shall be there at her side, advising, counseling, and keeping safe Royaume de France," Kell said, gripping Sylvie's shoulder with love shining in his eyes. It steadied Sylvie, despite her world becoming wholly changed. "For you. For the kingdom."

Lord Pike snorted. "How do you know she is *ready*, Father? Not even the Master Historian can quell what your subjects will think about this choice!"

"It will be up to Sylvianna to set them right then." The High King paused as Kell placed a vial to his lips; he drank from it and grimaced. "Farewell, Sylvianna. I wish I had known you as my brother knows you. My dreams are with you. And farewell, Kell, my first friend and brother. I will miss you."

"I will miss you too, my brother," Kell said, clutching the King's hand again. Though no mortal potion like Last Shade could kill the High King, it would free him of pain until his natural death arrived.

Long minutes passed. Sylvie reached out and placed her hand on Kell's shoulder, hoping to give her mentor some solace. The room, with its stinging hatred for her, fell away, and it was as if only the three of them existed. Alafair's breathing became so faint from the effects of the Last Shade that it was impossible to know if he yet lived. Then he gasped several breaths and finally lay completely still.

The room had gone quiet, with people either watching or lowering their heads in respect. With tears streaming down his weathered cheeks, Master Kell checked his brother's pulse and then announced, "The High King is dead." He placed his stepbrother's lifeless hand on

Lumière's hilt. Then he knelt before Sylvie, head bowed—a respect she had not yet earned.

Pontiff Scorus, his Citadel retinue, the Knights of the Ecclesia, and dozens of Goode family members—her family, she realized—knelt as well, save for a few who angrily took their leave of the room instead.

Of those around the bed, only Lords Pike and Idlor did not kneel.

"The High King is dead. Long live the High Queen," Kell said, his voice ringing throughout the room. All eyes were on her.

Sylvie stood, unsure what to do.

But with stunning clarity, she realized how dangerous her world had just become.

DONATO

3

re you sure there's no real way to know?" Sylvie asked, falling into her plush chair in the quarters she shared with Master Kell. She still couldn't quite grasp what Alafair—*her father*—had done and what it all meant. "If I'm safe from harm, I mean."

After Alafair passed into Annwn, Pontiff Scorus led a prayer, and then the bedroom emptied of everyone except a few. Kell and Sylvie waited in silence as the Pontiff led the Ecclesia knights in wrapping the body in a myrrh-scented white shroud. It took some time due to the various observances and prayers that had to be made. Then, together with a processional guard of thirty knights, they walked Alafair's body to the Citadel, where his remains would be cleansed and prepared for his funeral at sea. Afterward, Sylvie and the Master Historian strolled the High Garden under the stars. A Knight of the Ecclesia secretly warded them from the shadows, he told her, a bodyguard for the new High Queen to be. She did not mind. As the two strolled through the night, he answered as many questions as he could until they eventually arrived at the Masters Tower, where the routine of building the fire helped calm her nerves.

At times during their stroll, she'd had a hard time breathing, anxiety over her imminent life change falling on her. She wanted to flee the only world she had ever known; she had seen the crown's hardships while chronicling the High King's life, and now those difficult decisions and conflicts would become hers.

Now home where things were familiar, the fire warming her, Sylvie realized with sudden clarity that she had served the kingdom her entire life. It would be a betrayal of that life if she ignored this new calling and didn't answer it.

But the memory of steel buried in her chest lingered . . .

Master Kell prepared their kettle for tea, letting the fire do its work. Then he found a wooden splint and lit its end. "There is no prudent manner of testing, nothing that could make certain the magic that has kept safe Alafair and his descendants for decades is still working. Though I'm thinking on it, I'm thinking on it."

"The witch was real then," Sylvie mused, staring into the fire, its flames a dance.

"You doubted the veracity of my own written history?" Kell said with a short laugh as he lit candles to chase back the room's gloom. "That's not like you. I witnessed it with my own eyes. Felt the magic, saw my brother's wound close. Alafair would have died an uncrowned orphan of a royal family, and the world would have followed in that death, if not for the witch."

"Apologies, Master Kell. I did not doubt," Sylvie said. She needed to talk it out to make sense of it all. "I know the witch was real. I meant more about the magic that kept Alafair alive for so long. Does it mean I'm invulnerable too? And more importantly, did the witch know what she was doing? If so, why did she make the Goode bloodline long-lived? What purpose would that serve once Mordreadth was destroyed?"

"All questions that have plagued my life, Sylvianna," Kell said, taking a seat. The hearth burned bright, warding them from the night's chill.

"And beyond that," Sylvie said, "I thought I was an orphan. How is this possible?"

"Well, you *were* an orphan," Kell said, shrugging. "Not unlike Alafair. When he discovered his parentage, he wanted nothing to do with any of it. Save the world? Why him? He rebelled, as I think anyone would, given the circumstances. He eventually came to terms with it. You will too, my dear."

"Did you know? About me, I mean?"

"Did I know that your sire was my stepbrother?" Kell asked. "No, although I have always suspected. Alafair was a good man, but he did welcome a great many women to his bed after the Queen died. Lowborn, highborn, it didn't matter to him."

"My mother was a baker in the High King's kitchens, or so you said," Sylvie said, unsure what to believe anymore. "Is what you told me still true?"

"It is still true, Sylvie. Lovely jet-black hair, just like your own. And as I told you, she died in childbirth." Kell withdrew his pipe from the pocket of his robe and scraped it free of ash. "You were brought to me as a newborn. I never married. Too busy keeping the kingdom together after the destruction of Mordreadth and the chaos that followed."

"I was lucky then."

Master Kell shrugged. "I like to think we were a good match."

"In a way, you are my uncle. Though not by blood."

"No, not by blood," Kell said. "But some bonds are stronger than blood."

Sylvie nodded. It was something he had said often when she was a child. She had always looked up to Kell like a father. He was a man capable of great life lessons and stern but fair love. They had fought. They had laughed. She had received an education rivaling that of even the wealthiest merchant princes, with the understanding that she would one day take over his position. Most children were not so lucky.

"I understand why you wish to know about the witch and the magic she bestowed upon the Goode family," Kell said. "I know I'd want to know if I were in your position. Your Naming has incensed a lot of people, especially several of your half-brothers. To know if you can be killed or not would be great knowledge to possess."

"I have enough to worry about these next few days, let alone in all the days after," Sylvie said, the glares of Lords Pike and Idlor burned into her memory. "It'd be nice to know if murder is a worry I should also have."

Kell tamped smoke-weed into his cleaned pipe. "We could try a second test if you wish it." He patted his robe where he kept his dagger.

"But I might not like the consequences."

The old man grinned, the first hint of humor Sylvie had seen since the passing of his stepbrother. "You might not. Magic is fickle that way. Few witches can be trusted. Worse, at this very hour, some of your father's children are experimenting to see whether they are immune to death like he was. It is going to be a bloody few days."

Sylvie frowned. "What do you mean?"

"Well, how does one examine such a thing?" Kell asked.

"I suppose sticking a knife into someone's chest might do it," Sylvie said with a grin. When he didn't respond, she continued. "And since one cannot exactly do that to oneself . . ."

"Correct," he said. "I don't know this for sure, but I could easily see someone like Lord Idlor finding a lowborn son of Alafair's loins."

"And if magic no longer protects the family, that child will die," she said, horrified.

"Sad but true."

"I will do no such test," Sylvie said.

"Nor can we stop the others from trying. We cannot protect so many against the ill will of the few."

Sylvie thought about the new world she now occupied, one familiar and yet wholly different too. There was no way for her to stop any of her siblings from killing each other—not even the young who were easy prey. There were too many, and one could not prevent cunning machinations within the shadows. It made her realize how powerless she was even though she'd been Named.

"What happens next?" she questioned. "I know I will be crowned by Pontiff Scorus the morning after my father's farewell. But when will the funeral pyre be lit? Tomorrow? The day after? There is little information about all of this."

"The Covenant Codex of Saint Emmer is quite clear on the coronation and quite vague about the funeral," Kell said. "The coronation is to happen the day after the funeral, true. But grace has been given when it comes to the sea pyre. It merely needs to happen within a month." He paused, rubbing his beard as if expecting the answers to fall out of it. "I do not want my brother rotting that long, to be fair. He deserves better. I imagine preparations for the funeral will be two, maybe three days at most. The kingdom needs its High Queen. But it is largely out of my control. Pontiff Scorus will oversee the bulk of the duties now. My brother has fulfilled his."

"Did you know what Alafair had planned for me?" Sylvie asked.

"I wouldn't be much of a brother or counselor if he hadn't confided in me," Kell pointed out. "Yet the final decision was his alone."

Sylvie mulled over Master Kell's words. "Lord Pike would have done a fine job. Lord Idlor the same. Even Lady Erlina. Why not choose one of them? Why me?"

"Trust what Alafair said right before his end," Kell said, frowning at her. "I can share that my brother enjoyed your company a great deal. He learned as much about you as you did about him." The frown was replaced by a sly grin. "Though I'm trying not to take offense at your last question. I have taught you much since you were a babe. And you've been an apt student. I happen to think I've done a very good job with you."

Before Sylvie could respond, she heard a knock at the room's window.

"Ahh. I've been waiting for this," Kell said.

Curious, Sylvie watched her mentor open the window to the night. From the darkness, two tiny bodies flew into the room, circling it with dizzying speed. She sank deeper into her chair, unsure what she was seeing. Finally, the two creatures settled delicately near a plate with a honey crumble cake upon it, gossamer wings flexing rainbow hues. With stunning realization, she knew what they were, despite never having seen one before. Fae of the Twilight Lands. Sprites, from the look of them. One resembled an old, white-bearded man with wispy hair on his head. The other was much younger, beardless and broad-shouldered. Both appeared to be made from bits and pieces of the forest, their skin like bark and their clothing woven from moss and leaves.

Wonder replaced her initial fear as she observed them closer. The day had brought magic along with its grief.

"Well met, Grumtil, and friend, of course," Kell said, giving a short bow to their tiny visitors. "Pleased you could join us despite the sorrow of the day."

"Good evening, Master Kell the Historian," the older sprite said, tugging at a beard so long Sylvie wondered how it didn't hinder his flight. "Indeed a sad day. But also one of hope."

Sylvie knew the Fae rarely showed themselves to the world of Man. Her mentor kept stranger secrets than she could have guessed. She remained quiet, observing and listening.

"Yes, I have hope as well," Kell agreed, glancing at Sylvie before returning his attention to Grumtil. "And who accompanies you this evening? Your replacement?"

"I like to think no one can replace me." Grumtil sniffed.

"True, what was I thinking?" Kell grinned.

"You have always enjoyed antagonizing me. Like your brother. If you weren't so ugly, I would teach you manners." The old sprite crossed his arms over his beard. "I am sorry that the most important aspects of Alafair are no longer with us." He lowered his head, and a tear ran down his dark brown cheek. "He was my friend."

"You shared a bond. You were close. I think a refreshment is in order, if you are interested?"

Grumtil nodded. "We are. The journey was long." Master Kell went to the dresser and took a sewing kit from a drawer, withdrawing two wooden thimbles that he washed and then dipped into his tea. He added a sprinkle of sugar to each. The two sprites accepted them with nods and sipped the hot liquid.

The older Fae made himself comfortable on the arm of the historian's chair. "Master Kell, the journey was made more exhausting by the Court. The Elders are more interested in the drama of succession than what it means for the Compact. They are apparently not worried about these swamp vipers Alafair called his children. I am not so sure." He paused, considering Sylvie for the first time. "The Fae's obligation to the Covenant Codex is realized, though. Sizmor here was chosen. And while young, he serves with wisdom."

"Ahh, the Court of Elders," Kell said, shaking his head. "They do not see how tenuous the Compact is at all times. Nothing lasts forever, and if we let it, all that Alafair fought for could be undone. Even destroyed."

"So," Grumtil said, waving a tiny hand at Sylvie. "Your little apprentice has grown into a young woman. And she is the heir? Amazing."

"Please don't speak of me like I am not here, Master Kell," Sylvie said finally.

"Apologies, Sylvianna," her mentor said as he sat back down in his chair, teacup in hand. "May I introduce Grumtil Hodgemurkin. He is a Fae from the Twilight Lands and serves those of the Shadow Court who ensure that the Compact entered into by Saint Emmer of Man and Wise Belloch of Fae is maintained. They guard it, even as we do our best to uphold it here." He sipped his tea. "Grumtil was Fae advisor to the crown. He knew my brother better than anyone. Except me, of course."

"Grumtil lived here?" Sylvie asked, surprised. "I never saw him. And no one has mentioned him."

"My Lady," the old sprite said, bowing.

And then he vanished.

Before Sylvie could say a word, the sprite returned. A wry grin twisted Grumtil's face. "The Fae have many abilities Man cannot fathom. We are among you without your knowledge. Though the Covenant Codex of Saint Emmer does not allow my brethren to interfere in your affairs."

Sylvie leaned forward in her chair. "But you helped the High King? Does that not constitute interference?"

"It is the only relationship between Fae and Man the Covenant

Codex allows," Grumtil said. "I served faithfully all the years of High King Alafair Goode's rule."

"I did not know him," she said, regretting that her heritage had been withheld from her and a bit angry about it. "At least not the way you did."

"He was a good man. Prone to vices. But good, nevertheless."

"Yes," Sylvie said.

"You have many brothers and sisters," Grumtil continued, stroking his beard. "Brothers and sisters who would see you removed from ruling before you even begin."

"And therein lies my worry," Kell said, eyeing her.

Sylvie remembered the dagger-like stares she had received from those in the bedroom, their muttered curses. "Who are you most worried about? Pike? Idlor?"

"Pike is one, though he lacks the spine to do much more than whine," Kell said, waving that idea aside. "Idlor could be dangerous. He is friends with Pontiff Scorus too, which creates an unequal power balance within the kingdom. Scorus controls the coronation. That worries me. But honestly, there are too many threats to count. And some are smart enough to keep their interest in the throne secret until they make their move."

"Like?" she asked. Sylvie had few friends at court. The foreboding of that realization and how vulnerable it made her left her cold inside.

Kell shrugged. "Lord Kent, for one. He has always been a man possessed of keen intellect and quiet ambition. That's why it is so important for you to have eyes and ears in places you otherwise could not access. Sizmor will aid you during your transition, even as I will."

"Sylvianna Goode," the younger sprite said, inclining his head slightly. "I am Sizmor Darkinmoor."

Sylvie looked at Sizmor. "You are to be my Grumtil," she said. "Once I'm High Queen of the kingdom. I have questions about that. But first, how did you know to come here? The High King has only just passed into Annwn. How did this Shadow Court convene and send you so quickly?"

Kell stared into the fire, cup held before him but forgotten for the moment. "There are aspects to it that few know. As Master Historian, I am one of them. The Shadow Court is another. You will know these secrets now too, Sylvie. The moment my brother signed your name into the Covenant Codex of Saint Emmer, a matching signature appeared in the Covenant Codex of Wise Belloch. The Shadow Court became aware of that Naming and acted accordingly, voting on young Sizmor here to become the Fae's newest counsel to the monarch of Royaume de France. Our new sprite friend left the Twilight Lands and flew straight to us."

"Wait, there are two books?" she asked.

"There are," Grumtil said. "One book here with Man, one book in the Twilight Lands with the Fae. In this way, the Compact is maintained. When a change occurs in one book, it affects the other. Equal knowledge between equal partners."

"And this all started with Saint Emmer, Kell?" Sylvie asked, remembering her history and placing newly revealed pieces into the puzzle.

"Yes, and it has ever been so down through the ages," the Master Historian said. "Even when the Goode family did not rule, the stewards of Mont-Saint-Michel maintained the treaty. The peace between Man and Fae is of paramount importance. If the Covenant Codex failed to be renewed with a Naming and coronation, the possibility of war between Man and Fae would become all too real. And in that war a thousand years ago, the Fae could not be stopped."

"Yes, the sword Saint Emmer wielded was the only weapon Man possessed to keep safe the peace." Sylvie looked at the younger sprite, marveling anew at meeting the Fae. "How do you feel about all of this, Sizmor?"

The sprite puffed out his chest. "I was chosen to assist you on behalf of the Fae once you have been crowned High Queen of Royaume de France. It will be an honor to do so."

Sylvie knew little about ruling, only what she had read in history and philosophy books. She had wondered, earlier, whether she even wanted to be High Queen. Could she refuse the succession? How firm was the

Covenant Codex of Saint Emmer once her name was written there? The weight of responsibility would crush her if she were not prepared.

"Master Kell, this is all quite overwhelming," Sylvie admitted.

"I know it is, child," her mentor said, leaning forward and patting her knee. "I remember when Alafair discovered the truth of his parentage. It was daunting, to say the least. But I promise you this: I will prepare you for the coronation and be there while you rule. You also have Sizmor as a confidant, a spy, and wise counsel when you have need. The Masters will aid you as they deem fit. Even Grumtil will be here, at least until my brother is put to rest."

"But I know nothing about how to rule, Master," Sylvie said. "Are you not worried that Alafair made this decision in error?"

Grumtil replied, "The questions you are asking yourself are natural."

"I agree with Grumtil," Kell said, looking deep into her eyes. "I will add this. High King Alafair Goode knew people. He could read them. He did this with you these last few weeks as we worked on his memoir." He raised a finger as he did when he was about to make an important point. "I know you as I knew him. You have the same ability. You are learned. Strong. Capable. My brother's choice was wise."

Growing up, Kell's insights had always soothed her. They did so now, though she still worried.

"Relax tonight," Kell added. "Spend some time with that squire who is so fond of you. I will entertain Grumtil and Sizmor. Return here tomorrow morning, and we will help you realize what the rest of us see."

Sylvie nodded. "Thank you, Master Kell. You've always been there for me. I appreciate it more than you can know."

He nodded, smiled, and took another sip of his tea.

Sylvie took a deep breath, trying to relax, though her entire world and its future remained wholly changed. The position she had prepared for her entire life was quite different now. But with Kell by her side in the days to come, Sylvie knew she could overcome the hardships that would challenge her.

She'd simply listen to him and take one day at a time.

4

Sylvie awoke to the touch of fingertips on her naked back. "Good morn, love," Darian whispered in her ear.

Languishing in the warmth of his body next to hers, she drew a deep breath, content. A kiss graced her shoulder with a feathery touch. She smiled, opening her eyes. Sunlight entered the squire's small room through a slit in the wall, motes of dust swirling in the air. Most of the blankets were piled on the floor next to the narrow bed. Only a sheet remained, twined about her legs, hiding little of her nakedness.

She loved the feeling. They had hardly slept, but she regretted nothing. She kissed his lips. He returned the kiss, firm but gentle. She liked his lips, his chin, his strength. But her love for him went beyond the physical, even if that was how it had started. With his quick smile and wicked humor, Darian, squire to Sir Gwain, offered a refreshing contrast to Kell's serious studies. It's why she continued to share a bed with Darian when she otherwise would've grown bored.

She hadn't mentioned the High King's Naming, though bells ringing throughout Mont-Saint-Michel would have notified Darian and others of Alafair's death. Instead, when she arrived at his door late in the night, she pushed her way into his room and delivered a passionate kiss on his lips, wasting no time. He wrapped his arms about her and shut the door. She pressed him to the bed and disrobed, removing all pretense about why she was there.

Their pleasure had been hot and furious to start, but the second and third rounds they had taken their time, enjoying one another's touch in more intimate ways.

She rolled onto her back to view his handsome face above her. Sunlight played across his blond-red stubble. He smiled, green eyes kind.

In his hand, a cup.

"You went out this morning and got my favorite drink?" she asked, surprised she hadn't heard him leave.

Darian smiled, giving her the cup. "You deserve it. What got into you last night?"

"You did," she said, sitting up and taking a sip, enjoying the sweet juice. "Several times, as I recall."

He laughed. She loved the sound.

"That's not exactly what I meant, Sylvie," he said. "You were like a crazed highland cat when you knocked on my door."

"This cat may need more attention," she said, reaching down between his legs. When his manhood didn't respond, she let him go. "I thought a knight favored as many jousts as possible when a tournament came around?"

"Who would have thought I'd rather talk than fuck." Darian disentangled himself from both her legs and the sheet and sat on the edge of the bed, naked. Then he stood and relieved himself in the chamber pot in the corner of the room. Sylvie sat up, covering her breasts with the sheet and stared at his body.

"If you would rather talk," she said, "then you know what occurred yesterday."

"High King Alafair died," Darian said over his shoulder, his urine hitting the bottom of the pot with tinkling splashes. "The bells rang, after all."

"And did you hear the other news?" Sylvie questioned, watching him closely.

"Perhaps."

Sylvie sighed. "I should have known Sir Gwain would tell you."

"He didn't tell me about the Naming," Darian said, pulling on breeches and shirt.

"Then who?"

Darian grabbed her white robe and handed it to her. "Lord Idlor."

Sylvie shrank inward. Her dangerous present and uncertain future came crashing down on her again, with this man she had come to know now compromised in a way that made her feel dirty. She swung her legs off the bed and dressed herself, feeling the comfortable white robe fall upon her shoulders and, with it, some semblance of her own authority returned.

"What did Lord Idlor want?" she asked. "Did he come here? Or find you in the training yard?"

Darian took a deep breath. "He came here."

"Why? It wasn't to share news of the High King's death, I bet."

"Sylvie, I didn't want to be put in this position. Know that, my love," Darian said. He went to her, his calloused hands gently taking her own. "He came to me with a proposition."

"And?" she asked, feeling the very air around her poisoned by Idlor's visit.

"Surely you don't want to be High Queen. Do you?" Darian asked, his previous playfulness gone. "I mean, yes, he mentioned that you were Named Alafair's heir. That it was proven you were his child. It has . . . upset a lot of people." He paused and squeezed her hands. "And if I am to be fully honest, I'm one of the upset."

"It sounds like Lord Idlor came here with one purpose," Sylvie said, removing her hands from Darian's.

"You didn't answer my question," Darian said. "Do you want to be High Queen of Royaume de France?"

"I'm not sure what I want."

Darian paced across the small room. He turned and glared at her. "You just came here for one last fuck, is that it?"

Darian's barb missed its mark. Sylvie just shrugged. "You think I should give up the throne, don't you?" she asked. "For a prize that Idlor dangled in front of you, I bet. One you would use against my heart to help Idlor play his little game."

"I think you need to at least entertain the idea," Darian said, hands on hips. "There are other ways to lead a comfortable life aside from ruling the kingdom. Plus, if you were Queen, Pontiff Scorus would never let me marry you. You'd have to marry a prince or a Lord or something."

"You mentioned other ways," Sylvie said. "What did you mean by that? What did Idlor promise?"

"Sylvie, I love you. I want to marry you and have children with you. Lord Idlor is prepared to offer a large swath of his personal estate to create a new dukedom, one we could govern together and leave to our children one day, title and lands both."

She took a deep breath. "If I abdicate the throne."

Darian nodded.

"And you'd be knighted as well?"

"I would. Sir Gwain has said I am ready to take the trials anyway. I think I am too. The knighthood is a formality, though I would welcome it. Most knights are not given lands like Lord Idlor is offering."

Sylvie thought on it, looked at it from as many different angles as possible. It was a princely offer. Not only would they receive lands and titles but servants and workers. But whether Darian realized it or not, Lord Idlor had struck against her. If she had been younger, she would have stormed from the room. Instead, she cooled as Kell had taught her.

"What do you think?" Darian asked.

"I think I should be the one deciding the direction of my life."

"Wait, Sylvie, I didn't mean—"

"No, you just decided to do Lord Idlor's bidding."

Darian frowned. "For us. For our future!"

"No. For *you*," she spat.

"I think you really shou—"

"No one tells me what I *should* do, Darian. I have enough to think about without adding you to the mix. I'm leaving."

As she stormed toward the door, Darian stepped in front of her and grabbed the handle. "I was worried I wouldn't do this right," he said, opening the door.

Standing outside in the hallway, Lord Idlor, dressed in the finest clothing the kingdom offered, stood glaring at her. Sylvie saw the situation clearly. When Darian had retrieved her juice, he'd found the time to bring Lord Idlor to his chamber to ambush her. It left her even more furious.

Before Sylvie could utter a word, Idlor Goode pushed past her into the room, and Darian closed the door behind him.

Trapping her.

"Sylvianna Raventress," he said with a smile.

It took her a moment to register that Idlor had used her orphan's surname, as opposed to their shared one. And that Idlor knew about Darian meant he either had spies in Mont-Saint-Michel, or that her lover had told him.

She remembered a quote from Saint Emmer then, from when he was trying to form the Compact with the Fae: *The supreme art of war is to subdue the enemy without fighting.*

"Lord Idlor," Sylvie replied, trying to maintain the decorum that Master Kell had instilled in her. "This is an unexpected visit."

"But a necessary one," Idlor said. He found the room's one chair and took a seat, leaving Darian and Sylvie standing. Apparently, he did not intend to kill her, even if he could. "Yesterday saw the passing of the greatest King the world has known, rivaling even Arthur Pendragon. It also has demonstrated a need for family to come together. The kingdom needs us. We cannot be divided. We cannot show weakness now. Or ever. There are forces that would see Royaume de France undone. Strong leadership is required." He paused. "And that is why I am here now."

"Darian has told me your offer," Sylvie began. She knew men like Idlor. The expensive clothing. The perfectly trimmed pepper beard. Even his teeth gleamed. "It is a generous proposition. It speaks to how powerful you are as a man and as a son of High King Alafair Goode."

"I welcome you to consider it," Idlor said, leaning forward. Being so close to him made her almost nauseous. "I do not want to see the kingdom that my father built ripped apart. I will do everything in my power to prevent that from happening."

"A noble conviction," Sylvie said. "I will say this, though. Master Kell taught me well. The first lesson he ever taught me was how an offer always hides what the offeror wants."

"I see where you lead," her half-brother said, his grin deepening the crow's feet at his eyes. "You think I make my offer for personal gain."

"Becoming High King of Royaume de France would be gain, yes."

"There is no guarantee that Pontiff Scorus would crown me," Idlor said, waving her accusation aside. "My father had many children, evidently more than we knew of."

"Just so long as it isn't me, I take it." Sylvie bored her gaze into his. "I think you consider me weak because I am a woman. Or because you consider me lowborn. Or for any number of other reasons." She paused. "Do not consider me weak. That would be a grave error."

His smile vanished. "Quite the contrary. I understand why Father chose you. I find you talented and capable." He stopped and glanced from Darian to her again. "Nevertheless, a woman lacks the fortitude for Kingly leadership. Sometimes even a man—like Mikkel Goode, so long ago, driven by emotion—is a poor fit. There are times when a King's heart must be stone. And, as a woman, you lack that."

"Was Mikkel like a woman?" Sylvie asked, moving the conversation where she wanted it to go. "The stories I've heard said he was quite the fearsome man. Like you."

Lord Idlor's gaze narrowed. "Mikkel was mad for power. When Father had him silenced—even though it hurt him to do so—it was in service to the kingdom and its future."

"Master Kell shared details about Mikkel during my history lessons," she said. "A boy of extraordinary intellect and strength of mind. He became his father's First Knight, commanding a position reserved for the most chivalrous. But Mikkel wanted to carve out a life of his own. The conflict resulted in the only rebellion attempted against

High King Alafair Goode, one orchestrated by his own son." She paused. "How are you different from Mikkel? *Our* father made me heir to the crown. It was his wish. It seems like you are doing the same as our half-brother, just quietly and with a bit more nuance."

"I only want to rule as Father did," Idlor replied. He took a deep breath and shook his head. "I cannot simply take the crown from you. There were too many people in Father's bedroom when Scorus announced you, and they have already spread the news far and wide. But a woman is too much of an unknown for the Knights of the Ecclesia and the Masters. For the Church with its male priests, male Bishops, and male Pontiff. Even for the common folk, who will see you as weak just because you bleed several times a season. I will admit you have a tough mind, like Father. But it won't be enough. Let's stop being coy. Abdicate the throne. I do not care what you tell Pontiff Scorus and the family. Swear to me that you will do so."

She looked at Darian. "I must go. Master Kell will be waiting on me."

"Let me make this more plain," Idlor menaced, also standing. "Abdicate the throne or I will discredit you. Time is of the essence. Tomorrow night, our father's funeral pyre will be lit. The new ruler will be crowned the following morning. Preparations must be made with Pontiff Scorus for you to relinquish the crown." He paused, steely eyes upon her. "I suggest you consider the trajectory of your life."

"Threats are the actions of a desperate man," she said.

Lord Idlor stepped aside as she walked toward the door.

"Sylvie! Wait!" Darian yelled, reaching out for her. She ignored him.

In moments, she exited the building into brilliant sunshine.

"What you did to that boy, riding him like a horse, was . . . repulsive," a voice at her ear whispered, nothing there but air.

She almost yelped. Sizmor hovered over her shoulder, invisible to her and anyone looking her way. Sylvie took a calming breath. "*That's* what you were worried about? The sex? Not the attempt to steal the crown?"

"Well, that too, of course," Sizmor said. "I still feel ill, though."

"Oh yeah? Well, how do the Fae have sex?" Sylvie asked, not even wanting to know. Her head still spun from what Idlor had attempted.

With Darian's help, she cursed inwardly.

"I do not think a human can understand," the sprite said as they passed a group of children playing in Mont-Saint-Michel's grassy inner courtyard. "Let's just say it involves more play—days of it, sometimes—and less grunting and panting and sweating."

Sylvie laughed, needing it to calm down, she realized. "Master Kell and Grumtil said you are to be my counselor when I need it," she said. "What am I going to do about Lord Idlor? He is a powerful man who knows other powerful men. In other words, he is dangerous."

"Grumtil shared a great deal about the kingdom and its politics. Idlor did command Grumtil's respect. Still, the Lord endangers the Compact. That cannot be allowed."

"Is there even a way for me to refuse the crown?" Sylvie made her way into the High Garden. Privacy, shade, and blooming flowers in an array of colors always helped her find peace. She went to her favorite bench and sat. "Some way to erase my name from the codex?"

"That, I do not know. The magic of the Compact between Fae and Man is complex. Perhaps the Elders of the Shadow Court would know. Or Master Historian Kell."

Sylvie sighed. "It feels wrong to betray my father's wishes."

"If that is your choice," Sizmor said, "then accept it. Life is short for humans, and regrets are plentiful, from what Grumtil tells me."

"Speaking of Grumtil, where is he? Is he flying beside my other ear?"

"He is paying his final respects to High King Alafair Goode."

Sylvie wondered if her father had been close friends with the sprite. If so, the little Fae might have some insight. "I would like Grumtil's advice about this, yes," she said. "He saw much as an advisor to my father. He likely knows Idlor better than anyone."

"I think that would please High King Alafair," Sizmor said. "However, Grumtil flies back to the Twilight Lands upon the winds of the funeral pyre. There can never be more than one Fae present once a coronation is completed, so says the Compact. If I can find the time for Grumtil to speak with you before then, I will ensure it happens."

Sylvie nodded and closed her eyes, enjoying the sun on her face. Birds sang in the High Garden's willows, and children ran about laughing and screeching. They paid her no mind—they didn't even know who she was. She knew all of that would change soon.

"You have gone quiet," Sizmor said finally. "Is there anything more you require?"

"I think I am recovered from Lord Idlor," she said, shaking her head.

"What of your boy?"

Sylvie hadn't given much thought to Darian since she'd run out of his bedroom. "I know what I must do. But I have larger worries right now," she said. "I need Master Kell's knowledge. He understands more about the Covenant Codex of Saint Emmer than anyone else in the kingdom. He also knows Idlor, and will know how to counter what he's trying to do."

"Does this mean you wish to be High Queen of Royaume de France?"

"I do wish it," she said, not realizing the truth until the words had escaped her mouth. "Yes. I do. It is my duty. I will honor my father's wishes."

Sylvie got to her feet and began walking back toward the Masters Tower. She had chosen. Now she needed Kell's help dealing with Idlor. She climbed the steps two at a time, feeling the thrill of hope. She reached her quarters and was about to unlock the door when movement at the end of the corridor caught her eye.

She froze, uncertain. Outside the window, a shadow blocked the sunlight and then vanished.

"Who was that?" Sizmor asked at her ear.

"I don't know," Sylvie said. "But it is quite normal here. When I was younger, I moved about the castle roof regularly."

Finding the door already unlocked, she pushed it open.

The tea kettle was whistling and hissing. It continued to do so as she entered the living quarters she shared with Master Kell. She wondered why he was not attending it. Remembering the shadow outside the window, she crept in silently, the hair along the nape of her neck standing up.

In the main sitting room, between his plush chair and fireplace, lay Master Kell, the front of his white robe crimson, his throat slashed and a dagger buried in his chest.

She wanted to scream, but she remembered her Master's teachings. She moved across the room as cautiously and quietly as she could and knelt next to her mentor's side. His glazed eyes stared up at the ceiling.

Sizmor materialized on her shoulder. "Who would do such a thing?" the Fae whispered.

"I have a guess, but nothing matters without the facts," she said, tears stinging her eyes. She focused on steadying her breath. She wouldn't cry. Resolve mattered more than sorrow. The tea over the fireplace made her believe his killer had been familiar. Kell always offered tea to his guests, and since the kettle hadn't boiled out, the murder must have happened within the hour. Sylvie looked her mentor over and felt his flesh—still warm. She smelled the air above his open mouth—no poisons she could discern. Then she looked at the long dagger in his chest, a weapon he had gifted her long ago.

"My knife," Sylvie said, shaking her head. "A present, for passing my battle history trials. It was in my room."

"Someone wants this to look like you did it then," Sizmor said. The sprite pointed at the floor next to Kell. "What is written there, Sylvianna?"

She bent to examine the floor, where blood had been smeared into writing.

"'Mikkel Dung,'" Sylvie read. "He must not have died immediately from his neck wound. There is blood on his fingers, his hands. He wrote this before the blow to his heart."

"What does it mean?"

"Mikkel is the name of a rebel who wanted to take the throne before I was born. A son of High King Alafair who rose in rebellion against his father. Just like Alafair and the others, Mikkel could not be killed. The Dung part is perplexing."

"Did this Mikkel kill your Master, do you think?"

"Possibly. But if he did, why now? No, it doesn't feel right. Master Kell had been making tea for someone he knew. He would not have done so for Mikkel. No, this means something else." She paused. "And what is the meaning of 'Dung'? That's far more interesting."

"Maybe because Mikkel sounds like a proper shit?" Sizmor said with a straight face.

Sylvie ignored him. "What if Kell died before he could finish writing? And the smearing is someone trying to conceal what was written?"

"It makes sense."

Sylvie checked Kell's fingers. His hands and forearms were covered in blood, undoubtedly from attempting to stanch the wound at his neck.

She remembered what Idlor had said then. That if she didn't choose what he wished, there would be repercussions.

"I caused this," she whispered.

Just then, she heard a heavy door crash open.

Sizmor flew to the front entryway. "Knights of the Ecclesia," he yelled at her.

Sylvie ripped the dagger from Kell's chest. She had to escape. The knights would be in the corridor and would shortly be flooding into her quarters. She went to the window, threw it wide, and pulled herself out. The sun was blazing and the roof sizzling hot; she looked down and felt dizzy. She would not fall. She moved across the roof and through a maze of chimneys and smaller turrets and towers.

She wanted to cry for Kell. Needed to. But tears would blur her vision. She kept moving, the Fae creature hovering beside her. They needed to hide, and she knew many secret passageways through Mont-Saint-Michel.

"Where do we go?" Sizmor asked.

"Do you have any problem with stone and darkness?"

5

he lowest depths of Mont-Saint-Michel were as formidable—and dank—as she remembered.

Sylvie and Sizmor ventured deep into the castle's bowels, her torch held high to light their way as the two moved through narrow corridors that seemingly had no end, chiseled from the rock beneath the city. This was the world Sylvie had grown up in. As a child, she and her friends had explored the endless maze of the depths looking for lost treasure, or hunting deadly creatures from Fae stories. She knew these secret places as well as her own name, and now she was heading for a hidden door that led to the dungeons. There, long ago, she had spoken to prisoners who regaled her with stories of their ludicrous deeds or even tried to gain her help in breaking free—but she had never met anyone named Mikkel.

Now older, Sylvie wondered why such hidden cells were needed. Regardless, she pushed her musings aside; she returned to these depths only to discover who had killed Kell. Thankfully, he had given her the tools to unravel the mystery. He taught her knowledge found in books, but she also learned from meetings between the High King and dignitaries. Studied how to lead by example. To do right even if it meant failing. And to keep all options open, no matter how a situation looked. She knew her mentor had been trying to help her with his cryptic message in blood, but she had to tread carefully.

"You think Mikkel's down here?" Sizmor asked.

"I do," she said. "Kell was trying to help me. I firmly believe that. And someone unkillable like Mikkel would be kept in a place like this, with the worst criminals. It'd be where I'd imprison him if I were Alafair."

"It is also where you will likely end up if the magic upon your house remains and you are caught by Lord Idlor," Sizmor said.

Sylvie hadn't thought of that. She shivered, and not from the air's icy chill. "How attuned are your Fae senses to the natural world? I've heard so many stories about sprites, but I do not know what is real and what is Fae story."

Sizmor snorted. "We Fae are quite different from humans. We live in a world of magic that is largely invisible to your kind."

"Do you think you could find a hidden room down here?"

The sprite shrugged. "A hidden room within a hidden dungeon? Possibly. If one exists."

Sylvie held her torch high as they ventured through the secret corridors. She remembered every corner, crook, and cranny like old friends. Eventually, the carved rock ended at a wall built from stone blocks. She touched two places, as she had been shown by a boy her first time here. An unseen mechanism tumbled and clicked. The hidden door swung outward; the dark tunnel to the dungeons lay beyond. Sylvie held a finger to her lips. Sizmor nodded.

They stepped quietly into the tunnel, past empty cell after empty cell.

"What is that smell?" Sizmor whispered.

"Humans living. Humans dying."

"I hate it here. Oppressive and evil. We Fae do not have such places." Sizmor stopped in the air before her, and Sylvie had to halt. "Rather than look for a door or hidden room, wouldn't it be easier to see signs where someone has entered an area that they shouldn't be able to?"

"You can do that?"

"Sometimes. Though the air carries the least trace of passage. I might find nothing," the sprite said.

"I have a lot to learn about you," Sylvie admitted, suddenly sad her mentor would not be there to help. She had a lot of questions. Could one of High King Alafair's children starve, despite the witch's curse? Was that a natural death? She didn't know. But she doubted Kell would have sent her into the dungeons on a fool's errand. Mikkel had to be here. "See what you can find," she said.

Sizmor scouted ahead, sweeping the corridor from side to side. "There, Sylvianna." He pointed at a wall between empty cells.

It looked like just another wall of dark stone.

"How do we open it?"

Sizmor hovered next to the wall. "Here. I see the traces of many human handprints here. Use the palm of your hand, fingers out."

Sylvie pressed her hand on the cold stone, but nothing happened. She pushed harder and heard a series of clicks. The wall swung inward, creating a passage barely wide enough for her to use. She peered into a narrow corridor that vanished into darkness. She gave the sprite a look. He shrugged and flew ahead. The tunnel turned to the left, deep enough now to run behind the other cells. She saw flickering candlelight ahead, and then a door. The door was made of thick bars, rusty and old, but it was the large room beyond it that left Sylvie stunned. It was at least five times the size of the other cells and looked almost like a merchant's sitting room. Tapestries on the walls, tall shelves of books, a bed larger than any Sylvie had slept in, and a desk with quill, ink, and parchment. It was a room for a prince in a most unprincely place.

A man sat at the desk. Long salt-and-pepper hair hung lank over his shoulders and a thick beard hid most of his face. He wore a simple brown tunic that appeared quite warm over broad shoulders and a wide chest that was built for war.

It wasn't until they locked stares that Sylvie worried about Kell's message.

For those eyes burned with madness.

"Well," the man said. "It seems we have a visitor. And a beautiful one at that."

Sylvie let the flattery go. "We? Is there someone else in there with you?"

He shrugged. "I have so few visitors, I contrived someone to talk to. One cannot debate philosophy, power, or even love without a willing partner." He looked her over. "You are not here to feed me or remove my pot. You aren't supposed to be here at all."

"No, I am not," Sylvie said, taking a deep breath of cold air. "And I don't have long, either. Will you listen to me?"

"Do I have a choice?"

"You are Mikkel Goode," Sylvie said. "I am Sylvianna Goode, your half-sister. We share a father. In that way, we are bound. Master Kell also binds us. I was his student. Like you were."

"Then, Sylvianna Goode, you are educated. I like that," Mikkel said. "I do not like how you just used the past tense, though. Did you learn all you could from Kell and then leave him?"

"He's dead."

Mikkel looked away for a moment. "That is unfortunate. He was a good man. Perhaps the best I've ever known. This must have happened in the last few days?"

Sylvie frowned. "Why do you think that?"

"He visited me three days ago."

Visited three days before his death, Sylvie thought. She had not expected that, but it made sense. Someone had brought this stuff here.

"What did you talk about?" she asked.

"A question first," Mikkel said, a scarred hand tugging at his beard. "You could be anyone. How do I know you are Alafair's issue?"

"You likely cannot," Sylvie admitted. "I know I am, though. The High King stabbed me in the chest from his deathbed to prove to the Pontiff and all in attendance that I could not be killed."

"And therefore, it made you one of his children. Ah yes, that sounds like our father. Not a thing most people would lie about, that's for sure," he said. "I remember when I discovered I could not be killed.

I was eight. Knife to the chest, same as you. I pulled the blade out and killed the boy who had done it." He grinned, staring off at a past only he could see. "My first kill. Not clean, either. Tomas was his name. He was fifteen."

Sylvie shivered. She knew little about Mikkel. Master Kell had told her a great deal about his military victories as First Knight but not much else. She wondered if Kell had done that purposefully, to shield her from some truth.

"Why was Master Kell here?" she asked.

"To tell me that our father lay dying. Then yesterday, I felt the change in my heart the moment he died."

"You could feel it?"

Mikkel stood and walked to the cell door, folding his arms across his broad chest. "We are no longer unkillable. And a man who spent a great deal of time surrounded by death can feel when it is coming for him. It is a natural thing for a knight to know." He paused, considering her. "I expected armed knights to come for me the moment he died. A final parting gift for the hatred Alafair had for me."

While Mikkel's feeling could not be corroborated without violence to one of their persons, his words did make Sylvie even more cautious than before.

"I am not here to kill you. I am here for a different reason," Sylvie said. "Master Kell was murdered. He wrote your name in blood on the floor. It's what brought me here."

"That is sad news. Why would he write my name?"

"I do not know, but I learned to not second-guess him."

"I hope you learned that faster than I did," Mikkel said. "Who killed him? And why?"

"I don't know who did it. Though I have my suspicions."

Mikkel grabbed the bars with thick-fingered hands. "But you know the why."

Sylvie nodded. "On his deathbed, High King Alafair Goode made me his heir."

She expected him to laugh, but he just gathered his thick, greasy hair and twisted it into a bun upon his head. "The Naming. Our siblings must be quite chagrined."

"Lord Idlor attempted to bribe me to give up the crown."

"Ahh, Idlor," Mikkel growled, and pursed his lips. "Not the most cunning of the bunch, but he has power."

"He told me if I didn't refuse the crown, he would discredit me. And he did that by framing me as Kell's murderer. Sent the Ecclesia knights after me."

"Yes, that sounds exactly like Idlor. When our father needed help to dishonor me, Idlor was right there trying to gain favor with a handy lie about me conspiring to remove Father from the throne." Mikkel paused, shaking his head. "If you've been Named heir, I expect you've met Grumtil."

Sizmor materialized then, flying out of the cell.

"Well, well, a thief in the shadows," Mikkel said, eyeing the little Fae creature. "Grumtil's replacement for the new Queen, I would think. Spying on me, dear sprite?"

Sizmor landed on Sylvie's shoulder. "I was examining your bookshelves. You can learn a great deal about a man by what he reads. Or so Grumtil says."

Mikkel nodded. "True enough. How is old Grumtil doing?"

"He's deeply saddened by the loss of his friend," Sizmor said.

"That makes one of us," Mikkel grunted.

Sylvie stepped closer to the door. "You hated him, didn't you? Alafair, I mean."

"I did not hate him. He was my father and my High King. I devoted myself to his bloody cause with fervor and honor. Do you have Lumière? If you do, it will go a long way in securing the crown for that head of yours."

The thought hadn't even occurred to Sylvie. The famous blade had belonged to the Kings of history as far back as Kell's books had recorded, to King Halston Pendragon during the time of Saint Emmer. Forged from fallen-light, it not only carried with it the proclamation of kingship but was said to possess powerful magic on the battlefield.

"I know not where it is," Sylvie admitted. "I saw it when Pontiff Scorus moved our father's body to the Citadel. The sword lay on the King's chest, in his hands. The Pontiff and other Bishops of the Citadel have it for the funeral."

"Then it is with your enemies," Mikkel said.

Sizmor moved to Sylvie's palm. "As far as we know, Pontiff Scorus is a good man."

Mikkel snorted. "Do not believe it. Scorus helped put me in here too, when he was Bishop of Mont-Saint-Michel. Do not think he's an ally simply because he's a holy man. He will use Lumière as leverage, especially if he believes you should not be High Queen. Every man who gains power wields it for his benefit."

"Like you did?" Sylvie asked.

"You know not of what you speak, *girl*. I never abused my power."

"You merely tried to usurp the kingdom."

Mikkel laughed then, an echoing guffaw. Sylvie cringed, hoping the stone around them muffled the sound.

When he finished, he had tears in his eyes. "Thank you, Sylvianna Goode, for the laugh," he said. "Though perhaps crying would be more appropriate."

"What do you mean?"

"You are as wrong about history as you could be. Is that the tale Kell told you? Perhaps his mind grew soft as he aged. Worse, he protected his brother's role in it." Mikkel shook his head. "I did not want the kingdom. I was the High King's First Knight, the only honor I ever strove for after I saw my first tourney when I was six. By the time I was fifteen, I was one of the best warriors in the city. By nineteen, Father had dubbed me his First Knight. We finished quelling the outlying territories and unified the land under one banner for the first time. I was his man. In some ways, he was less a father and more a best friend."

"Then why did you turn on him? Master Kell told me your story but never explained the why of it all."

"Ah, Sylvianna. The why is never what you expect. If Kell never explained, then his silence on the matter is like a blaring trumpet of falsehood. Especially after the victor has chiseled his story into history. The why, you ask? Love. Love put me here."

"You tried to overthrow the crown . . . for love?"

"I did nothing save protect the love of my life." He turned away from her for a moment and cleared his throat. "After the Battle of the Three Immortals, by which the kingdom finally became one, I went home. Alafair said I had earned a rest. I took the offer. I went to take stock of my new landholdings. To set up the government of my province. If Kell taught you as he did me, you learned how best to lead. I went right to work." Mikkel sighed. "I should have listened more to bards. They sing of love happening when one least expects it. It was true for me."

"Who was she?" Sizmor asked before Sylvie had the chance. "She must have been quite the woman to capture a First Knight's heart."

"Chelle was unlike any woman I had met," Mikkel said. "A beauty, to be sure, but my feelings for her ran much deeper. She was intelligent. She had a wry humor that made me laugh more than I had a right to, given the death I had doled out. And she cared for what I attempted to build. We were happy."

"What happened?" Sylvie asked.

"I brought her to court. It pleased me to share our happiness with my friends in the Ecclesia. After so much bloodshed, believing a life after war was possible meant a great deal to me. Chelle charmed everyone, including the other women at court. She dazzled one and all."

"Did one of the other Ecclesia knights pursue her then?" Sylvie guessed.

"Not exactly. I could have dealt with that in a test of arms. No, the man you are asking about was our father."

Sylvie and Sizmor looked at one another. She most certainly had never heard this part of the tale, but the moment Mikkel shared it, she knew it to be true. She saw how the pieces of the puzzle fit perfectly. With the High King who lost his Queen and, to fill the void, bedded as many women as he could.

"I am so sorry," Sylvie said. "I had no idea. It must have been horrible."

"At first, I thought Alafair jested," he continued. "But then I saw how he changed toward me. And I saw how in error I was. Our father became infatuated with Chelle. First he tried to woo her without my knowledge. He did not get far. She spurned him as kindly as she could. When she told me of it, I knew I had to act. I sent her home to Bavar. Then I confronted him in private. He tried to tell me that Chelle misunderstood his intentions, then asked me to quell a small uprising in the north." He paused and rubbed his scarred hands. "It was a terrible time."

"Because the uprising was not real," Sizmor said. "A fool's errand to remove you so he could pursue your woman."

"Sprite, you cut to the bone. I was indeed a fool. There was no uprising. Alafair sent me north even as he traveled to Bavar to woo Chelle. Once I realized what he had done, I sent a raven with a note to my steward ordering him to bar the castle. Alafair had not been prepared for that. He hadn't brought an army. Unable to get what he wanted, he returned here to prepare the Ecclesia knights, while I prepared my army for what was to come."

"So . . . you weren't after the kingdom."

"Hardly. I was merely protecting my life and my love. The rest you know from what Kell taught you, I'd wager." He paused. "What would you have done in my stead, Sylvianna?"

Sylvie thought about it a moment. "I . . . I don't know."

"What happened to the Lady Chelle?" Sizmor asked.

"After the armies of the kingdom destroyed Bavar, Alafair had his way with her." Mikkel turned his back to them again. "He discarded her after that. Kell told me she left to join one of the abbeys in shame. The thought of her feeling any sort of guilt in it still angers me."

"And since you could not be killed, they put you here. In these dungeons," Sylvie said. "No wonder Kell continued to visit you. You were not in the wrong. But why didn't Master Kell teach me all of this? Was it banned by Alafair?"

"It doesn't matter. It is the past and what's done is done," Mikkel said with a dismissive wave. He walked over to his desk and straightened some papers and books, a nervous act that Sylvie also performed from time to time. "Nothing can undo it. I cannot regain the lost decades. I cannot unmake a nun once she has given her oath."

"You can help me, though," Sylvie said.

"How so?"

"Swear fealty to me as High Queen of Royaume de France."

Mikkel snorted another laugh and turned to face her. "I will say, you are tenacious. You will need that if you are to set right the wrong that has been done to you." He shook his head. "But I will not swear fealty again. Not until I learn how you would conduct yourself as a monarch. Perhaps I will consider your offer then."

Crestfallen, Sylvie hid how she felt. She needed allies. A former First Knight would make a powerful one—not only for his strength of arms but for the fact he knew Lord Idlor and the other snakes slithering for control of the kingdom. With stunning clarity, she realized she had no other options, no other friends, no one. Not even Darian, whom she could not trust.

"I see you did not understand my answer, not fully." Like Kell had been able to do, Mikkel read her easily, it seemed. "I merely said I would not swear fealty. I will aid you if you free me. You simply will not have power over me as a liege would."

"Very well. Where do we begin?" she asked.

"Lord Idlor will not be working alone. He could be working with any of our siblings. Or those of the Citadel. Or even the Masters. He is the first enemy you must stop, because he is known. The others can be dealt with later." Mikkel eyed her. "Before these dungeons became my home, I always found the best way to weed out the dishonest was to be direct. Being direct is unexpected. Sets people on edge. Gives insight into what they are thinking. We go to Idlor."

She nodded to the sprite, who flew to the door's locking mechanism and studied it. "And if he is wishing a crown upon his head, take the head. Leave the crown."

Mikkel grinned. "I like you, Sylvianna Goode."

Through some Fae means, Sizmor unlocked the cell door. Sylvie pulled it creaking open. Mikkel just stood there, eyes wide. Then he grabbed a dark cloak and pulled it over his head.

"I need a sword," Mikkel said.

DONATO

6

A light at the end of the corridor outlined the hidden door to Idlor's quarters.

After freeing Mikkel, the three had lingered in the dungeon to ensure a nighttime exit before going to gather supplies. Sylvie went to the kitchens first; they were empty, as she had hoped. She took cheeses, breads, and salted meats—enough to last them several days. Even sugar cubes for Sizmor. After that, she gathered two heavy blankets from linen closets and a black robe, which she changed into. She returned to Kell's quarters, which had been ransacked and the body removed, and took his elixirs and poisons for her canvas sack. Then, being careful of the Ecclesia knights guarding various entrances and exits, Mikkel led her to a small armory, from which he took a sword, daggers, and a thick leather vest. Confident they had what they needed, the three of them went back through the secret passages to the King's Tower. As far as Sylvie could tell, they had avoided detection.

The King's Tower housed not only the High King's quarters, on its uppermost floor, but also the royal suites of many of Alafair's children, including Idlor. If she could confront him without interference from the Knights of the Ecclesia, she was confident she could expose the traitor. The plan she had formed depended on her most.

Sylvie nodded to Mikkel and Sizmor before she pressed her ear up to Idlor's hidden door.

She could just make out voices.

"The Knights of the Ecclesia will be in place by then, yes?" Idlor was saying, but his words were faint, as if they were coming from the next room over. "All safety measures must be in place to maintain a peaceful farewell to my father. And I want them there during the coronation too. I do not want havoc when I'm supposed to reassure the kingdom."

"The knights will guard both ceremonies, my King," another male voice assured him. She had heard the voice before but couldn't place it. There seemed to be only the two men. It made sense. The fewer people who knew, the safer they were.

"Good," Idlor said. "Have you found Mikkel? Kell would not have written that name with his own blood if my half-brother did not remain in Mont-Saint-Michel. Mikkel is older now but just as dangerous. Do you think she searches for him? As an ally?"

"I do not know. My spies seek her even as the Ecclesia knights do. We will find her."

"She is smart and determined, which I can't really say of you. How *did* you rise to Bishop if you so underestimate your enemies?"

"My friends are well paid, and they outnumber my enemies, my King."

"Kell," Idlor cursed. "Even in death, he is a nuisance."

The other man snorted but said nothing more.

"If the magic that protected my father continued in me, I would not worry so. High King Alafair Goode never had to fear for his life. I do, it seems." Someone brought a fist down onto something solid, the sound echoing. "When that bastard whelp died at her mother's tit, it likely saved me."

"Useful to know, my King. Useful to know, for sure."

Sylvie took a deep breath, angered by the conversation and where it had led. Idlor had done exactly as the Master Historian surmised; her half-brother had tested the magic upon their house and found it lacking. The very idea of this man killing a babe in her mother's arms bolstered Sylvie's resolve even further. He had to be held accountable for what he had done, not only to Kell but to all those he'd harmed.

She steadied herself and triggered the door's release. A bit more light entered the tunnel. Then she nodded to Mikkel and pushed on the panel.

The room Sylvie entered was ornate, filled with art, fine furniture, a fireplace of dying red embers, and the thick odor of perfumed candles. The voices had come from an adjoining room to her left. To her right was probably Idlor's bedchamber. She crept silently to the bedroom and peered there, to make sure there was no one else present. It was empty.

She then made her way to the open room with the two men. Idlor sat behind a large desk, sifting through paperwork, three tall stained-glass windows behind him, the other walls covered in bookshelves. The second man sat across from him, scribbling notes into a book. He wore a simple robe with a large hood lying flat on his back. Rolls bulged at his neck and his bald head glistened in the candlelight.

That wasn't all. She saw Lumière lying across the desk between the two men, sheathed but unmistakable in its craftsmanship and beauty.

She steeled herself and stepped into the room. "Is that the High Queen's sword?"

Idlor glanced up. The other man turned too, and Sylvie recognized Pontiff Scorus. He gaped at her, his jutting lower lip trembling. The latter gave her more pleasure than it should have.

Idlor was not so surprised. He leaned back in his chair, hands steepled before him, watching her and the knife in her hand.

"Bold move, Sylvianna," Idlor said. "Most unexpected. As my door is guarded, it seems you've scurried in like a rat." He looked her over, eyes lingering a moment on the dagger. "Pray tell, is that the knife you murdered Master Kell with?"

"*I* did not kill him."

"Oh, but you did," Idlor said, standing. She could tell he hadn't slept much in the last two days by the dark circles under his eyes. "I told you. Choices have consequences. You chose, and that decision ended Kell's life. His blood is on your hands, not mine." He grinned, took Lumière from the desk, and held it up for her to see. "But that matters little. After your treachery was discovered, I took Lumière. I was always the most likely to become High King. Pontiff Scorus has already conducted the Rites of Kingship, witnessed by the Knights of the Ecclesia and most of the Masters. What's done is done. There is no changing it. I am High King."

Sylvie should have known Idlor would twist precedent to his desires. It changed little for her plan, though. The days ahead would be more difficult than she had anticipated, but she was ready for them. "Not when the truth is known," she said. "As I learned earlier today, the truth can never be buried, because there is always someone with a shovel."

"But how will you dig that truth up, Sylvianna?" Idlor asked, stepping around his desk. "Word has spread through Mont-Saint-Michel and has likely already reached the other cities and villages. You killed Master Kell. Knights of the Ecclesia—the most noble men in all the kingdom—saw you flee your quarters with your bloody dagger in hand. You are a murderer."

"Guilt. Innocence. Rumor. They are only words," she said, watching Pontiff Scorus heave his round body out of his chair. She did not see the Covenant Codex of Saint Emmer on the table, though, which meant she'd have to find it.

"Ah yes, your vaunted studies." Idlor chuckled. He unsheathed Lumière. "Philosophy will not save you."

"You are right about that, despite being wrong about so many things," Sylvie said. "You have Lumière. Yet you need the Knights of the Ecclesia to keep you safe during the funeral and public coronation."

"She's been listening to our plans," Scorus hissed.

"Listening is the first lesson a great ruler learns," Sylvie said, shaking her head. She pointed her dagger at Scorus. "You've forgotten that."

"And you've no one to keep you safe from me. A girl, alone, and without magic to keep her from harm." Idlor stepped from behind the desk, Lumière at the ready. "I have never liked killing, but I think I will enjoy it tonight."

That's when Sizmor materialized between them.

"Sylvianna Goode is not alone," the sprite said.

"Blasphemy!" Scorus yelled, pointing at Sizmor. He turned to Sylvie with an accusing finger, eyes bulging. "That thing is unholy! You're in league with them. You are a witch! My King, we need to kill her and that *thing* now. Now! Guards! Knights!"

Then Mikkel stepped into the room from behind Sylvie. Idlor froze, his bravado snuffed like a candle. The Pontiff paled.

"I will leave when my work is done." Sylvie nodded to Mikkel. "I've brought my brother here to verify that the witch's magic upon Alafair and his seed is indeed no longer."

The former First Knight of High King Alafair Goode moved into the room, a simple soldier's sword in his hand, eyes fixed on Idlor. Sylvie stepped back to give Mikkel more space to maneuver. Idlor moved away from his desk toward the windows. Mikkel said nothing. He crept steadily toward the desk and around its corner. Idlor raised Lumière before him. Sylvie doubted the man had held a sword since the kingdom's last battle almost three decades earlier. Mikkel hadn't wielded a sword in quite a while either.

On the other side of the desk, Scorus pushed up against the wall. He squeezed his rotund shape by his chair and stumbled to the suite's main door. Sizmor looked to Sylvie; she grinned and nodded. The Pontiff reached the key sticking out of the locked door. With shaking fingers, he fumbled to get the door open. "Knights! Knights! To me!" he thundered and pushed on the heavy door. It opened only a few inches, blocked by something on the floor outside.

"The knights on watch will not be joining us," Sylvie said. "My little friend here put them to sleep. You might as well come back into the room. We have much to discuss."

Sizmor waved a tiny hand and a gust of wind drove Scorus back into the room and slammed the door.

"Mercy. Mercy," Scorus said, quivering in fear.

"I wonder? Was it you who stabbed Master Kell with my knife?" Sylvie asked.

"He did it!" Scorus yelled, pointing at Idlor. "He did it all!"

Sylvie glared at Idlor. Mikkel stepped toward him. Idlor had to know Mikkel was one of the best swordsmen to ever step on a battlefield, but the elder scion held the fallen-light sword, a weapon capable of slicing through most materials. It would balance the fight between them.

Mikkel feinted. Idlor didn't fall for it. Mikkel stepped to the side. The two men circled one another before the stained-glass windows, their rasping breaths and Scorus's whimpering the only sounds in the room. The former First Knight grinned, his eyes bright. Sylvie realized Mikkel was enjoying this, a cat playing with a mouse.

Idlor must have sensed it as well. He roared and attacked, feinting left and thrusting right. Mikkel brought his sword up to parry—his first mistake, Sylvie thought.

Lumière shattered Mikkel's sword, shards exploding into both men.

Idlor swung Lumière back and forth, pushing his advantage. He brought Lumière against his weaponless enemy, hitting Mikkel's shattered sword at its hilt again and again, driving the larger man back toward the wall of books. His back to the shelves, Mikkel kept his broken blade in front of him, parrying each strike though it disintegrated with every hit. Just as Sylvie was about to shout at Sizmor to help, Idlor drove Lumière down at his foe—and this time Mikkel caught it with his sword's cross guard. The two men stood frozen, snarling hate.

Then Mikkel drove Lumière upward with one hand, grasped Idlor's sword hand with the other, and dug his thumb into his foe's wrist.

Lumière clattered to the floor.

"That was fun," Mikkel growled, discarding his broken sword. He grabbed the dazed Idlor and slammed his face into his desk. Blood welled up from a cut on the man's forehead. Then Mikkel turned him over and pinned him—knee on Idlor's chest and both of Idlor's wrists in his large hands.

Mikkel nodded to Sylvie. She approached, dagger firmly in hand.

"I will not grovel like Scorus there," Idlor said, blood seeping into his blinking left eye.

Mikkel's grin widened. "She isn't asking you to."

"I was doing what is best for the kingdom!" Idlor screamed.

Sylvie shook her head. "Then Master Kell would still be alive," she said, hardening her heart for what would come next. "He will live on in me, and I'll grant you one final lesson, to you from him. 'When a man lies, he murders a part of the world.' You lied. And there is only one way to deal with a murderer."

Bringing the dagger up so Idlor could see it clearly, Sylvie drove it down into his mouth and pinned him to his desk. Blood sprayed in crimson spurts as Idlor gagged and coughed. Its hot touch felt like a baptism on Sylvie's arms and face. She shuddered inwardly for a moment at the realization that as Idlor died, she confirmed her own vulnerability. But she didn't care. The battle lust for justice kept her focused solely on her foe. When Idlor tried to grasp her dagger, she pressed it harder into his mouth. Idlor died slowly, knowing that she had bested him. And whoever found his corpse would know not to cross her.

At last, the light in Idlor's eyes went out and his struggle ceased.

"For you, Father," Sylvie said, removing the dagger and wiping it clean on Idlor's finery.

"What would your father say?" Pontiff Scorus stammered, still cowering behind his chair.

"Master Kell was my father," Sylvie said, breathing hard from her efforts and prepared for more. "He raised me. I think he'd be proud. But if you mean High King Alafair Goode, he chose me to be his heir. And his heir, I shall be."

Sylvie nodded to Mikkel, and he retrieved Lumière from the bloody carpet. Then he walked over to Pontiff Scorus and slashed his thick white throat.

7

hey will find the bodies," Mikkel said next to Sylvie, arms folded over his chest. "The knights will wake from Sizmor's magic and realize they failed. Or the Citadel Bishops will come looking when Idlor and Scorus don't show up at the funeral."

Sylvie nodded, watching. They stood outside Mont-Saint-Michel's walls. From their cliffside vantage, they looked down on the ocean waves beating at the yellow-gray sandy beach, the water glimmering like a million fire diamonds. A large stone pier jutted into the sea, built for only one purpose—the funeral of royal family members. A large wooden boat with a single mast and furled sails stood at the ready, rocking gently, the day's final sunlight a swath of warm gold. On a tinderbox of dry wood and colorful flower wreaths lay High King Alafair Goode—He Who Once Wielded the Light of Lumière, the Final Bane of Mordreadth. Sylvie could see the regal finery the Citadel had dressed him in, his hands folded at peace upon his chest.

On the beach, the remaining members of the Goode family gathered alongside Masters, Bishops of the Citadel, and Ecclesia knights with their squires. Behind Sylvie, on the city's outer walls, commoners paid their respects. The sun descended toward the horizon where it would vanish into a salty sea—and the High King's funeral pyre would chase it, lit by a flaming arrow to honor the heroic man's life.

"I bet they're already looking for them. Might have even found them," Sylvie said, still viewing the ceremony. "It matters not. We have the time we need to set right the wrongs done."

"The Knights of the Ecclesia will hunt you," Mikkel said.

"They will. But they will fail."

"I like hearing calm certainty from you," Mikkel said, looking at her. "It is a powerful strength to possess. I will likely always be angry at Father, but I think he made a wise choice in Naming you heir. Holding on to that honor will be the difficult part."

"Without a Pontiff, no one can be crowned." Sylvie thought about the days ahead. She looked down at Lumière, sheathed and cradled in her arms like a baby. "The Bishops of the Citadel will clash over deciding who the next Pontiff will be. After that, he'll have to untangle the morass of rules and knowledge required to erase my name from the Covenant Codex of Saint Emmer, if it can even be done. In that time, I will prove my innocence and become High Queen."

"First, you must find the Covenant Codex of Saint Emmer," Mikkel said, appraising her. "It contains the proof you need. Scorus was a snake, but he was a smart one. It will be hidden. You may never find it."

"Or she could journey to the Twilight Lands and convince the Shadow Court to share the Covenant Codex of Wise Belloch," Sizmor suggested from her shoulder. The sprite had done well during the fight, and Sylvie now knew how valuable the Fae creature could be. "Remember, there are two matching copies. Though convincing the Fae to become involved in the political intrigues of Man may be far more arduous."

Sylvie barely heard him. She watched as the two most powerful Citadel Bishops gave their final benedictions upon the stone pier below, their shared song filling the evening air as they unfurled the sails and the boat began to move away from land into the great sea beyond. She agreed with both Mikkel and Sizmor. The days ahead would be hard ones. But she had to begin somewhere. She would have to learn everything about the Compact between Man and Fae, how the magic worked, and what problems could arise when no coronation took place at the expected time.

"That was quite beautiful," Grumtil said, the old sprite suddenly materializing to hover beside Sylvie and Sizmor. "I think High King Alafair Goode would be pleased. He is at peace."

"Did you do as I asked?" Sylvie questioned.

"I did as you commanded," Grumtil said, stroking his silvery beard, wings ablur. "The boy was shocked to see me hovering at his shoulder, but he left Sir Gwain's side when he heard you were nearby. He is headed here now."

"Did he alert Sir Gwain?" Mikkel asked. "Or any of the other knights?"

"No. He told Sir Gwain he had to piss in the dunes."

"Thank you, Grumtil," Sylvie said. "I owe you."

The old sprite bowed in mid-air. Together they continued to watch the boat drift from shore. Once the pyre was far enough out to sea, it would be set ablaze by Archery Master Kael. The ocean would consume what remained, spreading all that High King Alafair Goode had been to the far reaches of their world. It was a fitting tribute to a man who had saved it from the Great Darkness.

Sylvie soon saw the fruits of Grumtil's efforts. Darian had left the gathering below and now approached them on the cliff. The two sprites disappeared. When he saw her, Darian smiled, shaking his head in disbelief. She knew what she had to do. Yet as much as it hurt, she would do what was right by the kingdom.

"Darian, my love," Sylvie said, turning to him with a smile.

Dressed in his squire's best, Darian came right to her and wrapped his arms about her. She kissed him hard. Sylvie held the kiss for as long as she could. Fate would take care of the rest.

"I've been so worried," Darian said, rubbing her arms. He gave Mikkel a curious look but returned his attention to her. "I know you didn't kill Kell. I've been telling Sir Gwain and even some of the others that. But they won't listen. They have made up their minds."

"They have. Idlor used his poison well." Sylvie lightly touched his face, memorizing his handsome features. "Now it has spread."

"Why didn't you accept Lord Idlor's offer?" Darian pressed.

"Duty is an individual choice," she said. "High King Alafair did his duty by Naming his heir. I am doing my duty by accepting. Idlor thought he was doing his duty by protecting the kingdom from a woman. But as he said, choices have consequences."

"But we could have been together and still lived a fine life."

"It is not the life the High King wanted for me."

Darian frowned. "You aren't thinking this through, Sylvie. I think we need to go find Lord Idlor right now and straighten this out. Though no one seems to know where he is. The Pontiff too. They weren't at the funeral. It's like they just disappeared."

"Lord Idlor walked his own path, and that path has ended."

Darian took a step back. He looked at Mikkel and then at Sylvie. He blinked several times, took a deep breath, and shook his head. His cheeks reddened despite the cooling wind.

"I am sorry, Darian," Sylvie said. "Know that I loved you. Sadly, sometimes love isn't enough."

Horror twisted those features she had so come to love. He stumbled backward, tripping and falling hard on the dirt trail. She went to his side. She could have chosen to look away, to not view her handiwork. But Master Kell had taught her to take responsibility for all aspects of her life. She owed it to Darian to be there at his end, his death upon her lips when she kissed him. One of Kell's poisons, the antidote to which she'd swallowed earlier. His breathing became shallow, and he seemed lost in a daze.

A few moments later, Darian died, staring up at the sky.

"I see you have learned a difficult lesson," Mikkel said, nodding. "To rule, one must be dispassionate. Ultimately, he would have joined your enemies. He would have been used against you."

"I loved him," Sylvie said, wiping a tear from her cheek. She closed Darian's eyes. "Love is a powerful thing. Poets know it. Bards know it. You know it. Now, I know it. It makes me vulnerable. I cannot become the monarch Royaume de France needs me to be if my enemies have such an easy pathway to my heart."

"The world is only as bright as its darkest hole." Mikkel grunted. He said nothing more. She wondered if he was thinking of his long-lost beloved.

"What will you do now?" Sylvie asked him, still kneeling at Darian's side.

"You have given me my freedom. I never dreamed this day would come," Mikkel said, looking out at the sea. "They will never stop trying to kill you. You represent the power they all crave. One will succeed. At some point. Unless you steel your resolve and surround yourself with those you fully trust."

"I know. About that," Sylvie said, choosing her words carefully. "Before, you said that you would consider my offer of sworn fealty if you witnessed how I'd conduct myself as a High Queen. Will you now reconsider becoming my First Knight?"

Mikkel studied her. She gazed back. Long moments passed before he spoke. "Why would you do such a thing?" he asked finally. "I've done terrible things. I'm hated."

"You are hated for all the wrong reasons. Just as I am." Sylvie rose from Darian and stood at Mikkel's side. She put her hand on his forearm. "You are a good man, Mikkel Goode. History may not understand that, but Master Kell did. He wanted you to keep me safe. I offer you the title of First Knight for that reason. But I realize now he had one last lesson to teach. He wanted me to listen to your tale. To prevent it from happening to me. Love is a beautiful thing, but it can also be a weapon." She paused as she stared at Darian's body. "Without you, I might have fallen prey as you did. I thank you for sharing your story, despite the pain it causes you. I will never forget that."

Mikkel looked away, a light wind tousling his hair. Sylvie looked to the sprites, who had materialized once more. Sizmor shrugged. Grumtil waited, eyes curious.

Finally, her half-brother squared his shoulders and knelt before her.

"I would be honored to be your champion," he said, dropping his head to respectfully avert his eyes. "I will serve you and the kingdom faithfully as First Knight, to honor and protect the realm in life and by death, if need be."

Sylvie took Lumière and, rather than unsheathe the blade and touch his shoulders as was customary, placed the round pommel to his forehead.

She needed his new beginning to be different from the last.

"Rise, Sir Mikkel Goode," she said.

Mikkel did so. Sylvie breathed in the air, heavy with cool salt and coming night. It was a start. They watched the funeral pyre drift into the distance. Just when she thought Archery Master Kael wouldn't be able to reach the boat, he lifted his bow, lit the end of a large ceremonial arrow, pulled it back, and loosed it at the purpling sky, its fire an arc of flame.

Soon the boat was ablaze. A sting came to Sylvie's eyes. Not out of sadness for the dead, but for what High King Alafair Goode had given her.

At last, Mikkel rose and asked, "What will you do when our brothers and sisters fight for the throne, High Queen Sylvianna Goode? Not all of them will be as bold and forthright as Idlor. When word spreads about his death, they will conspire in the shadows. Even now, some likely plan a return to their lands, to raise armies and announce themselves as the true High King of the kingdom. What will you do when one challenges you? Or two. Or five. All blood-related with true claims to the throne."

"I will kill them," Sylvie said. "I will kill them all."

PART II

THE LIGHT-WEAVING PRIORESS

8

High Queen Sylvianna Goode waited in the Citadel, where Death was closing in.

It was not the death of old age that had completed the life of her father, High King Alafair Goode. It was not the death of vengeance that had destroyed her brother, Idlor Goode, who attempted to usurp the crown from her brow before her coronation took place. Nor was it the death of treason, which had found Pontiff Scorus as he abetted Lord Idlor, or the death of murder that had ended her lover, Darian, who dared to thieve her future in exchange for political gain. While the sun had set for her father in life's natural way—the ocean and its winds now scattering his ashes to the world—the others were destroyed by ill-conceived ambition, deserving of their fate. No, the death hunting her was of lawful justice, in search of which the Knights of the Ecclesia, who kept the kingdom safe, hunted a killer who could now die.

Sylvie sat in a secret reading room within the Citadel's library, one used only by the Master Librarian, and only in rare instances. She'd been in it twice before with Master Kell. The first time, they had observed an ancient manuscript reportedly written by Myrddin

Emrys, trusted advisor to Arthur Pendragon; the second time, it had been to view a rare prism crafted by light-weavers into the shape of a unicorn. The room hadn't changed since then. Bare walls. A chair. An oak desk. Parchment and a quill and inkwell. She'd be safe here, she had assured Mikkel; few would think to look for her in a library.

Her First Knight had left on an errand of great importance. He hadn't shared where he ventured. It left her in a precarious situation, though, one where she had to trust. She let Master Kell be her guide. She had to believe in him.

With his dying actions, he had delivered a First Knight to her.

She watched the small room's lone candle on the desk dwindle, as flame and time burned its wick through wax, thinking about her longtime teacher's last gift.

In that, Sylvie found solace.

"It is well beyond midnight now, Sylvianna Goode," Sizmor whispered in her ear. It was the second time he had made such a pronouncement.

"I know," she said, taking a deep breath.

"I do not think it prudent to stay here longer."

"We need to give Mikkel more time."

The sprite grunted. "What if he seeks out one of your enemies and exposes you?"

"He was honorable as First Knight during my father's reign," she said, unwilling to fall prey to the fears of the sprite. To do so would drive her to rashness. "He fought and bled for this kingdom, for my father. He will be honorable now that I freed him. You will see. Don't fret so, Sizmor."

"And if you are wrong?" the Fae asked. "He wanted Lord Idlor dead for a slight during their shared past. Now that Mikkel has his revenge, his plans may no longer align with yours."

Sylvie stared deeper into the flame, a single light in a sea of dark. She felt like the candle. "Then my tenure as Queen will be quite short-lived, my dear Fae. And our lives will be forfeit the moment this room's door is opened."

"I will not die that way," Sizmor sniffed. "I will fight."

Sylvie repressed a smile. She had only known the Fae creature for the barest of time, but she liked him.

"Let's hope it will not come to that," she said.

After the three of them left the cliff following Alafair Goode's funeral, Mikkel led them with haste back to the castle as night fell. Framed for the murder of Master Kell, anyone else would have fled Mont-Saint-Michel once they had dispensed justice on those responsible. Knights of the Ecclesia hunted her. To flee and live was a better deal than to be discovered and dead.

But Sylvie couldn't leave. She sought the Covenant Codex of Saint Emmer. It alone proved her legitimacy for the kingdom's throne. The last time she had seen the great book, it had been in the hands of Pontiff Scorus, who would have returned it to the Citadel. But none of her lessons had alluded to where the tome was stored. She only knew she needed it. By extension, Mikkel had left to discern answers. What he intended to do was a mystery even to her.

For without the Covenant Codex, her siblings would vie for the throne. The tome was the most powerful proof in Royaume de France in favor of the transition of power.

A soft rap at the door brought her back from reverie. With Sizmor chittering in her ear to be careful, she stood and took a deep breath before opening it barely a crack.

The sliver of light from the massive room beyond revealed a hulking shadow.

"It's me, my High Queen," a familiar voice whispered. "You may come out."

Sylvie snuffed the candle with wetted thumb and forefinger and stepped from the room.

As always, the grandeur of the Citadel's main library threatened to make her feel small. Stars winked through a giant circular skylight in the roof high above, but dozens of large candles set around the hall helped illumine thousands of books upon shelves, rows of empty study tables, and her First Knight now wearing the full plate armor of an Ecclesia knight while he cradled Lumière in his arms as if it was the most precious item to him.

Next to Mikkel stood a knight similarly armored, though not quite as tall or broad of shoulder. Fear pulsed through her. Worried Sizmor had been correct, Sylvie hesitated in the doorway of the secret room.

"Do not be alarmed," Mikkel said. His voice was a hiss within his steel helmet, but she could tell it was him. "All is well."

"You made no mention of seeking someone. Who is this?" she asked.

The second knight bent to one knee, the clink of his armor like pots and pans falling to a kitchen's stone floor. The sound left her even more on edge, as a lodestone drawing every guard to the library. "I am Lord Alent Loronn of Lyon. I served your father faithfully since I was a young squire. Now I am your humble knight, my High Queen."

"One of the good ones, according to Grumtil," Sizmor said at her ear.

"Rise, Lord Alent," Sylvie said. "No need for that here. We have more pressing matters than decorum." She had spoken to the Lord several times in the past and felt more comfortable in his presence now that she knew his identity. "You were always kind to me, even before all of this. But I fear what my First Knight has done by bringing you into this less-than-ideal circumstance."

"Lord Alent and I grew up together, fought together, and oftentimes recovered together after battle." Mikkel placed a gauntleted hand on the other's shoulder, a show of friendship. "Kell told me of Alent's rise as Legate to the Citadel, where he represents the Ecclesia. He is trustworthy. He is a friend to the kingdom. It is fortunate that, due to his rank, he was in the royal bedroom when Pontiff Scorus read your name aloud for all to hear after Alafair chose you as his successor."

"I am sorry I was unable to help you until now, though I'm not sure what I could have done," Lord Alent said. "The last few days must have been harrowing."

"That's one word for it," Sylvie said. "These are dangerous times, and you've been brought into that danger."

"I have survived worse," Lord Alent said, and Sylvie could hear his smile.

"I like that. I need survivors by my side," Sylvie said, turning to Mikkel. "Why did you seek him out? What's the purpose?"

"He knows where the Covenant Codex of Saint Emmer is housed."

Sylvie almost didn't believe what she heard. Hope rekindled after, she hated to admit, it had faded throughout the night. As they had made their way back to the city, she'd striven to remember anything from her time with Master Kell that indicated where the ancient book was kept. Nothing had come to the fore. She knew what everyone knew. For centuries, the Citadel and its Pontiff protected the Covenant Codex. But while the populace of Mont-Saint-Michel had access to the Citadel's main-floor church and library system, the areas above were forbidden and largely a mystery. Only the Pontiff, high-ranking officials of the Citadel, their staff, and other ambassadors—like Lord Alent—were given access. The fact that Alent Loronn had come to their aid seemed too good to be true.

"I think it best we move onward," Lord Alent said, glancing around. "The more time that passes, the chance we are discovered grows. I know the Ecclesia has focused on preventing you from escaping the city. Soon their efforts will look inward. There are only so many places to hide on this island."

Sylvie nodded, having shared his fears. With Lord Alent leading, she brought her new black robe's hood up to conceal her face and followed, with Mikkel bringing up their rear. Lumière remained with her First Knight—it wouldn't look out of place in his possession unless closely scrutinized—and they moved swiftly from the library through the maddening sprawl of hallways and corridors to a door steeped in shadows in the far corner of the floor. Only once did they have to hide upon leaving the secret room, when Sizmor heard an approaching group of four guards. After opening the shadowed door, they took a small staircase upward.

They encountered no one else once they entered the upper reaches of the Citadel. Lord Alent never deviated from his path. He guided them to the square tower that overlooked the city's central gardens, and from there deep into its heart.

"Are you sure he knows where to go?" Sizmor whispered in Sylvie's ear.

"Sprite, you can trust Lord Alent. Rarely do men change at our age," Mikkel responded, his voice dry paper rustling. "The religious men here decry change. Alent is not one of them."

Sizmor grunted. "How did he hear me?"

"It only takes one to listen, Master Fae," Lord Alent said with barely a look backward. The Fae's presence didn't seem to bother him at all, leading Sylvie to believe Mikkel had explained the sprite's inclusion already. "Now be quiet, please."

Walking as stealthily as his armor would allow, Alent stopped before a large set of doors that Sylvie didn't see until she was practically right on top of them. They were designed to mimic the stone of the walls, to remain concealed from everyone but those who knew they were there. Only an emblem spanning each door distinguished the entryway from the corridor: a carved image of Saint Emmer's sword, pointing downward with a shattered circle behind it. A single rose bloomed at the top of the symbol, its thorny vines twining about the blade's hilt.

"Bruyère," Sylvie said. She ran her fingers over the frieze. "The weapon that helped end the bloodshed between Man and Fae."

"Few have passed these doors," Lord Alent said. "If you like the artistry upon them, wait until you see what is within."

At that, the Ecclesia knight touched three thorns and three of the circle's fragments, each depressing into the stone. A series of clicks of some hidden mechanism sounded, and the doors opened outward on their own. Sylvie looked to Mikkel, who simply nodded back at her.

When Sylvie peered into the room, words left her. Inside, where hundreds of candles illuminated a room that could only hold several dozen people, the marble statue of a robed monk rose above all, dwarfing those observing it. The effigy of Saint Emmer held a large tome Sylvie recognized as a depiction of the Covenant Codex cradled in its handless left arm; held aloft in the air, raised high above the sculpture's head, was Bruyère. She took it all in. The monument had been designed by a Master craftsman, one capable of capturing the movement of the victorious moment despite the intractability of marble, where the stone stole the candlelight and glowed with the inner beauty and essence of its main character.

Above them all, a frieze of the archangel Michael had been carved into the ceiling, open hand outstretched and pointing with emanating beams of fallen-light, as if guiding Saint Emmer in the importance of his sacred duty.

Sylvie heard water then. It rippled quietly from beneath Saint Emmer's feet and down the stones at the base of the statue, forming a simple pool. Where the water came from or where it went, she could only guess, but it was a marvel to have such a fountain this deep in the Citadel.

"Who goes there?" a voice as old as an ancient whisper questioned.

Alent Loronn held up a hand before anyone could respond. "Aubert, it is I, Alent Loronn. Well met at this late hour," he said. "Keeping the candles lit against the darkness that follows the deaths of our dear Pontiff Scorus and Lord Idlor Goode?"

"Ah, a young sapling here to pray for those unfortunate, departed souls," Aubert said, his white eyes blinking in their direction. "It is indeed late and darker than usual. Hours mean little to me at this point in my life—I have seen many and too few remain—and I could not sleep with the sad, sad news." The old man stood on unsteady legs, his white hair wispy about his spotted head. "I will leave you to your spiritual duty and return to my cold bed. Let us pray the Ecclesia hunts down the killers."

Lord Alent nodded to the old man despite the latter's blindness. When the doors closed behind Aubert, Sylvie turned to Alent. "He is the caretaker of this room?"

"Yes. He is dear to me," Alent said. "To all of us. Soon he will adventure into Annwn."

"He sees much despite his affliction," Sizmor said, materializing.

"Indeed, he does, Master Fae," Lord Alent said, walking toward the statue. "Let's hope not too much. He is loyal to the Pontiff's seat and would not hesitate to sound the alarm at what I'm about to do."

Sylvie followed Alent between the pews, to stop before the great fountain. "This is an unbelievably beautiful work of art."

"It is. This is the Chapel of the Covenant Codex," Lord Alent said, lifting his helmet's visor. Sylvie remembered his blue eyes and graying blond hair, the combination accentuating his distinguished appearance. "It was sculpted in the decades following the Covenant. Few people are allowed to worship here. We are not likely to be bothered."

"And this is where the codex is kept?" Sylvie asked, skeptical. "It seems not protected enough for such an important item."

"When I reveal it, you will see."

At that, the Legate of the Citadel went to the edge of the pool and began to sing.

Sylvie recognized the melody—a hymn written by Saint Emmer. But the words of the verse and chorus were in a language she didn't recognize, one where each enunciated word held a beautiful lilt of hope and redemption. The song filled the chapel with resonant power, infiltrated the center of her being, and brought tears to her eyes. She realized she held her breath. Sizmor looked at her in surprise. He said nothing, but it was clear he knew something she didn't. Even the hard edges of Mikkel's face softened, the music affecting them all.

She realized that the sound of water had slowed. The pool below the statue's feet rippled with an inner light. Then the water parted before the watchful gaze of Saint Emmer.

Sylvie gaped at what appeared from the depths of the fountain—a chest made of the same marble as the fountain. It rose upward, water made solid somehow and holding it aloft.

And there it remained, waiting.

Lord Alent stopped singing. The chest continued to hover. He smiled at her surprise. "It is the 'Ballad of Wise Belloch' by Saint Emmer. Legend recounts he wrote it with Belloch in his presence, as they planned the Compact and the cease of conflict between Man and Fae."

"What language was that? I've never heard its like."

"It was the ancient Fae language of my people, Sylvianna," Sizmor answered. "We know the song too. Though a human voice singing it made my bark crawl."

"Probably more to do with my voice, Master Fae, than with a human singing it," Alent Loronn said with a wink. He went to the chest and unlocked its water-sealed gold catches. "Only the Pontiff, the Cardinal Bishop, and the Ecclesia Legate know the manner by which the chest can be revealed. This keeps the Covenant Codex of Saint Emmer safe, and we three ensure that if one of us dies, the knowledge is passed to the new member. Discovering and entering this room is difficult, but calling forth the Covenant Chest is impossible unless you know the 'Ballad of Wise Belloch' in his own Fae language."

Not only had Saint Emmer in death continued to keep safe the compact he had formed with the Fae, but those who had come after had created a marvel beyond what even the sculptor had accomplished. That level of foresight left Sylvie awed.

Then Lord Alent opened the chest's lid and reached in to pull forth the book. And paused. Heart sinking, Sylvie and the others went to the chest.

It was empty.

"No," Lord Alent breathed. He turned to look at the others. "I watched Pontiff Scorus return the Covenant Codex here after bringing the High King to the Citadel."

"Scorus must have put it somewhere else," Mikkel said, shaking his head. The thought had entered Sylvie's mind as well. "It wasn't in Idlor's suite. Maybe it's in the Pontiff's quarters."

"I sincerely doubt he returned the book here only to come back and take it again," Alent said, the worry in his voice mixed with fear. "There would have been no reason to do so. The Covenant Codex is our most sacred text. And with the Naming complete, he would have no further need of it."

"Then where is it?" Mikkel questioned, an edge to his words. "What of the Cardinal Bishop?"

"Wil Cornet was with me most of the time as we prepared the High King's body for his funeral," Alent said. "The Pontiff was there too. He held Lumière while we cleaned and dressed Alafair. No, the chance of it being one of them is small, if I am to guess."

"What of Aubert, that blind man?" Sylvie wondered aloud.

Before Alent could respond, Sizmor flew to the opened chest and, landing inside, touched the stone of the inner enclosure. His tiny face of green bark screwed up in disgust, as if he had just tasted an ale that had soured beyond drinkability.

"What is it, Sizmor?" she asked.

"A devastating darkness was here," the sprite whispered, his wings shivering from what he sensed. He knelt to place his palm on the chest's floor. "Something . . . dark. And twisted. I can feel it." He paused, concentrating, before his eyes shot open. "A Fae was here, unnatural in its creation and purpose."

"You can feel that?" Mikkel questioned.

"Yes, First Knight." Sizmor flew from the casket, features pained. He landed on Sylvie's shoulder where he quivered. "Sprites among the Fae have the ability to sense others. It's one of our gifts, one that sets us apart from the rest of my brethren." He paused, still considering the empty hole he had just left. "I have never felt such a void in the fabric of the air."

"Can you tell when the theft might have happened?" Sylvie felt her world crashing in around her all over again.

"Very recent. This night, I think."

"Can you tell what kind of Fae?"

"I have never felt its like. Strong and pungent. It's a magic I have not encountered before, yet is distinctly Fae," the sprite said, shaking his leafy head.

The room grew quiet. No one spoke. They looked to each other as if waiting for an answer that Sylvie knew would not come.

There was only one conclusion.

The Covenant Codex of Saint Emmer had been stolen.

DONATO

9

hen the outdoor air hit Sylvie, she shuddered and brought her cloak closer.

It had little to do with the coolness of the early hour or the fact she hadn't slept all night. As she and the others left the upper levels of the Citadel—careful not to fall prey to guards—a shadow of apprehension took root deep in her heart, slowly becoming dread. Mikkel seeking out Lord Alent and his connection with the Covenant Codex of Saint Emmer had been a blessing, one piece of good fortune amid a sea of terrible events beginning with the death of Master Kell and ending with her killing of Darian. But the hope sparked by finding the Chapel of the Covenant Codex had quickly been extinguished, stolen away as the book had been, leaving her with no path forward to reclaim her life and become the High Queen her father had wanted her to be.

One truth stood out among all others: there were forces aligning against her beyond those of family.

If the Fae were involved somehow, her enemies had doubled.

The weight of that realization pressed down on her.

"Morning is almost upon us," Lord Alent said, as they stood within the central gardens of Mont-Saint-Michel, the sky pinking to the east. "What will you do now, my High Queen?"

"I don't know," Sylvie said, having thought about it ever since they left the chapel. "I wanted the Covenant Codex to prove my Naming, so I could wear my father's crown, sit upon his throne, and make it my own. Now, I do not know." She paused and stepped up to Lord Alent, taking his hands. "I am in your debt. You have put yourself at risk for me, and I will not forget that."

"My High Queen," Lord Alent said, squeezing her hands back. "This is not something that will be easily sorted out. Without the Covenant Codex to confirm your name to the masses, there will be a power vacuum that will draw all interested parties. History recounts numerous kingdoms falling—not from invaders but from crumbling within amid power struggles. I know several of your siblings like Lord Pike and Lady Erlina will try to take advantage of the book's loss. And if the Fae are truly involved here, I see dark times ahead for you and the kingdom. Wars have started this way." He smiled despite the dire warning of his words, his eyes kind. "There are those who will join your banner, though. Count me as one of them. This farewell is not forever but, as Legate of the Citadel, I have a duty to maintain the stability of the Ecclesia and Citadel."

"Thank you, Lord Alent," Sylvie said, smiling back. She stepped aside then to let the two old friends say their farewells.

"Get over here, you old battle-ax," Mikkel said, the men gripping one another's forearms. "You haven't changed at all. Still that man with a powerfully deep heart."

"I have thought of you often, Mikkel," the Ecclesia knight said. "When I opened my door, I thought you a ghost. What your father did to you was wrong. I never thought you could be living beneath us this whole time. At some point, we must exchange tales over multiple ales."

"I would like that, Alent," the First Knight said, smiling.

"And you look good with that gray hair, though a cut would do you nicely," Alent said, grinning back. He turned to Sylvie again. "I will give you time to get clear of the Citadel and these gardens if that is your path. The less I know, the better. I must inform the Cardinal Bishop of the Covenant Codex's theft, though, and that will cast further suspicion on you. Few of the Ecclesia can be trusted to aid you; they will do their duty no matter what. I will do what I can to keep you safe, but at some point, they will find you if you are not careful."

"I know, Lord Alent," Sylvie said, touched by his words. She saw how his wrists were manacled by his position in the Ecclesia and the Citadel. He had done what he could. "I hope the next we meet, it will be under much better circumstances."

"Master Fae," Lord Alent said, looking to the sprite.

"Yes?" Sizmor said.

"Keep her safe. I'd really like to serve a High Queen."

With that, Lord Alent nodded and left, his armor clanking back toward the Citadel as the sun broke the horizon, its rays hitting the topmost point of Mont-Saint-Michel's King's Tower.

After Lord Alent had disappeared, Sylvie took a deep breath and turned to Mikkel.

"What now, my First Knight?"

"Everything Alent said is true," he said, rubbing his chin. "We took care of Scorus and Idlor, but there are a great many others of our family who will try to take the kingdom. We do have some time before that can happen, at least officially. Cardinal Bishop Wil Cornet is at the top of a short list for Pontiff, but confirmations like this are political and require many meetings to complete."

"And without a Pontiff, no coronation can happen, which gives us a short-term advantage," Sylvie said, thinking. "It's all for naught, though, if we have no lead. The Fae who stole the tome could have gone anywhere." She turned to Sizmor, who sat on her shoulder. "This is a question I hate asking, but could it have been Grumtil who stole the Covenant Codex?"

"No, I sensed no sprite magic in that chapel," Sizmor said. "And Grumtil is not large enough to carry such a heavy book. It had to be a Fae strong enough to do so."

"I know very little about the kinds of Fae inhabiting the Twilight Lands," she said. "That is your province."

The sprite looked as serious as Sylvie had ever seen him.

"I have been considering the thief, what kind of Fae could have done it."

"And?" Mikkel pressed.

"The Twilight Lands are filled with all sorts of different Fae. Even I have not encountered them all," Sizmor said, now hovering before them. "The Fae who stole the book is one I have no knowledge of. Therefore, I can rule out those I know. Given what I sensed, there *is* one type of Fae that matches my studies. A shapeshifter. A rare Fae, an amalgam of several dark Fae grown into one, stealing aspects of each. They are birthed in the very roots of the world. Few have existed. The Shadow Court outlawed their creation after Mordreadth used several for his evil. The most powerful Fae—like the Erlking—can create them. Witches can as well, though our records relate only one having done it. She who aligned with Mordreadth."

Sylvie frowned. "But why would any Fae be interested in another copy of the Covenant Codex? The Fae already possess one."

"The Shadow Court would not condone such a theft," Sizmor said, shaking his head. "Those on the Court dedicate their lives to maintaining the Compact between Wise Belloch and your Saint Emmer. It must be a Fae outside the Court's purview, and—"

"I will tell you why," Mikkel said, cutting off the sprite. "This Fae wants to stop you from ascending the throne." Sylvie and Sizmor looked at the First Knight, but he didn't seem to notice, his eyes as dark as thunderclouds as he stared back at the Citadel.

"The Shadow Court would do no such thing," Sizmor said, his finger chastising.

"Apologies. I did not mean that. Simply because a Fae shapeshifter stole the book does not mean it was at the behest of the Shadow Court," the First Knight said. "As you said, there are a great many Fae in the Twilight Lands, and all of them can't be aligned with the Court."

"True," Sylvie said. "Just like not all Goode family members are supporting my claim to the throne of Royaume de France."

"Right," Mikkel said.

"Well, Sizmor, is there any way to track the thief?" she asked.

The sprite contemplated this for a few moments. He closed his eyes, concentrating in a way she hadn't seen before. "I sense the thief left the chapel the way we came in." He opened his eyes and pointed. "The Fae left the Citadel and headed toward the front gates of Mont-Saint-Michel. However, the waking of the city and its people moving in and out of the gate has masked the changeling's leaving. I fear the book may have left already."

Sylvie's heart sank lower than it had already. "Then it is lost."

"There is another copy, you know," Sizmor said, bringing it up again as he observed a singing bird in the garden canopy above their heads.

Sylvie hadn't wanted to consider it earlier. Now she had no choice. The matching copy existed leagues away, in the heart of the Fae's Twilight Lands, in the blackest parts of Allemagne Forest east across the Vosges Mountains. The journey to retrieve the Fae's copy or have it copied in some way to reinstall Man's Compact would be arduous. It would leave Mont-Saint-Michel's throne unguarded, where she could not confront a usurper. Still, she had to consider it because, as of right now, it was her only possibility.

"He is right," Mikkel said before she could. "Though I hate to admit it. It would be quite dangerous, exposing you to your enemies if you were discovered beyond these walls. According to Alent, several of our brothers and sisters have probably already returned to their dukedoms. They will be looking for you. And there is also no certainty the Fae would welcome you."

"The First Knight speaks truly. I cannot vouch for your safety among the Shadow Court, or if you'd even be given audience. I must return there, though, and inform them of what has transpired. It is my duty," Sizmor said, his eyes downcast. "I do not want to leave your side, High Queen. But without the Covenant Codex, the Compact between Man and Fae is jeopardized. Erlking Hern the Hunter needs to know this, to prepare for any eventuality."

"Prepare for what exactly?" Sylvie was already dreading what the sprite would say.

Sizmor cocked his head to the side, as if it was obvious. "The appearance of this dark Fae, whatever it may be, and whoever created it. Dark plans drove the theft of the Covenant Codex of Saint Emmer," he said. "It could lead to a ruination of everything Wise Belloch and Saint Emmer created—and a return to war, of course."

Sylvie and Mikkel stared at one another. That thought hadn't crossed her mind. The battles between Fae and Man had spanned many seasons, leaving the continent broken and dying. If the Compact was not fully renewed by her coronation, within the allotted time, the war between Man and Fae could return, drenching the land in its blood and darkness. She couldn't let that happen. None of them could.

"Do we have enough time to travel to the Twilight Lands and back with Sizmor?" Sylvie asked.

"We do, if barely," Mikkel said, considering it. "If we leave now."

"Then it appears I have very little choice in this matter." Sylvie bowed her head in resignation.

"You could try to work with Alent," Mikkel suggested. "He has high rank among the Ecclesia as well as the Bishops of the Citadel. Sizmor could return to the Shadow Court to gain some understanding of what can be done about the book."

"It's not just a battle for our throne of Man. It could ultimately become a new war between Man and Fae, with the world of Man splintered and weakened at a terrible time." Sylvie shook her head, trying to see other ways forward but finding none. "We need the book as quickly as possible. It solves both problems."

Mikkel took a deep breath. "I see your point. Then we leave and head east," he said.

"Do you think we can exit the city without notice?"

"We could leave by boat, but the docks offer very little cover and nowhere to flee if the need arises. I think the gate is our best choice.

The sun is rising, and the day has begun. Traffic through the gate should increase as the morning wears on. We can blend in among those who are leaving. It is not uncommon for an Ecclesia knight to accompany a Lady during her errands. With the tide out, and once upon the sand bridge to Cliffside, we should be safe from those who hunt us."

"What about supplies? Money?"

Mikkel grinned at her. "The latter will lead to the former. And Alent was gracious."

They agreed with simple nods. Sylvie made sure her hair and face were concealed by her cloak's hood, pulling it tight, even as Sizmor disappeared. The First Knight replaced his helmet and strode toward the southern garden exit, which led to the kitchens, where she hoped the bustling bakers, cooks, and assistants would discourage the presence of Ecclesia knights. Soon the smell of fresh bread, frying bacon, and cooking eggs mingled with that of simmering lunch stews, leaving Sylvie's stomach growling after the night in hiding. Most of the kitchen staff nodded to Mikkel in his Ecclesia armor. Sylvie kept her head down, hoping to not be recognized.

Once beyond the labyrinthine kitchens, they reentered the morning sunshine on a winding cobblestone road that connected the castle with smithies, butchers, markets, bakers, warehouses, inns, apothecaries, cobblers, and other essential merchants that helped Mont-Saint-Michel thrive. There were also a handful of towers connected to the high outer wall that held the barracks, constabulary, and housing for visiting dignitaries. People were already out and about, going to work and running morning errands. It gave Sylvie hope that the masses would help mask them.

"The Ecclesia and city guards will be keeping an eye on the sand bridge," Sylvie surmised, thinking her way through the problem. "And when the tide swallows it today, they will be able to focus more on the docks."

Mikkel nodded, keeping his hand upon Lumière's hilt to help hide it. "Let's see what is happening at the King's Gate."

They continued to snake their way from the upper reaches of Mont-Saint-Michel to where the sea met the granite outcrop of the city's foundation. Few paid them any attention. They passed guardhouses and watchtowers without incident.

When they turned a final corner and saw the King's Gate, they stopped. Only one of the great doors stood open. Two Ecclesia knights wearing light armor—a tall redhead with high cheekbones and a shorter blond built like a tree stump—checked those leaving.

Beyond, the sand bridge awaited.

"Will this work?" she hissed under her breath.

"Doing the unexpected may be expected," Mikkel said. "There are no guarantees."

Getting closer to the knights, Sylvie saw they were young, even younger than she. They were only a year or two removed from being squires. They wouldn't know Mikkel, given his time imprisoned, and their inexperience could be the one boon she had.

The First Knight didn't deviate; he cut a path directly for them. He bypassed the small line of people waiting, getting glares. Sylvie followed with her head held high. She knew what her brother attempted, and she had a role to play if they were to win free. Though butterflies of nervousness flitted within her, she marveled at his courage.

The redheaded knight held a piece of paper, looking from it to each face that passed his way. His blond companion did most of the talking with those at the gate, shaking his head at his fellow knight as he let people pass through.

Only a few steps away, the blond knight's gaze narrowed on Mikkel as he approached.

"The line is back there, brother," he said, pointing.

"The line is no place for Lady Erlina's favorite niece," Mikkel said, much thicker at the shoulders than the redhead and towering over the blond. He looked like a thundercloud about to explode. "I am Lord Kusiak, and I have been given the great honor of escorting Lady Elwyn here to Lady Erlina's estates."

The young Ecclesia knights looked at one another and then at

Sylvie. She maintained her aloof attitude as if she were the most important person in the world. She did get a glance at the redhead's paper—a description of her.

"This one meets the criteria, Geoff," the redhead whispered to his companion.

Geoff peered closer at Mikkel. And again, at Sylvie. "Sir Aron is right, Lord Kusiak. You do understand that you match the descriptions of those responsible for the deaths of Master Kell, Lord Idlor, and the beloved Pontiff Scorus."

"I do, yet we are not them," the First Knight sniffed. "While I appreciate your zeal, think this through. Many members of the Goode family look the same. It is in their heredity."

"Still," Aron said. "We do not know you and cannot let you pass. We must notify Sir Gwain. He has taken responsibility for bringing the killers to justice."

Sylvie felt the entire situation crumbling. Since she had spent a lot of time with Sir Gwain's squire, Darian, he would know her immediately.

It would see them caught.

"Sir Gwain is even now meeting with the Cardinal Bishop concerning protection for the Bishops. One of you may fetch Lord Alent," the First Knight pressed with a sharp wave of his gauntleted hand. He knew the same as Sylvie that they needed to avoid Sir Gwain at all costs. "The faster the better. The Lady will not wait all day. And he will vouch for the purpose of our leaving." He paused strategically. "Though I am betting the Legate of the Citadel has far more pressing matters to attend to, given the tragic death of Pontiff Scorus."

The two knights looked at one another again. An unspoken uncertainty passed between them. Sylvie saw it in their eyes. Then they looked around at the people gathered, all of whom watched them, impatience at the delay growing.

The situation perplexed them, which had been Mikkel's plan.

"Brother Kusiak, safe journey to you," Geoff said, nodding to Aron. He gave a short bow to Sylvie. "And to you, my Lady. Apologies for the delay."

Sylvie nodded back and made sure to smile.

The knight looked away even as he flushed. Men could be so easily struck down by a smile, she thought.

"You do have an effect on people," Mikkel said as they took the wide King's Steps down to the sand bridge, passing even more people making their way to her home city. "Not unlike my Chelle, once upon a time. Similar smile and eyes, similar outcome."

"I'm not sure what Master Kell taught you," Sylvie said, grinning, "but he taught me to take every advantage that arises. If that means playful flirtation to an end, then so be it. Up to a point, of course."

Mikkel grinned. "He didn't teach me that."

"No need," she said. "Men have it easier in many regards."

"Yes, being this ugly is easy, easy, easy."

"Blame Father for that," she said with a short laugh, feeling her stress dissolve now that they had escaped. He reciprocated with his own guffaw. She sobered then, looking ahead. "I'm just happy we managed to get out."

"We need horses and supplies," the First Knight said.

"We will buy them in Cliffside?"

"That is my hope," he said. "Much can change in twenty years, and I have no doubt Cliffside is no longer the same. Still, there are universal truths concerning wealthy merchant princes and those organized lowborn who steal within the shadows. Oftentimes, there isn't much difference between them. We will find those who will serve our need."

It had been several winters since Sylvie had last visited Cliffside. In the past, when she had assisted Master Kell in trips beyond the island, it had been under the authority of High King Alafair and the Mont-Saint-Michel dukedom. Some trips were diplomatic for Kell, as he visited the other dukedoms of Royaume de France, managed trade disputes with neighboring countries, or even one time commemorated a beautiful library in Solstein whose creation he had overseen. Later, as his life ebbed, Kell preferred to remain within the castle, accepting visitors from far and wide rather than leaving. Sylvie had disliked being confined within the kingdom's capital city, but her love for Master Kell and understanding of what age does to the body quieted those feelings.

Now, with Mont-Saint-Michel behind her, she focused on the seaside city. Cliffside was founded before her ancestors realized that the island offered better protection from raiders and dangerous wyrms. The oldest buildings ringing the cliff were of the same pale granite used for the island's high towers, protective walls, and base that the ocean could never wear away. Over time, Cliffside flourished under the watchful gaze of the High King. As Sylvie and Mikkel walked the sand bridge and Cliffside grew closer, she marveled at the chaotic bustle of commercial activity that spanned the docks to either side of the bridge, as well as the crane-and-pulley systems helping to import and export products into and out of the city.

Midday approached as they reached the other side, the cliffs now dwarfing them. The tide had begun to return, and where the sand bridge ended, a large granite quay waited, deep and broad, with a large set of stairs cut into the cliff, filled with those trying to attain the town above as well as those leaving it.

"I've never had to take the staircase before," Sylvie admitted.

The First Knight nodded, looking upward. "You were always with Master Kell. You would have ridden the lift hoisted by windlasses."

"It would be unsafe to do so today, given the scrutiny of those operating the lift." Sylvie gestured at the metal encasing Mikkel's form. "How will you fare in that armor? It must be quite heavy. Will you be able to gain the top?"

"There is only one way to remove the rust from twenty years of being locked away," Mikkel said, taking a deep breath. "The workout will do me good. Though now more than ever I wish I was a sprite, with those wings of theirs."

"Best hope that tide doesn't come in quickly and drown you first," Sizmor said from the ether.

The Fae guide said it in such a way, Sylvie couldn't tell if he was joking. She expected Mikkel to retort, but she could see the First Knight already focused on the forthcoming climb. When they reached the quay and took the first steps upward, Sylvie stopped and looked back the way they had come.

Mont-Saint-Michel shimmered in the midday sunlight, its granite walls and spires glowing. She paused a moment to take it all in. The glory of the towers with their pennants flapping in the ocean breeze, the thickness of the island's walls keeping those within safe, and the swirl of seabirds gliding on unseen air currents. She'd always appreciated the beauty of her home, but it was different from such a distance. That's when she realized she might never see Mont-Saint-Michel again. But there was also the opportunity to become its High Queen, if she was brave and lucky enough to see this quest through.

She made a mental painting, hoping it would serve her well in the days ahead.

"You will return," Sizmor assured her, as if he could read her mind.

She nodded, feeling the burn of tears before they misted her sight. Rather than fall prey to the sentimentality that Master Kell always warned could cripple someone, she put her thoughts and effort into climbing the hundreds of stairs before her.

Mikkel went first. He slowed about halfway but he kept moving. Sylvie matched his steps. Since her youth, climbing the Masters Tower and other spires in Mont-Saint-Michel had toughened her leg strength. It made the climb easier for her than it otherwise would be. And even though Mikkel had dispatched Idlor Goode in a fight without breaking a sweat, it wasn't equal to climbing hundreds of steps when for twenty years no such opportunity had been allowed—especially bearing the weight of armor.

At the top of the stairs, though, he surprised her, not stopping. He ensured she was fine with a look before striding into a plaza where numerous people mingled around a fountain in the shape of the King's Tower across the bay. Several marketplaces ringed the outer edge of the plaza, each one offering refreshments and sustenance. Sylvie's throat burned for a drink, but Mikkel did not visit the merchants. Instead, he chose one of the streets that exited the plaza like a spoke on a wheel.

Sylvie kept close to her First Knight. Everyone was a threat, since anyone could recognize them and alarm the authorities. When she had visited Cliffside before, it had been with a retinue of Ecclesia knights to keep safe the High King's brother, and they had received a warm welcome every time with cheers and praise. Now she just hoped to be ignored and left alone.

The deeper they traveled into the city, the safer she felt. Until she realized that Mikkel had passed several stablemasters and numerous supply merchants, leaving her to wonder where her First Knight ventured and for what reason.

"We are being followed," Sizmor whispered at her ear, the sprite still invisible.

The feeling of safety she had just felt vanished like a bird in a rainstorm. "Who are they, and is it just one person or many?" she asked with a low voice.

"Children of various ages."

"You are sure?"

"Quite."

Sylvie tried not to draw interest to herself even as she glanced around to discover what the sprite sensed. She saw no one. But she trusted Sizmor and placed her hand on Mikkel's armored forearm to get his attention.

"Where are we really going?" Sylvie asked.

"I'm looking for someone. The right sort of someone, in fact," the First Knight said, his stride remaining purposeful, to the point that she struggled to keep up.

"Sizmor says we are being followed," she said.

Mikkel grunted. "Yes, I know. I'm hoping they will lead us to that someone." He turned to Sylvie, more somber, and pulled her into a shadowy alleyway. "Do you trust me?"

"I do."

"The man I seek . . . he does not follow the law of a High King or High Queen," Mikkel said, staring across the street at an inn. "He is a necessary tool but a dangerous one. I'm taking a risk in this, but it is a calculated one. We need mounts and supplies, yet we do not want to be discovered. Does that sound about right?"

She nodded, understanding his point. She had no idea what he saw across the street, but it kept his interest in a way that made clear he knew something she did not.

"There are those who live, work, and die in the shadows," Mikkel continued. "It's in those dark alleyways and seedy establishments we can remain anonymous while getting the items we need." Before she could ask another question, he pointed at the inn's sign. A boy leaned up against the wall below it, watching them. "The man I want is one I met long ago." He paused, putting his heavy hand on her shoulder. "You will see. Keep quiet while we're on the streets. The less we are seen and heard, the better."

Baffled by his riddling, Sylvie did as he requested. She trusted him implicitly, a bond that went beyond family. She looked at the sign and the boy underneath it. She saw nothing remarkable.

"Now, follow my lead. And be prepared to offer . . . whatever is needed."

She frowned, not liking the sound of that, but fell into step beside him as they crossed the street.

"You. Boy," Mikkel said, walking up. "Are you the leader of those who have been our constant companions since we arrived in Cliffside?"

"Maybe I am," the boy said, giving Mikkel a smug smile. There was a glimmer in his eyes, and he tossed aside brown hair grown longish. He appeared about five or six winters younger than she.

"You stand beneath the symbol of the Hawk," the First Knight said, eyes finding the sign where a knot in the wood appeared in the shape of a bird.

"The Hawk?" The boy laughed. "The Hawk is long dead."

The look on Mikkel's face turned stony. Sylvie worried he had placed too much faith in this one approach to win them the things they needed.

"Who replaced him?" the First Knight asked.

"Does it matter?" the other said.

"It does to me."

The boy's gaze narrowed on him. Mikkel towered above the other, but Sylvie saw no fear in the boy's eyes despite her brother standing over him like a mountain about to fall.

"How much money is it going to take to get a straight answer out of you?" the First Knight asked.

"I'm not for rent, hollow man," the boy said snidely, a disdainful reference to the armor. He looked Sylvie up and down then like she was a piece of merchandise. "Unlike your lady friend there."

It took Sylvie a moment to realize the child had just called her a whore. Or that she was one who purchased pleasures of the flesh from men, she couldn't tell. He stood there grinning at her like a court jester. While it should have rankled her, she found she couldn't be angry at the boy's audacity and infectious smile.

"I doubt you are not for sale." Mikkel hefted a coin bag the size of his gauntleted hand that he had produced from his bag. The boy's eyes lit up and then dimmed quickly as he tried to hide his interest. Money spoke to him as it did to so many in the world. "It just needs to be on your terms with the right price."

"Who is the woman?" the boy asked, pointing his chin at her.

"Questions get you no closer to this gold," the First Knight said, returning the bag to its place of concealment. "Now. Take us to the Hawk."

The boy laughed. It was a dark, throaty sort that held no humor. "Ha! Hawk you say. I told you the truth. Hasn't been a Hawk here for years."

"Then who do you work for?"

The street kid appraised him. "The Kraken rules these streets now."

"I see. The Kraken," Mikkel nodded. "Scary name."

"You are a smart one, hollow man," the boy said.

"You have a mouth on you, I'll give you that."

"Yeah, I've never been without it." The boy's grin widened. "Though it's gotten itself punched a few times for the shite things it says." He paused and then shrugged. "It's your death. That armor won't protect you, and neither will the beauty there. The depths of the Kraken are dark and grave."

The boy left the side of the building and sauntered down the street like he owned it. Mikkel and Sylvie followed. Noon had come and gone, leaving her hungry and perplexed. She trusted her brother with her life. Yet she also wondered why they needed the criminal element of Cliffside to aid them on their eastward search for the Twilight Lands. She realized then that those who had been following them had closed in to either side and behind, like feral hounds hunting a stag. It left her feeling exposed and confined.

"I worry about this choice." Sizmor echoed her thoughts.

"I'm worried as well, but we must trust," she whispered back to her guide. She caught Mikkel's eye, the First Knight showing no fear at all. "Why are we doing this? What purpose does it serve, seeking this Kraken?"

"Horses and supplies are only two things we'll need to survive the days ahead," Mikkel said. He kept his hand upon Lumière and a thundercloud on his mien, ways to discourage anyone who might take too much interest in them. "I have long been absent from the kingdom, and you know little concerning the ways of the real world. We will need information."

"And you believe this Kraken can offer all that we need?" she asked. "That seems like a lot to ask one man."

"One man can know and hold dominion over a hundred thousand others," Mikkel said. "A hundred thousand men can move mountains, if properly motivated."

"Sounds like we need a lot more gold," Sylvie pointed out. "That little bag won't be enough for all that."

"Is that what you just heard me say, Sylvie?" Mikkel questioned. "We just need the one man. The hundred thousand can come later."

"Still, this one man will want something."

"You are right, very astute, as usual," he said. "Then, as High Queen, what are you prepared to offer? As I said already, that's what I want you to think about."

Sylvie didn't understand what kind of offering her brother meant, but she tried to recall the history of the kingdom and its people. Every city possessed criminals that thrived on the misfortune of others. They were thieves. Assassins. Mercenaries. Whores. And others besides that she knew nothing about but who led a life very different from the one she knew. Master Kell maintained that all subjects had a role to play in the great scheme of life and the kingdom, but each subject was motivated by different reasons. When it came to the Kraken, she'd have to gauge the motives that drove him.

The boy suddenly veered off the main street and took an alley that ventured deep between four-story buildings—and came to a large mottled orange door set into a bricked wall. The day's light darkened, as though a cloud had passed between the alleyway and the sun. When the street gang cut off the entrance behind, Sylvie realized they were trapped.

Refuse and piles of human excrement littered the ground, and that combined with the strong odor of rotting flesh accosted her. She wanted to turn back before she retched on an empty stomach. Even Sizmor at her ear quietly lamented the smell humans created.

But the leading boy went directly to the alley door, its thick iron heavily rusted. He triple knocked, waited, and triple knocked again. The sound echoed deep in the close quarters. Soon the door opened, revealing a set of stairs disappearing up as well as down.

"My street name is Arn," the boy said simply. "Follow me."

He entered with a glance backward. Sylvie, Mikkel, and the invisible Sizmor did as they were told. The other street kids trailed them as well. Darkness swallowed them all instantly when the door closed behind, but the scrape of metal against metal created a bloom of light from a shuttered lantern that highlighted the faces of those present, the stairs, and not much else. The reek of the alley vanished, replaced by the sweet smell of lavender mixed with burning oil.

Sylvie looked about but did not see who had opened the door. Arn lit a new lantern from the first and took the stairs downward, the steps sturdy and sure. At the bottom, a hallway made of stone with numerous doors traveled deeper into the building. He opened a seemingly random door and welcomed Sylvie and the others to a room inside.

"Wait here," Arn said to Mikkel before placing his lantern on a large desk and vanishing through a different door. Sylvie looked about her. The room was of simple construction, the ceiling supported by heavy timbers and the walls blocks of stone. Floating shelves held a mélange of items she couldn't quite make out in the gloom created by the one light. The street children who had accompanied them prevented any escape through the doors.

When Arn returned, he was not alone. A tall, thin man entered the chamber. He wore a black leather duster of exquisite make, its stitching done in silver that glowed in the faint light. A black hood hid his features, only his chin exposed and showcasing a pepper-gray beard. Brushing back his duster but not taking it off, he went to sit at the desk. It took Sylvie a moment to realize something was off about the man: he lacked his left arm.

The one-armed man peered closer at Mikkel and Sylvie. The weak light was unable to banish the murk protecting most of his face.

"It seems time has a sense of humor," he said in a voice that seemed to carry all accents and none. Sylvie really wanted to see his face. "Light the wicks, Arn. Have no fear. We are in the presence of very special people."

Arn moved around the room to other lanterns. With each wick lit, the darkness within the man's hood peeled away, revealing striking green-yellow eyes, skin as black as any she had seen, sensuous lips, and a wry grin tugging at the corners of his mouth. If Sylvie was to guess, he was Afric, though his accent said otherwise. Rings set with various gems glimmered from his right hand, which he made sure to leave on the table for all to see.

"I know you. You know me. Let's dispense with the pleasantries, Kraken, if that's what you call yourself now," Mikkel said, hand resting on Lumière's hilt. "And lower that hood. No need for the dramatic flair here."

"Princeling, you no longer have power over me. Not here, not now," the Kraken said. He assessed the First Knight's words and demeanor, though, and eventually lowered his hood. He was a middle-aged bald man, thin like a knife when compared to the First Knight's armored frame. "But for the sake of our shared history, I sit before you, revealed. Let us speak plainly, as we once did."

"I appreciate that. You have not changed much," Mikkel noted with a nod. "Besides the lost arm and the different name."

"There are times when one must lose to gain," the other said, looking down where his left arm should have been. He shrugged. "As far as the name, the Kraken serves its purpose. Like that multi-armed Norge sea beastie, it denotes my reach, but is also an amusing title for a one-armed man. Don't you think?"

"The irony is not lost. And you've always enjoyed amusement." The knight looked to Sylvie before proceeding. "We have need of that reach. I am hoping we can come to an accord that is mutually beneficial."

"I bet you do," the Kraken said, eyes flickering over Sylvie. "Mikkel Goode, fallen First Knight of High King Alafair Goode. Imprisoned by your father for two decades. A princeling lost and in need." Then he looked at Sylvie. "And Sylvianna Goode, apprentice to Master Historian Kell and heir to the kingdom that High King Alafair Goode built. Also, alleged murderess. Yes, I know you. It is my place to know. There are many ways to attain power, but only through knowledge can power be maintained." He paused, considering them. "Now, let's get down to it. Do you need passage somewhere safe? Or a sanctuary in Cliffside? Or more fun yet, do you wish to join me after all these years, Mikkel? It would be like old times."

"Our paths diverged many years ago, and not by my hand," Mikkel said, his armored bulk taking up a great deal of the room. "We look for passage beyond Cliffside and east. If you feel like aiding an old friend."

"Altruism is a light you embraced and I rejected. It seems some things do not change," the Kraken said, eyes glimmering. "You aren't wrong about my feelings. I *am* considering what to do you with you, yes. I've never stepped foot on Mont-Saint-Michel, but I'm sure it has become a hive of chaos since yesterday. Were you in fact those responsible for the death of Idlor Goode and Pontiff Scorus?"

Mikkel nodded, eyes burning into the Kraken. "We are. I slew them. Both deserved it."

The lie was not lost on Sylvie. She had slain Idlor. But she saw the benefit of the First Knight's choice. It was his role to protect her—not just with strength of arms but in all ways that mattered.

"I haven't missed that arrogant certainty of morality you shield yourself with. It's true then. The immortality touching the Goode family is gone." The Kraken stared down at the rings on his hand. When he glanced up finally, it was with an emotion Sylvie couldn't identify. "The fact that you killed Idlor changes a great deal. It has left a vacuum. Lord Pike has filled it. He offers sizable rewards for your whereabouts."

"Is Pike trying to succeed where Idlor failed?" Sylvie asked.

"Why, do you wish to slay him too?" the Kraken questioned with a broader grin.

"If I have to, I will see it done," she said, and meant it with every part of her heart. "He has no claim to the throne. High King Alafair Goo—"

"I know, I know," the Kraken said, waving her words aside. His voice had an angry bite to it, like a hissing viper before it struck. "Virtuous hero High King Alafair Goode announced you as his heir during the Naming, and your name has been scrawled into the Covenant Codex of Saint Emmer. As I said, my reach is far and deep."

"You have spies everywhere." She spoke the obvious. It worried her. If she became High Queen, who could she trust in Mont-Saint-Michel?

"I counted on those eyes and ears, actually," Mikkel said before the Kraken could respond. "It's why I paraded us through most of Cliffside. To find you. Or your replacement."

"I knew the moment you descended the King's Steps," the Kraken said, glancing around at his gathered street crew, most of them young but a few older than Sylvie. "You wanted to get right down to it. Let us. You've brought something to barter for your lives as well as for my help, I presume? You aren't hoping for nostalgia and a shared youth to save you?"

"That is up to my High Queen," the First Knight said, looking to Sylvie.

"Every man has desires they cannot fulfill," she said, taking her cue from Mikkel and already having some suspicion of what the Kraken's next words would be. "Let us start there."

"There is little you have that I could ever want, my High Queen In Name Only. I have strong men, cunning women, and the young who will grow to become more. I have wealth. I have anonymity. I own this small but influential city. And other cities and towns in the kingdom feel my influence. What could you possibly offer me other than Lumière there? Or the delights of your body for several weeks? I doubt these are things you'd be willing to part with. Call me eager to know."

Sylvie took a step forward and placed her hands on his desk, infringing on his space, letting him know she did not fear him. All eyes fell on her, which was her hope.

"I can offer you one wish."

Silence pressed in around her, expectant and curious.

She knew she had offered the right thing.

"You have my attention," the Kraken said. "Tell me about this one wish."

"There are few things I can offer that you likely don't already possess, that much is true," Sylvie said, thinking her way ahead. "And you are correct. The sword is not available. My body is my own. But I am not without means, especially once I am crowned."

"What means would this wish entail?" the Kraken asked.

She knew she had him. She saw it in his eyes and heard it in his voice. "A wish, like the wishes from the Arabi's djinn of old," Sylvie said. "It must be a wish within my power, and it cannot be used to harm others. I can't very well become High Queen and have you wish for the Ecclesia army to wipe out Spania or some such, can I? Or take the kingdom's treasury. Or any number of actions that would harm the kingdom I am sworn to protect."

The Kraken nodded, thinking. "Very good. You bring up a worthy reward for my aid, though I can be quite creative when it comes to this life I live," he said, leaning forward, his eyes glimmering. "But I want *five* wishes."

The silence that had already filled the room grew until it weighted her down.

The bartering had begun.

"Two wishes," she countered.

"Since I am in a good mood and enjoying this very much, I'll accept four wishes," the Kraken said, sitting back once more.

It was a game. He knew how to play it. But she was not so easily beaten. "How many know your real name?" Sylvie asked the Kraken, each word enunciated and slowly said, looking to Mikkel, hoping her move on that game board would work. She took a risk, not knowing if her First Knight was familiar with that name or not. But all games posed risks, and she had to trust her instincts that the Kraken would not have given himself a different name if it had not mattered for a serious reason.

For the first time, Sylvie saw uncertainty in the man's eyes. She had guessed right. The Kraken narrowed his gaze at Mikkel, gauging him. The First Knight stood stonily, giving the other nothing, a game of pokra without cards. Sylvie heard the hissing of the lanterns in the death-still room. It was clear her words had been a dagger straight to the Kraken's legend that he had spent a great deal of time building.

It then occurred to her that the Kraken could try to overpower Mikkel and be done with them, a thought that left her cold.

Life was a risk. And she'd just gambled it.

"I'll say this. When I heard Alafair Goode's pick for heir, I found it curious. Now I have learned the why of it firsthand," the Kraken said, green-yellow eyes flashing lightning. He took a deep breath, and the storm in him calmed. "For the new High Queen, I agree to *three* wishes. In exchange for that extra wish, I proffer Arn Tomm as you travel. He's most cunning. He will keep you safe, thereby keeping my three wishes secure." He paused, a man holding the room hostage. "I have one more condition, though. When I want to cash in one of my wishes, I will be given access to you immediately, no matter what you are doing. If you are sleeping, you rise. If you are fucking, you halt. If you are eating dinner with the King of Norge, you leave the table. Do we understand one another?"

Sylvie thought it through. As High Queen, she would take part in matters of great import. What the Kraken wished could have serious consequences if he requested audience at a delicate time. But Mikkel thought they needed the Kraken's help. Without it, she'd never be High Queen in the first place.

"I agree to your terms," Sylvie said finally. "Do we have an accord?"

The Kraken looked around at those in the room. She could see him gauging his audience and how they would perceive the deal. He balanced it all with a calculation she could only guess at, probably years of experience in the underworld and the seediest of dwellers there.

Then he stretched out his one hand in agreement.

"We do, High Queen In Name Only," the Kraken said, taking her hand and squeezing. "Three future wishes that do not stretch incredulity, in exchange for my aid in safely attaining what it is you want. I must warn you, though. If you fail to uphold your end of this bargain, I know how best to wound you. This is not a threat. Merely a truth I wish you to know. Now. On to what is important. Where does your path lie so that I might be of the best use?"

"The Twilight Lands," Sylvie said. "The Shadow Court is my only option to set right the wrongs that have transpired."

The Kraken barked a laugh. "You are full of surprises. Are you sure you require such a path? That way lies death. The Fae do not tolerate our kind. And Arn would not be so sorely lost to death. From what I know of you both, you'd do quite well here under my watchful responsibility. I could use your talents. It would be a life of comfort, I can tell you that much."

"Thank you for the generous offer. I do not doubt it," she said, hands folded at her waist. "But I am set in fulfilling the final wish of my father."

"In that case, you will need to visit Clair-de-Lune Abbey."

Sylvie frowned. "Why call upon the light-weavers? What do they know of the Twilight Lands?"

"One must have light to illuminate the dark. Even one such as I, with so many spies, knows little of the Twilight Lands and what transpires there. I believe gaining counsel from the Prioress Superior at Clair-de-Lune would not hurt your quest in the least," the Kraken said, eyes laughing at her. The way he looked, Sylvie surmised he knew something, but she doubted he'd share. He then glanced at Mikkel, his grin returned. "And let's just say some pasts are worth revisiting to know if choices made bear sweet or rotten fruit."

Mikkel darkened at that. The First Knight sensed—as she did—that the Kraken played at some amusing game that only he knew the rules to.

"Very well, I can see the wisdom of seeking the light-weavers," Sylvie said. "What next?"

"A word of caution for you, a word that is free. There is a tempest brewing among the children of Goode, one that will inflict turmoil on Royaume de France and, worst of all, my place in it. War is not good for business," the Kraken said. "For now, follow Arn here. He will find the supplies you need as well as safe beds to rest tonight. Tomorrow morning, he will guide you from Cliffside. For good or ill."

"Thank you for receiving us, my once friend," Mikkel said to the Kraken. "It has been too long. It is nice to know that some hearts remain the same no matter the winters."

"Friends, always. But you and your High Queen are nothing more than an investment," the Kraken said, still smiling at some humor only he knew. "Safe travels, because one day I will come calling to benefit from those wishes." He turned back to Sylvie. "You have chosen an honorable man as your First Knight. Mikkel Goode would never suffer a fool twice, which leads me to believe you are not your father. Now go."

At that, Arn Tomm guided Sylvie and Mikkel from the room and, choosing a different door in the hallway, into a new part of the building and eventually back out into the warmth of the sun. Arn took several streets then, weaving this way and that, before arriving at a dilapidated inn on the eastern side of Cliffside featuring rotting boards, faded paint, and a broken sign declaring it the Untamed Pig. The boy took them inside to speak with the innkeeper, a man with ruddy cheeks and a portly nature who barely gave Sylvie or Mikkel a glance.

"Well. We survived that," Sylvie said after they closed the door to their room. She sat on one of the two beds, running her fingers through her hair, tugging to relieve the headache that had suddenly sprung to life. "You knew the Kraken well at one point. You called him friend. Was he part of the Ecclesia? A squire like you?"

"I knew him as a child, before I became a squire," Mikkel shared, shedding his armor a piece at a time. As he did so, he aged before her eyes. Some part of his past with the Kraken haunted him still, and it had followed him after the meeting. "We met in Marly-le-Roi. We were of similar age, and we stole wooden swords to slay imaginary wyrms and save princesses whose beauty could only be created in imagination. Alafair would spend weeks at a time there. Later, I found out Marly-le-Roi was the home to one of Alafair's favorite pleasure dens, one he had visited numerously in previous winters. Once we grew older and I apprenticed to Sir Holston, the boy who would become the Kraken realized just how different we were. That black skin of his, which was sadly upheld as a reason to disallow his admittance to the Ecclesia. He's held it against Alafair ever since. I was given every privilege; he was given nothing but heartache."

Sylvie listened to his words, but it was the unspoken that left her surprised and shocked at how incredibly cruel life could be for some.

"The Kraken wasn't your brother-in-arms then," she said.

"Not in the way you suggest. How do you think he survived the loss of his arm, a wound that would have killed almost any other man?" Mikkel turned his back to test the hot water of the tub for her. It would be heated for him again after she bathed.

Sylvie saw the truth then, as clear as the late-afternoon sunlight streaming through the second-story window. The one-armed crime lord liked that a bastard of Alafair Goode had been Named heir to the kingdom, no matter her gender, no matter her station.

Because the Kraken was one of Alafair Goode's bastards too.

DONATO

10

s your Fae guide, Sylvianna, I am appointed to counsel you in all matters," Sizmor said, sitting on her shoulder as she mounted the horse Arn had supplied her. "You should not seek the help of Clair-de-Lune. The light-weavers will surely kill you. Or worse, they will kill me."

Sylvie ignored the sprite, as she had done since he'd begun the argument upon leaving Cliffside. She was more concerned about her brother. Mikkel sat astride a massive charger, as unresponsive as the Fae creature had been talkative during their five-day journey to the small town of Fontaine, on their way to Clair-de-Lune Abbey. The villages they stopped at allowed them to learn from the Kraken's spy network what occurred in Mont-Saint-Michel and beyond, as well as gain new supplies. Mikkel had showed little interest in news during the ride, keeping to himself, some aspect of their meeting with the Kraken unsettling him. He had ignored Sylvie's attempts at engagement with him. Even now, as his burnished armor glowed in the afternoon light, darkness rolled over his mien, and there was nothing Sylvie could do about it.

Now they sat mounted—an unseen gulf between them—and waited for Arn to return from Fontaine. She had to admit she felt an impending sense of dread, a shadow on the light of her days. Whether it came from the Fae's worries, the First Knight's silence, or their traveling into the unknown Twilight Lands to the east, she couldn't tell.

For now, she had to deal with Sizmor, who would continue to argue as if his life depended on it. Which, according to him, it did.

"Master Fae, I hear your counsel and your worries." Sylvie breathed in the sweet air of the countryside, relishing the smell of fresh-cut grasses for hay. "The light-weavers of today are not those that your history recounts. Centuries have passed. Much has changed. Look to Arn Tomm as an example. When I asked you to reveal yourself to the boy, he barely flinched at your presence."

"The boy is being paid well to not flinch," Sizmor responded, wings shaking in agitation. "Did you hear not a word I said about the light-weavers. They killed Fae by the thousands during the Great War. And even after the Covenant Codex made peace between Fae and Man, they were unrelenting along the eastern borders of what would become Royaume de France."

"Again, that was long ago," Sylvie said, hoping Mikkel would come to her aid against the Fae guide. The First Knight didn't, which drew her ire even more. "You have nothing to fear while I am alive."

"That's what I'm afraid of," Sizmor grumbled.

On one side, she had a sprite who wouldn't shut up. On the other, a man who said nothing. *This is what ruling is like,* she thought.

Maddening.

"First Knight Mikkel Goode," Sylvie pushed, trying to get his attention, voice harsher than she intended. "Are you ready to talk about the Kraken yet?"

"He hears you, Sylvianna," Sizmor shared. "He remains deeply reflective, as he has been these last days."

"The sprite is correct, my High Queen," Mikkel said finally, taking a deep breath and letting it out slowly like a parent trying to find patience with their child. "Do not think I am ignoring you. I'm merely thinking about the best way to keep you safe while sharing what you want. The more you know, the more danger it puts you in. It is my job to keep you from such danger. I hope you can appreciate the dilemma that poses."

"The Kraken must know you'd tell me everything," she said.

"He also knows me as a man of caution, who will do anything to protect his liege," the First Knight said. "He knows I will balance risk versus reward."

"He knows you quite well then, if he knows that," Sylvie remarked, keeping her eyes on the outer edges of Fontaine as well.

"He does."

"Let me ask you this then," she said, taking a different angle. "The Kraken is a murderer. A thief. A lord of crime. You heard him. It takes knowledge to retain one's power. Like the throne. If I am to rule and continue doing so, it means knowing what you know."

"Sylvie!" Mikkel shot back, anger flashing in his eyes. Sizmor fluttered from fright, his wings shivering. It was the first such ire she had seen in her First Knight, and it was terrifying. It vanished as quickly as it arrived, though. "I am sorry, my High Queen. A knight is not meant to lose his temper. Not even on the battlefield, where such emotion can kill just as quickly as it can save. No, seeing the Kraken after so long has dredged up a great many memories." He paused, turning to look at her. "I need to stop treating you like the youth you appear but rather as a High Queen. I do apologize for that.

"Yes, the Kraken is those things you labeled him, and many more besides. But once upon a time, he was a boy named Lledimma Oka, born to an Afric courtesan named Nnenna, searching for his place in the world. I met him when we were both eight years old. Alafair had taken his yearly trip to Marly-le-Roi, and for the first time I was allowed to attend. I didn't know until much later that those trips were purely to indulge the High King's debaucheries." He paused, lost to memories that occurred decades earlier. "I remember Nnenna as exotically beautiful—ebony skin, long hair as dark as midnight, high cheekbones, a long-limbed grace with an inner power, and fiery eyes. She also had a terrifying wit with a tongue to match. Alafair made pleasure with many of the courtesans at Marly-le-Roi, but Nnenna was his favorite. And obviously had been for some time, as Lledi was the result of one of their unions."

"He's a half-brother to both of us then," Sylvie said. She had spent much of the previous days thinking of how she could use that if the need ever arose.

"He is," Mikkel said. "By the time Chelle was stolen from me and I was imprisoned, Lledi had already created the foundation of the empire he now rules. He's a man who has used the advantages of his birth and his inability to die to conquer the world. He is more than that, though. He is cunning. When we came to Cliffside, I hoped he'd be in town."

"Whatever happened to his mother?" Sylvie asked.

"I bet her life did not end well," Sizmor said, invested in the story and his worries pushed aside for the moment. "A man should not do the things Lledimma Oka has done while his mother is alive."

"That's not always true, Sizmor, but in this case it is," Mikkel said, eyes sad. "Once Nnenna grew older, Alafair cast her aside. He did that often in those days. It cost her everything. She lost her status among the other courtesans, and they banished her from Marly-le-Roi. With nowhere to go, she and Lledi turned to the streets."

"I bet that didn't sit well with Lledi," Sylvie said. "How old was he?"

"I was a squire then, so he had to be fourteen or fifteen winters," Mikkel said. "And no, it didn't sit well with Lledi. In fact, as I understand it, he burned down the golden palace where they used to live, where Alafair pleasured himself. From then, crime became his life."

"How did you know to look for him in Cliffside?" Sizmor asked.

"Kell visited me often and shared notable news, as I've said before. Lledi would come up every so often. A King is meant to bring law to the people. Lledi was outside that law, a thorn in the side of Alafair. There is some poetic justice there, I think."

Sylvie nodded. She thought about her father and the life he had lived. Sure, he had spent a great deal of his kingship rebuilding the kingdom after destroying Mordreadth as a youth. He had married and had children. Yet the man had been flawed, as so many were, fucking hundreds if not thousands of women over decades, resulting in children throughout the lands wherever he traveled. She felt bad for a man like Lledimma Oka, whose defining moment was being born to a woman who had caught the fancy of a High King who showed no interest in whether he existed or not.

High King Alafair Goode might have been a legendary King, but he had been a horrible man to father so many scions and disregard most of them.

She understood better why so many hated him.

"Thank you for sharing the Kraken's story. You've given me insight into who he is as a man, a subject of the kingdom, and what drives him. I cannot imagine the kind of life he's had to lead," Sylvie said. "Do you think I offered too much? The three wishes?"

"Not at all," her First Knight said. "In fact, you bartered well with such a man."

Sylvie patted her horse's neck. She hoped she'd never have to use the Kraken's past against him; after all, who knew what such a man was capable of if pressed. She focused on the present then, looking toward Fontaine. A dot in the distance left the town and trotted toward them, growing as it approached.

"What I just said stays between us and Sizmor," Mikkel reminded her, jaw set hard. "There is no need for Arn Tomm to know. And certainly, no one else. You want the Kraken on your side. The only way to keep him there is to keep his secrets too."

"I promise the knowledge is safe. Unless he betrays us, of course."

Mikkel nodded, eyes on the approaching man. When it became clear the rider was Arn Tomm, the First Knight let go his grip on Lumière and relaxed.

The boy reined in his mount, the horses nickering at one another in greeting.

"What news, Arn?" Mikkel asked.

"A great deal, none of it good," the boy grunted. He pulled free a waterskin from the side of his saddle and took a deep drink. "I found the Kraken's main envoy here, and she shared terrible news. Not like I needed it. The town is buzzing with war and multiple sources confirmed it. Firstly, the Ecclesia knights have given up looking for Sylvie in Mont-Saint-Michel. I surmise they think you escaped. Secondly, and because of that, many of the High King's children left as well, returning to their seats of power. Lady Erlina sent missives to every town in this dukedom, requesting able-bodied men of fighting age to join her army. Other duchies are raising their banners as well. There is no way to know the why of it all, besides the throne being empty."

"I had hoped my brothers and sisters would be more pragmatic than this. I guess I should have known better," Sylvie said. She had wished her father's death would not lead to conflict, but history recounted many times the children of a King had fought over the crown. "Who are the main players?" she asked.

"Lord Pike has formed an alliance with Cardinal Bishop Wil Cornet," Arn said, wiping his mouth. "Word is, Pike has most of the main Ecclesia knights with him, along with many Citadel Bishops. He's consolidating his power."

"Which also helped drive the others to flee Mont-Saint-Michel," Sylvie thought out loud.

"None of them are safe, now that the magic is lifted," Mikkel said. "Erlina. Yankton. Collin. Kent. I bet they all have fled Pike's side."

"They have gone to their dukedoms," Arn confirmed. "All except Lord Kent. No one seems to know why he's remained or what he's doing."

Sylvie and Mikkel looked at one another.

"Not just a civil war then between Mont-Saint-Michel and the mainland," she said. "But a war of siblings, one that will pit dukedom against dukedom and sunder the kingdom, destroying all that Alafair built."

"The Kraken was right," Sizmor said.

"He was right because he had already learned the plans of these people," Mikkel said, looking off in the distance. "That is his way. The Kraken has ears and eyes in every corner of this kingdom and some beyond."

"It seems the world's past has a strange sense of irony," Sylvie said, shaking her head. "It took a witch's magic to help Father defeat Mordreadth and prevent unending darkness from destroying all. Yet that same witch's magic created a kingdom filled with Alafair's children, each one with a direct claim to the throne."

"For me, it is more personal," Mikkel said, flexing his gauntleted fist. "For so many years, I could not be killed. I feel no different than I did before Alafair died, but it is a strange feeling, this fear of mortality."

"The other Lords and Ladies of House Goode are undoubtedly feeling the same," Sizmor said from his perch on Sylvie's shoulders. "Now that they can die, perceived power will be the only thing they believe will save them."

"Which makes them even more dangerous," Sylvie said. "Fear is a horrible motivator. They will risk others before themselves."

"When battle horns blow, men die," Mikkel added. "It's as simple as that."

"That isn't the worst of it," Arn said.

"I don't like the sound of that." Sizmor glowered.

"The Cardinal Bishop has had two secret meetings," the boy said, his eyes grave as he stared at Sylvie. "The attendees have been Lord Pike as well as the upper-echelon members of the Citadel. But one cloaked figure attended as well. The Kraken wished me to share this with you because he believes the mysterious figure is the Citadel Assassin."

Sylvie had learned a great deal from Master Kell about the history of the kingdom and its workings, but had never heard about this person. "Who?" she asked. "From the sounds of it, not only are Goode family members trying to usurp me—or worse—but now I have a Church Master assassin after me?" She felt one more wall encircle her. "When will the fun end?"

"Partially true," Arn said. "A Master assassin *and* his shadows."

"Shadows?"

"There are four shadows who aid the Citadel Assassin," Mikkel said. "As First Knight, I knew of the Citadel Assassin, but even given my high rank, I did not know who it was. That type of information is the province of the Pontiff, his Cardinal Bishop, and the Legate of the Citadel. No one knows the identities of the assassins, not even the Kraken, apparently. These four help the Citadel Assassin to deliver the death that has been Church-authorized at the highest level."

Sylvie took a deep breath, angry all over again. The life she'd hoped to build—the kingdom she'd hoped to rule—had dissolved in a matter of days. It was almost too much to bear. But with every new force amassing against her, her resolve hardened. She would fight or die. There were no other options.

"It appears you will earn your freedom in keeping me safe, Mikkel," Sylvie said, trying to bolster her courage in the face of such danger.

"I am your champion, no matter the title," her brother said.

Sylvie turned back to Arn. "What kind of reach does this Citadel Assassin have?"

"He has never failed, as far as I know," Arn said. "It may take time, but he always completes his mission. Once given an assignment, there is nowhere he and his shadows won't go. The very depths of the kingdom. The country over the mountains. Out to sea on a ship or to the islands. Wherever his mark goes, he and his shadows follow. Not all is lost, though. You have one ally in the Citadel. Apparently Lord Alent was the only person who argued against using the Citadel Assassin, requesting proof of who murdered Scorus and Idlor. But the Legate has limited authority when it comes to such matters, and he couldn't prevent it."

"Then we must get to Clair-de-Lune Abbey with all haste," she said. "And onward to the Twilight Lands. The sooner I return with some form of the Covenant Codex in hand, the sooner I can put this nonsense to rest. How many days before we reach the light-weavers?"

"Another three, if the weather holds," Mikkel said, gauging the sky. Dark clouds to the far west gathered, but it was difficult to decipher their ultimate direction.

"Do I need worry about this envoy you spoke to in Fontaine?" Sylvie asked Arn. "Does she know I am with you?"

"I was given explicit instructions to abide by the terms of your contract with the Kraken. That means keeping your secret," Arn said, taking another gulp of water. "No one knows you are here with me."

"There is no guarantee they don't know I'm here, though."

"In my line of work, only money guarantees anonymity," the boy said. "And sometimes not even then."

"If more money is offered, I can see that," she said, thinking. "This Citadel Assassin likely has his own network of spies and information-gathering, right?"

"Undoubtedly."

Mikkel grunted. "What's to stop your envoys from sharing news of your passage?" he asked. "Surely a boy from Cliffside traveling east and seeking information of the Goode family would be enough for these assassins to use."

"Let's just say the Kraken does not take kindly to those who counter his wishes," Arn said.

The boy said it in such a way that left little doubt what the Kraken did to those who crossed him. Still, there were no assurances, and if the Citadel Assassin or one of his shadows discovered these envoys in the towns they stopped at, it would lead them directly to her.

"I suggest we get going," Mikkel said, appraising the dark western clouds even as he clicked his tongue and pressed his heels into his mount.

"It's going to rain. I can smell it," Sizmor said.

Though seeking the Twilight Lands would have blanched the stoutest Ecclesia knight, Sylvie looked at the gathering blackness at their back and couldn't shake the feeling that the real danger was not ahead but rather behind.

11

he next morning before dawn, the storm found them.

Better the rain than the assassins, Sylvie thought as the first pelting drops woke her. She quickly changed her mind: she'd prefer to fight the Citadel Assassin than the clammy chill seeping into her bones. The morning was made more miserable by their lack of shelter, as they were currently crossing the interior plains of Royaume de France, with neither major forests nor craggy mountains for protection. The day passed in a blur of gray drudgery. When they stopped that night, she curled up in bedding supplied by the Kraken, under trees that were more like large bushes, trying to find a position that offered the most comfort. She found none. At some point she fell asleep, and when she awoke, lingering nightmares followed her into the new day along with a surliness she had not experienced in a very long time.

The next two days saw similar weather, though the rain changed to a persistent drizzle. Cold became one of her companions, ever present. Her horse, Marseau, plodded forward following Mikkel's charger, head held low with all the certainty of a creature heading toward its grave. Sylvie felt the same.

But in the early afternoon, the world brightened and the clouds parted. Patches of blue sky reclaimed the grim day, and the group began to dry out.

"Is that it?" Sizmor asked, pointing into the distance.

On a hill at the horizon, through a patchwork of farmland and shrubberies, Clair-de-Lune Abbey glowed in the noonday sun. A small town had grown up around it. A silver river ran between them, an oak forest growing along its banks and surrounding the abbey.

"The Voire River," Mikkel said. "We shouldn't have a hard time crossing it. Bridges litter this part of the kingdom. In fact, I see one there in the town."

Sylvie blocked the sun with her hand, looking where her First Knight pointed. "Lead the way," she said.

Mikkel clicked his charger forward. They rode their horses at a slow pace down the final hill toward the river, sweeping the countryside for any dangers. They saw their first person soon after, working the farmland around them. He barely paid them any heed. As they drew closer to the river, the town's buildings began cropping up, small at first and far apart but quickly larger and cramming up next to one another. All were made of oak timbers and white stone with roofs of orange tiles, some featuring ivy-like green coats. Flower boxes and shrubs added color, and the smells of baking and cooking permeated the air. People in the streets went about their business. Sylvie and her friends received some curious glances and several greetings, but no one asked after their affairs. She hoped none would remember them.

When they crossed the bridge, horse hooves clunking and echoing, Sylvie looked ahead at the abbey, its main tower spire tall, its three floors thick and imposing, all surrounded by a tall wall. A white-rock path sloped upward toward a gated entrance.

"I fear this place, Sylvianna," Sizmor said at her ear, the Fae creature invisible to the town's populace and those ahead at the abbey.

"The light-weavers are not a threat, I assure you," she said, trying not to belittle the sprite's feelings but knowing she would need him inside. "They are more interested in self-sacrifice and keeping to their studies than worrying about you."

"They killed my kind by the droves," the sprite said. She heard a deep anger and distrust in his words. "I wish I did not have to enter the abbey. My place is by your side, though, High Queen. I must warn you. I will do what I must to protect myself as well as you if it comes to it, if I feel danger from the light-weavers."

"You are very brave, sprite," Mikkel said. "You won't be the only one protecting Sylvianna, or our reason for being here. I will also see to it that nothing happens to you or Arn, Master Fae, to the best of my abilities."

Arn nodded, keeping his eyes on the surrounding gardens. The sprite said nothing else, but his determination was clear. Sylvie was pleased by her First Knight's words too. Her three companions were there when they did not need to be, and their resolve bolstered her own. She would need them all in the days to come.

Once Mikkel and Arn stopped conferring about which path would gain the gated entrance in the high warding wall, the First Knight led the way. The grounds were well cared for. Large oak trees along the Voire River offered shade, and small flowering bushes littered the area, clipped and kept healthy by an unseen caretaker. No one was about. Only birdsong accompanied the crunch of plodding hooves on white gravel.

Mikkel dismounted at the gate, one made from steel bars elegantly crafted. A large bell with a clapper waited to be rung. Sylvie and Arn slid down from their saddles as well, the boy taking her reins. To either side of the entrance, starbursts had been carved into the wall. Beyond, the abbey awaited with its gardens—green, lush, and vibrant in the sunshine.

Arn was looking up at the gate's stone arch, which was carved with ornate script. "I do not read well. What do the words say?" he asked.

"It is Old Norgi," Sylvie said, eyeing it. "It says 'Let the light guide.'"

"You will want this," Mikkel said, offering her Lumière, still sheathed.

"But why?" Sylvie had little training with weapons, and the sword was best held by the one who knew how to use it. "I am no warrior. And you may have need of it. We do not know if we will be welcome here."

"Another sword is there on my saddle," he said, extending Lumière to her. "Take it; you must have it."

"Again, why?"

Mikkel gave her a dark look, as if she were an idiot. "It is a sword created from the heart of fallen-light. Not only that, but it was forged here in this dukedom. The sword's history is a part of Clair-de-Lune's, and I am betting you will find a greater welcome for your station if you are the one who possesses it."

Sylvie hadn't considered that. "I see your point. I will take it, though I'll conceal it until it is needed," she said, taking the blade of her father—the symbol of her office—and keeping it cradled in her arms like a newborn. She pulled her cloak over its hilt. The sword revealed her identity; hiding that identity was of greater importance than ever before with the Citadel Assassin seeking her. "I must ask, though. Ever since the Kraken said we had to come here, you've seemed reticent. Dark, even. It's more than just seeing him again. Isn't it?"

"My High Queen," Mikkel said. "I've known the Kraken a long time. When he said we had to come here for counsel before our journey to the Twilight Lands, he looked right at me. He said it in such a way that leads me to believe he knows something I do not. He found great joy in what I do not know. So yes, I am worried."

"I saw it too. But what could be so worrisome about an abbey filled with smart and intelligent women?" Sylvie said with a grin. When he didn't return the smile, she sobered. "Whatever it is, Mikkel, we will face it together."

"I know, my High Queen," Mikkel said, nodding. "I just hope it isn't something that dashes our hopes for the journey we are undertaking."

"Who shall ring the bell?" Arn asked, returning their attention to the task.

With a sigh, Sylvie went to it. It should be she who requested audience. She took the clapper in her hand, looked at her companions, and slammed it against metal. The resulting peal broke the afternoon stillness, echoing throughout the grounds. Moments passed. Arn went to the gate and peered through the bars. When he backed away, he gave Sylvie a look that noted the bell had done its job.

A few moments later, a woman in a pale gray robe cinched at the waist by a golden cord, face hidden by a pale gray veil, appeared. Her clothing was a stark contrast to her glowing ebony skin and dark eyes. She stood with hands folded at her front, shoulders back, and gaze burning into them. She lacked the wrinkles of age but possessed the confidence of a woman much older. Sylvie respected that.

"Clair-de-Lune Abbey is not open to the uninvited," she said, appraising them.

Mikkel went up to the gate. He was about to say something, but when his hand touched the steel bars, a sunburst of light—swallowing the entirety of the First Knight in illumination—blinded Sylvie and was gone just as quickly.

It dropped Mikkel to his knees, where he shook his head, stunned, hand trying to clear the blindness that had overcome him.

"Do not touch the Lune Gate," the woman said, but her eyes held amusement at what had just occurred. "Try that again, Ecclesia knight, and you will discover how powerful the light can be."

Mikkel raised his hands in supplication, still squinting. "I meant no harm, and I am not here for myself, trust me on that." He regained his feet and turned to Sylvie, who joined him. "This is a woman you do not want to turn away, though."

The guard's eyes narrowed on Sylvie.

"And why would that be?"

"I am High Queen Sylvianna Goode," Sylvie said, standing as close to the gate as she dared. She lowered her hood and unwrapped Lumière, still cradled in her arms. The beautiful blade caught the day's sunlight and glowed ethereal, blinding in its own way.

The surprise on the guard's face could not be masked, and her eyes shone, as if she had just witnessed a miracle.

"Lumière," she breathed. "I will return with most haste."

"That will not be necessary, Ezel Fela," an old woman said from behind her, appearing as if by magic. She wore a robe similar in style to the younger woman's, but it was pristine white. She lacked a veil, though, her pale face worn with numerous wrinkles and eyes a light blue sparkling with mirth. "The light illuminates those who are in need, and there is great need here."

"Prioress Mother, I apologize with sincerity born of the morning's dawn. Do you wish my arm for the walk back?" Ezel Fela asked, backing away from the gate with eyes lowered in deference to the aged woman.

"Stop that poetic nonsense, as well as your posturing, or I will place you in the Dark Room for a day," the other snapped. "Do not mollify me, young acolyte. I am quite capable."

"Yes, Prioress Mother."

"Now, enough banter. Old bones make for impatient snark, High Queen Sylvianna Goode." The old woman's head tilted to the side as if she heard music from a great distance. "Do not think Ezel Fela uncouth. She means well, but youth's enthusiasm has a way of infringing on the most basic common sense. Welcome to Clair-de-Lune Abbey."

"I thank you for the welcome. I do not think ill of your acolyte," Sylvie said, trying to gauge the other. "Are you indeed Prioress Mother Agnes?"

The old woman winked at her. "You never can tell sometimes."

Then Sylvie noticed that the Prioress Mother's eyes weren't light blue but were in fact clouded by age or damage.

She was blind. Or close to it.

"We wish to speak to you and the Prioress Superior, if you'd have us," Sylvie said.

"Admittance is assured, but entrance may not be given," Agnes said, a riddle of some sort that made the woman cackle like a crazy person. With those words, she knocked her knuckles upon the gate's bars and withdrew from view behind the wall. "The light will guide your way if you have the ability to see it," she said, now hidden.

The gate swung open on its own. Sylvie glanced at Mikkel and Arn, wondering if they had any thoughts about such a strange woman. Neither said a word. Sylvie shrugged, stepping aside to let her First

Knight lead them through the opening. Arn followed Sylvie, taking the reins of the horses and bringing them into the abbey grounds.

Once through, Sylvie looked to ask the old woman what she meant, but both women were no longer there, as if they had never been. The pathway shimmered and seemed to curve away from the abbey suddenly, when it had appeared straight at first glance.

Sylvie blinked her eyes and the strange effect vanished.

"Where did they go?" Arn asked.

"Into the light, I expect," Mikkel grunted with a hint of mockery. "Though we know where we have to go, don't we?"

"Told you, Sylvianna. These light-weavers cannot be trusted," Sizmor said, hidden from view.

Uncertain what she'd just perceived, and wondering if the Fae was right, Sylvie shook her head and turned to Clair-de-Lune. She saw no obvious entrance, merely paths of white pebbles that cut through the verdant green of well-maintained grass and gardens. The abbey itself was a massive structure, built from stone and smooth slurry with one tower rising above all else from the building's end, a hand reaching for the sky. The design of the monastery was unlike anything she had seen before. Whereas most of the buildings in Mont-Saint-Michel were square or rectangular, with simple lines and small windows, Clair-de-Lune featured short walls cutting at strange angles with the tallest windows Sylvie had seen. She realized why then. The women of the monastery were dedicated to the study and application of light. It made sense that the light-weavers would want as much light from as many directions as could be created. It left her awed in a new way.

Sylvie strode ahead of Mikkel then, still cradling Lumière in her arms. The abbey gardens opened to them. The white pebble path twisted this way and that, crunching beneath her feet. She kept to the largest path that seemed to go toward the abbey, weaving beneath large rhododendron trees bursting with color.

She paused at a flowering bush, its blossoms large and brilliantly white beneath the afternoon sun. It was a flower she had never seen, like a cross between a rose and a lily.

"It is aptly named a lily rose," the Prioress Mother Agnes said suddenly, appearing out of nowhere. How she knew they were there, Sylvie couldn't comprehend. "The flower is capable of absorbing light in a way others can't. And it only seeds on one day a year, the summer solstice. It is quite rare. Like you, High Queen Sylvianna Goode." She smiled, tilting the flower gently toward her nose. "And it smells divine. Try it."

Sylvie leaned in. It did indeed offer a perfume not unlike honey mixed with pepper.

"It is a miracle in a garden of miracles," Sylvie said. She turned to the old woman. "But how did you disappe—"

The Prioress Mother had vanished again. The same shift of light had occurred.

"How is she able to do that?" Arn asked, frowning. He was clearly unnerved by the theatrics. So was Sylvie. "I swear I was just looking at her, but I have no memory of her arriving and leaving."

"Neither do I," Mikkel said. He took a deep breath. "She knows more about light and its abilities than anyone, I bet. She's been here since I was a boy, and she was old then. One does not live so long without learning a few tricks, Arn."

"Did any of you notice how the path changed?" Sylvie questioned. "It twisted this way to the lily rose, but now the walkway seems to curve a different direction than before."

"I saw no change," Sizmor said. The others nodded.

Wondering if her sanity had fled her, Sylvie left the lily rose and continued upon the path. She was a bit annoyed with the Prioress Mother, but it was her home and her rules. The strange glimmering in the air continued to blur the details around her—the world all color with no cohesive shapes. There was some strange magic at work, she realized, one that prevented them from finding the entrance to the abbey.

Sylvie stopped and closed her eyes. She heard her companions stop behind her. Sunlight warmed her face, a joyous feeling that calmed her. She thought about the abbey, its beautiful grounds, and what had transpired thus far. She heard Kell's resonant voice in her mind asking her to first diagnose the problem in order to find a solution.

She opened her eyes, doing exactly as she had been taught. They had been letting the path guide them to the abbey. But that path kept switching back into the gardens.

Inspired by an idea, Sylvie stepped off the white pebbles toward the abbey.

The moment she did, the path scooted over beneath her feet as if it had always been there. She turned to her companions.

The awe on their faces proved the others saw it as well.

Sylvie continued forward, ignoring the path her eyes saw for the one she saw in her mind. It curved around the side of the abbey, and as she grew closer, exhilaration replaced her initial confusion—until she slid to a stop, surprised by what she discovered on the other side of the magnificent building.

A massive fountain cascaded into the air, three tiers matching the floors of the abbey, the sound of water tinkling and chiming like music. The top tier misted fine droplets. The effect was stunning. Rainbows flashed all over the fountain, a kaleidoscope of color amid the white stone. It mesmerized. Sylvie sensed even Sizmor's wonder.

And again, Prioress Mother Agnes met them, sitting on the edge of the fountain. "You do possess an affinity for the light, Sylvianna Goode. That is well. That is well. Arcs of light are not unlike the arcs of one's life," she said, smiling as if her presence was the most natural thing in the world. "Filled with color that only the darkness can sap. Light will not be denied, though. It repels the blackest void if its strength is matched to the power of one's heart."

"Why do you keep riddling us? And what is that shimmering at the edge of my vision?" Sylvie asked, unwilling to take her eyes off the older woman for fear she might up and vanish again.

"Education is the key to both questions. As is having powerful friends and alliances," Agnes said. Then she whispered, as if it were a conspiracy only they could know, "And a powerful sword that sings to the light. Of course. Of course. Yes, of course."

"You are quite spry, for someone of so many winters," the First Knight said.

"An Ecclesia knight, so far from home, so far from the dark depths of Mont-Saint-Michel," the old woman said, a wide grin deepening her wrinkles. "Despite my eyes, I see much. How pleasant to see you again. A dungeon is no place for such a man. Yet I've never been a mother, though I have mothered. A calling of the light, you might say. Did you make someone a mother, knight? Did that mother save or damn the world?"

"She's quite mad," Arn said, shaking his head.

"Prioress Mother," Mikkel growled, annoyed. "We are here on very import—"

"Yes, yes, I know," Prioress Mother Agnes said. "Can't an old woman who feels the light but can no longer see it have a little fun?"

Questions in the form of riddles, words meant to confuse and confound. Sylvie was suddenly reminded of Alafair's last day, when he questioned his children in the ways of Lordship. She wondered if such conversation was the pure province of the old, who took pleasure in teaching the young through a means that seemed utter madness by the latter.

"Prioress Mother," a voice said.

Sylvie and the others turned. Acolyte Ezel Fela moved toward them from the back of the abbey, her movements smooth, her dark eyes fixed on the older woman.

"Yes, yes, what *is* it, Ezel?" Agnes asked, exasperated.

"Prioress Superior Sanna requests your presence," Ezel said, back straight and eyes sharp. "She also requests you stop badgering our new friends and guide them to the Prioress's Office where they undoubtedly want to go."

"Undoubtedly? Requests, eh?" the Prioress Mother asked, frowning. She sighed. She grew older then, shoulders more stooped, the light-hearted fun gone from her. "Well then, school is over. Come with me, High Queen Sylvianna Goode, if you dare."

Without another word, the old woman strode toward the abbey. The acolyte joined her. Sizmor grumbled in Sylvie's ear about the evil of light-weavers.

Sylvie paid the sprite no mind as she followed, keeping her gaze on the women in case they decided to suddenly vanish. She didn't want to lose them again. It didn't take long for Sylvie and her companions to arrive at a wall with large stained-glass windows to either side of two huge doors banded in steel and four times as tall as Mikkel. Ezel Fela waited by one of the doors, which already stood open.

"We would have found the entrance ourselves, Prioress Mother Agnes," Sylvie said with a grin, though wondering if she would have. The magic of the path had been no simple mystery to unravel. "Why the impressive show with the invisible but true path?"

"Would you have found it? Would you have? Do you know that? So certain? It's a test, my dear. Tests help temper the heart, build patience, and empower those who seek the truth," she said as she slipped through the doorway. "Tests are what keep us sharp."

"Our visitors do not need tests, Prioress Mother. They need food, rest, and answers," Ezel Fela said, her tone of voice holding nothing but affection. "I welcome them, as should you, without dilly or dally. Prioress Superior Sanna demands it."

"Fine. Fine. No fun for Old Agnes. The light welcomes you, Sylvianna Goode." The Prioress Mother sighed, her games now ended. Sylvie almost felt sad for the blind woman, who had clearly been having a great time at their expense. The elder light-weaver bowed. "In words and heart."

"In words and heart," the acolyte echoed. She glanced at Arn. "I will aid your companion with stabling your mounts."

With Mikkel a shadow behind her, Sizmor hidden, and Arn left outside with Ezel and their horses, Sylvie followed Prioress Mother Agnes. The old light-weaver guided them through a narthex with high ceilings that admitted the light from the large windows behind her, splashes of color on pale gray stone. Agnes shuffled ahead, certain in her direction, before taking a set of stairs upward. With each step, Sylvie became more aware of the silence permeating the halls. Even their footfalls seemed muffled, as if the abbey were holding its breath for something to happen.

Once on the second floor, and having taken several hallways, the Prioress Mother stopped before a large ornate door. An acolyte with the palest skin Sylvie had ever seen and no hair she could discern opened the entry. Agnes said nothing to the young woman as she moved through. Sylvie and Mikkel entered as well.

The first impression Sylvie had was of cascading illumination. The room was awash with light from a long bank of tall windows admitting the afternoon sun. It made the contents of the long, rectangular room hard to view, but she got the impression of an expansive desk in front of the windows, bookshelves lining the walls, and strange instruments of various sizes cluttering a large table on the right side of the room.

From the desk, a woman looked up at them. Sylvie could barely see her due to the blinding glare.

Sylvie was suddenly reminded of an angel on fire.

"Prioress Superior Sanna, you have guests," Agnes grumbled. She took a seat in a chair beside the desk, sighing as she eased into a well-used piece of furniture that looked no more comfortable than a boulder. "You could have let me talk to them longer, you know."

"I am Prioress Superior Sanna. Welcome to Clair-de-Lune," the woman behind the desk said, ignoring the Prioress Mother's pouting. She had a voice like silk, whispery and smooth. "I am pleased you finally arrived."

"You knew we'd be coming?"

The woman smiled. Now that Sylvie had grown accustomed to the bright light, she saw the woman before her looked neither young nor old but somewhere in between. "Not exactly. I just meant you survived Old Agnes over there. She can be frustratingly tricky at times." She paused, appraising Sylvie. "And you have been titled High Queen, though I am careful to call you that. It seems there are others who desire such a station. Is it true what the light tells me? That you have not been coronated due to machinations within Mont-Saint-Michel? That several members of the Goode family are no more, and that you possess a fabled weapon?"

Sylvie took out Lumière, showing the abbey's Prioress the hilt of the sword. "I am High King Alafair's heir, yes."

"I see," the Prioress Superior said, nodding. "But at what cost?"

That surprised Sylvie. "I do not understand what you mean."

"War has costs. I hope to learn of your reasoning for leaving Mont-Saint-Michel," Sanna said, eyes as hard as blue agates. "Once upon a time, this abbey was nearly razed to the ground, many of the women who lived here dying by the blades of those who followed Mordreadth the Great Darkness. High King Alafair slew that darkness with the sword you hold, but that occurred decades ago. Men forget war's evil and will always find excuses to battle. It is in their nature. Is that your nature too, as your father's daughter?"

"I had to leave Mont-Saint-Michel to win back a birthright I did not request," Sylvie said, a bit of anger woven into her words. "I did not choose this quest. It was forced upon me."

"You will see your father's last edict fulfilled then?" the Prioress Superior said, walking from the desk to stare out the nearest window.

"I hope with your aid, yes," Sylvie said.

"To know the light, one must embrace the light," Old Agnes said, cackling. "You have the light within you, young lady. I see hope. I see it despite my blindness. But do you?"

Sylvie had no idea what the old woman meant. The Prioress Superior said nothing, awaiting an answer to the older woman's question. Sylvie had already grown tired of the riddles but tried to keep her frustration from showing.

"I believe we each have power to change the world," she said simply.

"Pay the Prioress Mother no mind," Prioress Superior Sanna said. "Sometimes the light affects each of us differently."

"That's her way of calling me crazy," Agnes said, clucking her tongue. "I'm not crazy, though. Blind from seeing the truth of things that most do not."

When the Prioress Superior turned from the window, she gave Sylvie a steely look and then glanced at Mikkel. The two stared at one another a long time. The silence became tangible. That's when Sylvie took in her First Knight. He had turned the color of milk. He came back to himself almost as quickly, then he dropped to his knee, head bowed, armor glowing in the light.

"Apologies for my stare, Prioress Superior," Mikkel said, head still down.

"Rise, Ecclesia knight," she said, her voice now soft. With sadness? Wonder? Sylvie couldn't tell. "The past is a cold room, and our present is filled with light. There is no need for such formality between us, given that past."

Mikkel did as he was instructed. But he did not look at the Prioress Superior, preferring to avert his gaze to the rug at his feet.

"If your time is not already promised, I desire to walk with you this evening, knight," Prioress Superior Sanna said. "I know you to be a man of faith, light, and honor. I would learn the potential of this High Queen from you, if you would be so willing to honor me with your time."

Mikkel kept his gaze down.

"I could never say otherwise, Prioress Superior."

She looked at Sylvie. "Do you consent to this?"

"First Knight Mikkel Goode is at your service," Sylvie said, surprised the abbess would prefer to speak with him rather than her.

"Very well, one of my acolytes will collect the First Knight once you have been shown your quarters and have had the chance to refresh," Prioress Superior Sanna said. She moved to take Sylvie's free hand in her two. "Sylvianna Goode, find Clair-de-Lune at your welcome and disposal. No room is off limits, no part of our abbey closed to you. This is a place of worship and study. You may do both, one, or neither while in our midst."

"Thank you, Prioress Superior Sanna, it is an honor to be here," Sylvie said, squeezing the hands back.

The woman gave Lumière a cursory glance before smiling, the act melting the years from her, and Sylvie saw how beautiful she must have been when younger, like the dawn. "Very well. Once you have recovered from your journey and I consider what your First Knight shares, we will reconvene for a banquet in your honor and discuss the events of the world and its people. Find solace here, for the light warms as it guides. That includes your little Fae friend, who is also quite welcome here despite our shared histories."

With that, the Prioress Superior took a bell from her desk and rang it. The acolyte from outside the room answered and guided them out into the hallway.

"She is a smart woman, that one," Sizmor said at her ear.

"She is. And you are safe from these evil, no-good light-weavers," Sylvie said, shaking her head. She looked to Mikkel. He walked a step behind her, deep in thought. She would discover what was wrong with him once they were alone.

Taking them to a suite of rooms as decadent as any in Mont-Saint-Michel, the acolyte left them with a hot bath steaming and a tray bearing various berries and a pitcher of cool water. The acolyte would bring Arn to the rooms once he had finished securing and caring for the horses.

Mikkel ignored it all. He moved to sit on one of the plush chairs pushed up near one of the large windows and began removing his armor in a slow, methodical way that denoted he had no idea what he was doing.

He appeared a knight beaten—a man lost.

"I've never seen a man lose a fight so quickly. Already making an impression on the women here, I see," Sylvie said, trying to lighten her First Knight's mood.

"Do not take it as a slight, High Queen. I am your servant first and always," Mikkel said, taking a deep breath. It was as though he'd seen a weyr-ghost or aged twenty years. He kept removing his plate, freeing the man beneath. "I know her. She is the reason the Kraken smirked at the end of our meeting in Cliffside."

Sylvie frowned, not liking the sound of that.

"Who is she?"

His blue eyes shimmered with emotions Sylvie had not seen in the man before. "Someone I haven't seen for twenty years," he said, barely above a whisper. "A woman I've thought about every day since I was imprisoned by Alafair. The Prioress Superior Sanna is my Chelle."

With that, Mikkel Goode put his face into his hands and wept.

DONATO

12

he summons Sylvie expected by the next morning did not arrive for two days.

When Mikkel had returned from his night stroll with Prioress Superior Sanna, he'd had little new information to offer Sylvie. The two former lovers spent their time walking the gardens, enjoying the stars, and sharing their stories since they parted. For his side of the conversation, Mikkel related how his prison sentence had effectively ended his life. Chelle had had a difficult time after what the High King had done to her. Her grief drove her to Clair-de-Lune, where she changed her name, as every postulant did. The two did not dwell on the past, though, and soon the discussion turned to Sylvie and what had transpired after Alafair Goode died. Mikkel told Sylvie that he'd left nothing out, including their need for counsel from the wise women of Clair-de-Lune. In the end, the Prioress Superior had not said she would aid them in a fight between siblings. Sylvie worried that they had come to Clair-de-Lune in error.

To keep her mind off that, Sylvie spent her time learning more about the light-weavers. Those born to the ability of weaving light had existed long before Saint Emmer. A handful of light-weavers decided they needed a school to better organize their craft against evil—during their time as well as a prophesied future time when darkness would rise to overcome the light. The creation of Clair-de-Lune Abbey was the result. And over time, smaller abbeys of light-weavers spread outward to most of the major cities as well as along the eastern fringe of the kingdom, to help ward the land and educate its people.

A thousand years later, Mordreadth attacked the main abbey and razed it to the ground, hoping to destroy the power of the light and those who used it. But the light-weavers were strong by then, wielding a power the Great Darkness feared. The creation of Lumière, a sword forged from fallen-light in the days of Saint Emmer, was a testament to this power.

Not much had changed for Clair-de-Lune in the time since Alafair Goode destroyed Mordreadth and united a kingdom. They rebuilt their abbey from its foundations upward, the students studied, the light-weavers worked, and the world moved on.

Now Sylvie hoped she could gain the abbey's support, to retrieve a copy of the Covenant Codex of Saint Emmer.

And prevent a renewed war with the Fae and a civil war among siblings.

Since he had reported back to her on his meeting with Sanna, Sylvie had seen little of Mikkel. Sizmor told her that the First Knight remained largely in his room, though he had ventured out a few times to visit the garden alone. She worried over her melancholy brother. Despite not knowing him long, it hurt Sylvie's heart to see Mikkel in pain. All the while, she worried over when a new Pontiff would be chosen as well as the Citadel Assassin drawing closer to kill her. Time slipped from her like sand through fingers. Sylvie felt as if she were on the edge of an abyss that stared darkly at her, not knowing who would finally push her in.

When an acolyte no older than eight winters knocked on her door, Sylvie hoped the Prioress Superior had requested her presence.

Instead, it was an invitation to a banquet.

Now, dressed in a beautiful white gown of exquisite make gifted from Old Agnes, Sylvie took Mikkel's arm and left their suite for Clair-de-Lune's main hall. Sizmor accompanied them but remained hidden, the Fae still unwilling to show himself. Even Arn joined them, wearing black trousers, black tunic, and black leather vest like those gifted to the First Knight.

When they entered the nave of the abbey, she realized they were joining no mere banquet. The entire hall had been transformed. Tables ran the length of the walls, light-weavers standing with heads lowered in a show of respect as Sylvie passed by. Hundreds of large candles set in sconces blazed light, chasing all shadows from the room. A cheery warmth permeated the air as acolytes set out dishes, goblets, and cutlery in preparation for the feast. Lording over it all, the glass dome overhead glittered, multifaceted mirrors reflecting the scene below.

On a dais between the two transepts, Prioress Superior Sanna stood with Prioress Mother Agnes, both dressed in their finest.

Sylvie understood her part in it. This was for her. She'd seen High King Alafair in similar situations. She nodded to those light-weavers along her path as she made her way toward her host, keeping Lumière close, hoping to impress as much as remind the light-weavers of her reason for being there. That's when Sylvie sensed magic in the room, a gentle hum not heard but felt, like the feeling in High King Alafair's bedroom when he signed the Covenant Codex.

She stopped before the Prioress Superior and Prioress Mother. She nodded to them, feeling all eyes on her. Mikkel and Arn bowed low. Even Sizmor whispered encouraging words into her ear, mentioning how beautiful the hall appeared.

"I am Prioress Superior Sanna of Clair-de-Lune Abbey, and I am pleased to see so many familiar faces this evening. All may be seated," the Prioress Superior said, her voice echoing throughout the length of the hall. The light-weavers took their places, and once the sound of them doing so lessened, she smiled. "This is a blessed night beneath the light of the stars. It has seen friends reunited, a visit from the kingdom's High Queen in waiting, and we shall celebrate with food, drink, and merriness." She raised a finger. "It is more than a banquet, though. Prioress Superior Agnes has offered to weave a retelling of 'The Tragedy of Saint Emmer and Wise Belloch,' a story that, according to my archives, has not been told for over a decade. It is a story of bravery, honor, and history, of how two different peoples came to share peace. In this way, we remember Saint Emmer and the lesson he taught through his sacrifice.

"Until the Superior Mother is prepared, we shall feast. Welcome High Queen Sylvianna Goode, her First Knight Mikkel Goode, the squire Arn Tomm, and their Fae companion Sizmor. They are our guests, and they may take their seats to my right. We as light-weavers shall aid them to make safe the kingdom from all enemies—those within as well as those without. Let us begin!"

The Prioress Superior offered Sylvie and her friends their seats and, when those chairs were taken, sat down in her own. The light-weavers throughout the hall clapped, and then numerous conversations began. Women from hidden alcoves brought the first course, one of salads tossed in a lively strawberry vinaigrette, warm bread loaves slathered in salt butter, and a red wine touched by oak and vanilla.

"Did she just agree to our request for a light-weaver?" Sylvie asked Mikkel, leaning in so only he could hear and setting Lumière at her feet.

"I do believe she just did," the First Knight said.

"That's a huge relief, but I wonder at what cost," Sylvie said, unfolding a napkin to place over her legs and taking a small sip of the wine in her goblet. "Has Sanna changed at all since you knew her as Chelle?"

"She has and she hasn't," Mikkel said, stealing a glance at his former beloved. "In some ways, she is exactly as I remember her. I was surprised to see her here in Clair-de-Lune—Master Kell never told me what happened to her and I never asked—but that she holds such a position among the light-weavers is not surprising. She always had a great deal to offer the world, no matter her station. She has matured into a powerful woman."

"Twenty or so years and all she has been through would do that to anyone," Sylvie noted.

"I wonder if she looks upon me the same way?" the First Knight said. "Have I changed so much during my time of imprisonment that I am no longer the man I once was?"

"After all of these years, she still cared about you enough to trust your opinion of me," Sylvie said. She shrugged. "She could have ignored you and chosen to get to know me instead of taking you on that night stroll."

"It does strike me as odd that she hasn't met with you. I'm sure there will be time for it," he said, pouring water into his goblet instead of wine. "Still, it pleases me to see her doing well. Kell assured me that he would watch over her, see that Alafair didn't damage her further. That is all I knew. It was all I could take, to be honest. I understand war. Matters of the heart are a great deal more difficult."

Sylvie realized the kind of pain her brother had lived with for so long. The last few days had seen that pain dredged from the past and brought into the present's light. As if she had requested it, calming music began from one of the transepts, mostly stringed instruments providing atmosphere while people ate. The main course arrived too, one of succulent duck, braised potatoes, and an assortment of flavorful vegetables. Sylvie enjoyed it a great deal. Mikkel barely ate his food. Arn demolished anything brought to him. Even Sizmor made an appearance to gnaw on a cooked carrot sprinkled with sugar. At one point during the meal, an acolyte touched Prioress Superior Sanna on the shoulder and both removed themselves from the hall. Before she left, Sanna gave Sylvie a dark look and a frown, one that made Sylvie wonder if she had truly acquired the aid of the abbey.

When the Prioress Superior returned, she did so with several older light-weavers, each one walking to separate places throughout the hall.

Mikkel raised an eyebrow at Sylvie. "Curious."

"It is," she said. "Perhaps it is to help the Prioress Mother in her story?"

"The time has nearly arrived for the light-telling!" Prioress Superior Sanna announced, now returned to their table. Her voice ended the conversations in the hall. "The light and truth are as one to us. Those who lurk in the shadows live lives of lies." She paused, and the effect was not lost on Sylvie. "High King Alafair Goode passed through the light into Annwn recently, and Sylvianna Goode is his Named heir. She travels from Mont-Saint-Michel to seek the Fae of the Twilight Lands in a matter of importance to us all. Though not yet coronated, she has my full faith in the light." She paused again, eyes now on Sylvie. "Sylvianna Goode, Named heir of Royaume de France, do you wish the aid of Clair-de-Lune and one of its light-weavers for your arduous journey ahead?"

Sylvie was stunned by the offer, one made without a request. She nodded humbly, unwilling to sully the moment with words.

"I ask now," Prioress Superior Sanna said, her voice echoing thoughout the chamber. "Who among you will go with the High Queen and her companions?"

Sylvie was surprised when Ezel Fela rose from her table, the woman's dark eyes and sharp eyebrows challenging anyone else from doing the same.

"I will gladly go on behalf of Clair-de-Lune, to see our future High Queen safe from any and all harm," she said, her voice ringing.

"Do you approve of this, Prioress Mother Agnes?" the Prioress Superior asked.

"Ezel Fela is gifted and confident. I do," the Prioress Mother said, pushing herself up from her chair to stand hunched beside Sanna. "But I cannot let an acolyte of such will and talent go alone. I too shall go."

Murmurs echoed through the hall, surprise and worry filling the space between words.

"I say this for all to hear," Prioress Superior Sanna said, raising her hands for quiet. She turned toward the woman who once held her position. "The light has been with you a long time. A very long time, Prioress Mother."

"I hear the words beneath the words. Do not presume to tell me of the light, my dear," Agnes said, patting the younger woman's arm. "The light guides me just as it does you. I am old but I am strong in the light. I am strong enough to not only make the journey but see it through to the end of the light."

The Prioress Superior looked to Sylvie, real worry in her eyes. "High Queen Sylvianna Goode, what do you say? Does this meet your needs?"

She looked to Mikkel. He did not move.

The choice was her own.

"I accept all help willingly given in these trying times," Sylvie said, standing. It was the first time she had addressed a full body of people. A light sweat broke out on her skin, but she kept focused on the need at hand. "I thank you all for your hospitality these last days. If it is with the blessing of the Prioress Superior, I gladly accede to Acolyte Ezel Fela and Prioress Mother Agnes joining my First Knight and friends on this journey. It will be dangerous. But such times require courage in the face of atrocity." She realized sharing the truth might be best. "I hope to prevent this kingdom from tearing itself apart, due to my siblings disapproving of my Naming. It seems our two histories intertwine once again to hopefully form a new one."

Prioress Superior Sanna then grabbed her goblet and raised it. "Then I toast to your success. Keep our light-weavers as safe as you can, Sylvianna Goode. They are dear to us. To the valiant two!"

The room erupted in cheers, almost every woman raising her glass in salute.

"Now, Prioress Mother Agnes shall regale us with our tale," Sanna said, sitting again.

The aged woman left her table, taking stairs from the dais down to the main floor of the hall where a large space free of people or chairs existed. All eyes were on her as the light-weavers returned to their seats. A silence of expectation filled the hall.

The blind woman hummed then, her voice rising to a pitch that filled the room from its floor to its domed ceiling. Her hands wove in the air, her milky eyes looking up as if they could still see. The light brightened somehow to Sylvie. She had seen a light-weaver work before but not in such a grand scale.

Music and light joined, a great swelling, the story coming to life inside Sylvie's head.

Emmer stands at the top of the hill, one soul against a sea of hate.

From his vantage, he overlooks a forested valley to the east. On the opposite ridge, a dark stain makes its way downward. The Fae of the Twilight Lands come, and with them war. Behind him, the city of Rouen holds its breath, its citizens fled and only soldiers remaining. It is a dark time for the land. The war between Man and Fae has raged for seasons, with the armies of Man unable to prevent the inexorable encroachment of Fae from their shadowy woods into the lands to the west. No one knows why they've come, and nothing can stop them—not the cities of Man with high walls and moats, not rivers that crisscross farmlands, not even the Vosges or Alpz Mountains, with their snowy peaks touching the everlasting sky. The Fae have cut a swath of destruction spanning the distance from their Twilight Lands toward Mont-Saint-Michel.

No one remembers why the war started, only that it has resulted in hundreds of thousands of dead on both sides. More will die before its end.

The death pains the middle-aged monk. He feels every damage done, every soul sent to Annwn.

And the Fae will not relent unless he finds a way to stop them.

"Emmer, are you sure of this?" Lyelle walks up behind him, her white robe glowing in the early morning light. While he worries for them all, the light-weaver worries for him.

"Do we have a choice?" Emmer responds. "No number of swords, shields, or war machines have prevented the Fae advance. They will drive us into the western sea if we do not do something to stop them here and now."

Lyelle sighs as she twists her long blond hair into a braid, keeping the strands out of her face. As a light-weaver, she needs an unobstructed view. "A Great Darkness watches these events from the shadows. It is the prophecy our earliest light-weaver ancestors discerned. The light senses it. I sense it. For all we know, it drives the Fae battle madness. I just wonder if we've done everything we can. The blackberry seeds that horrible witch imbued with magic should be used only if no option exists."

"We've run out of options, Lyelle." Emmer can't keep his eyes off the approaching army of shadows and twisted creatures.

"The melding has never been done," she says. "It could kill you."

Emmer nods. He knows the danger. The risk. He doesn't want to die. But he must reach the Erlking Belloch of the Fae in some meaningful way, and all his efforts thus far have yielded no fruit. Missives have been sent; ravens have flown. Scouts with negotiation instructions waited for the Fae horde to overtake them in the hopes of coming to a compact of peace. None returned. The Great Darkness Lyelle is concerned about is secondary to the primary threat before them, he thinks. No matter. Emmer has prepared his soul for what sacrifice may be needed, but the monk still has a prayer he can reach the Erlking without it.

"I will not lose on behalf of Man due to a lack of courage," he says. "God does not shine on the cowardly."

"The light shall not die, no matter what you do," Lyelle argues.

Emmer takes a deep breath. "No, the light will not die. But if no one remains to see the light, does it truly exist at all?"

She chews over his words and says nothing to that. The forest in the valley below suddenly comes alive, limbs thrashing this way and that, the larger Fae creatures pushing trees aside for their brethren. Soon their stain will leave the wooded vale. It will begin climbing toward where Emmer and Lyelle wait.

Just like that, it begins. The first Fae leaves the forest under a darkening sky, his deer horns as black as obsidian, and where his legs should be, the body of a black stallion.

Belloch.

Emmer turns to look at the army at his back. Only King Halston Pendragon and his courageous warriors stand with Emmer and Lyelle, the monk having saved Halston as a child from the feverpox and the King prepared to return the favor or die. The other Kings of Man have fled. Emmer imagines most of them are purchasing ships to flee the continent. Faithless. Cowards. Halston would deal with them if given the chance.

Emmer is proud of those who ride with their King. Their fear is palpable and yet they stand, weapons drawn. With them, Halston's brother Sori, leading their only flank. Unlike his older brother, Sori is built for war, favoring their mother's side of the family. Broad shoulders. Height. Arms like tree trunks. He rides past them and nods to his brother, no need for words. They know how the other feels. Brothers always know.

"We won't be able to hold this tide back," Lyelle says when Sori is gone,

gesturing at the Fae emerging from the forest below. "You may lose your chance if King Halston's men are not able to slow the Fae."

"Do not worry so, light-weaver," King Halston Pendragon says behind them. He sits proud in the saddle, hand upon Lumière's hilt. Before the previous battle, Emmer convinced Prioress Superior Elana to give King Halston the fabled blade, hoping Lumière would turn the tide. They discovered it could do no such thing. "The bravery of my warriors and the leadership and might of my brother Sori will see the day won."

"The sword will keep the Fae from you, King Halston, but not your warriors," Emmer says. "It was created from fallen-light, to counter a darkness deeper than the world has yet known."

"I still feel better with it in my hand," King Halston says.

"That gladdens me. It will keep you safe." Emmer is hopeful. "The Fae hate the sword, hate its light. Perhaps you will be able to confront Belloch and discover what the Fae want when nothing else has worked."

The three of them continue to watch the Fae gather outside the forest. Given their vantage, Emmer doubts the Fae have not seen the monk, the light-weaver, the King, and his warriors above.

Once enough have gathered, the Fae rush toward them, the hill below awash in blackness.

"To war!" King Halston roars, Lumière drawn and waving in the air.

Horses ride by Emmer and Lyelle, warriors yelling battle cries and the stink of fear heavy on the afternoon. Lyelle grips his arm, whether from concern for their friends or to prevent him from leaving, he does not know. She understands what is at stake. So does he. This is their final stand. No other help stands between them and Mont-Saint-Michel. The day will see them victorious, or it will see them dead. There is no other outcome. The bonds of Man and the alliances of a dozen different Kings have fallen away, leaving a last desperate group of stalwart men and women to prevent the end of the life they know.

It is a dark day, but hope still burns inside Emmer's heart. It is a hope born of his conviction that he can make a difference when all others have failed.

It is a hope born of his faith.

Before he can think more on it, the black horde of Fae overrun King Halston's troops like a scythe through wheat. Screams and blood thicken the moment. Only the King is untouched, the light of Lumière bright and the Fae flood avoiding it. The scene is one from nightmare become real.

"Pull back! Sori, to me!" the King roars.

"No!" Emmer screams and pulls free of Lyelle. "Not yet. Get to Belloch. See what you can do!"

Even as King Halston rides toward the Fae Erlking and Sori brings his company into the fray from the valley's south end, Emmer pulls a length of steel from a sheath belted to the side of his brown robe. The blade lacks a hilt. It had been forged by the light-weavers as Lumière had been, the steel sharp and exquisitely made. Lyelle says nothing as he stares at its length. The time for warning words has passed.

"Will this work, Lyelle?" he murmurs, feeling the stirrings of fear for the first time.

"Even the light does not know," she says. "It is a melding of two disparate materials. It is possible this will be for naught. It is possible this will kill you."

Emmer watches as King Halston rides toward Belloch. Eventually, even Lumière cannot vanquish the Fae creatures protecting their Erlking, a wall of darkness howling in pain from the light but standing their ground to protect their leader. This is the closest Emmer has been to the Fae, and he's surprised by their appearances—each one features elements found in nature as part of their body. Bark forms skin, moss is hair, leaves sprout as armor. Emmer does not dwell on their alien look for long. He sees King Halston yelling, trying to get Belloch's attention. The former keeps it up while the latter doesn't appear to understand. There is an impasse while warriors and Fae die by the dozens and then hundreds.

"I have no choice, it seems. Death comes to us all, though I'd rather die fighting than giving up," Emmer says, taking a deep breath. He pulls free the magic-infused seeds, the small kernels glimmering black-purple beneath overcast skies. They feel ordinary as he rolls them under his thumb. "What is the best way to do this?" he asks.

"Put them in the dirt, cover, and place your hand over it," she says, kneeling with him.

Emmer does as he is told, unable to ignore the sounds of battle and dying. The earth is black and rich as he digs into it. He places the five seeds within and then covers them over. He pats the damp dirt and then places his right hand over the spot, palm down.

"Emmer!" King Halston roars. His warriors are dying.

The future of Man is dying.

The monk takes it all in. There is no turning back now. Sensing the truth as well, Lyelle places her hand over his. She says nothing. Instead, she calls forth her power with a deep hum, drawing light from the day to her. Her hand grows warmer until he feels like a sun is blossoming in the land by their will alone.

Then the pain begins. She pushes her weight onto his hand, holding him in place until he comes to terms with it. The heat enters his palm first, steady and throbbing, until it expands and extends into his fingers. Fiery pricks stab his palm, but he does not withdraw, unwilling to fail. His hand is on fire, but one look shows nothing out of place.

Emmer realizes that the pain is not relegated to just that hand. His whole body is connected to the seeds buried in the ground. He lifts his left hand, which holds the steel blade.

And almost flees from the horror. His hand is changing before his eyes. Fingers once used to bind leather books or serve the hungry are becoming something else—lengthening, losing their pink color and transforming into twining black-green vines bearing thorns that glisten with venom. His palm narrows and grows longer. Forearm bones writhe under his skin like snakes, misery racking his body as he feels them separate from his hand. It feels unending. An eternity of suffering. One he's not sure he will survive.

The pain suddenly dulls, leaving him panting. Exhaustion darkens his sight, but he fights fainting, knowing he is the only chance Man has to survive this day and those that will come after.

A sword, fused of fallen-light and the now missing part of his body, drops to the ground. He focuses on it, disbelieving. Where his hand used to be, a stump of new, pink flesh heals. Emmer bends down to pick up the weapon, wondering if it is even real. The flesh, blood, and bone of his left hand now form black vines tightly woven into the pommel, grip, and cross guard of a new sword. The steel is black, the hilt warm to his touch. With the help of Lyelle, the light of the blade has wed to the shadows of the earth—creating a weapon that Emmer hopes can reach the Fae in a way that Lumière could not.

He knows what he must do. Cradling his tender lackhand to his chest, Emmer strides forward, sword in his good hand, head buzzing with purpose. Man and Fae are both dying.

It is time to set right the war that sickens the land and its people.

With a nod to Lyelle, Emmer enters the battle, sword raised.

The Fae fall back from it as if it were Lumière. Through some part of the natural world now living within the sword, Emmer senses what the Fae feel. They rage at his human presence while they fear his existence. They believe Man threatens their kind by multiplying like rabbits. They have been told the end of the Fae is at hand if they do not fight. Amid what Emmer senses, Belloch is at the forefront of those thoughts, the Erlking doing what he must to ensure his kind are kept safe. The monk understands these lies even as he knows that Man has said similar things about the Fae. It is in both of their natures to fear the other; it is this idea that will undo them both at the end of all things.

Some entity has set the Fae against Man. Now a part of both worlds, he senses it all. It leaves him more fearful for what is to come.

Even if they succeed here, they could ultimately fail.

The monk focuses on the moment. He charges into the battle, and the Fae move away from his sword, hissing and snarling and angry at their inability to attack him. He realizes he has more to fear from King Halston's warriors, who can barely keep their mounts under control in an ocean of chaos. Through some form of communication that Emmer cannot see or hear, the Fae are coordinating their assault—and they are bewildered by him. He is unlike any son of Man they have encountered.

He can feel Belloch's frustration between the light and the shadows. The monk's presence draws the Erlking into the fray, closer and closer. The leader of the Fae is half horse, half bare-chested man, his skin dark and muscled, his eyes glowing red above high cheekbones. The deer antlers upon his head, used as weapons against King Halston's men, glisten with dark crimson and gore. The sight leaves Emmer sick, but he doesn't have time to contemplate the horror of it all. He brings his sword up, ready for what is to come.

"You," Emmer senses Belloch say. "Who are *you?"*

"This is not the way," the monk says, staring hard into the eyes of Erlking Belloch. Where once he would have been terrified, now a battle calm has overcome him. "This is not how I want things to be. Desist from your attack. Let us talk. I'd rather offer you peace than kill you or your kind."

"What is it that you wield?" the Erlking hisses, hooves stamping. "It is not of the world of Man."

"No, it is not."

Belloch growls low. Emmer can feel it in his chest. The Fae have slowed their assault and their eyes have turned on Emmer. He takes a breath, feeling the power of his and Lyelle's creation. Then he understands, the thought so impossible he can barely comprehend it. The Erlking controls his Fae through the shadows. The newly crafted sword is partly made of the shadows. The Erlking realizes what Emmer now knows—the monk can reach the Fae, perhaps even control them.

"Do not," the Erlking warns.

Before Emmer can respond, Belloch charges him, hooves pounding the earth, his visage a twisted mask of rage and fear. It leaves the monk almost paralyzed. None of King Halston's men are near. Lyelle is beyond aiding him. He has overextended himself and is at the mercy of the Erlking.

With a thought, Emmer confronts the Fae leader—not physically, but with his mind. He could have killed him; he could have made the Erlking do his will. Instead, he decides to prove his worth. The Fae's horse front legs collapse, sending the entire creature to the turf. Grass and soil fly. Emmer steps to the side, keeping the sword between him and his foe. He has no desire to kill the Fae leader; neither will he let himself be destroyed in the process.

Instead, he brings the tip of the black sword down and touches Belloch at his neck.

"Please, Belloch, be wise. I am not your enemy," Emmer says. "I am here to stop this madness before it swallows the whole world and us in it."

Belloch glares at him, defeated. He then stares at the sword, his red eyes flaring. He cannot overcome Emmer's will flowing through the sword into the shadows about the Erlking. The monk can feel the other's thoughts—his strengths, his fears. Tense moments pass. Sweating from exertion and fear of what Belloch might choose, Emmer prays to his god to not have to take this creature's life. Because he sees the end of the world if the Fae are fully destroyed.

"I accept," Belloch growls, his words thick with anger. "At dawn, join me here. Alone. We shall speak. My word is my bond, and my bond is shared with you now."

Emmer pulls his sword away from the other's neck and relinquishes his hold on the Erlking, offering the Fae Lord a hand. Belloch takes it, until it is no longer needed, and together they stand, the Erlking towering over the monk, both eyeing one another. A few moments pass and then Belloch turns, leaving the battlefield. The remaining warriors of King Halston cheer; the surviving Fae follow Belloch and fade back down the hill into the forest; and only the sounds of those dying or wounded fill the sudden silence.

Lyelle joins Emmer then. They watch the Fae disappear. After King Halston calls on healers from the rear guard, he dismounts and sheathes Lumière, his armor blood-splattered, his brow sweaty beneath his crown.

"You've saved us," the King says. "Both of you. You've saved us all."

"Perhaps," Emmer says. "Tomorrow will tell."

"What will you name it?" Lyelle asks, taking his lackhand to examine it. Her touch is careful, tender, and Emmer welcomes it.

"What do you mean?"

"The sword. Every sword of import is named, Emmer. And this one is certainly special. It deserves a name," Lyelle says. She lets go of his arm, gesturing at his remaining hand. "It would be ill luck to not do so."

Emmer lifts the weapon, having the time now to appreciate the sacrifice of his hand for his bargain made. The sword is an unusual weapon—created from two different worlds—the blade dull black steel with a hilt made from briar vines of different thicknesses. Swashes of strange light swirl through the metal of the blade. He squeezes the grip harder, testing its durability. The briar vines tighten like fingers forming a fist, alive in a way that an inanimate object shouldn't be.

"It shall be known as Bruyère," he says.

Lyelle nods, drawing her robe closer. There is a chill in the air. She leaves with King Halston to appraise his warriors and ensure that those who are wounded receive the care they deserve. Emmer remains, alone, considering what has transpired. Weariness draws him, but he ignores it. While he should care that he's lost a hand, Man has gained a greater gift than mere flesh can account.

There is much to be done. In the morning, he and Erlking Belloch will meet and become one within their peace. Emmer will bring a quill, ink, and as many parchment pages as he possesses.

Together, they will save the worlds of Man and Fae alike, creating a covenant codex.

And they will be as one forever.

The illusion shimmered and vanished. Sylvie shook her head at the sudden return of Clair-de-Lune, ready to weep from the gift she had been given. She had seen light-tellings before but never to such an extent. The clapping and cheers from the light-weavers in attendance matched her feelings. She had witnessed a great story, one she'd learned in her youth but never experienced in such a way. It left her in awe of the power Prioress Mother Agnes possessed. Sylvie found herself standing, clapping, as the others did.

When light blasted through the room, blinding her, for a moment she couldn't tell the light-telling from the real world.

"Get down!" Mikkel roared at her side.

Not waiting for her response, he pushed her chair backward, sending her sprawling to the stone floor behind. Confused, she gaped at him. He stood over her, drawing Lumière free from its sheath. More light filled the room, soundless and blinding. She squinted against it, holding her hands up, trying to get a glimpse of what was going on.

Mikkel stepped over her, sword up. She saw two bodies rushing toward them, faces covered, clothed all in black. They split apart, coming at Sylvie from different angles.

She knew what transpired; she would not be a victim.

She regained her feet, standing beside Mikkel, drawing one of his knives from his belt. Sizmor flew into invisibility. A resonant hum filled the air, seemingly coming from all directions as light-weavers gathered to combat the attackers. She felt Mikkel grunt before hearing it, something striking the First Knight so hard it staggered him. He spun to the side even as two more darts—that would have hit Sylvie if not for his protection—sprouted from his shoulder, the barbs deep in his black leather. A knife followed, its handle slapping Mikkel in the face. As he fell from the blow, one of the light-weavers the Prioress Superior had brought into the hall tackled Sylvie from the side, sending her sprawling away from her brother as another light-weaver slid on the floor to aid him.

"Lie still, High Queen Sylvianna. Do. Not. Move," the woman hissed, her breath hot. Then she started crying, brushing Sylvie's hair back from her forehead as if she had fallen prey to the assassin, even as others yelled that the High Queen had been slain. The light-weavers scoured the room and beyond for those who had invaded Clair-de-Lune.

Sylvie did as she was told, not moving. She stared at her First Knight—the scene too ghastly for her to look away. Mikkel lay stricken, the light-weaver probing where the darts had hit him, crimson creating a blacker black than the leather had been dyed. Beyond, she could just make out one of her attackers, limbs spread out awkwardly, unmoving.

Chaos made of movement and sound surrounded them, the deep hum still filling the air, and she could hear the sounds of light-weavers fighting the other assailant even as he managed to flee the room.

Sylvie looked back at her First Knight—her brother. Her heart sank. Tears sprang to her eyes, and she fought to get the light-weaver off her. She saw it was too late to save Mikkel.

Prioress Superior Sanna barked orders. The light-weavers moved to carry them out, to seek the assassin who had gotten away, to discover any others, to secure the abbey and the grounds, and to enter the town and learn where the assassins had come from. When the Prioress Superior finished her commands, she went to the fallen knight, hands clutched before her. Sylvie watched her kneel at his side, unable to ignore the truth. The hum Sylvie heard on the air did nothing to assuage the sorrow filling her heart.

Mikkel no longer moved. He did not breathe. He saw nothing despite his eyes staring up at the hall's beautiful dome.

The Citadel Assassin had found them.

And First Knight Mikkel Goode lay dead for it.

PART III

THE MAD-WHISPERING SAINT

13

igh Queen Sylvianna Goode stood on her balcony, and Death waited with her.

It was not the death of the night before her, where dawn closed in to lighten the eastern sky, sending the stars to their daytime graveyard. It was not the death of two light-weavers, who had confronted assassins in their abbey home and paid the ultimate price for keeping Sylvie safe from the machinations of her siblings. And it was not the death of First Knight Mikkel Goode, her brother and friend, who died honorably protecting her while carrying out his duty. No, the death accompanying her was unlike any other. Even as she cradled Lumière and gazed at the approaching dawn, she thought about Saint Emmer saving the land and her father Alafair Goode uniting it, and both men witnessing horrific death. They would understand. The death haunting her was one of memory—every vacant stare of every dead warrior, every final breath taken, every putrid smell of unleashed bowels—where she would relive it forever.

The cold of the morning matched the one within. She already wore her travel clothing under her black robe, ready to leave Clair-de-Lune. It was no longer safe for her anywhere if she could be found so easily by the Citadel Assassin.

It made her wonder if her choice to become High Queen at all costs was worth it.

Because Mikkel was dead, for his fealty to her.

"It is time we leave, my High Queen," Sizmor said. "The Prioress is ready."

Ignoring the Fae guide hovering next to her, Sylvie stared off at one star that refused to dim. It fought the coming dawn. It gave her hope amid the sea of darkness in her heart. Could she ever become that star?

"Sylvianna," the sprite pressed.

"I heard you, Sizmor," she said, feeling numb.

"He will be missed," the sprite said. "I know you cared a great deal for him in the short time you were together, but he protected you when there was need. He did his job. He would want you to do yours now."

"You sound like Master Kell," she snorted, unable to hide her derision. She swallowed pain, almost choking on unbidden tears. "I know all of that, Sizmor. It does not change the pain in my heart. He died for nothing."

Sizmor frowned but did not reply. Their previous conversations had gone like this one. Rather than argue and upset her further, he instead patted her shoulder.

A knock came at the suite door. Ezel Fela, who had helped Sylvie pack, answered it.

Prioress Mother Agnes shuffled in, heading to the balcony. Sylvie did not acknowledge her. She hoped the old woman hadn't come with more riddles. Thankfully, Agnes only put her hand on Sylvie's arm, an act that steadied them both.

"It is time we leave, High Queen," the blind woman whispered with a solemnity that touched Sylvie's heart deeply.

"It feels wrong for me to leave without saying goodbye to him."

"Sylvianna Goode, your First Knight would want you as far from this place as quickly as you can travel," Agnes said. "You must focus. Now."

"What the Prioress Mother says is true," Sizmor agreed. "Mikkel wouldn't want you waiting for the Citadel to finish its job."

Sylvie wiped tears from the corners of her eyes. The events of the previous evening played through her mind, over and over. She couldn't help it. After Mikkel had been struck down, and an acolyte whose name she didn't know kept her safe, Prioress Superior Sanna escorted her from the hall with two dozen light-weavers. Sylvie then saw a great deal she wished she could forget. One assassin dead. Two light-weavers unmoving except for the spreading crimson stains on their white robes. An abbey torn apart by its occupants in hopes of finding an escaping assassin. Once Sylvie had been escorted back to her rooms with Arn and Sizmor, Ezel arrived shortly after, requesting they pack their things in preparation of leaving before dawn.

It had given Sylvie busywork to do, keeping sorrow from overwhelming her. And below, in the depths of Clair-de-Lune, Mikkel lay in preparation for a burial the light-weaving acolyte assured her would occur after they had left.

Sylvie took a deep breath, knowing the Prioress Mother and her Fae guide were right. She thought about the light-telling and the lessons of Saint Emmer's life. Doing what was right sometimes meant sacrifice.

It was a difficult lesson to learn.

Still, she wished she could give a formal farewell to Mikkel, the first man after Master Kell who had believed in her Naming.

He deserved that much at least.

"I know you both are right," Sylvie admitted, nodding as much to herself as to them. "I would at least say my farewell to the Prioress Superior before we leave. She has been kind and supportive when she had no need."

"She is with your First Knight. They had a bond. She already knows how you feel, and I know her blessings go with you," the Prioress Mother said. "Come. Time is wasting, and the morning light will only brighten the new day the longer we dither."

"Arn will meet us with the horses?" Sylvie asked.

"He is already with them, yes."

With that, Ezel Fela took Sylvie's small pack and left the room. The others followed. The halls were empty, their footfalls whispers. Floating orbs placed periodically along their path lit the way for Ezel, whose shadowy form reminded Sylvie of a wraith from childhood stories. Once they gained the first floor, the acolyte said a few words, used a few gestures, and a floating orb of her own creation manifested, bright enough to light the passage as it accompanied them. Without waiting, she took them to a wooden staircase twining downward, the light leading the way. It grew colder as they traveled deeper into the abbey, an entire labyrinth of passages and rooms existing below to purposes Sylvie could only guess at. The Prioress Mother had no problem keeping up. Her spryness belied the age written on her face.

After what seemed an eternity of walking through darkness, they came to a thick door. Ezel Fela produced a skeleton key and unlocked it. Swinging wide on rusty, squeaking hinges, the door exited to a long tunnel that cut through the bedrock Clair-de-Lune sat upon. In the far distance, Sylvie could just make out a gray square that brightened as they approached.

"A new dawn is before us, Sylvianna," Prioress Mother Agnes said.

The stone of the tunnel ended even as the land met them, mud and pebbles at first and soon a set of stairs that cut through grass as they lifted toward the horizon. Above, Sylvie could just make out evenly spaced trees. She realized that she looked upon an orchard of apple trees sprawling along a rising hill to the east. The trees were well maintained, though the fruit had not ripened to the point where it could be picked and consumed. Soon they were in the orchard itself, the smells of mulch and growing things offering her solace. Through the limbs around her, Sylvie could make out a much larger set of trees on the highest hill beyond—twisted trunks holding up broad boughs of a much older orchard.

When they exited the first orchard, she saw three figures and horses to match waiting underneath one of those ancient apple trees, the pinking sky behind casting them in dark relief against the growing morning. Puzzled, Sylvie was about to ask who they were when she recognized the robed woman—and the man she was with.

Sylvie was running before she knew it.

"Mikkel!" she yelled, running to him, her tears trying to blind her.

Heart ready to burst and legs burning from her climb, she threw her arms around him. With a laugh, Mikkel accepted her hug, her enthusiasm almost bowling him over even as he wrapped one strong arm about her. When Sylvie peeled herself away, he looked embarrassed. Sylvie didn't care. "I am safe. I am well," he said. "I am happy you are fine too, my High Queen. I worried for you all night."

"But how . . . ?" Sylvie asked, at a loss for words. "I mean, I saw you. You were dead. And why was I lied to?"

"No one lied to you, Sylvianna," Agnes said, eyes twinkling. "You just weren't told the whole truth."

"It was a necessary subterfuge," Prioress Superior Sanna continued, her demeanor just as pleased as the older woman's. "I pray you can forgive us. We did so for your future safety and that of your First Knight." She gestured at Arn. "And friends, of course."

"How will this work, though? Surely the Citadel Assassin will learn of this. Won't the shadow who fled know they did not finish the job? Won't they know I'm still alive?" Sylvie questioned, still trying to come to terms with the moment.

"We let that shadow escape," Prioress Mother Agnes said, before slapping her knee and cackling loudly.

"You did *what*?!" Sizmor exclaimed.

Sylvie also couldn't believe it. "Why would you do that?"

Arn cleared his throat. "I thought the same, Sylvianna Goode. But then I realized someone had to share the news with the Citadel Assassin of your apparent demise. It's the only way to keep those sons of bitches from coming for you further."

"But I was still alive when that shadow bolted," Sylvie said, shaking her head.

"Sometimes what we see is not exactly what is real," Prioress Superior

Sanna said, removing her arm from about Mikkel's waist and stepping forward. She hummed some small piece of music as she made several gestures with her hands. Light bloomed on the ground before them all, coalescing into a light-telling image of Sylvie as she lay upon the hall's floor in Clair-de-Lune. Just like Mikkel had, she stared upward, unbreathing and seemingly devoid of life, several darts sticking out of her neck.

The horror of seeing herself dead became surprise as she saw what the light-weavers had done the previous night.

"It was all an act?" Sylvie asked, incredulous and angry at the same time.

"An act that came at a terrible cost," Prioress Superior Sanna said, eyes sad. "Two light-weavers were killed last night. That was true enough. My friends. My loved ones. They died so that you may live. The cost is borne by you. Repay it by what you do hereafter. The light prepared their way to Annwn, but we as an abbey and as a world are lesser for their loss and sacrifice."

Sylvie approached the other and stopped in front of her, the gravity of what had transpired the night before heavy within her heart. "Prioress Superior Sanna, the losses of Clair-de-Lune can never be undone. Yet I promise you, as High Queen of Royaume de France, I will do all within my power to ensure their losses are not in vain." Tears came unbidden to her eyes. "I will forever be in light-weaver debt for the life I still live. And I also promise to hold accountable those who ordered the assassination attempt against me."

Similar tears formed in Sanna's eyes. "Ruling is not easy, Sylvianna. You have seen with your own eyes here in Clair-de-Lune how difficult it can be." She paused and smiled. "I hate to say it this way, but let's pray you remain dead a long time."

"If the Citadel Assassin and our siblings believe you buried, I think that will aid us in the coming days," Mikkel said.

"Do you think we are safe?" Sylvie asked, turning to him. "For a while, at least?"

"I do," the First Knight replied. "But we must leave soon, and remain clear of towns and cities from here to the Twilight Lands. If we are not more careful than we have been, the Citadel Assassin will not be fooled for long."

Sylvie turned to the Prioress Superior. "I know you've lost a great deal by my coming to Clair-de-Lune. You have supported my claim to the throne of the kingdom. I will not forget that." She glanced at Agnes and Ezel. "I do have to ask, though. You've already lost so much. Are you sure about these two amazing women traveling with us to the Twilight Lands? I can't imagine it *not* being dangerous."

"Ask them, Sylvianna Goode," Sanna said, amused. "They are their own women."

Sylvie turned to them. "I fear your coming will endanger you more than if you stayed. The Citadel Assassin notwithstanding, the journey is still long, and the Fae of the Twilight Lands may not be hospitable to your kind. My companion Sizmor has shared the history of animosity between you and the Fae."

Ezel looked to Agnes. Some form of communication seemed to pass between them, through a bond Sylvie could only guess at.

"We know the dangers, Sylvianna Goode," Ezel Fela said, with Prioress Mother Agnes nodding in agreement. "We are going."

"It is settled then," Sanna said to Sylvie. "High Queen Sylvianna Goode, there is much more to say and not much time to do so. I'll share this, though. Listen to the Prioress Mother. Listen to our best acolyte. Between them, they possess a wealth of knowledge and strength in the light. You will need that light if you are to return from the Twilight Lands." She stepped up to Sylvie and gripped her hands in her own. "After speaking at length to your First Knight, I fully believe you are the right choice to lead this kingdom. In you, I see the light. War already threatens all dukedoms. Despite Clair-de-Lune Abbey sitting within the borders of Lady Erlina's duchy, we will stand by you when the need comes. And if you ever have need of me, I will be there at your side as quick as the light can speed me."

Sylvie nodded, squeezing Sanna's strong grip. It was easy to see what Mikkel had loved about her. Compassion. Clarity of thought.

Strength of soul. "I thank you for that. The reassurance is much appreciated."

"The light of the morning is here, blessed be it," Sanna continued, closing her eyes to enjoy the sun's warmth. She opened her blue eyes and they sparkled. "It will share your path and guide you. I hope you gain what you need. With the kingdom beginning to fracture, gaining that Covenant Codex is necessary to heal what is being wounded even as we speak."

Sylvie looked at the coming morning. The uppermost edge of the sun had broken over the mountains and dark forests ahead. Color returned to the world, a wash of beauty reminding her of what she fought for. Hope returned. She knew the road ahead would be difficult—a road that could kill her at any twist or corner—but she had to trust in herself and in those around her. They believed in her even as she believed in them. She had no army. She had no magic. Her friendships and her wits were all she had.

"I will set right this wrong, Prioress Superior Sanna," Sylvie said. "Or die trying."

"We all die, my High Queen. Just make sure it is for the right reasons." A grin tugged one corner of Sanna's lips.

With that, the Prioress Superior stepped to the First Knight. Mikkel stared into his once-beloved's face. Sylvie saw the couple they had been. Powerful in their love, connected by strength of purpose and deed. It made her think briefly of Darian and what could have been, but she swept that feeling aside, preferring to enjoy her First Knight's happiness as he gazed at his Chelle, her face shining back.

The world needed love more than ever.

"Do keep yourself safe, you old battle dog," the Prioress Superior said to Mikkel. She touched his cheek with tenderness. "The lives we lived are done. All we have is what is before us and what that means for everyone."

"I will cherish these last few days, Chelle," he said back. "Your light goes with me."

With that, the Prioress Superior let go the First Knight and, with a nod to Sylvie, left them, descending the hill back to the tunnel. No one spoke. Only birdsong filled the morning silence, and an occasional impatient stamp of a horse hoof. The Prioress Superior went to mourn those the abbey had lost and lead its women toward a light that had almost escaped Sylvie at Mikkel's death. She hoped to be as strong as Sanna one day.

"She cares for you, you know," Agnes said.

Sylvie expected the words to be directed at Mikkel. Instead, she was surprised to see the blind woman glancing her direction.

"It's nice to have friends," Sylvie returned.

"The past is a jumbled puzzle only gifted minds can piece together. Fortunately, I have one of those minds," the Prioress Mother said with a low chuckle, tapping her temple. "I foresee our treasured Sanna will be far more important by the end of this. For you. For the kingdom. For the living. I chose her as my successor, and she has never let me down."

"She has always been remarkable," Mikkel said, taking the reins of his horse in hand and mounting. "It is time to leave. Do you agree, Arn, that we should stay clear of towns and cities? I do not care for a repeat of what happened last night."

"I agree," Arn said as he aided Agnes into the saddle of a dappled gray horse so short it was almost a pony. "Last night, after ensuring Sylvie was safe in her room, I went into the town. I found no one aligned to the Kraken. Found his mark but no one answering it. It was like they'd vanished. I worry the Citadel Assassin and his shadows discovered the Kraken's agents there, either kidnapping them or killing them and leaving them in a gutter. Either way, if they can do that in a town this remote, they can do it anywhere. Best to be cautious." He shrugged. "It seems you have no more need of my services."

"I still need a squire," Mikkel observed. "I rather like you, Arn. Mouth notwithstanding."

Arn Tomm rolled his eyes. "If that's how I ensure the Kraken's investment is maintained, then so be it. I like the horses."

"News will be hard to come by, since we're staying away from people," Sylvie said. "Once we talk with the Shadow Court in the

Twilight Lands and get what we need, we will have to make for Mont-Saint-Michel with all haste."

"We know armies are already mobilizing," Mikkel said. "Every day will see an escalation. It might be quite difficult to make our way back."

"That's why we must be swift," Sylvie said, already turning her horse.

The others followed, all of them leaving the orchard and entering the morning sunshine. Mikkel took the lead, Lumière covered once more and strapped to his saddle. The First Knight was back in his armor and sitting proud in the saddle, his back a little straighter than before. Sylvie could hardly measure the gift of his return. She would have struggled onward without him—her resolve to fulfill her Naming not in question—but it would have been far more difficult for her to complete the journey and acquire the Covenant Codex. He brought a wealth of knowledge about the kingdom and their siblings, and his presence was a rock for her amid a stormy sea.

"I can feel your happiness, Sylvianna," Sizmor said, the sprite riding the horn of her mount's saddle and looking up at her.

For the first time in several days, she felt it would all work out.

14

izmor spotted the galloping column of warriors late that same afternoon.

As everyone peered across farmland that would eventually become vineyards the farther east they traveled, Sylvie watched and waited to see where the soldiers traveled. In the northwestern distance, the long line of horses appeared to be heading in a similar direction but not directly to them. No one said a word. The companions had nowhere to hide, with few trees and no rivers carving into the land nearby. One of the front-leading warriors carried a tall standard, its cloth flapping in the wind, but Sylvie could not make out the image on the flag. They were within Lady Erlina's dukedom but close enough to Lord Kent's home that it could be warriors from either house.

Then the group of warriors switched direction. Soon their leader's horse was no longer broadside but arrowing in their direction.

"Here they come," Sylvie said, already fearing the worst.

"I will handle this," Prioress Mother Agnes said, her head tilted as she listened to the approaching soldiers. "Few men at any age know how to handle an old woman with steel in her. I am an elderly lightweaver. Mikkel will be my escorting knight. Arn his squire. Ezel, my assistant. And you, Sylvie, are my granddaughter. Sizmor, vanish. You cannot be seen."

"It's as good an idea as any I have," Sylvie admitted even as her Fae guide disappeared. She looked at Mikkel. Her First Knight simply shrugged and checked that Lumière remained hidden while his other sword was easily accessible.

The thunder of horse hooves pounding sod grew until Sylvie could view the flag and the image emblazoned there—the phoenix of House Goode gripping red grapes on a sea of white.

The standard of Lady Erlina's dukedom.

"Well met, travelers!" the warrior at the fore said, reining his mount in. He was a big man like Mikkel, broad through the shoulders and waist, though younger, and his hair and beard aflame. The warriors at his back spread out in a half circle, eyes intent on Sylvie and her friends. None of them wore heavy armor but rather chain mail and hardened leather. "Who are you and where do you venture?" he asked.

"Well met, warriors!" Agnes said, her voice rising over the tumult caused by so many horses in one place. "We are come from Clair-de-Lune, just this morning, and we are pleased the weather is holding. For the moment, at least."

"Old Mother, do you lead your companions?" the first warrior questioned.

"As well as I can. It is with utmost importance that I travel."

"Why would a light-weaver leave Clair-de-Lune?" the captain questioned. None of his warriors had weapons drawn, but all the men were intently listening to the exchange. "It is your home, after all, and riding is hard even on a young body."

"Do not begrudge an old woman the freedom found at the end of her days," Agnes said, her voice as hard as the steel Mikkel wore. "Though you are right. We left Clair-de-Lune this morning, and I do not look forward to sleeping on the hard ground or even in an inn's creaky, bug-infested bed. No, I do not do this for fun or with ease. My granddaughter there, the last fruit from my first and only marriage, has brought me awful news. My son is gravely ill. I hope to ease his suffering with the aid of my acolyte here." She gestured to Ezel. "The knight and his squire are hired from our town, to ensure my safety at the request of the Prioress Superior."

"I'm sad to hear of your family's hardship. But you are going to need a great many more knights to be safe these days. One is not enough." The redheaded man rubbed his bearded cheek. "Perhaps you do not know, but war has come to the kingdom."

"Is that so?" Agnes grunted. "That brings great sadness to me. War is rarely an answer, even at the worst of times. I was a young woman when High King Alafair Goode vanquished the Great Darkness and united our kingdom. I witnessed death on a scale few have. How did this war come to be? Who has taken what sides? I would know."

"I am Captain Boden Allard. We are bannermen of Lady Erlina Goode," the leader said, nodding to Agnes. "She has raised her army to keep safe her dukedom. Others of the Goode family are doing the same. The High King is dead. His Named successor has murdered and deceived Lord Idlor and Pontiff Scorus, and now the throne is devoid of an heir. Lady Erlina has returned home, to prepare."

"I do hope our beloved Lady Erlina is not involved. She has ever been gracious to the light-weavers," the blind woman said. Sylvie noted her honeyed words and saw what the Prioress Mother was doing. "Mistress Avril is one of our best, and she has long been a fixture at the Lady's court. I do hope she is safe. Do you know her?"

"I do. She brings us wonder with her light-tellings and wisdom," he replied. "For now, Mistress Avril is safe. Soon none of us will be, though."

"Who else has raised their bannermen?" Mikkel asked.

Captain Boden gave the First Knight an appraising look. "It is said Lord Pike has raised the largest army, one with the blessing of Cardinal Bishop Wil Cornet and the Ecclesia knights. They have already engaged in skirmishes along Mont-Saint-Michel's southern border with Lord Collins's dukedom, though we have no news what will come between them. One quelled skirmish thus far. But that will not be the end. Lords Yankton and Kent have also left Mont-Saint-Michel. It is assumed they are preparing even as Lady Erlina."

"Royal children, all brats," Agnes spat, feigning annoyance. "Do none of them remember their histories? Children of Kings destroy kingdoms more than enemies do. It is too bad the High King couldn't keep his sword between his legs. Now matters are much, much worse. Which child killed Lord Idlor and Pontiff Scorus?"

"Some royal bastard," Captain Boden said. "A woman even."

Mikkel growled. "Must be *some* woman, to have done that."

"She had help. Obviously," the captain said. "The former First Knight from twenty years ago, or so I'm told."

Sylvie kept quiet, listening, trying not to draw attention to herself. She appreciated how Agnes and Mikkel were handling the situation. There were too many warriors to overcome, and the horse Agnes rode upon could never outrun them. Words were their only way to win free.

"Well, at least you are sworn to one of the best of those Goode children," Agnes said, clucking her tongue. "Why are you not at your duchess's side? I would think she has need of you more than ever now."

The captain shrugged. "We are under orders to sweep the countryside, not only to call more warriors to Lady Erlina but also to look for Lord Idlor's murderer and her consorts."

"Ahh, that makes perfect sense. Murderers must be brought to justice."

"Indeed. And with that, I'm afraid you'll have to come with us," Captain Boden said.

"Now you wait one moment, Captain Boden," Agnes said, words become as sharp as razors. Though blind, she stared in the other man's direction with an angry frown. "I will not be jostled further in the saddle and taken away from my bloodline. We are clearly not those you seek. And my son has need of me. I only hope it is not too late." She paused, looking to Sylvie and then back again. "I am too old and too tired. You will have to fight and kill me if you plan on taking me to Lady Erlina."

The grin that spread across the captain's face slowly melted when he realized the old woman was not joking. Paralyzed, he didn't know what to do. He glanced around at his men, who mostly turned away from him. Sylvie wanted to laugh but she kept her amusement hidden.

The old woman did have steel running through her.

"Grandmother," Sylvie chastised.

"I know, dear, my blood has run hot," Agnes said, sending her blind eyes in the direction of Captain Boden. "If you are truly so concerned about me, you could accompany us to Tanarick, where my son and granddaughter live. Keep us safe, not only from brigands and the like, but also Lord Kent's men. Once I have visited with my son and aid him, then we can come with you."

"Indeed, and we would be honored with such a request during normal times," the captain said, considering his options. "But Tanarick is not within Lady Erlina's dukedom. We have no authority there and shall not start a conflict."

"True, true, I tend to forget where such borders lie," the Prioress Mother said, tapping the side of her wrinkled face with her finger. "Well, it is safe to say at the very least that we would enjoy your company this evening, sharing fire and food. And safety in numbers is a fine thing during these ill times, it seems."

Captain Boden glanced over his company. They did not appear harried or tired, and the condition of their mounts suggested they had not been gone long from Lady Erlina's house. "The day winds down and a longer reprieve for rest may be in order to keep my men salty," he said, nodding. "Yes, let us visit further. I'm enjoying your company and conversation."

"And the fight," Agnes said with a grin. "Let us not forget about our duel to the death."

The captain laughed. "Let us not forget that either."

"I recommend we stop at the next rill we come to, Captain Boden," Mikkel said, eyeing the setting sun and pointing to a thin sliver of silver winding through the upcoming countryside. "We could make camp there. Fresh water for us and our mounts."

"What are your names?" the captain asked.

"I am Arienna," the Prioress Mother answered. "My granddaughter there is Aslyn. She is of age if you have any handsome warriors looking for a fine but fiery wife." She grinned, making Sylvie quite uncomfortable. "Ezel is my light-weaving acolyte. Protecting and guiding us are Joffe and his squire Ravaul."

"Perhaps your acolyte may share a short light-telling with us," Captain Boden said. "If she is willing, of course."

"I'd be honored, Captain Boden," Ezel said, inclining her head.

"Well, this is most unexpected," he replied, rubbing his hands together and smiling. "Let us help you set up camp. It's the least we can do for the hospitality."

"Lead the way, Joffe," Agnes said.

Mikkel kicked his horse into a canter, with Agnes, Sylvie, Ezel, and Arn following. The warriors at their back did so as well. Sylvie marveled at what had just occurred. The Prioress Mother had done a wonderful job at pretending to be other people entirely. Sylvie just hoped it would be enough to free them fully from her half-sister's men.

Otherwise, they were lost.

DONATO

15

ylvie sat with Agnes, Ezel, Mikkel, Arn, and Captain Boden, along with his second-in-command Jace, each with a bowl of rabbit stew, tubers, carrots, and onions brought by Lady Erlina's men. With multiple fires to warm them, Mikkel had shed his armor. Arn helped him with his gear, playing the part to perfection, and now they sat together as they would if they were truly knight and squire. Sylvie took note of it and did the same for the Prioress Mother, doting on the older woman and worrying over her as a family member would. Ezel remained quiet, Sizmor invisible. The sun had already disappeared into the west, its light fading even as stars replaced it. The world around them seemed to slow, and it was hard to believe a war brewed in the kingdom. As they ate their meal together, the moon appeared over the horizon, sharp like a sickle to fight off the stars for attention.

Insects buzzed and Sylvie kept optimism close to her heart.

"Captain, what is Lady Erlina wishing from all of this?" Mikkel gestured at the warriors sitting around their fires. "I realize she is capable and is an heir to High King Alafair just as her siblings are. But is war worth it?"

"That is difficult to know, as she has said little," Captain Boden said, pulling a chunk of rabbit from his bowl and slurping it into his mouth. "I am not her only captain to be sent into the dukedom, I do know that."

"Alliances will be made, politics will be played," Agnes said. "It's what Man does."

Captain Boden shrugged. "I have an easier time of it. I do what I'm asked to do."

"Even if what you are asked to do aids the darkness?" the Prioress Mother asked.

The captain chewed on that even as he tore into a chunk of hard bread. "I hope that our Lady Erlina knows more about what is going on than a lowly soldier like me or Jace," Boden said at last. "Therefore, if I feel the Lady is honorable and has the best intentions for our duchy, yes, I will carry out my duty."

"There is the problem with Man right there," Agnes snorted.

"And what is that, Old Mother?"

"Not thinking for yourself, my dear boy," the blind woman said.

"Grandmother, how did this come to be? This war, I mean?" Sylvie asked, to discover not only what the captain might think but also what the Prioress Mother thought. She hadn't had time to talk with Prioress Superior Sanna, but the blind woman had been alive so long, she might have insight into what was tearing the kingdom apart besides the botched coronation.

"What do you mean, child of my child?" Agnes questioned, frowning. "When there is power to be wielded, there will always be those who wish to possess it."

"I know, Grandmother," she said. "But the kingdom is filled with children sired by High King Alafair. It seems to me that he had too many scions, all of whom could not die. There are stories in Tanarick about the royal family. Wasn't there some magic that has made this situation even worse?"

"That history is known," Ezel Fela answered, ending her silence. Her dark eyes stared into the fire, and for a moment Sylvie thought she might not say more. "The witch. She who used magic to save a young Alafair before he became King. That magic did not end with his survival, but rather followed his seed into his sired line. We study this at Clair-de-Lune in support of the light. When I learned the history of the Great Darkness and the boy King's fight against Mordreadth, I always wondered why a witch would become involved. Was she helping to save the world? Or was she trying to end it? She was not part of Saint Emmer's prophecy about who would destroy the Great Darkness. If she hadn't healed the boy and imbued his line with a form of immortality, would he have triumphed over Mordreadth anyway?"

"Are you contending that the witch meant to destroy the world? That is quite different from every story I've heard." Captain Boden shook his head. "And that was almost eighty winters ago. How could she know what her actions then would create now?"

"It is a theory at Clair-de-Lune," Ezel said. "Those who use magic use their craft with care and purpose. It is not out of the question that she knew what she was doing beyond the moment."

"How could she know the High King would fuck so many women?" Captain Boden asked, clearly annoyed. He waved his hand. "This is academic and pure speculation."

"Men are often led by what's between their legs," Ezel said, breaking apart a piece of bread and putting it into her mouth beneath her gray veil. "Especially those with wealth and power. One does not need be an oracle to know how a poor boy who became King would act."

The women around the fire laughed. The men didn't.

"Not much is known about that witch," Agnes admitted finally, having finished her rabbit stew. Mikkel took the bowl and added it to his emptied one. "Even her true name is lost to the annals of history."

"Back to the point," Sylvie said. "What if the witch intended all of this?"

"I echo my captain. I think it's impossible," Jace said. The young warrior was handsome, hair black and eyes green. "Besides, what would a girl from Tanarick know of such matters?"

Captain Boden put a hand on the young warrior's arm. "Let her speak," he said. "No need to belittle."

"I just hope the battle doesn't come to Tanarick," Sylvie said, ignoring Jace's barb. "Either way, the witch's action has brought us to war—indirectly or directly. I pray it ends quickly."

"We will likely never know about the witch, so why even discuss it," Mikkel said. "War is an act we have no control over either, though perhaps Lady Erlina is trying. Let's hope calmer minds prevail when it comes to the empty throne of the kingdom."

"From what I have heard, Lord Pike would not discuss the throne's succession. He believed it to be his and his alone," Jace said. "That's why Lady Erlina left. Probably why the Lords of the other dukedoms left as well, to form their armies."

"War is coming. Death will follow," the Prioress Mother said sadly. "None of it is necessary. It hurts this old woman's heart."

"Since that's probably true, do you think Lady Erlina shouldn't fight for her right to the crown?" Captain Boden asked, eyes narrowing on Agnes.

"No, not at all, Captain," Agnes said. She shrugged. "I merely state that killing is killing, death is death, and does it matter who doles them out? We might as well have let the Great Darkness win, if that's the case. What separates us from Mordreadth?"

"I see your point," the other said, taking the ladle and scooping out more stew from the pot over the fire. "Yet here we are. Us few could solve the world's problems in a day."

"Captain Boden, you seemed surprised that a woman could kill Lord Idlor and Pontiff Scorus," Sylvie said, curious to know how the captain felt. She had discovered she liked him, but that didn't mean she trusted. "It seemed you were suggesting a woman couldn't be High Queen. Yet you believe full-heartedly in Lady Erlina. Is that not a problem for you?"

"Now, Granddaughter, let's not start a war with the captain. As I said, war is not the way," Agnes said. She grinned at Captain Boden then. "You see, I told you my granddaughter there was feisty."

"And I see where she gets it from," he said, already into his second helping. "It isn't a problem for me, though I can see why you'd think that. I suppose Lady Erlina has proven herself a capable steward of her father's legacy. I would not continue being one of her bannermen if that was not true."

"Would that mean you'd bow to a High Queen?" Jace asked, frowning at his captain.

"Possibly, though such a woman would need to have steel running through her veins," the redheaded man said. "A lot of it. Lady Erlina does."

"Ultimately, it does not matter," Mikkel said, walking toward the rill to clean the two bowls he held. He turned momentarily and said, "The past is the past. No point arguing it now."

Silence returned until laughter from the men sitting around one of the nearby campfires echoed to the stars. Based on Captain Boden's comments, Sylvie understood she had a lot to prove. Even if she took the throne back, men would despise her, for no better reason than that she bled several times a season. It made her furious. Yet this was the world she lived in, the one she would one day rule. It gave her more pride that her father had Named her heir, that he could believe in a High Queen despite his philandering and the pain he had brought numerous women during his long life. Perhaps it had been his way of making up for it, though she had a hard time accepting that idea.

Her Naming could have been as simple as Alafair not liking his other choices.

Mikkel returned with the wet bowls. "Captain, where will you go from here?" he asked, sitting back down.

"We will continue onward through the duchy," Captain Boden said. "Seeking able men to fight for the dukedom. After we finish our sweep through this countryside, we will perhaps ride west and stop at Clair-de-Lune briefly to request any help Prioress Superior Sanna may offer. Then we will visit the other towns along the Voire River before returning home." He paused, considering the knight. "She will want your sword, Joffe. After you carry out your duty to see Arienna to her ill son and return to Clair-de-Lune, I request on your honor that you will ride to Lady Erlina's court with all haste. You look strong. Young enough still. We will need you in the days to come."

"On my honor, I will do what is best for Lady Erlina's dukedom," Mikkel said, patting Arn on the leg. "My squire as well."

"It sounds as though you do not intend to come with us," Agnes said, eyebrow raised. "Or ask us to go with you?"

The captain licked his greasy fingers again. He sat up straighter and did not speak until he had finished chewing rabbit meat. "You are not murderers, you are not thieves," he said. "I would stake the honor of my house on that. I have mulled this over during our dinner, keeping an eye on you and your companions. Worry sits heavy upon your granddaughter there, and it is clear you care a great deal about her. You are who you say you are. You are not who we seek."

Sylvie kept her surprise and excitement in check.

"But I say again, Joffe"—Boden held up a finger like a warning—"I would very much like to see you on the training field after you return from Tanarick. See what kind of mettle is within the metal, as they say."

"I'd welcome that," Mikkel said, grinning.

"Beware, though, they don't call me the Red Bear for nothing," the captain said with a punch on Jace's shoulder. "Isn't that right?"

The younger warrior rubbed his arm and just shook his head.

16

he morning dawned gray and chilly, low clouds having arrived overnight.

Rolling out of her blankets, Sylvie stretched, body aching. She had barely slept. Being surrounded by her half-sister's guard left her on edge in a way that prevented relaxation, despite apparently winning their freedom from Captain Boden and his warriors the night before. Most of the warriors around her were awake, some bringing their fires back to life, others already cooking. Sizmor was not with her, having chosen to sleep in a shriveled oak tree nearby. Arn had aided Mikkel as a dutiful squire would, the First Knight reapplying his layers of leather and steel for the day's ride. Ezel and Agnes were just rousing, their robes already dirty from a day on the road.

Sylvie yawned, shaking off the terrible sleep. She was just pleased the ruse supplied by Agnes had worked so well.

After everyone had eaten and the campsite had been reduced to no more than charred spots of ash, Captain Boden ordered his men to mount.

"Farewell, Old Mother," he said, swinging up into his saddle. "I enjoyed our conversation. May we meet again, if only to continue the wit and banter. If you ever desire to visit Mistress Avril, do call on me. I would introduce you and your wisdom to Lady Erlina, and I know she would find you a refreshing change to the politics of Mont-Saint-Michel."

"I thank you, Captain Boden," Agnes said, nodding. She walked up to his horse and whispered some words Sylvie could not hear. Then she went and patted the captain's boots as if they were the head of a child. "I will certainly visit once my son has regained his health."

"I hope he recovers," the other said. "It is unnatural to lose a son so young." He looked at Sylvie. "Make sure your father survives so this visit may occur."

"I will, Captain," Sylvie said, worried the lies were written all over her.

"The light will make it so," Agnes said. She stepped away from the horse and took Sylvie's arm. "Farewell, Captain Boden."

At that, the warriors lifted reins and put heels to their horses. The group cantered away into the west toward Clair-de-Lune Abbey, standard flag flapping.

Sylvie took a deep breath. It was like an explosion coming out.

"Well," she said, watching the warriors disappear. "I was sure we were doomed."

"The light aided us," the blind woman said. "That and a plausible story that tugged on the heartstrings of even one such as the Red Bear."

Sizmor materialized in the air, free to do so now that Lady Erlina's warriors were gone.

"I thought light-weavers always told the truth," the sprite said, as if some betrayal had occurred.

"We light-weavers change our names, in case you did not know, Master Fae," Agnes said, her smile broad. "Who's to say the names I gave us are not our true selves?"

"What of the stories? They were lies," the sprite shot back.

"Perhaps I twisted the truth a bit," Agnes admitted.

Ezel Fela laughed at that. The sprite frowned and grumbled.

Arn cleared his throat. "We may have another problem. When

Erlina speaks with her captain and hears his report, she may discover her captain's error. There are few people who appear as you both do, Sylvie and Mikkel. The black hair. The blue eyes. The builds. Everything. And together at the same time."

"Let's be long gone from here by then," Sylvie said. "Between the Citadel Assassin and Erlina's captain, we've been lucky."

"Luck vanishes the moment it is relied upon," Arn said, climbing into his saddle.

"Let's not rely then," Agnes agreed.

They made their way east and by the late afternoon were climbing ever-growing hills that would become the Vosges Mountains, a short range barely larger than the hills they climbed but snow-speckled at their top just the same. The Vosges Mountains ran north and south along the eastern kingdom, a simple natural border between Man and Fae. Master Kell said they were part of the Alpz Mountains, which could not yet be seen but was described as icy, jagged knives puncturing the sky. And between the two mountain ranges nestled the Allemagne Forest, cradling a wild and dark territory comprising the ancient Twilight Lands. As she rode, Sylvie loved seeing the Vosges Mountains and could only imagine what lay beyond. She found beauty in the nature about her—so different from the ocean coastline of Mont-Saint-Michel—and despite the weather growing cooler as they climbed, she was excited to be making progress once more.

They spent the night in a large grove of pines. The boughs hid the travelers from view and the needles below offered a soft reprieve from sleeping on hard ground. Upon waking, it was so unseasonably cold that Sylvie added one of the coats supplied by the Kraken to her layers, her breath producing clouds on the air. The only companion who seemed unaffected was Sizmor, who had begun to be more open to the accompanying light-weavers, even laughing with them in one moment of levity. Mikkel guided them now, the First Knight knowing more about the terrain from his travels, and Sylvie found him humming at times. She wondered if it was the result of seeing Chelle again, the mountain air, or both.

Late in the afternoon, they made their way through a gap to the other side of the Vosges Mountains. It happened so quickly that it took a perceptible slope to their descent for her to realize it. She reined her horse to a stop, peering deep into the shadows about them. With the day's failing light, she felt eyes on them. They hadn't seen anyone during their travels, though small plumes of smoke could be seen at times far in the distance, either homesteaders or other travelers. The feeling unnerved her.

"Do you feel that?" she asked in a low voice as she dismounted and began laying out her bedroll beneath a thicket of pine trees, her eyes taking in the breadth of the view. The valley was larger than she had expected, the Alpz Mountains now visible but still so far away they could barely be discerned. Below them spread a green forest so thick and wild she could barely make out the silver ribbon of a river cutting through it to a large lake at its center.

"We are now on the other side of the Vosges," Ezel Fela said, joining Sylvie, also staring into the gloom of approaching night. "The Fae perhaps?"

"The wood," Sizmor corrected. The sprite gazed down at the Allemagne Forest. "The Shadow Court knows we are here. If you light a fire to cook and warm by, the entirety of Fae will know we are here. We are connected to the land in a way that Man is not. What occurs within our borders is known due to that link."

"We will most certainly have a fire," Mikkel said, already gathering the necessary fuel while Arn watered and cared for the horses. The First Knight didn't have to go far, the pines creating a vast dry space beneath their boughs that was filled with fuel.

"We are safe from the Fae," Sizmor assured them, wings flexing on a branch above.

"That may be," the First Knight said. "I do not take risks, though. Remember: a changeling stole the Covenant Codex from the Citadel. That creature—and whoever is using it—is still out there. I'd rather be prepared for the worst and have fire as one more weapon at our disposal in case it is needed."

The sprite shrugged, but Sylvie saw the First Knight's wisdom. She had almost forgotten about the changeling, being so focused on fleeing Mont-Saint-Michel, winning support at Clair-de-Lune, the shadowy presence of the Citadel Assassin on their heels, and eluding Erlina's Red Bear. She realized that everything hinged on the Covenant Codex. Once she was crowned High Queen of Royaume de France, she'd have the resources to counter her siblings, fortify the kingdom her father had unified, and then ferret out the changeling's master and discover what ill purpose had been set against her.

Once they had eaten a simple meal of hard bread, summer sausage, and blue cheese gifted them by Captain Boden, they settled into their bedrolls around the small fire, the stars visiting from a clear sky.

It was then that a sweet sound entered the night. Sylvie sat up to discover its source. It seemed to be a humming lullaby. Then she glanced up into the pines, seeing Sizmor resting on a bough filled with needles, the sprite creating the song. Sylvie's guide stared off at the Allemagne Forest with shining eyes.

Soon words joined the small Fae's music, clear and distinct like the bubbling mirth of a rill over smooth stones:

Aware, beware the birth of Man
They scream and cry for the longest span
With parents who raise babe with dishonor grim
The best way to end Man is to open splay him
Before they grow into the Man they'll become
Willing to kill any Fae who succumb

Aware, beware the lives of Man
They steal and rob and sully the land
Without a care for the Fae of the world
Man would see us destroyed and burned
Brought low by fire and steel and spite
Careful go the darkness unto the light

Aware, beware the death of Man
The lives they live are short but with plan

In the darkest wombs of evil's home
They share their hatred from birth to loam
Each Man multiplying tens more from their den
To continue the war against Fae again

"That was a rather depressing song, Sizmor," Agnes said, lying close to the fire. "Though you sang it lovely. I wish we had known of your gift sooner."

"I chose the song for a simple reason," the sprite said, looking down on them. "Man is not welcome here. Not now, not ever. I am safe as a steward of the Covenant Codex and chosen by the Shadow Court. In the morning, I will visit the Court and request a long audience with them on behalf of Sylvianna. They may wish to see her; they may turn me away. Worse, those on the Shadow Court who hate Man and the Compact may take offense to our entering the Twilight Lands and attack us. It is a risk, and one I hope you all see clearly."

"I do wish to speak to the Shadow Court, Sizmor," Sylvie said, sitting up and wrapping her arms about her crooked knees. "Do you think that is possible?"

"Possible, yes," the sprite said. "Not likely, though. As the song says, Fae are taught at a very young age the power and evil of Man."

"But the Compact keeps peace between us," she said.

"That is the only reason I say it is possible," Sizmor said. "Rest. You may need it. If I return from the Shadow Court and you gain admittance, it is quite the walk to the pavilion."

Everyone laid down to sleep, with Sizmor keeping watch as he had done since they left Mont-Saint-Michel. Sylvie listened to the others faintly snoring even as she observed the stars slowly spin their way through the heavens. It was some time before she fell asleep, her mind considering any number of different possibilities for the coming day. What would the Shadow Court be like? Would they aid her? If they denied her access to an audience, what would she do? What *could* she do? Would they have any answers for who sent the changeling thief? Could they even share their copy of the Covenant

Codex with her? Or copy it in some way? If they couldn't, would the Compact end? It was all too much to consider, the unknown making for restless slumber.

When Sylvie awoke the next morning, her friends were still asleep. Sizmor watched her from above, but he said nothing. She sat up, wiping the grittiness from her eyes, the chill morning fully waking her. She couldn't remember much of her dreams, but they had been filled with shadows, four red eyes watching her with gleeful madness from a void so dark no light could penetrate it. She hoped it was not a precursor to the day ahead, and she tamped down her anxiety before it betrayed her worries to the others.

She stoked the embers of their fire until flames licked dead pine branches, and her companions woke to her making breakfast.

"I will leave you now," Sizmor said. "I will return."

"Share with the Shadow Court that the High Queen of Man wishes to speak with them in a matter of utmost importance to the worlds of both Man and Fae," Sylvie said, trying to sound official. "Invoke Emmer and Belloch, if you need to. I come in peace and good will."

Sizmor nodded and flew along the slope down to the forest.

Where he vanished into the darkness.

The rest of the companions arose and ate breakfast, the lightweavers in a close discussion with one another that Sylvie could not hear. Arn spent time cleaning Mikkel's armor, an act he had grown to love, while the First Knight sharpened his sword. Birdsong accompanied them, pleasant and soothing to the heart, and Sylvie almost felt like they were there for leisure rather than under the direst of circumstances.

The sun was just peeking through the forest when Sizmor returned.

"They will see you, though not the others," the sprite told her.

Sylvie stood, stretching her back. "That bodes well at least. Do you think they are open to the request I will make? Did they ask the reason for this visit?"

"I felt it wise to let you speak. And they did not prompt."

Sylvie nodded, thinking. "Very well. Let's go now. Time matters."

"If my being by your side jeopardizes your request, please take Lumière, my High Queen," Mikkel said, retrieving the sword still in its wrapped blanket to conceal it from knowing eyes. "It is your badge of queenship, but it is more than that. It should have some effect on the Fae if you should be harassed or even attacked."

Sylvie thought about that. "I worry the Fae will view it as an affront to their history. Will it not have the opposite effect of what I'm trying to achieve?"

"I agree with your First Knight," Agnes said. "The sword will keep you safe, at least safer than any other weapon or shield we possess." She glanced up at Sizmor. "Master Fae, how does Lumière make you feel when you are around it?"

The sprite shivered, clearly repulsed by it.

"I hate it."

"Yet its presence does not harm you?" Agnes said.

Sizmor frowned. "No. It just makes me want to disappear from its view."

Sylvie took Lumière from Mikkel, its weight reassuring. If it brought no harm to the Fae but repelled them in a way that kept her safe, it might make the difference between staying alive and not. She had no idea how the Shadow Court would treat her, even given her Naming. Taking precautions made sense.

"I will take it," she said. "It is my sword, as High Queen. And I visit the Shadow Court as High Queen of the kingdom. Do you think the Fae will understand, Sizmor?"

"The Fae will not like it, Sylvianna," Sizmor said. "I think you should leave it behind. I don't care what Mikkel says."

"It is settled. Sylvianna will take Lumière," Agnes said, quieting the knight's forthcoming reply to Sizmor with a look. "The Fae cannot abide the blade. Which might give an advantage if your safety is in question." She paused. "Now. I would speak with Sylvianna and Sizmor. Alone," she added, the old woman accepting Ezel's aid in regaining her feet. "Let us walk a ways."

Sylvie went to Mikkel. "I will be safe. Have no fear."

The First Knight nodded. He didn't look like he believed her.

Sylvie left him and, accepting the Prioress Mother's arm to steady her, made her way down the hillside meadow they had camped at the edge of. Sizmor followed, flying next to them. Agnes said nothing. Sylvie wondered what the blind woman wished to say away from the others. She hoped the light-weaver had no intention of coming with her.

At the edge of the Allemagne Forest, Agnes stopped and turned to Sylvie. "I speak to you now not as an old woman, but as a light-weaver whose sight is only within the light now." Her white robe absorbed the morning radiance and glowed against the darkness of the wild wood ahead.

"I'm listening. I value your insight," Sylvie said, meaning it.

"There is much we do not know in all of this," Agnes said, concern etched deep in her face. "Prioress Superior Sanna shared the knowledge she knew, most of it acquired from Mikkel. Where you go, death follows. Master Kell. Lord Idlor. Pontiff Scorus. The Citadel Assassin. The light-weavers who gave their lives to keep you safe. The brewing war of the six dukedoms against Mont-Saint-Michel. It has ever been so for the office of High King. Or in your case, High Queen. Your father understood it. He understood it all too well. The darkness and the light have battled since the world was young, and I fear the darkness has left Alafair's grave to fight the light once more. I believe very black days are ahead, not only for you but for all of us.

"Master Kell was no fool," Agnes continued. "I knew him, though not as well as you, perhaps. I trust his teachings in you. Yet that education is not as complete as you might think. The world is vast—I had to learn this in my youngest days at Clair-de-Lune—and knowledge has a way of coming to us when we need it." She pulled back the blanket covering Lumière's hilt and touched it as a mother does a newborn baby. Tender. Reverent. "Do you know the forging story of this blade?"

"It is made of fallen-light," Sylvie said, thinking back on what she had been taught. "That light fell from the sky and was forged in

Erlina's dukedom into the weapon it is now. Of the Goode line, King Halston carried it first. It is the symbol of my heritage, my house."

"That is a very good summary," the old woman said. "But it lacks. The metal burned as it fell from the sky, crashing near the site where my abbey would be founded. That metal was forged into this sword. But the fallen-light wasn't found by chance. The metal burned as it struck the earth—and it called to the light-weavers of Clair-de-Lune like a bell rung. It summoned, was retrieved, and those light-weavers oversaw Lumière's creation by one of the greatest blacksmiths to ever lift hammer to anvil."

"It *called* to them? *Summoned* them?" Sylvie asked, puzzled. "What do you mean? This isn't more riddles, is it? I'm not sure if I can stomach that."

"A riddle is merely truth wrapped around itself," Agnes said and smiled. "You will discover your own truth soon enough. But to answer your question, yes, the fallen-light called to them. There is no other way to say it."

"How is that possible?" Sizmor asked. "The sword's not alive."

"Is the light alive, Master Fae? Is fire alive?" the Prioress Mother asked, her words like those a teacher speaks to a student. "The fallen-light arrived from the skies, a gift. From whom or for what reason, we may never know. I have read the diaries and journals of the light-weavers from that time, and they corroborate one another." She paused, considering the hilt, and patted it again. "There is much about Lumière we do not know. But this much I do know. It called to the light-weavers. The metal wanted to be found. *Needed* to be found. In that way, it *was* found. Forged. And it is yours at this moment."

"What does this have to do with the Twilight Lands, the Shadow Court, and what I'm about to do?" Sylvie asked, ready to leave and enter the forest. "Surely you tell me all of this for a reason beyond a history lesson."

"Just this." Agnes raised a finger just like Master Kell used to do. "Trust in Lumière. Its creation from the light, by the light, with the light has created a powerful tool for you in the days ahead. Be yourself and be true. That is important. But you are about to enter the darkness of the Twilight Lands, and there the future will be seeded—for good or ill." She closed her eyes and turned to face the forest, as if she were trying to sense what lay within it. "It is a world unto itself, I can feel that much. But even I, with my decades of life, know very little of the Fae. I can feel the pervasive darkness in the valley and forest, though. This will not be easy for you. I want you to be prepared for it. To prevent the ugly war that comes."

"Thank you for your counsel," Sylvie said. "What advice would you give me, based on what you do know about the Fae?"

"Only this ancient saying among us light-weavers," Agnes said, her milky eyes seeming to shimmer. "'Sometimes the darkness can show you the light.'"

"Are you suggesting Lumière may respond to the darkness?" Sylvie asked. "Like Sizmor said, it's not as though the sword is sentient."

"That is not what I said," Agnes said, shaking her head. "I'm not saying Lumière will respond to the darkness. I'm saying the sword may respond to your need against the darkness within you. We all have both sides within our hearts—the light and the dark. There is darkness in you, I have seen and felt it. Yet there is also light, and the sword will respond to it."

"Like the light-weavers feeling the fallen-light," Sylvie said, understanding what the old woman meant.

"Just so. And Sylvianna, you will do well. It is in your nature to make the hard decisions for the best outcome. I would come with you. So would Ezel. But the Fae have chosen who may accompany you. And there are many ways for us light-weavers to aid you, even from afar," Agnes said cryptically. She turned her blind gaze to the sprite who sat on Sylvie's shoulder. "Sizmor, keep her safe, at all costs. In this, you must not fail."

"Sylvianna is my ward," Sizmor said. "I will see no harm come to her."

Agnes placed one aged palm on Sylvie's cheek. It was dry and leathery but tender. "We will be waiting for you, Sylvianna Goode. Ezel and I will sit in the light today, try to gauge your progress, and meditate for your safe return. Farewell."

Sylvie nodded, and without looking back, and with Sizmor leading, she entered the Allemagne Forest.

17

rom the moment she entered the dark wood, Sylvie wanted to flee.

It wasn't the fact that the morning light faded behind her to a dull gray that leached color from the world. It wasn't that she could see only so far in any one direction before she saw nothing, an impression of darkness closing in. It wasn't the ancient trees about them, their limbs so intertwined and heavy with foliage that they blotted out the sky and their gnarled roots reached for her like hands ready to haul her screaming into the depths of black soil. And it wasn't the sudden lack of birdsong or insect buzzing or the humidity that clung to her like a sweaty blanket after a fever, the air heavy with moisture and filled with the odors of rotting vegetation and growing mushrooms. After all, she had been in darker and danker places beneath Mont-Saint-Michel, and none of what she saw or sensed there had frightened her.

No, Allemagne Forest was alive in a way she'd never felt within another wood. It seemed to repel her. The world had existed a long time before her birth and would exist long after she was dead, but Allemagne Forest seemed older somehow than everything, making her feel so inconsequential she wanted to run back home where things made sense.

Despite the feelings the forest instilled, the tree limbs and heavy brush parted for them as Sylvie and her guide passed, leaning away as if her humanity were anathema.

"Is the forest doing that at your behest?" Sylvie asked, shivering.

Sizmor stopped flying ahead and waited for her to catch up. "Not exactly. You have been approved by the Shadow Court. Therefore, you are allowed to pass."

"All of this is some sort of wall then? A barrier to keep Man out?"

"You will see," the sprite said.

Sizmor flew ahead. Sylvie pressed on, careful not to trip on any roots or large stones along her path. She realized she gripped Lumière like a lifeline, her hands and arms rigid as they held her one weapon.

It helped steady her amid the unknown.

After what seemed like an eternity, the darkness at the edge of her sight lifted, color replaced the gray, and the feeling of being watched dissipated. She breathed a sigh of relief even as the path ahead opened and the silver surface of the valley's lake appeared through the bracken with the blue of the sky above sharing its light.

"Erlking Hern of the Shadow Court welcomes you to Miroir Lake," Sizmor said.

"Did you speak to them about me personally? Who I am? That I'm an ally? Do they hate me?" she asked, worried.

"*Speak* isn't exactly the right word," the sprite said. "No words were exchanged. It's more like an awareness of one another and the Shadow Court. It is hard to explain if one is not Fae." He paused, landing on her shoulder. "And yes, I shared that though you are Man, you are not a harbinger of ill intent. Is that what you wanted?"

Sylvie nodded, looking around. "That's as good a way to say it as any. Where are they?"

"They await. Come," Sizmor said, launching from her shoulder. "I do not know how long the Fae will tolerate your presence."

Sylvie did as instructed, following the sprite beyond the last few trees of the forest and into a flat meadow that circled the entire lake, one filled with blue grasses and numerous flowers blooming despite the return of the Vosges Mountains chill. She closed her eyes, drawing in a deep breath of optimism, enjoying the feel of sunshine on her face. Birds sang to one another, so many varieties of trills and chirps that Sylvie wished to see them all. She discovered she just wanted to sit down and forget her reason for being there, but a warning within her heart advised her not to fall prey. Some magic was at work, one opposite from what she had experienced in the outer section of the forest.

"It's beautiful here," Sylvie said.

"There is more beauty here than a human heart can fathom, Sylvianna," Sizmor said. "Still, you will see very little of it. You are the first child of Man to walk this lakeshore in centuries; you will likely be the last child of Man to walk these shores for centuries more."

"Where does this Shadow Court meet?" She saw no buildings, no pavilions, no amphitheaters, nothing that struck her as a meeting place.

Sizmor didn't answer. They moved around the edge of the lake in the meadow, the day warming as the sun reached its zenith, the scent of blossoms infusing the air and bees beginning to buzz. She kept expecting some strange Fae creature to appear, but none did. She began to worry that the Fae of the Shadow Court had decided against meeting with her.

"They are gathering," Sizmor said finally, gesturing ahead.

Sylvie stopped, gazing where the sprite indicated. Two ancient weeping cherry trees stood within the lea, separate from the forest, their branches wide and limbs falling low, filled with thousands of blossom buds that had yet to open. The boughs of the two trees were so thick and intertwined that they produced a dark shade beneath, one Sylvie had a hard time penetrating. And in that shadowy area, she saw a horse with long mane, long legs, and a bright stab of light upon its head.

No, she quickly realized. Not a horse.

It was a unicorn.

Before she could say anything, the magical creature faded and vanished.

"Was that . . . a unicorn?" she asked, stunned.

"That was a marvelous sight indeed, Sylvianna, and quite rare," Sizmor whispered, awe in his voice. "That bodes well. Several have found sanctuary within the Twilight Lands and roam freely. That was Peagle, the oldest among them."

"I have no words," Sylvie said.

"If you made Peagle curious, perhaps you'll survive today's meeting with the Shadow Court after all," a familiar voice said behind them.

Sylvie turned, already smiling.

"Grumtil!"

The old sprite hovered in the air before them, arms crossed, wings a blur, and a smile breaking his mossy beard apart. She had last seen him when the former representative from the Shadow Court had paid his last respects to High King Alafair Goode. Grumtil had then returned to the Twilight Lands—his service complete.

Seeing a friendly face in unfamiliar territory settled her nerves in a way Sylvie had not expected. Two Fae allies were better than one.

"I wish this was under better circumstances, young Sylvianna," Grumtil said, his features dour once more. "Sizmor shared what transpired in Mont-Saint-Michel. A pity the Goode family is set on destroying itself, and taking the kingdom into the depths of darkness. If not corrected and you are not officially crowned High Queen within the allotted time, the Compact between Man and Fae will be broken. It will be as a boulder thrown into a pond: the ripples will spread as a tidal wave, affecting all. Only you and Sizmor can set right the wrong that has been done. That begins here."

"Do you think the Shadow Court will aid me?" Sylvie asked.

"Difficult to say," Grumtil said, shaking his head. "Do you remember what I told you in Master Kell's suite? The Shadow Court has its own politics. There will be some members of the Fae who loathe you, and some who will be indifferent. I doubt any of them will like you. You have a difficult audience ahead."

"You know much more about the Court than I do, Grumtil," Sizmor said. "Man's copy of the Covenant Codex has been stolen, and I sensed it was done by a Fae changeling. There is much more going on here than a coronation or sibling rivalry."

Grumtil tugged at his beard, thinking. "I am not sure how the Court will react to that news. It should worry them all. Yet most of the members on the Shadow Court were not present when Emmer and Belloch made their pact. There will be dissension. Young Sylvianna Goode will have to be quite persuasive."

Sylvie straightened. "I am prepared, Grumtil."

"Let us find out," the old sprite said, flying toward the shadowy area where she had seen the unicorn. "Come."

As Sylvie and the sprites approached, the shadows beneath the cherry trees began to change, to coalesce and expand, to take on shapes as varied as those found in nature. That wasn't all. Thick roots from the trees thrust upward from the ground, snaking around one another, until Sylvie noted that they were creating the bones of a stage for her and a wide, half-circle table within the drooping branches above. Smaller roots joined the larger, filling in areas and making them smooth. The day had grown still—she heard no animals or lapping of the lake against its shore or wind in the trees. The shadows she had first seen were settling behind the table of the newly erected pavilion, spaced out evenly like the Citadel's Pontiff and Bishops during spiritual tribunals.

Sylvie glanced around, looking for more Fae. She saw none besides the sprites. She realized with a poignant need that she wanted to see the unicorn again. But she surmised that such a creature would only be seen if it wanted to be.

Instead, she focused on the shadows, as they shimmered in and out of reality. Then the falling cherry branches behind the table parted. A giant Fae stood proudly within the shade of the cool pavilion, tall and slim, his upper half in the shape of a muscled and pale-skinned man, his lower half that of a black stallion with gleaming coat. Upon his head sat what looked like a crown of thorns until Sylvie realized it was not a crown but antlers with many tines, the bone alabaster white. When the centaur shimmered again, Sylvie blinked, unsure what she was initially seeing as the man above—by some sort of Fae magic—separated from the horse below, his naked white body stepping out of his equine self to sit at the table in front of her.

Other Fae appeared then from the cherry trees, some featuring antlers of their own, others taking on forms found only in the forest. All were unique, all were difficult to view. For unlike the sprites, whose forms mimicked a human's head, two legs, and two arms, the Fae before her had multiple arms or legs and were made from ferns, tree branches, gnarled bark for skin or smooth, and various animal parts.

"Please, Sylvianna Goode," Grumtil said, offering her a way forward. "Step within the pavilion and have your plea heard."

Sylvie took a deep breath and did just that, still cradling Lumière.

And waited.

Once the remaining Fae had joined the table and each sat within the shadow cast by their outer form, the first to appear from the weeping cherry trees stood again, his eyes suddenly blazing red in her direction without fear or worry.

"Child of Man," the Fae said, his voice quiet and deep like an approaching thunderstorm. "I am Hern the Hunter, Erlking of the Twilight Lands, King of the Fae and Lord of the Shadows. You have requested audience. We have answered."

Sylvie bowed while she gathered her thoughts. She scanned the Shadow Court's members. Some observed her with interest; others looked anywhere but at her. She called on years of Master Kell's training during visits with dignitaries like High King Alafair.

She would be calm, collected, and clear.

"I have traveled far and under great duress to seek your counsel and aid, powerful members of the Shadow Court," Sylvie began, her words coming easier with each one spoken. "As you likely know, High King Alafair Goode has died. He Named me his heir, to be crowned as the first High Queen of the kingdom of Man. The name Sylvianna Goode is written in your copy of the Covenant Codex, and in that Naming

I hope to fulfill my duties and honor the Compact that has existed so long between Man and Fae, as set down by Emmer and Belloch."

The Erlking held his hand up at that.

"Rerell," he called.

Sylvie stopped, confused, until a Fae so slender and tall a stiff breeze would have sent him tumbling appeared through the cherry tree branches, his long fingers bearing the Fae's copy of the Covenant Codex.

Hern took the massive tome—one that mirrored the copy of Man—and opened it. Red eyes reading, he then closed the book, and Rerell vanished with it again.

"You are so Named. Go on," the Erlking said.

"Thank you," she said, pleased to see that the object of her journey existed and was readily at hand. It gave her hope that she could win what she needed from the Fae. "Upon my Naming, I was charged with a murder I did not commit. One of my half-brothers—another scion of the former High King—fabricated evidence and falsely accused me, attempting to steal the throne. He did not care if the result would be the breaking of the Compact between Man and Fae. He did not care if it went against our father's last wishes. I dealt with him as he deserved.

"But another conflict arose while sorting out the allegations," she continued, ready to share her travails in their entirety if need be. "I witnessed my father sign Man's copy of the Covenant Codex. Others saw it as well. Yet my brother's poisonous accusations took root in our kingdom and have spread. To dispel them, I sought the Covenant Codex of Saint Emmer, as proof of my Naming. But when we visited its location, we discovered it gone. Taken by a dark creature Sizmor sensed to be a changeling."

"Is this story true, Master Guide?" Hern asked Sizmor, his balefire eyes burning into the sprite. "Has the Covenant Codex of Saint Emmer been stolen from the possession of Man?"

"I can confirm it," Sizmor said. "The thief of the Covenant Codex of Saint Emmer left an aura of such darkness I could barely breathe while in its presence. The Fae that took the tome is of the darkest kind, the evilest of sorts. Once it gained the outdoors, I could not track it. Gone, along with the book."

"Changelings haven't existed for centuries." The Fae sitting to the Erlking's right spoke in a deep rumble like stones breaking against one another. He possessed a barrel chest like a tree stump, his skin bark-like with little oak-leaf twigs growing from him. "The Shadow Court has not authorized such a willful, natural affront since the battles against Man."

"True, Chreek, the Shadow Court has not," a female Fae said, the one member on the Shadow Court who had not looked upon Sylvie with clear disdain. She had horns similar to the Erlking's but she was short and waifish in comparison, vines of ivy here and there and doe ears twitching annoyance. "There are others in this world that can form, mold, and unleash such a creation, though. It is not a secret known only to Fae."

"Chreek and Secil," the Erlking chastised with a hiss. "The Shadow Court has been convened to offer this child of Man audience. Let us proceed without interrupting."

"We may discuss it separately then, my Erlking, as I believe discovering who is creating changelings—if that indeed is what young Sizmor sensed—is important," Secil said, returning her gaze to Sylvie. She smiled, her smooth features pale. "We have not yet learned what this Sylvianna Goode wishes of the Shadow Court."

"I am here before you at the gravest of hours," Sylvie said, taking control once again, hoping her honeyed words and good faith would raise her merit with the Court's members. They clearly did not trust her. "I beseech you to aid me in acquiring a copy of the Covenant Codex that I can use to clear my name, take the throne, and set right the wrongs perpetrated by my wayward half-brother." She paused for effect. "Then, like you, I can turn my attention to the mystery of the changeling and discover who pits Man against Fae again."

"I am named Brose," a Fae with black eyes, smooth black skin, and dark green moss for eyebrows and beard said in a deep baritone. "You state there have been wrongs, plural. What occurs in the world of Man now besides that which you have shared?"

Sylvie inclined her head to Brose, the first to share his name. "The kingdom my father united is breaking. A civil war is brewing between his children, many of them intent on gaining the crown," she shared. "They do not care that I am so Named. They care only about their selfish ambitions, and taking advantage of a situation that should not be. As I stand here, my brothers and sister are raising their armies. It is only a matter of time before war shatters our kingdom."

"You request a new edition of the Covenant Codex," the Erlking said, frowning darkly. "Or aid in discovering the whereabouts of the thieved copy."

"I believe in maintaining the peace between Man and Fae," Sylvie said. "A peace that is long-standing and beneficial for both of us. In time, if I cannot prove my legitimacy with your help, one of my siblings will seize power and control Royaume de France."

"And if that happens?" the Erlking asked.

"The pact between Man and Fae will be broken," Sylvie said, shaking her head. "And the victor among my siblings may turn their armies toward the Twilight Lands."

"We are safe here," Chreek spat. "We have nothing to fear."

"War of any kind damages the fabric of the world, Chreek," Secil argued, the ivy leaves of her body shaking in anger. "Let me remind you that we live in that same world."

"Battle and death come only to the ill-prepared and weak," the Erlking said, turning to Secil. His eyes blazed. "We are neither of those."

Secil shrugged. "Still. I believe the Compact between Belloch and Emmer prevents war, sorrow, and death."

"Yes, death. Let us speak of death," Chreek snorted. He turned back to Sylvie. "You came with two light-weavers of Man, did you not?"

"I have traveled far with their aid, yes," Sylvie said, unsure how to answer the question to her best benefit. She knew she couldn't lie. "They are my companions, and they mean the Fae no harm."

Chreek sat forward, his intensity flooding the space between them. Sylvie already hated him. "That was not the case once," he said. "Like our Erlking, I was on the battlefield when Belloch failed to overcome the wiles of Man. Belloch did what he could to save the Fae that day, yet he shackled our future in irons." He turned to the Shadow Court around him. "I do not trust this woman who trusts light-weavers."

The reason for her visit was devolving into something other than she'd hoped.

"The light-weavers are honorable and kind," Sizmor spoke up from her shoulder, his words surprising Sylvie. The sprite had made his hatred for light-weavers known. But now he spoke on their behalf. "They have not harmed me. They have the High Queen's interests at heart."

"There is no way to know if those interests are *our* interests," Brose put in, showing him to be neutral. "How are we to know this, child of Man?"

"I also vouch for Sylvianna Goode," Grumtil said from the side of the pavilion. "Her father was an honorable King, one I served for almost a century. He chose her as his heir. She has shown herself to be of the same quality as her father."

Sylvie nodded to the old sprite, thanking him with her eyes.

"I do trust our sprite brethren, who judge character better than the most astute among us," Brose said, dark eyes running the length of the blanket in her arms. He pointed at the sword with his chin. "What do you carry with you, young Sylvianna Goode?"

She did not unwrap it. She knew the history of Lumière and how it might unsettle those who observed her. "It is the sword of my father, High King Alafair Goode," she said, refusing to name Lumière. "The badge of my office as High Queen. My First Knight required me bring it, in case I had need."

"You have concealed it. Show us," the Erlking demanded.

Sylvie took a deep breath and did as requested. She undid the heavy cloth wrapped around Lumière. The sword captured the light of the afternoon—even within the cool shadows—and it gleamed silver, gold, and steel among the Shadow Court.

No words were uttered, but she felt the Fae's anxiety, like the fear instilled by a bee before it stings. Finally, Chreek stood, stocky form quivering with ire. With a thick finger made of bark, he pointed at Lumière.

"That blade is a horrible blasphemy," he hissed, his anger filling the pavilion.

"Stay your seat, Chreek," the Erlking commanded. Once the Fae returned to his shadow seat, the Erlking turned back to her. "Do you threaten us with that sword?"

"No, no," Sylvie said, covering it back up. "It is the badge of my office, one that proves my identity, at least in part. I am not here to harm you. I am here requesting help."

"You brought that weapon here with intention," Chreek said, unwilling to let it go.

"I am not the one who wielded the sword against you so long ago," she argued, her words terse. She settled her nerves, calmed her demeanor. "Again, I am not here to harm."

"The King of Man with the Monk of Man slaughtered many of my kinfolk that day," Hern the Hunter growled, muscles along his jaw bunching. "Despite the centuries, I remember that sword's might. I feel it now. It is not a memory I hold as cherished, child of Man. Why would you ever feel it wise to bring it before the Shadow Court, among those it harmed so long ago?"

"As I said, my First Knight wished me to carry it, to ward against any attempt on my life—changeling or other," she said, chin held high. "I will say this, though. Saint Emmer and Wise Belloch joined despite their differences, and Lumière was there at that time too." Sylvie tried to assuage the anger, pain, and resentment the Shadow Court held for Man. "It helped bring peace between our two worlds. I regret what it did to Fae at that time, but that was then. This is now. Our world is different. And while I do not know this to be true, since I did not know him, I'm not King Halston, the man who wielded Lumière that day."

The Fae members of the Court looked toward the Erlking. Before he could respond, Chreek was already leaping at the chance to fight her.

"I was there that day as well, child of Man," the stocky Fae said. "It was a peace brokered by attrition. Belloch was forced to peace. Emmer had his own sword that day, one as reviled as the one in your arms. Belloch did not come to peace because it was the right choice. That cursed black blade of Emmer's did that. And behind him, a King of Man, with *that* sword." He pointed an accusing finger, like a dagger, at Lumière. "*That* King slayed many of my kin with the weapon in your grasp."

"I did not come here to argue with you. I did not come here to fight. Members of the Shadow Court, I'm trying to prevent more war!" Sylvie said, becoming angry herself. "And I need your help. Why would I kill you? You have my word that is not my intention. You have nothing to fear from me."

"A child of Man's word is not worth the breeze used to utter it," Chreek sneered.

"Chreek!" Secil shot back, her eyes glowing white with anger.

"You know nothing of true death, Secil," Chreek said, waving a dismissive hand in her direction. "You are young. You weren't there the day the idea of the Covenant Codex was birthed. You haven't seen what I've seen. What our Erlking has seen. What friends we lost that day, to never again walk these woods. We are to put our trust in this child of Man when Man has never given us cause to trust? I say we end this woman, bury the sword in the deepest of hollows, and be done with it. It would prevent harm from befalling the Fae ever again."

"Silence, Chreek. You have spoken your feelings clearly," Hern the Hunter said, the Erlking then raising his fingers to steeple them before his glowing eyes. "I must think on this. *We* must think on this. There is no clear path ahead. I would receive counsel from the Shadow Court as well as others of the Fae I trust. We will reconvene later to judge the child of Man's wishes."

Shadows quickened about Sylvie, a tightening noose. She blinked, wondering why her sight had darkened when the others didn't seem to notice.

"Do not send her to the labyrinth. You must stop this madness!" Sizmor yelled, flying to each member sitting along the root-made table. "The Covenant Codex is sacrosanct. To ignore High Queen Sylvianna Goode's request is to invite war and death for Man and Fae alike!"

"Belloch would not condone this," Grumtil agreed, pleading. "The Shadow Court can take winters to come to its decision."

"That may be the case here," Hern the Hunter said. "Yet you are not Erlking. I am. I am charged with the safety and longevity of the Fae. I think Belloch a fool for falling prey to the wiles of a Man like Emmer so easily. This child of Man has offered no legitimate reason for the Fae to aid her in claiming the throne she desires. Yet I am willing to consider her plea if I can come to some understanding of how *she* may aid *us*."

"What do you need in exchange for that?" Sylvie asked, trying to keep the desperation from her question even as the shadows quickened around her.

"There is nothing that Man can offer Fae," Secil said, her demeanor sad.

"You would let the Covenant Codex end?" Sylvie pressed, anger bolstering her resolve.

"No, it will not be the Fae who break Belloch and Emmer's compact." Chreek's face was hard and flat like stone. "This child of Man does so. When this ignorant female does not fulfill her obligation, the Compact that has shackled us in chains for millennia will be broken. The world of Fae will be free once more, to forge its own path."

"I have spoken my choice for this day," Erlking Hern the Hunter said, unmoving in his seat, his eyes swirling with liquid gold until it was all Sylvie saw. Some sort of magic acted on her; she heard his words but could barely comprehend them as the world about her lost shape. "I alone will decide the fate of the Fae."

As she lost her ability to understand why she was there, Sylvie tried to recall what Agnes had said about Lumière, the light, and the darkness, but she couldn't remember the light-weaver's sage words.

Instead, she withdrew Lumière, the sword capturing what light remained, and focused on it to keep herself from falling into the abyss created by the Erlking's magic. The Fae of the Shadow Court hissed at the blade's revealing light, some fleeing the weeping cherry tree while others remained stonily in place. The Erlking stood and stepped backward, his naked form an indistinct blur until it rejoined with the black stallion.

Fighting what was happening to her, Sylvie raised the sword up as if she could invoke some aspect of its legendary power.

"I will not leave this Court until you hear me!" she screamed, gritting her teeth against the Erlking's power.

"You are correct. You will not leave," the Erlking said.

"Imprisoning her will do nothing but make matters worse," Grumtil yelled, the sprite siding with Sylvie.

"You will be dealt with, sprite," Chreek smirked. "Being among Man for so long, you have become just like them. Weak. Without Emmer and his sword, without this child of Man and *her* sword, the Fae will finally be free."

Darkness filled Sylvie's vision, even the brightness of Lumière unable to chase back the gloom befalling her. She tumbled from the day, dumb to her identity, the burning eyes of the Erlking following her into the void.

Then she knew nothing, not even her name.

DONATO

18

ith a throbbing head and bitterness on her tongue, Sylvie awoke to warm sunshine on her face and sweet birdsong filling the day.

She sat up, groggy. When she remembered what had transpired at the Shadow Court, rage filled her veins, strength to fully wake her. She gained her feet, looking around. She stood within a meadow of green grass and blooming flowers, insects buzzing about her and thick white clouds slowly moving through an azure sky so bright she could barely look upon it. The Erlking and the other members of the Shadow Court were not present, though their hatred of her and all things Man remained like splinters in her heart. Of the sprites, there was no evidence. It was as though some magical force had knocked her out, picked her up, and deposited her in some wild part of Allemagne Forest, without word or consent.

Then she realized she still held Lumière, the sword gripped firmly in her right hand, the blade no longer as bright as it had been in the shadow pavilion.

Cursing, Sylvie first folded the blanket at her feet. She sheathed Lumière.

"Where the hell am I?" she asked no one, looking around. "Sizmor!" she screamed.

But the Fae guide did not appear. Only silence answered her call. She took more time to view the meadow. Circling its fringe, the dark wood of Allemagne Forest grew, the trees tall and thick, their limbs meshed so tightly they formed a barrier Sylvie saw could not be infiltrated. She sought a way out but discovered only a single passageway exiting the lea, the trail lined by the same wild wood. She left by the nature-made passage, coming to two new paths that branched in different directions. Bramble vines with thorns as large as her thumb prevented passage in any other direction.

She took the left passageway, heart hammering, wondering where the Erlking and the Fae had put her. After only a few moments of walking, the passageway ended at a bubbling spring, its waters vanishing back into the land. She took a drink, letting the cool water remove the terrible taste in her mouth. She took another drink, realizing it might be some time before she'd get the chance to do so again.

Then she backtracked. She returned to the corridor that went to the meadow and took the other path. She had more success there, finding multiple branches leading to other areas within the Twilight Lands. But when she came to another dead end, she remembered what Sizmor had said and realized the awful truth of her situation.

The Erlking had put her in a labyrinth, with walls of savage nature surrounding her.

Effectively, she was a prisoner.

Keeping her composure, Sylvie ventured deeper into the Fae's warren, going this way and that, turning back sometimes but always moving forward. As the afternoon waned, Sylvie found she had become wholly disoriented. Her travels hadn't been in vain, though. She'd found a small lake with drinkable water, an orchard filled with all sorts of sweet fruit she enjoyed, and a field of grasses so tall she could bed down comfortably. When she found the lake, she kept better memory of its location, venturing back and forth as she sought the other places, until she knew where each one was in relation to the others.

At no time during her quest for freedom did she find anything resembling an exit. She knew Sizmor and Grumtil would be doing what they could to free her, to make the Shadow Court see the error of what they'd done. Mikkel, Agnes, and Ezel would begin to worry. But she couldn't rely on anyone else. Not now. It was on her to win free if the Compact could be saved in time.

Sylvie placed her hand on Lumière, wondering if the sword could help. It warmed at her touch, not unlike how it had responded in the presence of the Fae. She knew so little about the weapon. The knowledge she possessed came from legend and history, the battles it had helped High King Alafair win, the war it had stolen from the grip of Mordreadth the Great Darkness. She knew the Fae hated it, some aspect of its fallen-light anathema to them. But could it help her now?

Within the part of the labyrinth that contained the lake, Sylvie walked up to the walls of Allemagne Forest and stared at them, thinking. She brought Lumière forward, hoping the sword would somehow penetrate the wood's darkness and create an opening like Sizmor had done when they traveled into the Twilight Lands. No matter what she did—sticking the fallen-light blade toward the forest or trying to cut the foliage in hopes of making a path—nothing worked. She surveyed the immediate area, searching for any way the lake's waters might leave the wood. She found nothing. The Erlking's prison was as impenetrable as any stone wall with iron bars.

Frustrated, she had to come to terms with her situation. She was a prisoner, locked away behind Fae's nature. She had little to help her—Lumière, a blanket, and the clothes she wore. She yelled in hopes of reaching Sizmor, Grumtil, Mikkel, or the others, but her voice fell dead. It was as though she had been buried, without chance to dig free, to slowly suffocate with no one in the world the wiser. All while failing to achieve her reason for coming—to gain the Covenant Codex and become High Queen.

Hope bled from her like the tears that had started to roll down her cheeks.

"Now, now. What could be the reason for such sorrow?"

Sylvie spun, raising Lumière with both hands, prepared for Chreek or one of the other Fae who wished her ill. Through the shimmer of her tears, she had a hard time focusing on the man who stood before her. Barely able to comprehend it, she wiped her vision free.

Then she realized who it was. She had seen the man before, but only in paintings and on a singular sculpture in the Citadel's Chapel of the Covenant Codex. He was not as tall or as lean as he had been portrayed on canvas or in marble, and his beard had become quite long and tangled, but artists had been able to capture his likeness well enough for her to know him. She felt as though she had left her world and entered legend, where anything was possible.

"You can put Lumière down, I will not harm you," he said, smiling kindly at her, his good hand holding the nub where his left hand had once been.

Sylvie blinked again, trying to make sense of it all.

The man before her was Saint Emmer.

19

o reason to gape, young lady," Emmer said, his voice musical and deep.

Sylvie blinked her surprise away. Centuries had passed since the Covenant Codex had been struck between Saint Emmer and Wise Belloch, centuries in which whole generations were born, birthed the next generation, and died, only to have it all start over again. In that time, the Citadel had grown and its Bishops had canonized Emmer, the first man given sainthood. Since then, his words, philosophy, and wisdom had spread throughout the land, giving people hope, bringing a sense of belonging to one's dark days. Growing up under Master Kell's tutelage, Sylvie had learned a great deal about how to be decent, moral, and strong in the face of adversity. Much of it due to Saint Emmer's writings and teachings.

Yet here he was, a real person, robed with hood lowered. Was she facing a Fae glamour or illusion?

"Is this some kind of trick?" she asked, unwilling to lower Lumière fully. "You cannot still be alive. It's been—"

"Almost a thousand years?" Emmer finished, chuckling. "Yes, it has been a very long time."

"Then how? How is this possible?"

"First, whom do I have the pleasure of meeting?" Emmer asked, amused.

"I am sorry. This is all just very strange." She took a deep breath. "I am Sylvianna Goode, from Mont-Saint-Michel, heir to the throne of our kingdom."

Emmer glanced at the sword. "What surnames would your forebears have held in the past? Do you know?"

"The only one I know from history is Pendragon," Sylvie answered, thinking of her studies with Kell. "If you are who you say you are, you knew one of them."

"I did. Halston," the saint said, eyes sparkling suddenly. "This is all quite intriguing. If that be true, you have done impossible things already. You could not be here if you hadn't. Possessing Lumière. Entering the Twilight Lands. Suffering the wrath of the Erlking, if I am to guess, since you are in this labyrinth with me. Yes, you've made the impossible possible. Is it such a stretch that I'm capable of the same?"

"Those things pale in comparison to living so far beyond your natural years," Sylvie pointed out, still unsure what to think.

"Not all is as it appears when you look at me, Sylvianna." Emmer's eyes became grave. He turned away from her. "Come with me. As you carry Lumière, I would hear your story even as I share mine."

The man who purported to be Emmer left the lake then, his gait loose and free as he headed toward the path into the woods. Still stunned, Sylvie forced her legs to move. If he had wanted to harm her, he could have done so already. She sensed no ill will from him. She worried his long imprisonment did not bode well for her freedom but hoped that by showing trust she might discover a way free.

The man took several turns, and soon they had traveled beyond the area Sylvie had memorized. Unsurprisingly, it all appeared the same—implacable walls thick with thorny vines, limbs, and roots. After a long walk, they entered a glen unlike any she had seen. Six cedar trees grew to great heights, spaced out evenly to create a circle of sentinels dwarfing the Allemagne Forest's labyrinthine walls. And in the middle of the glen, a granite boulder sitting within a small pool of water. Thrust into the boulder was a sword with a black blade and a hilt constructed of thorny brambles wrapped around one another.

Sylvie had seen paintings of the blade many times.

"Bruyère," she said, marveling at it.

"It would be unwise to touch it," Emmer warned, his dark eyes on her. "It does not take kindly to unwelcome fingers."

Sylvie walked around the edge of the pool, the shade beneath the massive cedar trees cooler than the rest of her prison. She wouldn't get close to the blade. "Are you saying the sword is . . . alive?" she asked.

"I know much time has passed since I walked beyond the Twilight Lands, and I did not leave behind a great deal of knowledge when it comes to Bruyère. I had a year's time to create the Covenant Codex and catalog other aspects of that work, and I thought information about the sword would not matter as it is connected to me and, therefore, can never be used by another," Emmer said, nodding as if to assure himself he'd made the right choice. "Let me just say that the sword is made from several living elements, and like all living things, it is capable of choice."

"What would the sword do to me if I touched it?"

Emmer held up his arm with the lackhand. "Who knows? The brambles that make up the hilt are alive in their own way. I just wish you no harm. I can't be sure what the sword would do to you, and I feel we might not want to test it, yes?"

Sylvie nodded even as she flexed her left hand.

"She possesses Lumière," Emmer hissed then, his voice low and even deeper.

Sylvie stopped walking, taken aback by the change in Emmer. He stared coldly at her. There was some aspect to his gaze that had turned alien, quite different from a moment earlier.

Then his mien changed again, like a ray of sunshine finally winning free of a slow-moving black cloud.

"What is wrong with you?" Sylvie asked, confused.

Emmer shrugged. "I do apologize for Belloch," the saint said, his voice soft again. "He can be a bit testy at times."

"Testy, you say," Emmer growled low, features twisting. Belloch had returned. *"Only because I've been living in your stinking carcass of Man for so long. I would rip it apart if I could."*

Sylvie stepped back, fear twisting her insides. Belloch had been Erlking of the Twilight Lands during Emmer's time and the Great War between Man and Fae. History recounted him as a mighty being. Feeling the other's animosity, she understood why.

"You are safe," Emmer said then, voice kind, hand and lackhand outstretched before him as if trying to prevent her from fleeing. "Belloch and I have been shut away from others for so long that sometimes simple manners escape him."

"I am so confused," Sylvie said, trying to understand what was going on. "You and Wise Belloch joined all those centuries ago? In one body? While you've been imprisoned here in this maze of the Twilight Lands?"

"Hear that," Belloch whispered. *"She thinks me wise. You should listen to this one."*

"If that's all you heard, Belloch, you may wish to listen more," Emmer said, shaking his head. He returned his attention to Sylvie. "My apologies. The best humor he can summon is of the wryest variety, I'm afraid."

"I see that," she said, still unsure about their dichotomy.

"I suppose you are owed some level of explanation, though I'm unsure what history has said in my absence. It has been a very long time," Emmer said, stroking his beard with his fingers. "Humanity has always been good at rewriting its own bloody past. I doubt that has changed since my time of exile in the Twilight Lands."

"You are Saint Emmer, considered one of the most important historical and spiritual figures of our lives. We read your words often," Sylvie said as if it were the most obvious thing in the world. "You are a hero to one and all. You saved Man."

Emmer looked down at the nub of his left wrist. "I am no hero. I have done many things I am not proud of, young Sylvianna." He spoke so sadly that it almost broke Sylvie's heart.

"Is that why you are locked up here?" Sylvie asked, unsure what to say.

"Heavens above and fires below, no," Emmer said, chuckling. It was a pleasant sound that helped soothe Sylvie's frazzled nerves. "Part of the Compact between Man and Fae demanded it." He paused, considering her anew. "I will begin with what I know and address any questions that may arise. To answer your first question, Belloch and I made a mutual pact that neither of us could return to our people to help maintain the peace between Man and Fae. I'm sure you know the story of your forebear, Halston Pendragon?"

Sylvie nodded. "You had the light-weavers bequeath Lumière to him. He was the first of my line to carry this sword I hold."

"That's right, though he did not want that responsibility," Emmer said.

"He still slew many of my kin that day, Emmer," Belloch snarled. *"He liked wielding it well enough."*

Emmer returned, anger in his eyes. "Regardless, Belloch and I spent several seasons together, working to define the peace we were brokering between Man and Fae. It took a great deal of time. During those months, we arrived at many specifics—historical and otherwise—that would become the Covenant Codex. We included King Halston along with Hern the Hunter in our discussions, to build a level of consensus between our peoples, so it wouldn't appear that the only reason Belloch aided in the pact's creation was because of Bruyère and my influence over him."

"As if such influence were possible," Belloch added, snorting. *"I fell to you in battle. All saw it. With those swords of yours, you could have destroyed all Fae. I made a choice to keep safe my kin."*

"Thank you, Belloch," Emmer said.

"That's why we call you Wise Belloch," Sylvie said, knowing the Fae creature within Emmer could hear her words.

"Again, I like her, Emmer."

"During our numerous discussions, though, it became clear that the Fae would not trust such a compact with Bruyère remaining in the hands of Man," Emmer said, nodding as if convincing himself anew. "Hern the Hunter wanted me imprisoned; King Halston wanted Belloch beheaded for the death of his warriors. You see the compromise before you, a decision Belloch and I agreed to."

"The peace between Man and Fae has been long-standing," she said, getting a clearer understanding of what had occurred so long ago. The history books and legends did not recount what Emmer was telling her now. "What you both accomplished has resulted in a safer world for all."

"We have been imprisoned here ever since, without keys to undo the lock," Emmer added, looking around him. "We do not lack for much. The labyrinth is large and filled with wonders, many we have not discovered yet. Though speaking with you has made me realize how much I miss an earnest conversation."

"I can see the wisdom of your choices." Sylvie shook her head, though, awed and unable to comprehend what living centuries would be like. "The Fae live much longer than Man. Is that how you are still alive, Emmer?"

"I keep him alive," Belloch said. *"Without my magic, he would die. And me with him."*

Sylvie looked at Bruyère. Once, when she was a little girl, Master Kell had brought her before High King Alafair to officially meet the monarch as Kell's new apprentice. The King had treated her kindly—with soft words and warm smiles—giving her sweet treats while relating the tale of Lumière and the destruction of Mordreadth. She remembered being awed by his story and the blade, along with the King's magical ring, Vérité, and the shield Pridwen. But seeing Bruyère made her realize history had entered the present, and she had become the steward to set right the wrongs. Her efforts affected more than just her own future; her efforts could change the lives of hundreds of thousands of people.

"Now, Sylvianna Goode," Emmer said, cocking his head, considering her. "What brought you to these Twilight Lands? With Lumière, no less."

"That is a long story," she said, unsure where to begin.

"We are ready," Emmer said.

"I am the Named heir of High King Alafair Goode, he who slew Mordreadth the Great Darkness and united a kingdom under one banner," Sylvie said. "There is a great deal to discuss about that, but my proper coronation has been thwarted while my brothers and sisters scheme." She took a deep breath. "Now, even as I am here, the kingdom is fracturing, my siblings vying for the throne. War and bloodshed have come, and the only way to set it right is to prove my Naming, take the crown, and bring justice to those who deserve it."

"The very thing I have come to fear all these years has come to pass," Emmer said, looking down at his lackhand.

"I tried to warn you of this, Emmer," Belloch said quietly. The fire in the other's eyes dimmed as if the realization of what it meant had just been discovered. *"It took longer than I thought but it remains true."*

"You did, my old friend," the saint said, shaking his head. "We knew a compact that instills peace between Man and Fae would be difficult to uphold." He stepped around the pool, looking at Bruyère as he said, "I must ask, though, Sylvianna Goode. You have a copy of the Covenant Codex. It should be written there, for all to see, concerning your Naming. For all to know. Why weren't you able to prove it?"

"Given my older brother Lord Idlor's accusations against me, I had to have the codex. But when I went to acquire it and prove the Naming beyond any shadow of doubt, we discovered the book had vanished."

"The Pontiff of your world should have offered it freely," Emmer said.

"Pontiff Scorus became compromised by Idlor," Sylvie said. "Through bribery or friendship, I do not know. It matters little at this point. I put the Pontiff and my wayward brother to death."

"Again, the fear I had," Belloch said. *"Fae do not mislead like Man. What happened to the book?"*

"My sprite guide, given after my Naming, said it had been stolen by a Fae," Sylvie added. "A changeling, if he is right."

"No Fae would create a changeling," Belloch argued. *"Why bother, during a time of peace?"*

Sylvie shrugged. "Someone who doesn't want peace?"

Emmer didn't move. She could tell the two entities within one body were silently talking with one another. She stood, waiting.

"If a changeling is involved," Emmer said, "then there is more occurring than the splintering of a royal family."

"I can understand the actions of my siblings. Power and the way it corrupts is known," Sylvie said. "But none of them could create such a beast. Who then?"

"Do you have any insight into it, Belloch?" Emmer asked.

"The Fae are unlike Man in many ways," the Fae creature whispered through the man's lips. *"Yet in some ways, we are very alike. The hunt for power amid politics blights Fae even as it does Man. Factions exist within the Twilight Lands, their motives differing. One such faction could have created the changeling and used it to undermine the Compact between Man and Fae, in hopes of wresting control from Hern the Hunter and supplanting his seat of power."*

"Chreek had no interest in hearing my story, let alone helping," Sylvie acknowledged. "I can tell you that. He was quite awful."

"He hates Man more than I do," Belloch said with a short bark of a laugh. *"I am not surprised."*

Sylvie nodded. "You are saying someone within the Fae could create a changeling without the Erlking's consent or help?"

"There are others who could also accomplish it," Belloch said. *"Witches. Warlocks. Even magi from the east could likely create one."*

"There is no way to know then," she said, annoyed. "Which brings me back to the reason I am here. I need the Fae's Covenant Codex, or a new one for Man. I can use it to prove who I am to undo the damage that's been done in the kingdom. Once I've done that, I can turn my energies to discovering who is attempting to renew the war between Man and Fae."

"You are quite focused on fulfilling your father's decree that you become High Queen. That is admirable," Emmer said. He raised a finger, like a teacher about to chastise a student. "Yet what would be the purpose of stealing Man's Covenant Codex? Forget the changeling, which is just a puppet. What does this puppet's master intend with the theft? Why take this step? Why not just kill you outright and be done with it?"

Sylvie hadn't considered that, always thinking the answer to such a question would lie within the Twilight Lands. There were numerous possibilities, she realized. She took her time, analyzing what Emmer asked, thinking about each step she had taken since leaving Mont-Saint-Michel. The Kraken and his underworld. The visit with the light-weavers and the Citadel Assassin's attack at Clair-de-Lune. Even entering the Twilight Lands. She saw nothing there.

Then she realized where she had ended up after those events, what she held in her hands, and who stood before her.

And the other sword, glinting dully in the afternoon light.

"No," Sylvie breathed, too stunned by what she thought to articulate it. Not immediately. It left her dazed, daunted. It left her frightened beyond anything she had dealt with thus far. The truth carved its way into her heart like a chisel into marble.

"What, Sylvianna Goode?" Emmer asked, frowning.

"This is who you hope to lead Man?" Belloch growled. *"She is daft. Look at her."*

Sylvie ignored the former Erlking, her mind spinning. She thought back to Clair-de-Lune and the story Prioress Mother Agnes had brought to life with her light-weaving talents. She saw the tale again in her mind. It solidified what she had come to suspect.

"The changeling. It would have been created by someone or something with the power to do so, right?" Sylvie said. She had a hard time even saying the words, but she swallowed her fear, countered it, and continued. Emmer nodded for her to go on. "Such an entity would likely know a great deal about magic, right?"

"That would definitely be the case," Emmer said. "Those who practice such arts study for many years."

"Witches. Warlocks. The Fae. Yes, we've been over this already," Belloch said.

"I've been so focused on getting a copy of the Covenant Codex that I hadn't considered the chessboard with all of its pieces—and how they've moved," Sylvie said, feeling stupid. She wanted to curse herself, but it would do no good. "Stealing the Covenant Codex kept me from proving my Naming, true. That's all I thought about. Yet it had a different result as well. What would such an act accomplish if I discovered it was a changeling who had stolen it?" She shook her head, getting angrier as she spoke. "The thief would know I'd need the Covenant Codex. That I'd do anything to get it back."

"That you would blame the Fae," Belloch said.

"No. Well . . . yes, but no," Sylvie said, speaking faster as the puzzle pieces fell into place. "What if the book's theft was meant to send me here?"

"And?" Emmer asked, eyes narrowing. "Why would that benefit this puppet master?"

Sylvie shook her head. "Where am I right now? And with what?"

Belloch laughed then, his dark humor bubbling out of Emmer's mouth like a cauldron heated to a boil.

"You have been jailed," the Fae creature said. *"Along with both swords of Man."*

Sylvie wanted to scream her rage. Instead, she lifted Lumière up. "Lumière and Bruyère, two powerful weapons that helped bring peace and prevent war are now—"

"No longer part of that world," Emmer finished, taking a deep breath, shoulders slumping and gone rigid as if a great weight pressed down on him. "You carried Lumière here."

"As the master of the changeling could easily predict. Lumière is the badge of my office. Of course I would bring it with me," Sylvie said, fire running through her. "I must get out of here. *We* must get out of here. Can you call the Erlking? Wouldn't he listen to you?"

Belloch shook his head. *"I do not have that ability. If he visits, it will be of his accord."*

"No help will come from that direction—not soon, I would wager." Emmer eyed her. "You said friends journeyed with you. Do any of them have sway over the Fae of the Twilight Lands? Could you get help from beyond these prison walls?"

Sylvie thought about it. She had little with her. Only a saint with a Fae creature within as company, both of whom were impotent as far as she could tell. And Bruyère, which she knew little about.

"Could Bruyère buy us freedom?" she asked.

"No," Emmer said. "It is made of nature but has no power over the natural world."

"Without Sizmor here, I have no way to reach those friends," she admitted, tendrils of defeat worming their way into her chest. The futility she felt lent a heavier weight to the stillness that encompassed them.

Her absolute failure festered in her like a wound.

"Then I hate to say this, Sylvianna Goode," Emmer said finally, eyes sad. "If what you surmise is true, you are never getting free. And the world of Man and Fae alike will burn for it."

20

ith dawn brightening the east, Sylvie huddled within her blanket, thinking.

It had been a long night. Despite Emmer creating a simple bed of soft grasses upon a raised platform of stones for her to rest on, Sylvie hadn't slept well. The previous day had ended with the saint scrutinizing her conclusion, and asking her repeatedly to explain the events that led her to the Twilight Lands. Each time, they arrived at the same end—she, fallen into a trap intended to remove one of the most powerful weapons from Man. Sylvie grew angrier and more helpless as they talked. Even as Emmer cooked a dinner of fresh quail, potatoes, and spinach—accompanied by a jug filled with water so sweet it tasted like wine—she fell deeper into darkness. And upon going to bed, she held Lumière next to her like a lover, gazing at the sword, the faint light of the stars that swirled above creating a dull shine on the weapon that did nothing to free her from lamentation. Her thoughts cycled through anger, guilt, resentment, hope, and right back to anger when no new ideas presented themselves.

There was a chance the Erlking would leave her here, to spend the rest of her days trapped, to die. It would give Fae like Chreek the chance to attack Man and finish what had been started by Belloch centuries earlier.

When sleep finally did arrive, Sylvie found no comfort in it, her dreams plagued with dark, twisted trees crushing her with unrelenting, grasping roots.

Sylvie couldn't ponder it all anymore. She had to go for a walk.

She rose from her makeshift bed as the sky pinked. She stretched and took a drink from the jug. The cool water flowed down her throat, a refreshing way to start the day. She took an apple from a nearby boulder serving as a table and bit into it, letting its tang satiate. Then, retrieving Lumière, she left her sleep space, already happier for the action of doing something.

Of Emmer there was no sign, his bed vacant.

Rather than wait for him, she trod the labyrinth, memorizing her way, until she had returned to the meadow where she first awoke within the maze. Standing an arm's length from the dark wall of vegetation, Sylvie unsheathed Lumière. She hacked at the vines and limbs first. The sword cut deep, but the forest healed itself as quickly as it was cut. She knelt to the earth, to see how the trees and vines multiplied so easily and readily; from what she saw, they grew like other plants, with deep roots in the black soil. Sylvie used her hands to dig down as best she could, to see if she could somehow tunnel underneath the wall. But when she reached the roots, they slashed at her, drawing blood.

She stared upward, wondering if she could go over the walls. Sheathing Lumière and tucking it into her robe's cord, she grasped the nearest branch that could hold her weight—and began to climb. The twisted limbs of the trees offered many hand- and footholds, each one strong enough to bear her weight. Sylvie grinned, seeing a way out. But after she had climbed more than two heights of a man, the vines within the wall came alive, snaking toward her, and she realized with horror—when one curled about her arm—that they intended to either wound her with their sharp thorns or push her away to fall. She struggled as other vines grabbed her, until she realized she had to drop.

Sylvie hit hard, her legs buckling, thrown backward by her momentum. Lumière, positioned on her back, pushed hard into her body. She twisted in agony even as her vision swam within black undercurrents. She lay still for a time, breathing hard, looking up at the sky as if it too imprisoned her. She couldn't cut her way out with Lumière. She couldn't tunnel. She couldn't climb. She realized, with dull certainty, she couldn't escape.

Then she focused on one of the clouds high above. It was large, like others around it, its underside dark and quite threatening by all appearances. There was nothing remarkable about it; it was like many she had seen in her life. Yet how its upper reaches captured the early morning sunshine and glowed white captured her attention. Like its siblings, the cloud slowly moved eastward, unfettered, the white of its billowing heights rising above the darkness of its bottom.

With stunning clarity, she realized there might be a way to help her friends find *her*. She sat up, still gazing at the cloud, thoughts tumbling. She thought back on what Agnes had said before Sylvie and Sizmor entered the Twilight Lands.

Sometimes the darkness can show you the light.

Sylvie withdrew Lumière from its sheath. She placed the blade upon her crossed legs. Gripping the hilt, she let her wish pour into her hand. She closed her eyes, focusing on the sword, its feel, and its place in the world. The metal was warm beneath her fingers.

Tingling began, as if her hand had fallen asleep and was coming back to life.

A feeling of eagerness infused her.

"Good morn, Sylvianna Goode," Emmer said from behind her, his feet barely making noise on the soft moss that seemed to grow richer along the edges of the forest walls.

"To you too, Emmer," she said, opening her eyes and turning. "And you, Belloch."

"What are you attempting?" the former Erlking asked, his voice like gravel beneath feet.

"I do not know, but I must try something—anything—to win free,"

Sylvie said, returning to face the forest wall. "I've tried everything. But Lumière was forged from fallen-light by a Master blacksmith with light-weavers present. Before I entered the Twilight Lands, Prioress Mother Agnes shared that the light-weavers of your time had sensed the fallen-light when it fell to our world. No, that's not what she said. She said the fallen-light *called* to them."

"And you are hoping that Lumière may call the Prioress Mother here?" Emmer asked, considering it.

"That is my hope," Sylvie said. "She is a force of nature herself. I am hoping her light can break apart this darkness, create a path, and free me."

"Little is known about fallen-light," Emmer said. "If anyone can unlock some mystery it possesses, it'd be someone from the House of Pendragon."

Sylvie closed her eyes once more, feeling the sword. She went inside herself, keeping Lumière at the forefront of her thoughts. She recalled the light, how it played across the hilt and the blade, the tingling, and tried to connect with the fallen-light forged into it. Then she thought about the light all around her and beyond—the sun warming her back, the beauty of an azure sky after a thunderstorm, the glitters on the ocean waves outside her island home, and the rainbows she'd seen arcing through Clair-de-Lune's fountain. She thought about Lumière connecting to all of that light and molded her thoughts with her need to draw Agnes to her.

Before she understood what was happening, Lumière warmed to a furnace heat that would have been uncomfortable had it burned her hand. It didn't, though. She opened her eyes and saw the blade glowing with the new light of day.

Some part of her separated from her body then, an aspect of herself she hadn't known existed, which now bloomed with argent light. It traveled beyond her, took a part of her. She still perceived the sword, the meadow, Saint Emmer, the flowers springing up out of the moss and grasses, and even the dark walls of the forest.

But then, like iron to a lodestone, the light within her brightened to

Lumière's call, and she shot toward the Vosges Mountains. The sense of duality, of being in two places, intensified. Within a moment, she saw Mikkel, Arn, Sizmor, Agnes, and Ezel at their campsite. They were in discussion. Before Sylvie even thought about how she'd reach one of the light-weavers, Agnes smiled and turned her eyes up to the sky.

They were filled with wonder.

Then the light vanished, and Sylvie returned with a shock to her body. Almost toppling over, she gripped the grasses around her to keep the world from spinning out of control.

"Are you fine?" Emmer asked, strong hand holding her upright.

Sylvie sucked in air, steadying herself. "I . . . I went outside myself," she said. "Yet I was here too."

"Lumière is a blade made of wonders. I am not surprised," Emmer said. "Still, it took a toll on you. Please rest. I have little apothecary means to heal here. I will be right back."

Emmer returned with the jug of water and a bowl of ripe blackberries. Sylvie accepted them gratefully, throwing a few berries in her mouth, their sweetness and the water steadying what remained of her strength.

"*What now?*" Belloch asked.

"I think the Prioress Mother sensed me. She isn't far away, just outside this forest labyrinth if I am to guess," Sylvie said, feeling strength return. "I have no way of knowing if she can aid me or not, but I had to try. Perhaps she'll be able to tell my Fae guide where I am and he can do something about it."

"A light-weaver is a powerful creature," Emmer said, nodding. "If she is anything like those I once knew, she will not rest until she's exhausted every opportunity to find you."

The three of them sat in the midmorning sunshine—a High Queen, a saint, and a former Erlking. Sylvie glanced down at Lumière. The sword winked at her. She knew the blade had slain Mordreadth the Great Darkness, the horned evil unable to withstand whatever fallen-light properties had been forged into it. Yet it left her wondering what else the sword could do—and whether she dared discover what those abilities were. She shuddered, remembering how it had split her awareness apart. It hadn't been pleasant.

When noon came, Emmer stood. "Feeling restored at all?" he asked.

"I do feel better," Sylvie said, grateful. She sighed, looking at the top of the wall. "Before you arrived, I tried to cut my way out, tunnel under, and even climb over. Allemagne Forest prevented every attempt. What is the purpose of having such a labyrinth? Why do the Fae need such a place?"

"Once, long ago, it imprisoned any member of the Fae who broke their oath to the Erlking and the Twilight Lands," Belloch hissed, eyes flashing red. *"Now, it is clear Hern the Hunter either has no such dissent within the Fae, or he deals with usurpers, liars, and the like the same way Man does—with death. The maze has little use now, besides—"*

"Do you hear that?" Emmer interrupted, the switch between the two entities happening instantly and the saint holding up his hand for silence.

Sylvie heard nothing at first. Then the cracking and shattering of tree limbs and trunks came to her, each concussion reverberating in the air and eventually in the ground at her feet. She rose, still holding Lumière, and backed away from the prison wall. Emmer did the same, coming to her side. While the sun shone down on them, the darkness from the forest intensified, as if the trees and vines were bunching closer together to hoard a treasure or keep it secret. The foliage began to sway this way and that, alive in a horrifying way that went against the very nature of nature. The ground rolled at her feet, the roots of the labyrinth shuddering in their soil. Then the very branches Sylvie had climbed split asunder as if giant hands forced them apart.

And a unicorn stepped from the new opening. It glowed incandescent, muscles rippling beneath his coat as if he were shrugging off the effects of the labyrinth. The Fae creature snorted and tossed his mane, his white horn flashing in the sunlight. The darkness of the day fell away, replaced by warmth.

"Peagle," Belloch whispered, bowing.

The unicorn stepped up to Sylvie, his gaze steady. There was a depth of age in Peagle's large blue eyes that stilled her heart. Awed by his appearance and unsure how to behave toward the Fae beast, Sylvie almost missed seeing the old woman following in the unicorn's wake.

"Agnes!" Sylvie yelled, running to her.

The Prioress Mother emerged from the woods, the power of the light-weaver emanating from her, her robes still dirtied but bright like the unicorn. Her song filled the meadow from lips pinched in pain, the music's command over the light resonating like a tuning fork. Agnes made small motions with her hands as if she touched the very fabric of the universe. When she exited the darkness, the path behind her remained open despite the forest straining to close the gap.

Then the old blind woman collapsed into Sylvie's arms. She gently lowered Agnes to the grasses and flowers, fearing the worst. For the first time, the Prioress Mother seemed as frail as her age, nothing more than ancient bones within wrinkled skin. She breathed shallowly, her milky blue eyes staring upward.

"What have you done?" Sylvie said, setting Lumière aside and cradling the old woman's head in her lap.

Agnes grinned, her sparkling eyes the only youthful thing about her still. "I did what was necessary, Sylvianna Goode. You called, I answered. Lumière did the rest. What is done is done. My end was foreordained by the light, and I've always heeded the light's call."

"It is not your end. Can you get up?" Sylvie breathed, trying to work her arms under the woman's to leverage her into a sitting position. "We likely do not have much time before the Erlking discovers what you and the unicorn have just done."

"I cannot," Agnes said, only her face animated. It was as if the forest around them had leached her indomitable strength. Agnes turned her head then and saw Emmer. A smile lit her face. "Saint, I have felt your light and your darkness at twilight. I did not know it was you but now all is revealed."

"Prioress Mother, it is an honor to meet you under such a dire circumstance," Emmer said, nodding his head in reverence. "I knew several light-weavers once upon a time. They were like you. Selfless. Strong. And filled with love."

"This Fae creature aided me, Sylvianna," Agnes said, gesturing with a weak finger. "To live my last moments in the presence of such wonder and puissance is a powerful way to enter and become one with the light."

"Love draws love, Prioress Mother," Emmer said. "Love is the way."

Agnes smiled before turning her attention back to Sylvie. "The path I have created will win you free of this place. Sizmor is just on the other side of this wild wood, and the others await your return. They are unmolested. That will not remain true once the Fae discover you have fled." She paused and gripped Sylvie's hand tight. "One thing. While working within the light, I sensed a great darkness in these lands. Deep. Pervasive. Elusive. Ancient. Beware, Sylvianna. You are in the gravest of dangers while you remain here."

Sylvie looked to Emmer. The concern written on his face gave credence to what the old light-weaver said.

"I haven't come this far to fail now," Sylvie said to Agnes. "Thank you for the warning."

"Remember, there is light within you. It has always been there. You used it just now with Lumière. Find comfort and strength there," the Prioress Mother said. "Now go."

Tears sprang into Sylvie's eyes. "How many must die to save the kingdom?"

"Many," Agnes breathed. "Yet your mettle will see you through. Do what is right. That is all the light demands."

"Sylvianna," Emmer urged, eyes narrowing above a deep frown.

"I will share with the Prioress Superior what you have done today," Sylvie said, gently taking her blanket, bunching it up, and placing it beneath Agnes's head. "Songs will be sung of your life and your sacrifice. You will be remembered."

"Go," Agnes said, weaker still. "I can keep the pathway open for you but only for so long. When my strength is gone, so goes the path."

Sylvie turned to Emmer. "I need you by my side. I need allies in this."

"The Compact fails if you do not complete your coronation,"

Emmer said, shaking his head. Then his eyes started darting back and forth. "Belloch agrees. Await me."

By the time Emmer returned—in possession of Bruyère—Agnes's eyes were closed. Sylvie still held her hand and life still flowed through the old woman.

But it was clear she slowly failed.

"I won't forget you, Agnes," Sylvie said, kissing her leathery cheek.

The Prioress Mother squeezed Sylvie's hand one last time and let go. Picking up Lumière, Sylvie moved toward the break in the labyrinth. Emmer followed on her heels. She stopped to glance back one time. Peagle knelt before the light-weaver, placing his finely molded head on her legs, round eyes closed and horn glowing, comforting her in some way Sylvie felt in her heart. It made her gathered tears tumble down her cheeks even as she turned to flee. She would make the Prioress Mother's end mean something—even if it killed her.

Sylvie hurried ahead, unsure how much time she had. She could feel Allemagne Forest straining to prevent her escape, the leaves and branches quivering around her, an occasional barbed vine trying to stab her before being pulled back into its foliage by whatever power Agnes wielded. The maze wall was thicker than she had expected: she couldn't see the end of the path she was on—until the corridor turned abruptly to the right. Suddenly, the wood ended and she rushed into another flowered meadow, one that spread over a hillside.

"Sylvianna! You are alive!" Sizmor screamed, flying to her and hugging her neck. Grumtil was also there, nodding his approval.

"I am. *We* are," she said, looking at Emmer.

Before she could say more, the sentient forest slammed back together like stone hitting stone, the path they had taken to freedom gone.

"She is gone," Emmer said sadly.

"The Prioress Mother sacrificed herself?" Sizmor said, eyes bewildered.

Sylvie nodded. "So that we may make a difference. There is a great deal to discuss. But not now. Sizmor, I need you to guide me to the Erlking."

The sprite gave her a look as though she had gone mad. "Do you think that wise? Hern the Hunter will merely throw you back into the labyrinth."

Sylvie looked at Bruyère in Emmer's hand. "He won't with that around."

Sizmor shrank behind her; Grumtil frowned darkly. They both shivered in the presence of the black sword.

"Is that what I think it is?" Sizmor asked.

"Do not worry so, little sprite," Belloch chuckled. *"You are safe from Emmer."*

"Who was that?" Grumtil asked, even more incredulous.

"Again, it's a long story," Sylvie said. "Can you get us to the Erlking or not?"

Sizmor nodded. "I can show you to his dwelling. He will not be pleased to see you. Or that sword, I bet. You still wish to discover a copy of the Covenant Codex?"

"I do," Sylvie said. "That is not all, though. I need to form an alliance with the Fae that goes beyond the pact Emmer and Belloch made. Again, we cannot discuss it now. Time is short. Lead the way."

Her Fae guide shot ahead, the late-afternoon sunshine beginning to vanish behind the Vosges Mountains. Grumtil followed him. Shadows were lengthening, and Sylvie didn't want to be caught in the Twilight Lands after dark. It helped that she held Lumière, and Emmer had retrieved Bruyère, but that didn't mean they were safe from harm. In fact, the swords might draw more ire from the Fae and create a far more dangerous situation than they could handle.

The sprites led the way along a path that twisted and turned through Allemagne Forest. They'd wait until Sylvie and Emmer caught up before flying ahead again, wings a blur as the sun sank into twilight. They were still walking when night fell, the moon breaking through gaps in the canopy to light their way. Woodland animals who enjoyed the night scurried around them as they passed, though Sylvie only heard them. Fiery purpose running in her veins, she moved quickly, the fear of being caught mixed with her desire to win free of the Twilight Lands, find the Covenant Codex, and form a new alliance with the Erlking.

By the time they reached the lakeshore where the Shadow Court had been held, the darkness of night had fallen upon them fully like a shroud. Stars winked at them, watching as they traveled along the edge of the lake beyond the pavilion into new territory for Sylvie.

"I feel eyes upon us," Sylvie said, the feeling sending a shiver up her spine.

Sizmor stopped. "I feel nothing. Are you sure?"

"Is it the Erlking?" Sylvie questioned. "Do you think he will listen?"

Grumtil looked beyond Sylvie to Emmer. "With Bruyère returned to the world, Hern the Hunter will listen. He will be compelled to. He will see the wisdom of maintaining some semblance of peace between Man and Fae, now that those two swords are free." He paused, looking from face to face. "But still, if we assume there is an ancient machination involved in all of this—one going back to the time of the Great War and the melding of Emmer and Belloch—then there are powerful forces at play. Who is it? A fallen angel? A rising demon? A wizard or sorcerer or witch? Or is it some Fae even I've never heard of?"

"It is the one piece in all of this puzzle we know nothing about," Sylvie admitted, and Emmer nodded in agreement. "I've thought of every text I can remember reading, hoping for revelation to present itself. Nothing has."

"Once we return to the world of Man, I will aid you in discovering more information," Emmer said, tugging at his beard. "Perhaps a set of aged eyes on old pages in musty libraries could be some use."

The companions made their way from the lake into the dark depths of the forest. Sylvie kept Lumière free, wishing Mikkel was there. The First Knight was attuned to danger, able to sift it out. But before long, she entered a break in the wood where a lone oak tree as old as the world rose before them, limbs wide and thick, its reaches high, its leaves so dense that they hid the canopy's interior—except for one opening where Sylvie could just make out the shape of walls and windows grown from the tree itself.

Below the limbs, a series of boulders bloomed from the earth, vague shapes in the night.

"Won't the Erlking have guards protecting him?" Sylvie asked.

"We Fae are not so distrusting as Man," Grumtil said, keeping his eyes on the surrounding shadows. "He is strong without such need." The sprite frowned so deeply even Sylvie saw it in the moonlight. "Though I do not see his horse Slipnir nearby. Odd."

"And beware," Sizmor added. "The oak tree before us is not like others of its kind. It is alive and can cause great harm."

"Of course the tree is alive," Sylvie said. "Aren't all trees?"

"Sizmor means the tree protects the Erlking's domain when he is not present," Grumtil said, flying next to his young successor. "The tree will come to life and kill any creature that attempts to break into the Erlking's home. If he is not here, we must be wary."

Sylvie looked to the oak. "Let's hope Hern the Hunter is there then." They approached slowly, moving through deep grasses up to Sylvie's knees. She relied on the sprites to keep her safe—this part of the world unknown to her in all its magical and mystical facets—but it also pleased her that Emmer walked beside her, Bruyère held at his ready. It gave her hope that she could acquire what she needed—both the book and an alliance—then win free of the Twilight Lands and return home.

"Something is not right," Emmer said, slowing his gait. He brought Bruyère up as if to ward off some grave peril.

Sylvie did the same, peering through the gloom. Grumtil flew ahead, remaining clear of the oak's branches, trunk, and roots, circling the area. Sizmor went the other way, finding his way around the boulders that erupted from the land like a giant's fingers. Then the young Fae flier swooped to the ground, froze in space for one moment, and promptly shot up, almost hitting the tree and forgetting his own warning.

"No," Sizmor breathed.

With Grumtil flying to where the other sprite waited, Sylvie and Emmer joined them. What she saw left her puzzled, until she realized what she stared at was not one of the stones toppled by some earlier force but something else entirely.

Slipnir, the black stallion that formed the Erlking's lower half, lay dead.

Throat ripped out.

Eyes rolled back white.

And tongue lolling from his mouth.

"What could have done this?" Sylvie questioned, the grisly scene almost choking her. The horse's blood slicked the whole area around her, making the grasses at her feet sticky. Every instinct inside told her to flee—yet she needed answers.

"It is recent," Grumtil said, hovering close to the carcass. "Still quite warm."

The hairs on Sylvie's arms and neck rose. "There is a chance the killer is still here," she whispered. "Where is Hern?"

They all glanced upward, into the limbs and leaves of the oak.

"I will go," Grumtil said.

"No," Sylvie said. "We stand a better chance if we are all together. We have weapons that can protect all of us."

The elder sprite did not argue. He did go to the tree's trunk and touched the rough bark there. The oak did nothing.

"He's here," Sizmor confirmed. "Though . . ."

He left the rest unsaid. They were all thinking it. Emmer took the lead, brandishing Bruyère as he took a series of leafless limbs, grown at intervals around and upward along the tree's trunk, as steps to attain the upper reaches. Sylvie followed, with the sprites to either side. She held her breath. The darkness that had swallowed her life ever since she had been Named heir rose inside her; every step she took, the suspicion that this would be one more failure grew, until she imagined what she'd find above.

After several spirals around the tree's trunk, the group entered the foliage, the world reduced to dark greenery. Small orbs of light hung suspended near a door that stood open, with more illumination within the Erlking's home.

"It is I, Grumtil, my Erlking," the old sprite said, flying slowly inside.

The others followed—and froze.

The Erlking's abode had comforts Sylvie had thought could never exist in a home grown from a tree—furniture, bookshelves, books created from strange materials, a simple kitchen, and a side room where she could just make out a bed hanging from the ceiling.

But she barely saw them. Two cups steamed, undisturbed, from the room's windowsill overlooking the land outside. But the rest of the room appeared as though a tornado had ripped through it.

Horror gripped Sylvie then. Dark green blood splattered everywhere, gruesome and sickening. In one corner, the upper half of Hern the Hunter lay. In another corner, his legs.

The Erlking had been riven in two.

DONATO

21

o, no, no," Sylvie breathed. "What . . . what is this?"

The companions stood, stunned and horrified, the silence in the air like the calm before an approaching thunderstorm. Never had Sylvie felt more impotent. The gruesome scene before her changed everything, in ways her mind raced to comprehend. Hern the Hunter had not supported her, but he had not completely denied her request. He could have been an ally if she'd been given time to discuss the situation with him alone. That would never be, now. Even as the stink of his freed innards assailed her, the realization of how the Erlking's death affected her future left Sylvie wanting to cry, lash out, or both.

"I will tell you what this is," Grumtil replied, hovering over the dead Erlking. "It is an action similar to what happened to you."

It took Sylvie a moment to realize what the sprite meant. "The darkness Agnes spoke of," she said. "She was right. I was right. The Fae did not steal the Covenant Codex from Mont-Saint-Michel. Some other evil sets its will against us. Against us all. Man. Fae. Everyone."

"The kingdom of Man is leaderless," Sizmor said, nodding. "The Twilight Lands of Fae are leaderless."

"Who could be doing this?" Emmer walked the room, Bruyère at the ready as he checked the rest of the domicile. "No one else here."

Before Sylvie could answer, shadowy movement from the roof opening above flickered at the periphery of her sight.

"Beware, Sylvianna Goode!" Belloch roared, rushing her.

Sylvie had just enough time to sense darkness falling upon her as she was flung to the side by the saint. A black and twisted figure landed, far enough away it couldn't reach her easily, red eyes glowing like hot coals blown to life. It crouched low upon two crooked hind legs, howling hatred, splaying wide four arms connected at two shoulders ending in fingers clawed like daggers.

"Changeling!" Grumtil screamed.

The creature bunched and launched itself at Sylvie. Long, extended jaws snapping, it drove her to the floor of the Erlking's home. Just in time, she got Lumière up between her and the creature, the sword hot in her hands. The changeling howled at the sword and its form began morphing into new ones, all taken from nature and the animals living within it: teeth like a giant black bear one moment, the wide gaping mouth of some cat the next. Only its eyes remained the same, hot and angry and burning red fire. Sizmor threw dust at the creature, catching it unaware, the gritty stuff flaring to life the moment it touched the changeling's skin. Fire raged along its form from the sprite magic and it mewled low, in pain, but not enough to drive it away from Sylvie.

With a need born of survival and will, she kept Lumière before her face like a talisman. The blade glowed an ethereal, blinding white. The longer Sylvie held it, the more she felt herself drained, some part of the sword needing her strength to maintain the power it displayed in her defense.

What transpired inside her, though, seemed to have a cumulative effect on the changeling. As she weakened, the light expanded until only the changeling's claws were upon her. It still snarled and snapped at Sylvie, though, still hating the light, still trying to reach her around Lumière.

Then the weight of the changeling left her as it flew to the right.

Emmer stood over her, Bruyère's black blade bloody. The saint's eyes were not on her but on the changeling, who struggled to rise, a deep, dripping slash in its side exposing ribs but already disappearing as though no blow had been dealt. The saint moved to end it.

"No!" Sylvie screamed, getting to her knees. "We need it alive!"

Emmer stopped, his lips whispering something she couldn't hear. Whether it was the saint or Belloch or both having a conversation with one another, Sylvie couldn't tell. He brought Bruyère up again, though, shielding Sylvie from the Fae creature. The effect was immediate. The changeling's eyes went wide—before it leapt for the doorway.

To escape.

Emmer leapt after, and a dark mist permeated Bruyère, the sword a dark swath absorbing the orb light about it, a dark reverberation on the air between blade and unnatural beast.

The changeling flopped to the ground as if struck. It crouched low, mewling, trapped.

"Is the sword commanding the changeling?" Sylvie asked, breathing hard and regaining her feet. "Are we safe from it?"

"Bruyère has control of it. For now. It is incredibly strong; evidence of its master's skill," Belloch hissed, stepping up to the dark creature. The eyes of the changeling burned at the former Erlking, jaws snapping, four clawed hands trying to reach him. *"Ask what you will. I will compel it to answer."*

Before she could do so, the changeling screamed—the sound so horrific it nearly drove Sylvie to the floor—and then lost form, lost substance and connection, its limbs separating like pieces of a quilt pulled apart to hit wetly on the ground, flesh and muscle falling away from bone, until only a crimson slop of quivering flesh remained, the stench of its insides making Sylvie want to vomit and flee.

The eyes hovered above the creature for a time, though, burning at Sylvie. She stared back, aghast. Then the flames winked out like snuffed candles even as its heavy head hit the floor. She thought she saw the approximation of a grin spreading across the changeling's face before disintegrating along with the rest of it.

"Why did you do that?" Grumtil yelled, the sprite flying to confront Belloch.

"I did nothing," Belloch growled. *"Its master did that, not I."*

Sylvie wanted to rage—at the remains of the changeling, at Emmer, at the sprites, at the entire world and its cruelty and hardship—for any information she could have gleaned from the changeling had now vanished.

Just then, another Fae materialized in the doorway. Sylvie breathed relief when she realized it was a Fae loyal to the Erlking.

Rerell. The Seneschal of the Shadow Court.

"The Erlking," he whispered, terror in his eyes, backing away. "You did this!"

"No," Sylvie said at once. She lowered Lumière. "We discovered a plot to harm both Man and Fae. With the help of Belloch and Emmer, I escaped the labyrinth in which Hern the Hunter placed me. And the situation is so dire, both Belloch and Emmer accompanied me, to overcome the unknown evil will set against us all. The sloppy remains on the ground there . . . that changeling . . . attacked us after it killed the Erlking." She paused, staring hard at him. "Why are *you* here? It seems very convenient that you arrived just as we did."

"Belloch?" Rerell said, frowning. Gills at the side of his neck Sylvie hadn't seen before fluttered as he stared at Emmer. "That cannot be."

"It is I, Rerell, enslaved to this Man's body," the former Erlking said. *"Though I do not look like my former self, I assure you it is I. You would be wise to listen."*

"Can you prove such a statement?" the Fae requested.

"The loss of your sire, Ramall, during that battle with Man so long ago still grieves me," Belloch said, head lowered. *"He was one of my closest allies. Not even Emmer knew that."*

Rerell bowed to Emmer and Belloch. "I am convinced."

"Why are you here?" Sylvie pressed, ignoring the reunion.

"I always take tea with Lord Hern," Rerell stammered, gesturing at the two cups by the window. "We discuss the events of the day and decide upon the importance of the next one."

"I can confirm it is a long-held ritual for the Seneschal," Grumtil said.

"Very well," Sylvie nodded. She looked to the Erlking's remains, fearing what would happen if the Fae decided she was at fault. "What will happen now? The Fae need a leader."

Grumtil grunted. "I am just pleased we all survived that." The sprite glanced around the room and shook his head, tugging at his beard. "We bring the Shadow Court here, to view what has taken place. Then it will convene, to name a new Erlking."

"It is not a simple process," Belloch warned. *"It takes the members of the Shadow Court three or four seasons to finalize a choice."*

"It is mentioned in the Covenant Codex," Emmer added. "Man and Fae are quite different in how they approach a coronation. A month for Man; a year for Fae."

"A year?" Sylvie stammered. "I cannot wait that long to speak with the next Erlking."

Grumtil shrugged. "It is our way."

The odor of the dead changeling suffocated even the silence in the room. Rerell went to the top half of Hern the Hunter—eyes darting at them as if he'd be attacked at any moment—and then knelt. He picked up the two sets of horns that had sloughed off the Erlking's head when he died. They were black and shimmered in the orb light. Sylvie saw a tear roll down the thin Fae's cheek; it touched her that the Fae were not all that different from Man.

"Rerell, I came here for a copy of the Covenant Codex," Sylvie said, keeping her voice soft and steady, trying not to scare the Fae while thinking her way out of the debacle. "I told the Erlking and the Shadow Court the same. I need the book." She paused, considering the pile of offal on the floor. "Now, matters are worse. I need the book but for both of our peoples. For we have a common enemy that threatens us."

"I will do no such thing," Rerell whispered, eyes flicking from

Sylvie to Emmer. He stood, towering over everyone. "It will take the Shadow Court convening to discover the truth of which you speak. It will take the Erlking to decide what is to come of the book."

"Sadly, we do not have time for that, Rerell," Emmer said, gripping Bruyère until his knuckles whitened.

"Listen to my words, Rerell, and heed them well," Belloch added. *"Do this. I confirm it. Retrieve the book. It will be one small part in setting right what has been done."*

"What if you are merely a pawn, Belloch?"

Belloch barked a laugh. *"Have I ever been a pawn? You once knew me. I know you hear me within my words."*

Rerell looked from Sylvie and the sprites back to Emmer.

"I do," he admitted.

"Move, then," Belloch ordered. *"We have little time."*

With a furtive look backward, Rerell left. Long moments passed. Sylvie was about to ask Sizmor and Grumtil to locate the Seneschal when the Fae returned, holding the book she had come hoping to acquire. He went to Emmer, who accepted the book. "I will give this to you and no other, Belloch. I could very well be executed for this. Do care for it. I would prefer you request it from the Shadow Court, but we both know what would result in that situation."

"We know," Grumtil said. "Chreek and perhaps several other members of the Shadow Court would use this for their own gain. They would imprison all of us and use it as leverage to gain favor with the new Erlking. When Sylvianna Goode and the Fae are not enemies."

"Whoever sent that changeling is the true enemy," Sylvie argued. "The Shadow Court *must* be made to see it. I need the Fae on our side."

The sprites looked to one another. Emmer frowned.

"If you remain, Chreek will see you returned to the labyrinth, with no Erlking to counter his desires," Sizmor argued, shaking his leafy head. "Is that a good path to take? Is the reward worth that kind of risk?"

"What if Belloch spoke to the Shadow Court?" she asked, looking to Emmer.

"It would not matter, Sylvianna Goode," Belloch said. *"The Shadow Court would consider me compromised, being within a Man's body. I would not be trusted."*

Sylvie saw what they meant, the realizations striking her like a fist in her stomach. She was caught. Damned if she did, damned if she didn't. The trap had been laid and the choice before her was one of anguish.

"You are right. I cannot risk it," Sylvie admitted. She turned to the Seneschal. "Rerell, you are welcome to join us. Once the Shadow Court learns of what has transpired here, they may not look kindly on you. You could be named an accomplice to Man. I doubt that would go well for you. Too many have been harmed for me; I do not wish it to happen to you. Though I cannot say for sure those in my kingdom wouldn't fear you—creating an even more difficult situation for you to deal with."

"I am the Seneschal of the Shadow Court," Rerell said, gills fluttering. Long-fingered hands steepled before him, he looked upon her with stoic resolve. "I have served for centuries. I survived the period when Belloch resigned his Lordship. I will survive this." He paused, gesturing at the dead changeling. "I will share this news. Perhaps the Shadow Court will ally with you when they discover the true nature of the Erlking's death."

Grumtil flew to the doorway. "We best go. Time is short."

No one said a word. They filed out of the Erlking's abode and took the steps through the massive oak back to the ground. Emmer held the Covenant Codex, his lackhand arm hugging it to his chest like a baby—sure and tender. The sprites spread out, scouting their way forward, to keep them safe. Soon they returned to the dark woodlands of Allemagne Forest and gained the pathway winding west, to the Vosges Mountains, the First Knight, his squire, and the light-weaving acolyte ahead.

Though she understood the reasons for haste, it pained Sylvie to leave. She should have been pleased. She had acquired the Covenant Codex, as she had planned. And not only that, but she had gained Saint Emmer and Wise Belloch as allies. Yet she felt hollow.

She now understood that a dangerous foe had set its sights against Man and Fae alike. The menace couldn't be known or seen, but it was out there, waiting.

They walked through the night, the sprites leading. Exhausted from lack of sleep and the day's turmoil, Sylvie continued onward, unwilling to slow. She would not fail. She *could* not fail. The world she knew had collapsed around her. Only she held the knowledge of what had transpired; only she carried Lumière and had managed to discover Bruyère. She would take back her father's crown, share the clues she had uncovered with her siblings, and root out the evil set against them all.

The grade sloped toward the Vosges Mountains, the forest still thick around them. It seemed to take forever to win free of the Twilight Lands. Then a barely perceived shift in the light drew Sylvie's attention behind her. There, faint brightening occurred, the approach of dawn. And after a few more steps forward, she spotted a faint orange light ahead through the trees.

The early morning fire for Mikkel, Ezel, and Arn.

Sylvie quickened her pace despite her legs burning. Mikkel rose from his log seat, his surprise becoming happiness. Ezel also rose, her eyes moving between those who approached. She hung her head then, her dark eyes above their veil sad, realizing the gravity of the world's loss.

Sylvie nodded to Mikkel, who returned the greeting. They no longer needed words to communicate. She went to Ezel instead, placing Lumière on the ground, and hugged the other in hopes of sharing grief.

"How did she die? Was it a worthy death?" The acolyte's dark eyes shimmered as she gripped Sylvie's arms.

Wiping away her own tears, Sylvie related everything that had transpired since she had left the campsite—and how the Prioress Mother had saved them when they had no options left.

"It is the light's will," Ezel said. "Agnes knew it better than anyone. When she felt the sword on the day's sunshine, she knew she had to try and reach you. That you couldn't escape on your own. That you needed help only a light-weaver could offer. I tried to go in her stead. She wouldn't have it. Agnes did this for you. Let's hope her loss isn't in vain."

They held one another. The light-weaver recovered quickly and, slightly embarrassed, stepped away to help Arn prepare the horses.

"Emmer and Belloch, this is my First Knight, Mikkel Goode. My half-brother. I trust him with my life. You can too."

"You have the book. We should get moving," Mikkel said, already dousing the fire with water and then moving to gather their things. "We must win free of these mountains and put distance between us and the Twilight Lands. From what you said, the Fae may hold you responsible."

"You've been fine here?" she asked.

"Worried about you," he said, then shrugged. "Guess I had right to be."

Sylvie turned to find the older sprite. "Grumtil, will you be joining us?"

He nodded. "I am already out of favor with the Shadow Court."

That pleased Sylvie. She needed all the allies she could get. Once the horses were prepared and their belongings strapped down, they left the campsite on horseback, Emmer with Bruyère riding Agnes's mount. Arn took the lead, while Mikkel brought up the retinue's rear, the First Knight keeping his eyes on Allemagne Forest for any sign of pursuit by the Fae. By midmorning, they were cresting the pass of the Vosges Mountains, the kingdom of Man awaiting on the other side.

Sylvie halted, feeling eyes on her back.

She looked over her shoulder.

There stood Peagle, long horn glowing faintly in the rising sunshine. The unicorn did not move but simply stood there, ethereal, its big, liquid eyes luminescent. He then watched them depart, and Sylvie was filled with the mournful sorrow emanating from the beautiful Fae creature—but also strength for what was to come.

Then the unicorn faded from sight as if it had never been.

"Was that what I think it was?" Arn asked, blinking.

"That is a powerful omen to witness," Belloch said. *"Peagle does not appear for just anyone."*

"I hope it improves our future," Mikkel said. "From the sounds of it, we will need it."

Sylvie thought about the goodness of the unicorn—and the evil that had stared at her within the Erlking's home. Before the changeling had dissolved, its fiery eyes had seemed to separate and hover above the body, the malevolence controlling the creature perceiving them one last time before blinking out.

"Are you all right, Sylvianna?" Sizmor asked, hovering beside her.

"Nothing is right," Sylvie said, shaking her head, aware the others were watching her with the same concern. "Remember the eyes of the changeling as it disintegrated?" She looked back the way they had come, as if she could return to the scene and discover the truth. "I could feel the malice in that creature. Ancient. Powerful. And it . . . came from nowhere and everywhere. I can't explain it. Even as the changeling disintegrated, I thought I saw that horrible mouth grin one last time and the eyes hover outside its collapsing body—almost as if it had two sets of eyes altogether."

"What kind of devilry do you think it was?" Arn asked.

They all looked to one another. Soon they were watching Emmer, who seemed to be having one of his inner dialogues with Belloch, his eyes darting this way and that, a sweat breaking out on his forehead.

"I sensed it. Tell her, Emmer," the former Erlking growled finally.

Emmer looked from face to face as if trying to find another answer. Not finding one, he finally turned toward Sylvie, a darkness in his eyes she hadn't seen before.

"Sylvianna Goode, the entity controlling the changeling was a witch."

EPILOGUE

ylvianna Goode breathed the warm afternoon air, settling her dark thoughts.

The day sprawled before her, not a cloud in the sky. The group had spent the night near a bubbling creek, able to finally relax after fleeing Allemagne Forest. The farther from the Twilight Lands they got, the safer she felt, though so many questions remained. While they ate a simple dinner around a small fire, Sylvie and Emmer shared everything they had learned. It helped her put puzzle pieces together. Yet the truth of the situation remained: a witch had set her will against Man and Fae alike and was willing to see all the world burn if need be. And that wasn't the only storm ahead. She was returning to a kingdom at war.

It left her sad in a way she hadn't felt since the death of Master Kell. A part of her was happy her old mentor couldn't see what had become of the kingdom he had helped forge. When her father had Named her heir, Sylvie knew it would be difficult. But not like this.

And the witch was out there somewhere—plotting and hating.

At least Sylvie had found the Covenant Codex, Emmer and Belloch, and not one sword but two to counter the evil that had sprouted from long-sown seeds.

It would have to do. For now.

"Company approaches us," Mikkel said, shielding his eyes from the late-afternoon sun.

Sylvie saw what he meant. A column of dust rose in the distance, growing larger. After a while, it became clear who had found them, the standard at the head of the mounted warriors familiar.

"I doubt we will be able to lie our way out this time," Arn said, snorting.

The sprites vanished. Sylvie took the lead, moving her horse to the front. Mikkel waited alongside her, sword drawn.

He prepared for the worst even as she hoped for the best.

Lady Erlina rode directly to them, slowing her horse from a canter to a walk. The beard of Captain Boden Allard flamed beneath the sun. Dozens of warriors formed the column behind him—weapons glinting. Sylvie was aware that the soldiers all looked at her.

Lady Erlina shook her head when she saw her. "I might have known."

"Sister," Sylvie greeted.

"Well, well, looks like I won't be imprisoned in a dungeon after all, Lady Erlina," Captain Boden said, the Red Bear grinning through his bushy beard.

"Do not be so quick to think so," Erlina shot back angrily. She turned back to Sylvie and her brow darkened further. "Sylvianna, what are you doing in my dukedom? You managed to evade my captain once before, because he is clearly daft. Why remain?"

"Surveying my kingdom," Sylvie said, shrugging. "Though I do miss the salty wind of Mont-Saint-Michel. I think we will return home soon."

Lady Erlina grinned without humor. "I think not. Not even Mikkel can help you now. He is mortal, and he is outnumbered."

"We have no intention of fighting you," Sylvie said. "Or your men."

"That is wise," Erlina said, looking from Emmer to Ezel and then back to Sylvie. "A member of your party is no longer with you. An old light-weaver. Where is she?"

"Prioress Mother Agnes died in Allemagne Forest, protecting

Sylvie," Ezel Fela said, the acolyte sitting straight in her saddle, eyes dark with power. "Respect her sacrifice."

"I am sad to hear that," Captain Boden interjected, though he drew ire from his duchess. "She was quite formidable. For a liar and a cheat, she was amusing in her own way. A pity. I looked forward to seeing her again."

"Quiet, Captain," Erlina ordered. "You grow soft with sentiment. You've lost your steel."

Captain Boden shrugged and said nothing more.

"Lady Erlina, we must talk. Soon and at length," Sylvie said, hoping to disentangle herself from her sister. "There is much you do not know. Much the *others* do not know. Evil has returned to the kingdom. Bickering and squabbling between us will do nothing but embolden that evil."

"What she says is true, Lady," Emmer added. "Time is short, and we must be steadfast."

"Who is this man who thinks he may speak to me without being spoken to?" Erlina asked, eyes flashing.

Sylvie thought about lying. Then she decided there was no reason to hide the truth.

"He is Saint Emmer."

Captain Boden laughed, and his men did the same. Humor filled the afternoon. Emmer wasn't amused, though.

And neither was Erlina. "Lies," she scoffed. "You are no different from Idlor."

"She is a great deal different from Lord Idlor," a man said loudly, trotting upon his white mount from the rear of the warriors. He sat high in his saddle, shoulders back, his short-trimmed beard showing more gray than brown. It was his eyes, though, that captured Sylvie. They were the icy color of a winter sky free of clouds but contained a twinkling mirth that made him appear a great deal younger than his winters.

"Myrddin Emrys, you come when not called and not at all when needed," Lady Erlina growled, clearly annoyed. "If I could force you to leave, I would. Stay out of this. It is a family affair and is therefore none of yours."

"The future is my affair, and I will do as I see fit. I am pleased to see Emmer and Belloch here." He nodded to the saint. Then the man—whose name Sylvie could not believe to be true—inclined his head toward her. "Lady Sylvianna, I trust you are as well as can be, given your last few days and your current situation?"

"Myrddin Emrys? Do you mean like the Merlin from before even Saint Emmer's birth?" Sylvie questioned, unable to believe it. "From the time of Uther and Arthur Pendragon? It's not possible. You'd be over a thousand years old."

"I would think a woman who has met Peagle would not begrudge the possible," Myrddin Emrys said. He smiled, though, and when his wrinkles deepened, it was like a sun rising, as if no danger existed in the whole world, despite the armed men around them. "We shall convene soon, you and me, once we arrive at Lady Erlina's residence. We have much to discuss."

"You will have no such access to her," Erlina said. "Unless I deem it necessary."

Myrddin Emrys said nothing more. He merely sat in his saddle and grinned all the more.

"What do you plan on doing with us, Lady Erlina?" Sylvie asked. She spoke up so her voice carried over the multitude of warriors. "I am the rightful heir to High King Alafair's throne. He Named me thus. Not you nor Myrddin Emrys nor anyone else can change that."

"I can change it by taking you prisoner, of course," Erlina said, ordering her warriors to spread out around Sylvie and her friends. "Pike will be quite interested in this."

Sylvie couldn't believe it. "You are allied to Lord Pike?"

Erlina laughed, a sound with no amusement. "You are so young. Naive. You have much to learn." She turned to her captain. "Bring them all. We ride hard for home; I will not sleep outdoors again. Or I'll chop that beard off your face or your head from your shoulders with it."

Captain Boden roared his orders. Sylvie looked to her companions. They stared at her as if she could do something about it. She was at a loss, though. She turned her stare at Saint Emmer and the man named Myrddin Emrys—the former shrugging and the latter giving her a quick wink, his lack of worry confusing her more. She sat her horse, unable to come up with a solution, and realized maybe she didn't have one.

Besides the witch being out there somewhere, the thing Sylvie feared most had come true.

One of her siblings had found her.

HERE ENDS Book One of Old World Tales.
Book Two, *The Witch-Wiled Wizard,* will reveal more
about Sylvianna Goode and her loyal companions as
they attempt to discover the witch behind the fracturing
kingdom and what evil intentions are driving them.

GLOSSARY

Agnes—nun, light-weaver, and Prioress Mother (formerly Prioress Superior) of Clair-de-Lune Abbey

Alafair Goode—High King of Royaume de France, He Who Wields the Light of Lumière, the Final Bane of Mordreadth; served as High King for nearly a century, his long life granted and protected by the gift of a witch

Alent Loronn—Knight of the Ecclesia and Legate of the Citadel at the time of High King Alafair Goode

Allemagne Forest—forest in the Twilight Lands, just across the eastern border of Royaume de France

Alpz Mountains—a sky-high mountain range that runs east-west to the south of Royaume de France and the Twilight Lands of the Fae

Annwn—the Otherworld or Afterlife, where Arthur Pendragon is said to reside still

Arn Tomm—teenaged street thief, works for the Kraken and serves as squire to Sir Mikkel Goode

Battle of the Three Immortals—historical battle in which the kingdom of Royaume de France became one

Belloch—Erlking of the Twilight Lands in ages past, also known as Wise Belloch

Bishops of the Citadel—leaders of the Church in Mont-Saint-Michel

Boden Allard—captain of soldiers serving Lady Erlina and her dukedom; nicknamed Red Bear

Brose—Fae, Elder of the Shadow Court

Bruyère—sword of Saint Emmer, used to end the Great War between Man and Fae

Cardinal Bishop—first among the Bishops of Mont-Saint-Michel

changeling—a shapeshifting Fae, created rather than born or grown, very rare

Chelle—partner of Sir Mikkel Goode before his disgrace

Citadel—fortress built on Mont-Saint-Michel; also refers to the spiritual/religious institution headquartered there

Citadel Assassin—secret role directed by and protecting the Bishops and the religious institution of the Citadel

Clair-de-Lune—town at the foot of the hill on which Clair-de-Lune Abbey sits

Clair-de-Lune Abbey—primary home of the light-weaver nuns

Cliffside—mainland city that lies just across the sand bridge from Mont-Saint-Michel

Collin Goode—Lord of Royaume de France and son of High King Alafair Goode

Compact between Fae and Man—agreement forged by Saint Emmer and Wise Belloch and documented in the Covenant Codexes held by the leaders of Man and Fae

Covenant Codex of Saint Emmer—Man's copy of the magical tome that contains and continues the Compact of peace between Man and Fae; twin to the Covenant Codex of Wise Belloch

Covenant Codex of Wise Belloch—Fae copy of the magical tome that contains and continues the Compact of peace between Man and Fae; twin to the Covenant Codex of Saint Emmer

Darian—squire to Sir Gwain in Mont-Saint-Michel and lover to Sylvianna Raventress

dukedom—one of the seven political divisions of Royaume de France, which are currently led by a direct (legitimate) descendant of the House of Goode

Ecclesia—the ruling council and political institution, headquartered in Mont-Saint-Michel, that rules Royaume de France under the aegis of the High King

Elders of the Shadow Court—members of the ruling council of the Fae in the Twilight Lands

Emmer—monk at the time of the Great War between Man and Fae; sainted for stopping the war, writing the Covenant Codex along with Erlking Belloch, and thus creating the Compact of peace between Man and Fae

Erlina Goode—Lady of Royaume de France and eldest daughter of High King Alafair Goode

Erlking—title of the ruler of the Twilight Lands and premier of the Shadow Court

Ezel Fela—acolyte nun and light-weaver at Clair-de-Lune Abbey

Fae—long-lived denizens of the Twilight Lands with a close connection to nature visible in their physical forms and their communication with each other

fallen-light—a meteorite of rare metal, not found naturally occurring on earth

Great Darkness—an entity of great evil, antithesis to the light

Great War between Man and Fae—historical battle in which the Fae nearly drove Man into the western sea, before being stopped by King Halston Pendragon, Saint Emmer, and their magical swords Lumière and Bruyère

Grumtil Hodgemurkin—Fae, a sprite, spent nearly a century as the Shadow Court–assigned advisor to High King Alafair Goode

Gwain—Knight of the Ecclesia

Halston Pendragon—King of Royaume de France at the time of the Great War between Man and Fae

Hern the Hunter—Erlking of the Shadow Court at the time of High King Alafair Goode

Idlor Goode—Lord of Royaume de France and son of High King Alafair Goode

Kell—Master Historian and stepbrother to Alafair Goode

Kent Goode—Lord of Royaume de France and son of High King Alafair Goode

Knight of the Ecclesia—a knight belonging to the military organization that guards and serves the Ecclesia

Kraken—a master of spies and criminals currently residing in the city of Cliffside

light-telling—a method of storytelling, available only to light-weavers, that uses the power of the light to immerse the viewer in images and emotions

light-weaver—one who wields the power of the light

Lumière—sword forged from fallen-light by the light-weavers of Clair-de-Lune Abbey and wielded by Kings and High Kings of Royaume de France from Halston Pendragon to Alafair Goode

Masters of Mont-Saint-Michel—academics who pursue knowledge and oversee the education of the kingdom

Mikkel Goode—son of High King Alafair Goode and once Knight of the Ecclesia and First Knight of Royaume de France, now disgraced

Miroir Lake—lake in the middle of the Allemagne Forest, in the Twilight Lands

Mont-Saint-Michel—island and fortress home of the Citadel, the Ecclesia, the court of the High King of Royaume de France, and the people of the city that supports them

Mordreadth—the Great Darkness who attempted to enslave the world but was instead destroyed by Alafair Goode

Morgause—a witch; also called Gwyar or Anna

Myrddin Emrys—sorcerer and trusted advisor to King Arthur Pendragon, nearly a thousand years ago

Naming of the Heir—political and magical ceremony in which the High King announces his successor and inscribes their name in the Covenant Codex of Saint Emmer

Peagle—a unicorn

Pike Goode—Lord of Royaume de France and eldest son of High King Alafair Goode

Pontiff—supreme leader of the Bishops of the Citadel in Mont-Saint-Michel

Pridwen—the High King's shield, made from the scale of a dragon

Rerell—Fae, Seneschal of the Shadow Court, keeper of the Covenant Codex of Wise Belloch

Royaume de France—kingdom ruled by the High King in Mont-Saint-Michel

Sanna—nun, light-weaver, and Prioress Superior of Clair-de-Lune Abbey

Scorus—Pontiff of the Citadel at the time of High King Alafair Goode

Secil—Fae, Elder of the Shadow Court

Serath the Shadow—an assassin

Shadow Court—the ruling council of the Fae in the Twilight Lands

Sizmor Darkinmoor—Fae, a sprite, newly assigned advisor to the Named heir of High King Alafair Goode

Sylvianna Raventress—apprentice to Master Historian Kell of Mont-Saint-Michel, Named successor to High King Alafair Goode

Twilight Lands—the lands of the Fae; a wild, dark, and wooded territory

Vérité—the High King's ring, a truth circle

Vosges Mountains—a low mountain range that runs north-south along the border between Royaume de France and the Twilight Lands of the Fae

Wil Cornet—Cardinal Bishop of the Citadel

Yankton Goode—Lord of Royaume de France and son of High King Alafair Goode

ACKNOWLEDGMENTS

Adrian Collins

Who published the first iteration of Sylvie's grimdark tale

David Alpert

Who wouldn't take no for an answer

Robert Kirkman

Who built Skybound Entertainment with the creator first in mind

Alex Antone

Who oversaw this project with knowledge and counsel

Adriel Wilson

Who made the Kickstarter run smooth, smooth, smooth

Nat Sobel

Who championed the book as agent and first reader

Terry Brooks, Jacqueline Carey, Wesley Chu, Robin Hobb, Tamora Pierce, and Anna Smith Spark

Who spent their precious time reading the earliest of drafts

Rachelle Longé McGhee

Who kept everyone on task, including me

Betsy Mitchell

Who brought decades of SF&F editing experience and friendship to the fore

Magali Villeneuve

Who painted a cover even the best Mont-Saint-Michel artists would be envious of

Donato Giancola

Who imagined the Old World in ways I never would have thought of

Nate Taylor

Who agreed to illustrate the graphic novel and ended up in a straitjacket for it

Robert Napton

Who adapted my words into the graphic novel and wound up in the cell next to Nate

My readers

Who take a risk every time I publish a book and yet remain enthusiastic

And finally . . . Kristin Speakman

Who will forever be the most powerful light-weaver in my life

KICKSTARTER BACKERS

Thank you doesn't even begin to express the appreciation I have for the following people (as well as those who did not wish to be named) who supported the Kickstarter campaign for this book and helped make it a success. I am sincerely grateful.

A. Cline • A. Treamayne • A.C. Gray • A.L. Humphries • Aaron Dilday • Aaron Granofsky • Aaron Hollander • Aaron Markworth • Aaron Reidy • Abilash Pulicken • Abra Roth • Ace • Adalyn Ruth Reynolds • Adam Holliday • Adam Loster • Adam Nielsen • Adam Tannir • Adam Wilson • Adam Yarbrough • Adele Pugsley • Adinah Denisse • Adrian Collins • Adrián Francés • Adrienne Eve Gonzalez • AFiteNite • Agnès Metanomski • Ahmed Edwards • Aidan Moher • Aiden • Aiden "Odin" Auty • Akul Singh • Al Pa • Alan • Albert L. Hoyt III • Alec Miller • Alejandro R. Sedeño • Alen Dubinovic • Alenthor101 • Aletia Brauer-Meyers • Alex Figueras • Alex Helm • Alex J • Alex Perry • Alex Whisenhunt • Alex Zeisig • Alexander Denley • Alexander Dickinson • Alexander Nelson • Alexandre • Ali T. Kokmen • Ali Tuttle-Easton • Alice Bentley • Alice Elder • Alicia Hintzen • Alisa • Alisa Chan • Allen Barnhill • Allison Grier • Allison Marie Caron • Ally Shilo • Alma Molinari • Alvaro Erickson • Alysses R. • Amber de Haan • Amber Marshall Lucas • Amber W • Amelia Ray • Amy S. • Andi Scott • Andrea Bicego • Andrea Juneé • Andrea McNeil • Andrew R. Crawford • Andrew Martinez • Andrew Olsen • Andrew Springer • Andrew Jacob Torres • Andrew Williams • Andrew Wright • Andy Adams • Andy Barbieri • Andy Bennett • Andy Bolland • Andy Holcombe • Andy & Ben Rock • Andy 'Alundil' Wintle • Ane-Marte Mortensen • Angel Brandner • Ángela • Angela Gray • Angela Ross • Angela Tucker • Ann Holland • Anna • Anna Emenheiser • Annabelle Kinnear • AnnaMarie • Annie W • Anthony Atthowe • Anthony F. Del Sandro • Anthony Gonzalez • Anthony Juan • April Bendickson • April D. Moore • April Morgan • Ariane Sears • Ariel • Arielle A. Haddad • Aris • Ashley • Ashley Gibson • Ashley Hatter • Asta • Atit Patel • Aubrey & Dylan • Audrey S • Austin Kile • Author Dave Barrett • Author Michael J. Sullivan • Ayantu R. • Azhwi

B J CLIFFORD • B Kieth Cooper • B. Letsinger • Bai Loki • Baird Searle • Bambam Aquino • BanesKnightfall • Banshie R. • Beki Romeis-Markham • Ben Jacobson •

Beni Cheni • Benjamin Akers • Benjamin Hatch • Benjamin Hopman • Benjamin Huang • Benjamin Molina • Benjamin Ryan • Benjamin Spademan • Benjamin Suan • Berta Batzig • Bet Zyx • Beth • Beth Dean • Beth Holley • Beth Tabler • Bethany Vann • Bethany Wood • Bev Nelson • Bhelliom Demian Rahl • Bill Bosley • Bill Cornette • Bill Fannin • Bill Oconnell • Billy • Billy Clawson • Billy Taylor • Blake Hansen • Bob Milne • Bobby McKnight • Bodhi Kish • Boe Kelley • Bonk! • Bonnie Ross • Brad Rohrer • Bradley Roar (bookswithespresso) • Brady Brewer • Branden Prentice-Brooks • Brandon Baratono • BRANDON EASTON • Brandon Fite • Brandon Hall • Brandon J. Neal • Brandy Yeazell • Braydon Roberts • Breanne Iseler • Bren Andrew Aguirre • Bren the Librarian • Brenda J Hand • Brendon Grimm • Bret Harris • Brett Samek • Bri Weiss • Brian Becker • Brian Bolvin • Brian Gold • Brian Gressler • Brian Horen • Brian Meadows • Brian Noonan • Brian Weicker • Brian Whiting • Brian, Kay & Joshua Williams • Brittney Nowicki • Brock Sager • Brook Freeman • Brooke Pownceby • Brooks • Bruce F. • Bruce Villas • Bryan Adams • Bryan Hill • Bryan Wood • Butch Hanson

C Sperry • C Taormina • C. Corbin Talley • C. Harris • Cait Greer • Caitlin • Caitlin Aha • Caitlin Kelly • Caitlin Northcutt • Caitlin Steele • Caleb E. Durrant • Caledonia • Callum Paff • Cam Thomas • Cameron Morris • Cameron Rush • Can Acar • Carissa Badenoch • Carl Plunkett • Carol • Caroline Luu • Carson K. • Carver Rapp • Cary Meriwether • Casey Beck • Casey Mahoney • Casie Powers • Casper • Casper Wong • Cassandra Baubie • Cassandra Rose • Cat Parker • Catherine Holmes • Cathleen Atela • Catie Murphy • ccrider • Cecil Mathis • Chadrick Hess • Char Clinger • Charles M. Gatlin, Jr. • Charles E Goodrich III • Charles Jackson • Charles Mc • Charles J Munn III • Charles Norton • Charley Hearn • Charlie • Charlie Grayson • Charlotte • Charoi • Chase de Groot • Chelsea Persen • Cheryl Costella • Cheryl Karoly • Cheryl Ruckel • Chip Page • Chris • Chris Bernardo • Chris Bristow • Chris Crowe • Chris Gaboury • Chris Gerber • Chris Harvey • Chris Haught • Chris Hoover • Chris Marp • Chris Messer • Chris Prew • Chris Schwartz • Chris Smith • Chris Vodraska • Christi Sch • Christian Bonilla • Christian Dos Reis • Christian Tempro • Christin Smith • Christina Szemethy • Christine LePage • Christine Skolnick • Christoph van Dommelen • Christopher Adolph • Christopher Birkinbine • Christopher Horn • Christopher R. Perry • Christopher Taylor (ThePapaTee) • Cillian O'Neil • Cindy Beehler • Cindy Rouch • Cindy Zapawa • Claire Ramsey • Claire Rosser • Clarissa Ching • Claudia Aguirre • Cliff • Cliff Winnig • Cody Perry • Cole Holman • Collin M Johnson • Connie Lee Lynch • Connor Bradley • Connor Wesley Frye • Corey Peterson • Corky LaVallee • Corwin Mead • Cory Miller • Cotina S. • Courtney • Courtney Getty • Courtney M • Craig • Craig Cawley • Craig Dyson • Craig Massey • Crestienne Bertrand • Crystal F • Cynthia Conner

Dale A. Russell • Daleth • Damian Gordon • Damien Child • Damon Morton • Dan Andrews • Dan Dalal • Dan Grove • Dan Holland • Dana Silber • Dane Northrup • Daniel W. Ahrens • Daniel Ashwell • Daniel Diez Blazquez • Daniel Edwards • Daniel Govar • Daniel Griffith • Daniel J Holman • Daniel Kirwan • Daniel S. Lee • Daniel D Magnan • Daniel 'Iowa' Mears • Daniel Merchant • Daniel Milton • Daniel E Roberts • Danielle Sherman • Dannel Stanley • Danny Kriegbaum Laursen • Danny Lundy • Danny Pearman • Darcy Harrison • Darian Pedford • Darko Z302 • Darren • Darren Pallant • Darth •

Dave Baughman • Dave Nee • Dave P. • David Bobbitt • David Charlton • David A. Dick • David H L Edwards • David Gonyeau • David Guiot • David A Harris • David Hummel • David K. Leighton • David F. McCloskey • David McEwen • David J. Moran (Tyrik of Delonvale) • David Noller, HMBT • David Parish • David Perry • David Renback • David Mark Roberts • David Robinson • David Roth • David "Honorary Knight of the Word" Salchow • David Tai • Davyd Coe • Dawn M.C. Webb • Dawn Marie • Dead Fishie • Dean Marconi • Dean Whirley • Deanna Zinn • Deb McKelvey • Deborah Hedges • Deborah Torrance • Deborah Yerkes • Deleva Stanley • Denis Gagnon • Denise Fuentes Alcaraz • Dennis Parslow • Derek • Derek Devereaux Smith • Derrick Bucey • Derrick J. Ranostaj • Diana E. Garcia • Diana Vecchio • Diego Avendano-Morineau • Diff • Dipin Nayee • Djerri Nuijen • Dominic De La O • Dominique Knobben • Don Forster • DonnyJr (DefiantGod) • Dorothy Raniere • Doug Erling • Doug Thomson • Douglas Cline • Dr. Chris Yeary • Dr. Nina Semjonous • Dr. Ray Barker • Drew Rhoades • Drew Ricketts • DrLov1n • Duane Powell • Dudley Pajela • Dumah Die • Duncan Wilcox • Dustin Warford • Dylan Underhill • Dyllan McCartin • Dyrk Ashton

E • E.M. Middel • EClaire • Ed • Eden • Edresa Ramos • Eduardo Soriano • Edward Abbott • Edward Kenyon • Eileen • Eileen Walling • Eilliam Goodwill • Elaine Elias • Elena Maureen Martinez • Elijah M. • Elizabeth Illyia-Noelle Allen • Elizyann Taylor • Ellen • Elyse M Grasso • Em • EM Saffel • emanuele iacono • Emerald • Emilie Woog • Emily "Missy Boo" Adams • Emily Omizo Whittenberg • Emma Adams • Emmanouil Paris • Emmanuel MAHE • Emperor Milano • Eoin Fagan • Eric Burnham • Eric Chase • Eric Deutschbauer • Eric Krul • Eric Lienhard • Eric Matson • Eric Porter • Eric Quartetti • Eric Stamber • Eric Vilbert • Eric Werner • Erich Rau • Erin @ WonderLesch • Erin DeBiase • Erin Richards • Erin Walyor • Esko Lakso • Evan Miller • Evan W. Anderson

F Scott Valeri • Fabian • Fatima Fayez • FawnoftheWoods • Felqrom • Fidelio Hawkeye • Flora C. Possumtail • Folletto • Francis • Francis Floyd Occena • Francis Wallace • Franck Picardat • Frank Iasparri • Frank Jur • Frank Klein • Frank Wright • Freddie Moriarti

G. Fisher • Gabriel Rivers • Gabrielle • Gabrielle Camassar • Galen W Miller • Gargoyle • Garth C. Almgren • Garvin Anders • Gary Todd Heath • Gary Lombardo • Gary G Nordmann • Gary Olpin • Gary Olsen • Gary Phillips • Gaurav • Gavin Fast • Gelar Phahla • Gene Farley • Gene McLaughlin • Genesis • Georg Egger • George J. Wheeler, Jr. • Gerald P. McDaniel • Gerard White • Gerda März • Gianna Claudio • Gidon Uriel • Giles Arms • Gina P • Giulio Torla • Glen Vogelaar • Glenn M Tharp • @GoGeekGirl • Goose • Gordon Tellefsen • Graham Dauncey • Grant B. • Graverazor • Greg Bergerson • Greg Hansford • Gregory Alix • Greybear • Griff Massey • Griffin

Håkan Ståby • Hank • Hannah M • Hansi • Harley Hannon • Harold van Bolhuis • Harper Ethan • Harvey Howell • Heather • Heather A-W Prestenback • Heather Bessman • Heather Cooper • Heather Harrington • Heather Joyner • Heidi K. Allen • Heiko Koenig • Helen McMillin • Helen & Glenn Stratakes • Helmut Köhler Mendizábal • Hennie Giani • Herm Wong • Hex • Hilary • hms • Hollie Lillico • Holly Bowers • Holly Marie • Hope Terr • Hugh • Hugo Essink • Humphrey Huang • Huntyr Green

Ian Bannon • Ian Bauer • Ian Greenfield • Ian Harvey • Ian Meason • Ian Visintine • Ilia Danilov • ILIYAN ILIEV • Ironsoul • Isaac Ben-Ezra • Isaac 'Will It Work' Dansicker • Isabella Schlorer • Ishmael • Island Richards • Ivan Jones • Izo

J LaBelle • J R Forst • J. M. Kelzenberg • J.D.L. Rosell • Jack Baer • Jack McGuire • Jackie A. Ogle Pencka • Jacob H Joseph • Jacob Magnusson • Jacob Malevich • Jacob Watt • Jacqueline • Jake Dietsche • Jakob Barnard • Jalle Van Goidsenhoven • James • James Ball III • James Danko • James W. Hutchinson • James M Joyce • James Kennamer • James Kralik • James Lagos-Antonakos • James Martin • James Matson • James Montanus • James Morrison • James Rao • James Robblee • James Rukstalis • James F. Schutt • James Zheng • James-Neil A. McCabe • Jamie Ayers • Jamie Mynott • Jan Dierker • Janet • Janet Dray • Janet Lam • Jaques Retief Andre • Jared Ferguson • Jarret Dahms • Jasmine Morgado • Jason • Jason Breining • Jason Burt • Jason 'XenoPhage' Frisvold • Jason G. Gray • Jason Marsala • Jason Martin • Jason McDonald • Jason Perfetto • Jason Smith • Jason Templeton • Jasper • Javier Heredia • Jay Lofky • JD Hall • JD Hobbes • Jean M Pearce • Jean Sitkei • Jean-François Lacroix • Jeannie Born • Jeannine Cheney • Jeb Wieland • Jedidiah Blake II • Jeff • Jeff Ahlstedt • Jeff Granger • Jeff Meiring • Jeff Pena • Jeff Thacker • Jeffrey S. Gardner • Jeffrey M. Johnson • Jen • Jen Burns • Jenetic • Jenn M.K. • Jenn Strohschein • Jennalyn Davis • Jennifer • Jennifer Colton • Jennifer L. Pierce • Jennifer Wilson • Jennine • Jenny Busby • Jens Helvig Dahl • Jeremiah Jo • Jeremy Brett • Jeremy Howard • Jeremy Patelzick • Jeremy Pinske • Jeremy Rametes • Jes Golka • Jessica Br • Jessica H Davis • Jessica M Fee • Jessica Jett • Jessica Maass • Jessica Meade • Jessica Smith • Jessica Wilcox • Jezza • Jill McGillicuddy • Jim Bassett • Jim Ryan • Jimmy Guikema • Jiunn Tai • JL Franke • Jo Jo • Jo PM • Joan Digney • Joanna Rennix • Joanna Schaff • João Gilberto Lamarão da Silva • Jodi Buckett VanWormer • Joe Anders • Joe Burgert • Joe Field • Joe Kaplan • Joe R. • Joe Scheuer • Joel Dupont • Joel Lee Liberski • Joel Rosen • Joel S Trabado • Joey Linzey • John M Allen • John Caboche • John F. Chattaway • John Conlan • John Ewalt • John Franklin • John Gilligan • John Hodgetts • John Iadanza • John Idlor • John Nicholson • John Osmond • John Riggs • John S Roberge • John Sabia • John C Spainhour • John B Spinks • Johnny B • JohnPG • Joi Tribble • Jon Berlinski • Jon Brenas • Jon Lie • Jon Marshburn • Jon Schneider • Jonathan • Jonathan Adams • Jonathan Daysen • Jonathan Hamm • Jonathan D. Hashimoto • Jonathan Hutchinson • Jonathan Livet • Jonathan Mendonca • Jonathan Olsson • Jonathan Piedmont • Jonathan Salvin • JonathanF • Jonny Nilsson • Jonny Walker • Jordan Hibbits • Jorge Cordero Martínez • Joris Maes • Jörn Flath • Jose Javier Soriano Sempere • Jose Rojas • Josef de Castro • Joseph S. Fleischman • Joseph W. Germano Jr • Joseph Kinkead • Joseph Nephew • Joseph Pritchard • Joseph Reininger • Joseph Rice • Joseph Steck • Josh • Josh Gambill • Josh Herndon • Joshua Arnold • Joshua Beardslee • Joshua Bradley • Joshua Callahan • Joshua Copper • Joshua Furman • Joshua Hardy • Joshua Kensler • Joshua McGinnis • Joshua L Roe • Joshua Smith • Joshua Smith • Joshua Stingl • Joshua Struss • Josie • Josie Noble • Joyce Bashford • Joyce & Gary Phillips • Judy Hudgins • Judy Vandagriff • Juha Tuominen • Julian Del • Justin Barba • Justin C' de Baca • Justin G • Justin Greer • Justin James • Justin Lloyd • Justin S

K Stoker • K. Florence • K. Vick • Kaden • Kahleb Kensinger • Kaitlund Zupanic • Kang930 • Karen • Karen Cobbley • Karen Kaplan • Karen LeDuc • Karen M • Karin Holt •

Karishma Patel • Karissa Tedrow • Karl Ansell • Karlo Openiano • Kasper Grøftehauge • Kassidee • Kat • Kat James • Kate Joy • Kate Mackay • Kate Stuppy • Katherine Lee • Katherine Randall • Katherine Shipman • Kathleen O'Hara • Kathryn "Aryn" Bennett • Katie Gale • Katie Pawlik • Katrina Hamilton • Katrinka • Kay Finnegan • Kay Martens • Kayla Bafrali • Keidy Zuniga • Keith Dolan • Keith E. Hartman • Keith West, Future Potentate of the Solar System • Kel • Kellmar • Kelly Flynn • Kelsey • Kelsey Hart • Kelsey Stenberg • Kelvin Neely • Ken Roberts • Kenneth E Baker • Kenneth E. Bragg • Kenneth Geary • Kenneth Hoppe • Kenneth J. Lindsey • Kenneth Skaldebø • Kenny • Kent Barnes • Kent Clark • Kerry aka Trouble • Kerry Stubbs • Kevin Bell • Kevin Chang • Kevin A. Fidacaro • Kevin Gliner • Kevin Grønberg Poulsen • Kevin McNaught • Kevin Pittman • Kevin G Scott • Kevin Sluss • Kevin Welch • Kevin Z • KHALED AHMED KHALIL HUSAIN • Kid Metroid • Kim Alice • Kim Brodie • Kim Edströmer Sandelin • Kim Pham • Kim Wand • Kimberley Dubberley • Kimberly • Kirasha Urqhart • Kits Knight • Kjell van der Kroon • KnavishOsprey • Kneena Levert • Kolby Durocher • "Korina" • Kramer Walz • Kris Alexander • Kris Spiesz • Krishna Patel • Kristen & Eric Terlep • Kristian Handberg • Kristin Gallagher • Kristin Linnen • Kristin Taggart • Kristina S. Reynosa • Kristopher Ecklof • Kristopher Jerome • Kristy Kearney • Kristy Lorenz • Kristy Van Wyhe • Krysti • Krystina Roupe • Kurt Johansen • KurtD0g • Kyle Baker • Kyle Montcrieff-Prokop • Kyle Mowatt • Kyle Niemeyer • Kyle Spencer • Kyle Webster • Kyle A. Yawn

L Wills • Lady Gonzales of Aragon • Lark Cunningham • Lars Bess • Larson Steffek • LAT • Laura E Winfree • Laura Miller • Lauren • Lauren McKee • Lauren Potts • Lauren Wu • LAURENT SCHAEFFER • Laurie M Edwa • Laurie Harper • Laurie Schuberg • Laurie Seftn • Law Wizard • Lawrence Lynn • Layton Alley "Night Panda" • Leah S • Leah White • Led Emmett • Lee & Michelle Sharp • Lela • Lemuel Yap • Leonid Levitsev • Leonie • Leslie Anne Rogers • Leticia S • Lexilemp • Liam Simmons • Lidor Sorkin • Lindsey Stockstill • Lisa • Lisa Fraley • Lisa Krenn & Jenson Heaton • Lissette Buckley • Liz • Liz Williams • LordTBR - FanFiAddict • Lorenzo G • Lotta D. • Louis Maurati • Louis Rayomond • Lowell Ziegler • Lucas Carlberg • Lucas Nicholes • Lucas Rackley • Luis Kathleen Penn • Luke Baker • Lyn Kaufmann • Lynne Everett • Lyon • Lysal

Macdonny • Maciej Piwoda • Maëva Touchet • Maggie Dominiak • Maggie Wright • Maid Christa McNiehot • Malfor • Marc Andrew Kramer • Marc Rasp • Marc Schäfer • Marek Fukas • Margaret St. John • Margo Sterling • Maria & Dee • Maria Rosaria Monticelli • Maria T • Maria Vitoria Nunes Lemes • Marie Goursolas • Marie James • Marie-Helene Ayotte • Marilyn Reid • Mario Poier • Marissa Scudlo • Mark • Mark Bloom • Mark Dewees • Mark Flemmich • Mark Geier • Mark Hindess • Mark Holt • Mark Larson • Mark Matthews • Mark Newton • Mark Roberts • Mark Vach • Marko S • Marlow Woodman • Marnie Kiener • Marnilo Cardenas • Marte Myrvold • Martha Carr • Martial M • Martin Burcombe • Martin Gamma • Martin Key • Marty Moon • Marvin Langenberg • Mary Alice Kropp • Mary B. Allen • Mary Gaitan • Masky or Trevor • Mathieu Lefebvre • Matt • Matt Barnes • Matt (Doc) Bowman • Matt Brantley • Matt H • Matt Johnson • Matt Moran • Matt "Catapult" Wang • Matthea W. Ross • Matthew Alton • Matthew Cleverdon • Matthew Cunha • Matthew Hess • Matthew Pebworth •

Matthew Pemble • Matthew Siadak • Matthew Stepan • Matthias • Maurice G • Maurizio Mineo • Max B. • Maxime Gregoire • McGuire Uccello • Megan I • Megan Marsden • Megan N. Quinn • Mekel • Melanie Arndt • Melanie B. • Melissa Barber • Melissa A. Garcia • Melissa M. Hernandez-Alvarez • Melissa Hirschfeld • Meredith Carstens • Meryl M. • Micah Jones • Michael & Crystal • Michael James Boyle • Michael Breland • Michael J Brown • Michael Butler • Michael Cummings • Michael D'Angelo • Michael DeCuypere • Michael DeLong • Michael "Dancermike" DeMeritt • Michael DeVaughan • Michael L. Emerson • Michael Heintz • Michael Jenisch • Michael Leai • Michael B Mitchell • Michael Sacropski • Michael H. Sugarman • Michael Sweitzer • Michael Ude • Michał Kabza • Michel Robert • Michele G. • Michelle • Michelle B • Michelle Rodriguez • Michy Maynard • Midnightm • Miguel A. • Mikael Mortensen • Mikalantis Vecchiarelli • Mike Johnson • Mike Ketchen • Mike Klein • Mike Lannon • Mike Parsons • Mike R. Pomeroy • Mike Scott • Mike VanKammen • Mikey Dubs • Mikkelsen • Milliebot • Min Liu • Ming Shui • Minzoku • Missy Beal • Mitchell Butterfield • Mitchell Tyler • Mitsy Docter • Molly • Molly Miller • Molly J Thomson • Monika Binkowska • Morgan Alston Thomas • Morgan Fraser-Heetbrink • Mortimer C. Spongenuts III • Mossytoes • Mrinal Singh Balaji

N. Scott Pearson • Nadia • Naomi Kay • Naomi Mahala • Naomi & Peter Riba • Natacha Lima • Natalie Gillespie • Natalie Hill • Nate, Sarah, Owen & Kate • Nathan & Denita Zelk • Nathan Beins • Nathan Van Dyck • Nathaniel Adams • Nathaniel Black • Nathaniel Blanchard • Nathaniel James Luyong • Neil & Irene Shapiro • Neil Musser • Ni • Niall Price • Nicholas • Nicholas Bowers • Nicholas Keslake • Nicholas Peck • Nicholaus Chatelain • Nick Catalano • Nick Nelson • Nick Newman • Nick Toepper • Nicolas Lobotsky • Nicoline Diana • Nik Mennega • Nikki K. • Nikki Robert • Nikkii Thompson • Niklas Henningsson • Nilah • Nina Anne • Nirkatze • Noah DeHaan • Noah M. Bruemmer • Noah G. • Noah S. Lowenstein • Nolan Turley • Norman P. Gerry • Nyx Kahanovich

Oliver Greytome • Olivia Adams • Olivia Smith • Ot

P. Arthur Geisler • P. Karns • Padraig Ayre • pagesandpotions • Parker • Pat Spanfelner • Patrick • Patrick Bächli • Patrick Couch • Patrick Ernst • Patrick L Hayde • Patrick Heffernan • Patrick High • Patrick King • Patrick McCook • Patrick Skaggs • Patrick Swenson • Paul Charlebois • Paul Emigh • Paul Everingham • Paul Hranko • Paul M. • Paul Niedernhofer • Paul Perez • Paul Stansel • Paula Evans • Pavel Tyšlic • Penelope Rose • Penny Ramirez • Pete Flannery • Peter Gnodde • Peter McQuillan • Peter Rado • Peter Rubinstein • Peter Schnare • Phil Hucles • Phil Miller • Phil P • Phil Wallace • Philip Alldredge • Phillip H • Phillip Steele • Phillip Wood • Pierce • Pierce A. Erickson • Pierre G. • Pierre Guittonneau • Piet Wenings • Pieter Willems • Posey Sanders • PunkARTchick *Ruthenia*

Queerfin • Quentin Foster • Quimbey • Quinn Giguiere

R.A. Fedde • R.D.Solomon • Rachael • Rachel • Rachel Burkell • Rachel W Martin • Raeleen • RagManX • Ramón Terrell • Randi Dwan • Random Yarning • Randy • Randy Chrust • Raymond E. Feist • Razaq Durodoye • Rebecca B • Rebecca Kronenfeld •

Red Waldron • Remon Waasdorp • Ren G • René Kristensen • Renee Weekley • Reverend Mothman • Rgr375th • Rhonda Moore • Ricardo Monascal • Rich Reading • Rich Rodriguez • Rich Thomas • Rich Velez • Richard L Fellie • Richard Erik Larsen • Richard Lebrun • Richard Novak • Richard Parker • Richard Resnick • Richard T. Ritenbaugh • Richard Schwartz • Richie Greenbaum • Richie P • Rick Brose • Rick Brown • Rickey King • Ricky Lyn Mohl SR. • Rik Geuze • RJ Hopkinson • Rob Armstrong • Rob Crosby • Rob F • Rob Holland • Rob McPeak • Rob Sheffield • Robert • Robert K. Barbour • Robert James Bruce • Robert Antony Hughes • Robert Kusiak • Robert Lightsong • Robert McGeary • Robert Migchelbrink • Robert Thompson • Robert W • Robin Hill • Robyn Burnette • Rod Cressey • Roe Jivers • Roger Jared • Roger Mortimer • Roger Plath Jr • Roland Roberts • Roman Yeremenko • Ronald H. Miller • Ronald Redden • Ronald L. Weston • Rose Pendleton • Roseking • Rosie Vincent • Rosta Viktorin • Rowan • Royce Ogburn • Ruaidhrigh • Rufo • Ruhi • Rui Ferreira • Rumen Ganev • Russ & Melody Champagne • Russell Lindsay • Ryan Berry • Ryan Briggs • Ryan & Rebecca Filkins • "Ryan Garms" • Ryan Groh • Ryan H. • Ryan LeDuc • Ryan Maloney • Ryan Ragan • Ryvix

S M Muse • S. Busby • S. Felske • S. Marie Grimaldi • S.K. Nicholanus • Sabine MacMahon • Sadie Cocteau • Sam • Sam Leigh • Sam M • Sam Pickerel • Sam VanSantvoord • Samantha Goodwin • Samantha Handebo • Samantha Landström • Samantha Ranz • Samantha Whitney • Samuel Frick • Sandra K. Lee • Sandy L. Egger • Sanzaki Kojika • SaraBeth Roberson • Sarah B Carey • Sarah G • Sarah Haskins • Sarah Kasson • Sarah Palmer • Sarah Perez • Sarah Richards • Sarah Schroeder • Sarah L. Stevenson • Sarah E. Troedson • Sarasvathi Kannan • Sasha Bridges • Scott Casey • Scott Dell'Osso • Scott Frederick • Scott Hinshaw • Scott MacEwan • Scott R. • Scott Rarden • Scott Sizemore • Scott Slinde • Scott Sweeny • Scott Wiggins • Seamus Sands • "Sean Carr" • Sean Doescher • Sean L. • Sean Lynch • Sean Meichle • Sean Stanley & family • Sean Stockton • Sebastiaan Henau • Sebastian Allocca • Sebastian Barwinek • Sebastian Bretschneider • Sebastian Kleinschmidt • Sendeu • Seow Wan Yi • Serafina • Seraphina Maurer • Sergey Kochergan • Seth Scott • Seth Lee Straughan aka TrashMan • Shaanan • Shabana • Shadow • Shadrick Para • Shanda • Shankar Viswanathan • Shanon M. Brown • Sharon J Eastridge • Sharon Kepford Ogan • Shawn Biancucci • Shawn T Huffman • Shelley • Shelley Barra • Sherri Crimmings Vincent • Sherry Marcolongo Barker • Sherry Sheggrud • Sigrid Rowe • Silver • Simon & Cherloria • Simon Dick • Simon Felline • Simon Payne • Sir Ralex • Skandranna • snail • Solar Kane • Solomon Stone Romney • "SomersSKetch" • Sonya Anne • Sophie Lyall • Soren Haurberg • Spencer Wright • Spyrl • Stacy Miera • Stan Edwards • Stefan Lind • Stefan Mason • Stefani Anderson • Steffan P. Arndt • Stelios Koutrakis • Stephanie Fischer • Stephanie Martin • Stephanie Powell • Stephen J. Cassell • Stephen Cobb • Stephen Corby • Stephen Hoarau • Stephen Pretty • Stephen Sutton • Stephenie Morales • Steve 'El Queso Grande' Drew • Steve Thornton • Steven Brodb • STEVEN CONNELLY • Steven Ede • Steven Makai • Steven Nicoll • Steven Ribaudo • Steven Sabatke • Steven Saund • Stine-Mari • Stuart I. Chenkin • Stuart S. Ng • Sue DeNies • Sunpreet Kiran • Surfnerd • Susan Abenilla-Brown • Susan, Tom & Anthony Ferrara • Susan K. Jolly • Susan Rackley • Susan J. Voss • Suzanne Stitz-Bernescut • Sven

Tako • Taliesin Morgan • Talli • Tammy Kaufman • Tania Clucas • Tania Richter • Tanja Æltringham • Taylour • Telrúnya Ereinion • Tenille Desjarlais • Teran K • Teresa Telesco • Terry Adams • Terry Callan • Terry Davis • The Antosiak Clan • The beer man • The Bugge family • The Gilpin Circus • Thomas Burbine • Thomas Legg • Thomas Maguire • Thomas G. Maybin • Thomas Probst • Thomas Santilli • Thomas D. White • Tia Frances Allen • Tiffani Sahara • Tim Brugman • Tim Correll • Tim J Doel • Tim Harwood • Tim Jordan • Timothy J. Bennett • Tina & Marco • Tinman • Tino Fahrentholz • Tobias • Tom Branham • Tom Dean • Tom Farmer • Tom Snyder • Tom Stephens • Tomasthanes • Tommy • Tommy Noftle • Tomte Family • Tony • Tony Hamlin • Tony Page • Tony Pedley • Toto • Tracey Grzegorczyk • Traci • Tracy Fettig • Tracy Frost • Tracy Gius • Tracy Schneider Morstad • Travilogue • Travis Brannan • Travis McElroy • Trev Williams • Trip Space-Parasite • Tristan Howard • Tristen B. Conner • Troy Saunders • Tucker Thurman • Tuffin • Twila Price • Tyke Beard • Tyler Cheek • Tyler DeHaan • Tyler Spencer • Tymothy Peter Diaz

Ulrich Fricke • urs hiller

Valentin Gelb • Valentina Volpi • Valerie Winters • Velizar Dragoev • Viannah E. Duncan • Vic Turner • Vicki Hsu • Vicki Lindberg • Victor Rova Morgan • Vidur Paliwal • Vincent Grippa Jr • Vincent Mak • Vincent Rocco • Virginia Anderson • Vlad Wunschl • Voglet Cédric • VoidLies418

Wade Leibeck • Walter Eadie • Walter J Montie • Wayne Fullmer • Wayne Seto • Wayne Smith • Wendy Emlinger • Wesley Mattice • Wesley Wilson • Whitney Jordan • Wilfred W. Wu • Wilfredo Quiles JR • Will Ritchey • William M Lucero • William Martin • William Moe • William Schneck • William A. Tomlinson • Wilma Jacobs • Wyatt Kelley

Xahun Wisprider • Xan Dawson • Xiomara Reyes

Yankton Robins • Yaromir Kniese • Yasmine • Yosindu • Yukihiro Uchizato • Yuri Samandar • Yurii "Saodhar" Furtat • Yusa • Yve Budden

Zach Bettis • Zach Harney • Zach Lay • Zach Rhodes • Zachary Beauregard • Zachary Lambert • Zack Griffith • Zack McFarland • Zak Kanoff • Zeb Berryman • Zeth • Zhaxtbrecht • Zyraphyre

Shawn Speakman is the author of *The Tempered Steel of Antiquity Grey*, *Song of the Fell Hammer*, and *The Dark Thorn*, an urban fantasy novel Terry Brooks called "a fine tale by a talented writer." He is also the award-winning editor of two *Unbound* and three *Unfettered* anthologies. An avid fan of SF&F, he owns The Signed Page and Grim Oak Press, where he is surrounded by books. He currently lives in Seattle, Washington, with his wife and two sons.

ShawnSpeakman.com
Facebook.com/AuthorShawnSpeakman
Twitter: @ShawnSpeakman
Instagram: @ShawnCSpeakman

GrimOakPress.com
Facebook.com/GrimOakPress
Twitter: @GrimOakPress
Instagram: @GrimOakCommunity